#1 *New York Times* Bestselling Author

SHERRYL WOODS

LOVE

HARLEQUIN
BESTSELLING
AUTHOR
COLLECTION

**HARLEQUIN®
BESTSELLING
AUTHOR
COLLECTION**

Recycling programs
for this product may
not exist in your area.

ISBN-13: 978-1-335-40631-6

Love
First published in 1992. This edition published in 2022.
Copyright © 1992 by Sherryl Woods

Plain Admirer
First published in 2013. This edition published in 2022.
Copyright © 2013 by Patricia MacDonald

For questions and comments about the quality of this book,
please contact us at CustomerService@Harlequin.com.

Harlequin Enterprises ULC
22 Adelaide St. West, 41st Floor
Toronto, Ontario M5H 4E3, Canada
www.Harlequin.com

Printed in U.S.A.

CONTENTS

Also by Sherryl Woods

Vows

Love
Honor
Cherish
Kate's Vow
A Daring Vow
A Vow to Love

The Sweet Magnolias

Swan Point
Where Azaleas Bloom
Catching Fireflies
Midnight Promises
Honeysuckle Summer
Sweet Tea at Sunrise
Home in Carolina
Welcome to Serenity
Feels Like Family
A Slice of Heaven
Stealing Home

Visit her Author Profile page at Harlequin.com,
or sherrylwoods.com, for more titles!

LOVE

Sherryl Woods

Prologue

Sunlight streamed through the stained-glass windows of Boston's Whitehall Episcopal Church early on the morning of June 21, as three glowing brides walked down the aisle—one of them very pregnant.

Jason Halloran stood next to his father and grandfather in front of the altar and watched the three generations of women come toward them. He was every bit as nervous today as he had been a year ago, when he'd waited alone. Today, however, Jason was worried that his wife might not make it through the renewal of their vows without going into labor. Dana had a habit of bucking tradition.

As she had done on their original wedding day, Dana caught his eye and winked. The unexpected audacity in the midst of the solemn occasion brought an immediate smile to his lips. His wife was as uniquely irreverent as ever, and he was as enchanted with her now as he had been then.

He glanced over at his grandfather and saw that Brandon's normally fierce expression had gentled as he regarded his wife-to-be. Jason knew this day was one his grandfather had dreamed about for close to fifty years. It had been suggested by Brandon and his beloved Elizabeth that all three generations of the Halloran family use the occasion as a chance to give thanks for the blessings of their marriages.

Brandon's voice held steady, but there was a sheen of tears in his eyes as he gazed at Elizabeth Forsythe Newton, whose adoring eyes never once left his.

"I, Brandon, take thee, Elizabeth, a woman I loved and lost and have been blessed to find again, to be my wedded wife. I promise to cherish thee all the rest of my days."

Next the minister turned to Jason's parents. Kevin Halloran looked shaken as he kept his gaze fastened on the lovely, gentle lady who'd been his wife for nearly thirty years. They had met as children, fought for the same causes in the turbulent sixties and loved each other with equal passion and exuberance. Later they'd found themselves changing. Jason knew the road had not been easy for his parents, but they had survived. Today was their chance to tell the world and each other that time and change had not destroyed the foundation of their marriage.

Jason saw his mother's hand tremble before his father enfolded it in his own.

"I, Kevin, take thee, Lacey, a woman who has stood by me through hard times and good, who has provided love and understanding, I take thee again to be my wedded wife. For the blessing of your undying love, I thank God. For the joy of our family, I thank you. And I promise to honor you and all that you have meant to me all the rest of my days."

Jason heard the heartfelt commitment in his father's voice and knew that it mirrored his own deep feelings of commitment for his wife. The last year with Dana had been filled with joy and laughter, with unpredictability and unstinting love. She was a woman who had learned in childhood to reach undaunted for the elusive brass ring and to hold on tight. She faced each new day with optimism and determination, and she had given him the same joyous—if occasionally unorthodox—outlook.

When their turn came, Dana handed her bouquet of spring's brightest wildflowers to Jason's mother, then placed her hands in his. Her eyes shimmered with tears, but there was no mistaking the strength of purpose in their sapphire depths. Her generous mouth curved into a smile that radiated warmth.

His voice suddenly choked with emotion, Jason began slowly, "I, Jason, take thee, Dana, to be my wedded wife all over again."

He felt the reassuring squeeze of her hands, and his voice steadied. "I thank you for a wonderful year filled with the unexpected. As we await the birth of our first child, I pray that he or she will be blessed with your imagination and your generous heart and guided by your sense of loyalty and your love of family. And today as all of us reaffirm our vows before God and our friends, I promise to love you and care for you and our children all the rest of our days."

As he said the special vows he'd labored to put into words, Jason thought back to that incredible winter day when Dana Roberts had come bursting into his dull, predictable life and changed everything.

Chapter 1

Boring. Predictable. Tedious. As he crossed Boston Commons, Jason Halloran ran through an entire list of adjectives describing the way he felt about his so-called charmed life. He might have blamed his mood on the heavy, overcast skies that promised snow by nightfall, but he'd been feeling this way for weeks now. He knew his state of mind was one of the reasons for this lunch today with his grandfather. Brandon Halloran had lost patience. Jason had been ordered to appear at Washington's Tavern at noon on a Saturday for what would no doubt be a stern lecture intended to snap him out of his doldrums. Jason didn't hold out much hope that it would work.

At the corner Jason paced impatiently, waiting for his tall, distinguished grandfather to stride through the weekend throng. The blustery winds cut right through his topcoat made of Halloran Industries' finest cashmere-and-wool blend. Shivering, he glanced at his watch and realized that he was early. Brandon Halloran was a creature of habit. He would not appear until precisely noon and it was now barely 11:30, another indication of the boredom of Jason's days. After picking up the new VCR he'd ordered earlier in the week, Jason had then rushed to get to the one engagement on his calendar that held any promise of challenge.

The VCR weighed a ton and there was no point in freezing to death while he waited, he decided after several more minutes. So he headed for the restaurant. Inside the overheated tavern with its elegant antique mahogany bar, gleaming brass fixtures and private, well-cushioned booths, Jason shrugged out of his overcoat and slid into the booth that was reserved daily for his grandfather's use. A waiter placed a Scotch and water on the table mere seconds later.

"Shall I bring you something more while you wait?" the dour-faced man inquired. He'd looked exactly the same since the first day Jason had come here with his grandfather nearly twenty-two years before. Jason had been six at the time and had been dressed in his best suit in honor of the occasion.

"Another one of these," Jason said, finishing the first drink in two gulps.

"As you wish, sir."

Jason caught the faint sniff of disapproval as the waiter retreated. It would be just like old Giles to feel duty-bound to cut him off. Jason's gaze followed the elderly man as he crossed to the bar, his back ramrod stiff as he placed the order. Once assured that the drink would be forthcoming, Jason surveyed the other occupants of the tavern—the handful of people who'd sought refuge from the cold even though it wasn't quite lunchtime.

The usual stuffy crowd. Even on weekends everyone had an uptight, button-down look about them, he'd decided until his glance fell on the woman at the end of the bar. For the first time in ages he felt a stirring of interest. Among those dressed in Brooks Brothers basic black pinstripe and those sporting academic tweeds, she stood out like a vibrant wildflower in a field of grass.

Her boots caught his attention first. They weren't the elegant Italian leather boots favored by the style-conscious women in his crowd, but heavy black boots suitable for riding a Harley-Davidson. Even so, they couldn't disguise the long shapely legs they covered to midcalf. Black jeans, faded nearly to gray, kept his attention as they hugged slender, boyish hips. The jeans nipped in at an impossibly tiny waist, where a bright orange sweater with a jagged thunderbolt of purple was tucked in. A black leather jacket completed the ensemble. Again the style was more suited to motorcycles than a Rolls-Royce.

Jason was both appalled and fascinated, even before his gaze reached her incredible, heart-stopping face. Her skin was pale as cream, her features delicate. Full, sensuous lips looked as if they'd just been kissed to a rosy pink. Short blond hair stood up in spikes, not from some outrageous styling, he guessed, but from a nervous habit of running her fingers through it. The result was part pixie, part biker.

The look in her eyes was definitely streetwise and every bit of her attention seemed to be as riveted on him as his was on her. Though he couldn't explain the attraction, he was jolted by the first genuine excitement he'd felt in weeks.

Forgetting all about the second Scotch, forgetting the

boredom, forgetting just about everything, he slid out of the booth and crossed the tavern's wide plank floor. At twenty-seven Jason knew all about seduction, all about provocative charm. It was the one thing at which he was very successful. His walk was deliberately slow, paced to increase the mounting tension already sizzling between them. He kept his gaze locked with hers and felt another shock of pure adrenaline when she didn't blink, didn't look away. That serious, hard stare remained boldly fastened on him.

Jason was two steps away from her, poised to introduce himself, when she came off the barstool in one fluid, graceful motion—and slammed a fist into his jaw. Before he could recover from the shock of that, she was all over him, pummeling him with more fury than skill, landing just enough blows to assure him she was deadly serious. Her colorful curses turned the bar's genteel air blue while an expectant hush fell over the room.

If the respected Halloran image hadn't been deeply ingrained in him since birth, Jason might have laughed with sheer exhilaration at the unexpectedness of the attack. As it was, he knew if his grandfather caught him brawling with a woman in public, Siberia wouldn't be far enough away for him to run.

Jason hadn't boxed at Yale for nothing, though even that hadn't quite prepared him for the unprovoked fury of this tall, lanky stranger. He dodged her next well-aimed blow, which had obviously been intended to do serious harm to his masculinity. He grabbed one of her arms and pinned it behind her, then latched on to her other wrist. Pressed tight against her and all too aware of every inch of invigorating contact, he looked straight into wide eyes that had turned an exciting, stormy shade of blue. Amusement tugged at his lips as he murmured, "Have we met?"

Apparently she was in no mood for his dry humor. Muttering another string of curses, she hauled off and kicked him. When Jason gasped and reached down to rub his injured shin, she twisted free and came at him again. Obviously she wasn't nearly as familiar with the Marquis of Queensberry rules of fighting as he was. She got in two or three more solid shots before he wrapped his arms around her from behind and held her still, his blood pumping like crazy.

The bartender hovered nearby, obviously in shock. The tavern probably hadn't seen this much action since the Revolutionary War. "Should I call the police, Mr. Halloran?" he inquired with an obvious air of dread at the stir that would cause.

Jason felt the woman stiffen in his arms. "I don't think that will be necessary," he said, then added more softly for her ears alone, "Will it?"

Her shoulders sagged in defeat. "No."

Jason had learned the hard way not to trust her docility. "If I let you go, will you come with me quietly so we can talk about whatever's on your mind?"

When she failed to answer, Jason chuckled. "So, you can't bring yourself to lie. That's good. It's a basis for trust."

Eyes flashing, she glared at him. "I wouldn't trust you if you were the last man on earth."

"I wonder why, since to the best of my recollection I've never had occasion to lie to you."

"You're worse than a liar. You're scum. You're evil."

Her voice rose with each charge, which seemed to fascinate the rapidly growing crowd of onlookers. The words cut far more than the flying fists. Hallorans were rarely humiliated in public. Jason could just imagine how the gossips would enjoy the news, which he had no doubt would spread like wildfire by evening. It would probably make the Sunday papers as well. The faint amusement and exhilaration he'd felt vanished, replaced by a sense of growing outrage. Who the hell was this woman and where did she get off calling him scum? he wondered indignantly.

To his growing fury, it sounded as if she was just getting started. In fact, she might have gone on berating him, but Jason decided enough was enough. He ended the tirade by clamping a hand over her mouth and nudging her firmly across the room and into the booth. She gasped as her knees buckled, but she sat. Just to be sure she stayed until he could wrestle some answers from her, Jason wedged himself in beside her.

"Start talking," he commanded in a low voice.

"I have *nothing* to say to you."

"Amazing. Not more than sixty seconds ago, you couldn't shut up." He rubbed his aching jaw and wished for the first time in his life for a little anonymity. Too many people seemed as interested as he was in her answers. She disappointed them all by remaining stonily silent.

Jason had plenty of experience in social graces, but this situation defied the conventions. To the best of his recollection no one had ever defined the etiquette for chit-chat following an unprovoked attack by a woman he'd never seen before in his life. If she'd been a man, he could have slugged her back and felt avenged. As it was, he felt a little like Perry Mason stuck with a reluctant witness.

"Dammit, you owe me an explanation," he said, sensing as soon as the words were out of his mouth that they were wasted.

"I owe you nothing." The spark of fury in her eyes hadn't dimmed a bit.

Jason sighed. Something told him right then and there to send her packing, but he couldn't bring himself to do it without satisfying his curiosity. "Okay, let's try this another way. How about a drink?"

"Not from you." Patches of color on her cheeks emphasized her indignation.

"Fine. You can pay for it."

"With what? Sammy gave you every dime I had saved."

Jason stared at her, startled by the depth of her anger and the unwarranted accusation behind it. Despite his own conviction that it was time to cut his losses, he was undeniably intrigued by the puzzle she represented. The women he knew did not enjoy scenes, much less creating them. This woman appeared totally unfazed by the stir she'd caused. If anything, she was itching for another round, still righteous in her fury. At least in that they had something in common—he was charged up enough to do a full bout with her.

"Who the devil is Sammy and why would you think he gave me your money?"

Apparently startled by his blank response, she studied him thoughtfully, then shook her head. "Nice act. You're really good. For a minute there, I almost believed you."

The sarcasm had a nasty sting to it. Even considering the source—a wacko woman he'd never met before in his life—Jason was offended by the attack on his honor. "I'm not acting, dammit. I'm losing patience. Who is this Sammy?"

She shot him a look of pure disgust. "I told you I'm not buying it. You know perfectly well who Sammy is."

With a sense that he was in over his head for the very first time in his smooth, well-ordered life, Jason tried a little deductive reasoning. "Is Sammy your husband?"

She shook her head.

The response cheered him in a way that probably didn't bear close examination. "You're too young to have a son who's stealing cash from the cookie jar," he decided.

"I'm not as young as I look."

"Sorry. Of course not. You're probably ancient—maybe even twenty-five."

"Twenty-three."

"Like I said, ancient. So what's the story with Sammy?"

She huddled in the corner of the booth, as far from him as it was possible to get in the confined space. Her expression settled into a mutinous glare. Whatever her problem with him was, apparently she hadn't thought much beyond beating the daylights out of him.

"Hungry?" Jason inquired politely, hoping to catch her off guard by trying a different tack. She ignored him.

"No problem," he said then. "I've got all afternoon." To prove it he settled more comfortably in the booth and took a sip of his drink.

Her eyes widened at that. "You can't keep me here all afternoon."

"Oh, but I can," he said mildly. "You can talk to me or you can talk to the police. I'd say we have enough witnesses to make an assault charge stick."

"I'll swear you were coming on to me."

"I was coming *over* to you. There's a big difference."

"Where'd you get your law degree? In jail?"

"No law degree. No jail."

There was a faint glint of curiosity in her eyes before she banked it and fell silent again.

"I'm waiting," he reminded her.

"Sammy's my brother," she said finally. "He's only sixteen, which makes what you did particularly reprehensible."

It was a start, but the woman definitely had an attitude. She clearly intended to be stingy with her information. "So your sixteen-year-old brother stole your money?" he prodded.

"Every cent I'd saved for the past three months," she confirmed wearily. Her fingers swept through her hair, leaving more spikes.

Jason was filled with the sudden and astonishing urge to find this Sammy and pummel some sense into him. "Haven't you ever heard of banks?" he asked instead, astounded by the notion of someone leaving large amounts of cash lying around the house.

She gave him a scathing look. "It was in a bank. Well, it *was* in a cookie jar actually."

"Which means when Sammy turned larcenous—or hungered for chocolate chip cookies—all he had to do was lift the lid."

"Okay, it was stupid," she admitted, abandoning her hair to fiddle with a napkin. Little strips piled up in front of her. Her gaze rose to clash with his. "It didn't seem to make much sense to go to all the bother of opening an account for a couple hundred bucks. I have a checking account to pay the bills, but this was just savings. If I'd put the money in the checking account, I'd have used it to pay the rent or the electric or something."

Jason didn't like the picture he was getting of a

woman struggling to make ends meet, only to be taken advantage of by her no-good kid brother. Where were her parents? Why weren't they disciplining the brat? He barely resisted the urge to reach in his pocket and replace the missing money. But he figured that was the surest way he knew to get another punch in the mouth.

"Where do I fit in?" he asked. "What makes you think Sammy gave me your money?"

"I found this VCR in his room. He told me he bought it."

"From a store?"

She regarded him accusingly again. "No, from some man he met on the streets. He was supposed to see the guy again today. The guy offered him a deal on all sorts of fancy things—stereos, computers, who knows what else—if Sammy would go in with him."

Incredulous, Jason was beginning to get the whole ugly picture. "What the hell are you suggesting?" he demanded indignantly. "Surely you didn't think I was dealing in stolen property and recruiting your brother to help?"

He could see from her expression that that was exactly what she'd thought. It was the last straw.

He leaned in close and lowered his voice. "You've made a mistake, okay? If you leave quietly, right now, we'll forget this ever happened."

"I have no intention of staying quiet about this, mister. You won't get away with it. Men like you are a blight on society, a disgrace to decent people."

"Men like me?" Jason repeated. Now his voice was climbing to the fishmonger level of hers. "*Men like me! What the hell would you know about me?*"

"I know that you were willing to use my brother, that

you played on a kid hungry for a little money and attention."

Jason raked his hand through his hair and tried to control his temper. Another five minutes of listening to this woman's outrageous accusations and he might forget all the rules of propriety and...and what? Hit her? Hardly. Give her a stern talking to? That would certainly terrify her. He faced the fact that he was stymied, unless he could get to the bottom of this story.

"Maybe we should start at the beginning," he said very slowly. He was gritting his teeth. "Why did you assume that I knew your brother?"

"You were right where Sammy said you'd be," she said defensively. "You stood on the corner down the block, right under the old clock. You had another one of those VCRs. The exact same model. It said so on the box. It was obvious you were waiting for someone, so don't even bother trying to deny it."

Jason prayed for patience. "I bought that VCR less than an hour ago. I can show you the sales slip." He got it out of his pocket and waved it under her nose. She didn't look impressed.

"And I was waiting for someone—my grandfather. We're meeting at noon for lunch and I was early. I thought about waiting outside, but it was too damned cold." He shook his head at the ridiculousness of her mistake. "Can I give you a bit of advice? Next time be sure of your facts before you attack some stranger in a bar. Otherwise, you're likely to land yourself in jail or worse."

She regarded him defiantly. "What makes you think I'm not sure of my facts now?"

Jason realized that she was absolutely serious. He hadn't convinced her of a thing. On a day when he'd decided nothing would ever surprise him again, the idea of being considered shady and dangerous held a certain insane appeal. "You honestly think I'm a thief?"

She shrugged. "You could be. Just because you're wearing fancy clothes and talk smooth doesn't mean you're honest. Some of the biggest crooks I know spend a bundle on clothes."

"And the sales slip?"

"If you're any good as a thief, you can probably forge that."

"You're very cynical."

"I've had to be."

To his utter astonishment, Jason found that he wanted to ask why. He wanted to spend the next twelve hours talking to this woman, finding out what made her tick, explaining that a kid who'd knowingly bought a stolen VCR probably couldn't be counted on to lead her to the thief. He wanted to discover the source of all that fierce determination and protectiveness, because one thing was perfectly clear—she didn't blame Sammy for his crime. She blamed the man who'd lured him into it. He wondered if anyone stood up for her the way she stood up for her brother. He wondered about parents and lovers. He wondered a lot about lovers and cursed the notion that there might be one.

He dragged a hand through his hair. It was obvious he was every bit as nuts as she was.

She was sitting perfectly still beside him, as alert as a predatory jungle creature waiting for a chance to spring on some unsuspecting prey. Jason looked up and then caught sight of his grandfather striding across the tavern. Even though his hair had gone silver and his shoulders were slightly stooped, at sixty-eight he was an impressive man. No one could mistake Brandon Halloran for anything less than the distinguished, *legitimate* businessman he was.

Hallorans had been held in high esteem in Boston since the first one had made his way over in the 1800s. Brandon had done his part to see that the image of respectability remained intact. As he stopped to talk with one of his cronies, Jason could just imagine the wild tale he was hearing about his grandson's latest escapade.

"Okay, whatever game you've been playing, it's over now," he said with finality. "I want you to leave before my grandfather gets over here. And if I hear the slightest hint that you've continued to spread these lies about me, I'll slap you with a slander suit that will make your head spin. Is that clear?"

He moved out of the booth to let her pass. She slid across the seat and stood up. Instead of going, though, she stood toe-to-toe with him, undaunted. Her chin jutted up a defiant notch and her hands went to her hips.

"I'll leave," she said. "But don't think for one minute that I'm intimidated by the likes of you. And as long as we're issuing warnings and threats, you might remember this—if you come near my brother again with one of your shady deals, I'll turn you over to the cops. Is *that* clear?"

With his grandfather approaching, Jason didn't have the option of telling her exactly what he thought of a woman who managed to get her facts so incredibly screwed up, then tossed around slanderous charges.

"Oh, I think we understand each other," he muttered.

She nodded. "I'm sure we do."

She cast one final glare in his direction, then whirled

around and stalked off, leaving both Jason and his grandfather staring after her.

"Who the devil was that?" Brandon demanded.

"Some lunatic."

Brandon's gaze narrowed speculatively. "What'd she do to get your dander up?"

"Nothing." Jason slid into the booth and gulped down the remainder of his Scotch.

"Oh, really? Last time a woman got me that hot and bothered, I asked her to marry me."

Jason's horrified gaze shot to his grandfather. "I don't even *know* that woman."

Brandon shrugged, his expression pure innocence. "Maybe you should get to know her. Mind you, I don't know the whole story, but judging by what I've heard in the last five minutes, she'd give you one hell of a run for your money. Seems to me you could use the challenge."

"Granddad, if I ever need the skills of a matchmaker, remind me not to come to you for advice. That woman would drive a saint to drink."

Brandon eyed the empty glass in front of Jason and nodded complacently. "Yes, indeed. A regular hellion. You could do worse."

"Frankly, I don't see how," Jason said. "With any luck, I'll never see her again."

Sammy Roberts was sprawled on the frayed living room sofa watching television when Dana got home. He spared her an all-too-familiar sullen, hostile glance then returned his attention to the thirteen-inch screen where black-and-white images flickered weakly. At least she knew that set hadn't been stolen. She'd bought it herself. Sammy would have gone for color.

Still shaken by her encounter in the bar and worried sick by what was happening to her brother these days, she crossed the room in three quick strides and snapped off the TV. "We need to talk."

"Again? I got nothin' more to say."

Filled with determination and furious that she might actually have made a complete fool of herself earlier, she pulled up a chair in front of him and sat on the edge. "Well, I do. I want you to tell me again about this man who sold you the hot VCR."

Sammy sighed heavily and stared at the ceiling. A hank of limp hair hung down in his eyes. Dana barely resisted the desire to brush it off his face. She supposed he was just being a teenager, but he'd grown increasingly resentful of any suggestions she made about his clothes or appearance. It had nearly killed her when he'd shaved one side of his head to crew cut length and left the other side long, but she'd bitten her tongue and chalked it up to his need for self-expression. She'd seen at least a half dozen other boys in the neighborhood sporting equally horrifying hairstyles.

"Dammit, Sammy, I want you to talk to me."

"He's just a guy."

"How old? How tall? What's his name?"

"I figured you'd know all that by now. Didn't you find him and turn him over to the cops?"

"No, I did not," she answered truthfully.

There was no mistaking the relief in Sammy's eyes. He'd been scared when she'd stormed out of the apartment earlier, not for her, but for himself. He'd obviously feared retaliation, but he'd been wise enough to know there was no way he could stop her.

"Sammy, the man belongs in jail. What he did—what you did—was wrong."

"So turn me in," he said with the sort of smug bravado that made her want to shake him. He knew she wouldn't do it, knew that she was a soft touch where he was concerned.

It had been seven years since she'd taken on the responsibility for raising Sammy. He'd been nine and she had just turned sixteen when their ne'er-do-well father had vanished for the last time. Their mother had died two months later, of a broken heart as near as Dana had been able to tell. Dana had been more concerned with survival than with a medical diagnosis that was too late to do anybody any good.

It had taken every ounce of ingenuity Dana had possessed to keep herself and Sammy two steps ahead of the social workers and out of the legal system. She'd conned one of her mother's friends into posing as a legal guardian, whenever the need arose. She'd even trumped up some very official-looking documents to make it all appear legal. Since Rosie hated authority and had always wanted to be an actress, she'd been more than willing to step in occasionally and present herself as the responsible adult in the household. Overworked school officials had been easy enough to fool.

The scheme had turned out just fine. Dana had worked hard, taking any job she could get, from waiting tables to mowing lawns. Sammy had helped out after school and she'd even managed to take night courses until she'd passed her high school equivalency exam. Right now Sammy had only two more years until graduation. The Roberts kids had done okay so far.

It was only in the past year that Sammy had begun

rebelling, wanting more than she could give, more than he could earn. He was a good kid, but he'd done without for a long time. She couldn't really blame him for wanting all the fancy things his friends took for granted. Yet that didn't mean she was about to condone his buying stolen property.

"What does this man look like?" she repeated. Though she wasn't entirely convinced that the man she'd accosted in Washington's Tavern was innocent, she wanted to be certain. As she'd told him, she wasn't impressed by his clothes, his smooth talk or that sales slip he'd waved under her nose. The seemingly refined grandfather had made her pause, but she supposed it was possible the whole family was involved in a well-paying life of crime.

Still, she hadn't expected a thief to have eyes that could melt stone, gentle gray-blue eyes that had at least momentarily filled with compassion once he'd gotten over the shock of that reasonably accurate left hook to his jaw. She would really hate to think she owed the guy an apology. In fact, she would hate like heck to have to see him again at all. He'd made her nervous in a way no man ever had before, a way that guaranteed trouble even for a woman who considered herself an expert at dodging it.

"I didn't pay that much attention," Sammy said evasively.

"Then how did you expect to meet up with him again? Was he supposed to find you?" She couldn't keep the sarcasm out of her voice.

Sammy squirmed uncomfortably. "Yeah. No. I don't know. Come on, sis, gimme a break."

Dana sighed. This was getting her nowhere. "Was he tall? About six-one?"

Sammy shrugged.

She thought of the man's wind-tousled golden hair and deliberately asked, "Dark hair?"

"Yeah, I guess."

She studied Sammy's pale face, but couldn't for the life of her tell if he was lying or telling the truth. What difference did it make? She wasn't going to turn the guy in, not when she was still so uncertain of his identity. She might as well let it go for now. She cupped her hand around Sammy's chin and forced him to meet her gaze.

"If one thing comes into this house without a proper sales slip from a regular store, I will personally turn you over to the police and let them deal with you. Got it?"

He didn't look nearly as intimidated as she might have liked, but he mumbled an affirmative response. Dana nodded. "Okay. I've got a design presentation to do this weekend, if I'm going to have a prayer of getting that ad agency job."

Dana took twenty dollars from her purse. She didn't want Sammy to get the idea she was rewarding him for his dishonesty, but she really needed the peace and quiet. "Why don't you call one of your friends, maybe take in a movie? Stop at the store on the way home and buy something for dinner, maybe spaghetti. I'll make homemade sauce."

For the first time since their fight over the VCR she'd discovered in his room that morning, Sammy's expression brightened. He wrapped skinny arms around her for a quick hug. "You're okay, sis."

Dana sighed. "You're pretty okay yourself. Don't forget the onions and green peppers and be back here by six-thirty."

"You got it."

As soon as he left, Dana pushed aside all her doubts and worries. The only way to deal with Sammy—with any teenage boy, from what she'd seen in the neighborhood—was to take each day as it came. She couldn't panic over each and every failure. If she did, it would mean conceding that she had done the wrong thing by trying to raise him by herself. No matter how bad things got, she refused to believe that they would have been better off separated and placed in a couple of loveless foster homes.

With a sigh she got out her art supplies and set up her drawing board in front of the living room window. The light was terrible in the dreary apartment, but at least she had a view. It was better than the cubbyhole she'd been assigned to in the back room at the printing company. It was there that she proofread type and, if she was lucky, designed an occasional cheap flyer for the dry cleaners down the block or the bookstore two streets over.

On Friday she'd applied for a better job in the graphics department at an advertising agency. Despite an impressive portfolio, they had required that she do an actual assignment before offering her the job. She pulled out the materials she'd been given by the art director and began to read about the textile manufacturing company that was looking for a new corporate logo to jazz up its staid image.

By the time she'd read the first half dozen pages of the company's annual report, she suspected that their idea of a more modern image would be a nudge into the twentieth century, not a daring leap into the twenty-first. It was the sort of assignment she'd hated in her night school design classes. It required little imagination and even less skill to create a bland logo, which would be barely distinguishable from the old one that had satisfied for the past hundred years.

Dana flipped through the rest of the report. She had just turned to the last page when she felt her heart screech to a halt, then begin to hammer.

"Oh, hell," she muttered under her breath as she stared at the page of photos of the company's corporate executives. Unmistakably, right in the middle and listed as the head of marketing was the man she'd accused just a few short hours ago of being a thief: Jason Halloran—as in Halloran Industries.

Oh, God, why hadn't the name registered when the bartender had mentioned it earlier? Why hadn't she made the connection in time to retract her stupid charges?

With a sense of urgency she flipped to the front of the report and took another look at the letter from the chairman of the board. She'd skipped over it before, not even glancing at the accompanying postage-stamp-sized photo. The only difference between this distinguished-looking older man and the one she'd brushed past this noon was the fierce expression on his face. This morning he'd merely looked stunned.

"Oh, hell," she repeated as weariness and a sense of doom spread through her. Leave it to her to ruin a perfectly good job opportunity.

Chapter 2

Dana stood outside the glass doors of the small but prestigious Lansing Agency for the better part of a half hour Monday morning, trying to work up the courage to submit her work. She knew the logo designs were good. She wanted the job more than almost anything she could ever remember wanting, except maybe a real home complete with fireplaces and window seats and ceilings tall enough for a storybook-style ten-foot Christmas tree.

But more than any other time in her life, she was gut-deep scared. Scared she would get the job and fail, equally terrified that she would have to meet Jason Halloran again and be fired on the spot.

She had spent the entire weekend alternately working on the presentation and staring at his picture, reminding herself that he hadn't called the cops on her, remembering that brief instant of compassion she'd seen in his eyes as she told him all about Sammy and the stolen VCR. Though he wasn't all that old, Jason Halloran struck her as a man who'd known some pain, who'd learned the value of forgiveness. It was there in his eyes, showing up when he was trying his best to appear stern and unyielding.

Obviously he'd been embarrassed, but that was hardly terminal. And anger faded…eventually. Maybe he wouldn't hold what happened in Washington's Tavern against her. If he was as chauvinistic as most men, he'd probably already chalked her crazy accusations up to some female idiosyncrasy and dismissed her as a flake.

Dana sighed. That might get her off the hook with him, but it sure wouldn't land her this job. Her designs would have to do that.

Ultimately her confidence in those designs had given her the courage to show up at the agency this morning. That and the realization that a lowly design person was unlikely ever to meet with the client. For all she knew this logo assignment had been a fake, nothing more than a way to test her skills. It was possible that lots of companies did that. She'd never gotten this far in the interview process before.

Bundled up against the snowy day, but shivering just the same, Dana opened the door to a blast of warm air and low music. Inside she quickly removed her leather jacket. It looked thoroughly out of place with her brand-new spike heels and her one decent, professional-looking outfit. After half a dozen unsuccessful interviews, she'd finally realized it was her unorthodox appearance, rather than her designs that were her downfall. She'd found a sedate skirt and sweater on sale the previous weekend. So far they'd brought her luck, in the form of this second interview, which probably proved a point about appearances meaning every bit as much as talent in this business.

Glancing into a mirror, she decided she looked boring but presentable, except for her windblown hair. She tried taming it with her fingers, but the cropped style refused to be tamed. Shrugging, she gave up and walked across the lobby's thick gray carpeting to the reception desk. Wobbling a little on the unfamiliar heels, she couldn't resist glancing back to see if she'd left footprints in the thick pile.

On Friday she'd been too nervous to note the contrast between the reception area, with its subdued lighting, modern furniture and pricey artwork, and the brightly lit chaos closed away from public view by glass bricks and a curved wall painted a muted shade of peach. Today as she was directed to John Lansing's office, she took in each detail, trying to imagine herself a part of the cheerful confusion and resulting creativity.

Seated in John Lansing's office, she waited nervously for him to return from a conference with his art director. She tried to tell herself that this job wasn't the only chance she'd ever have. She reminded herself that just last week her boss at the printing shop had told her she could expand her duties and take on more special jobs for local stores, if she wanted. They would split the extra income. He'd get seventy-five percent, for overhead he'd explained, and she'd get the rest. She hadn't laughed in his face—she couldn't afford to. But she hadn't said yes, either.

John Lansing and Lesley Bates rushed in finally, amid a flurry of apologies. Lansing, a devilishly handsome man in his mid-forties, and Bates, a sleek, stylish woman in a severely cut suit and discreet but obviously expensive gold jewelry, stared at her expectantly. They were both so polished, so sophisticated that Dana had to fight the urge to check for runs in her hose. She noted every detail of the art director's attire for the time when she could afford to dress that way.

"What do you have for us?" the agency founder asked, giving her an encouraging smile.

Dana opened her portfolio and pulled out a half dozen designs. As she started to spread them on Lansing's desk, the art director shook her head. "Let's hear about them one at a time. Tell us the reasoning behind each one. You might as well get used to making a presentation."

Swallowing hard, Dana nodded and picked up the first design, a subtle alteration of the present logo. "From everything I read about the company, it seemed likely that they're not looking for a drastic change," she said, managing to sound confident even though she was quaking inside. She detailed the reasons behind her color changes, the minimal updating of the design itself.

Though their expressions were impassive, she took heart. She ran through four more alternatives, each bolder and more creative than the one before. The last, in which the company's name would be embossed across an artistic swatch of fabric from its latest collection, had the substance, fluidity and style that she was convinced was both an exciting and impressive change from the current outdated design. The embossing would give it a texture she thought suitable for an internationally prominent manufacturer of rich textiles.

She caught the subtle exchange of glances between Lansing and his art director. "I love it," Lesley Bates said finally.

"So do I," Lansing agreed, taking a closer look at the final proposal. "You've captured exactly the look they need. But you're right about Halloran Industries. The old man is not looking to do something this drastic. He'd be happier with the first one."

"I'm not so sure about that," Lesley countered. "I've always had the feeling that Jason's the conservative one. Brandon didn't get where he is by avoiding risks."

"What about Jason, then? Since you can't go over his head, do you think you can convince him?" Lansing asked the art director.

Lesley Bates shook her head. "I honestly don't know. For one thing, he's not all that interested in anything going on over there these days. From what I hear, he's bored and making no pretense about it. I doubt he'll be the least bit interested in rocking the boat. He's certainly not going to put his faith in someone with little formal training and no experience."

Nor was he likely to put his faith in a woman who'd labeled him a liar and a thief, Dana thought with a sinking sensation in the pit of her stomach. She listened to the arguments pro and con on her designs, trying desperately to hear something that would indicate for certain that she would get the job even if Jason Halloran turned down her designs. She didn't like having her fate linked to the whims of a man she'd publicly insulted.

Unwilling to leave the decision to chance, she decided she had to do something and do it fast to convince them she was the sort of bold, assertive designer they owed it to themselves to hire.

"Let me talk to him," she said impulsively. Of all the limbs she'd ever climbed out on, this was by far the most dangerous. It was also a mark of her desperation. "If I sell him, I get the job."

John Lansing smiled. "I like your attitude, but you're taking a big risk and an unnecessary one at that. It's up to us to convince the client."

Dana fought to hide a grim smile. He had no idea how big a risk she was offering to take, both professionally and, in some way she couldn't quite define, to her own emotions. She took a deep breath. "It's worth it. This could be the break I've been praying for. I believe in these ideas. If I could sell you, don't you think I could convince him?"

"Could you give us a moment?" the art director asked. "Leave the designs and wait just outside."

Dana nodded. Outside the office she paced and paced some more, wishing she dared to kick off the uncomfortable heels. Though they'd sounded enthusiastic about her work, she wasn't sure that they were equally excited about hiring her. She'd sensed the unspoken reservations. The art director had come right out and said she was an amateur. Her ideas, though, were bold and new. Even they couldn't deny that.

Still, she sensed that a lot more was at stake for the Lansing Agency than she'd realized. Maybe she'd put them into an untenable position by suggesting that they send a mere novice over to Halloran Industries. It didn't matter, though. Her audacity was just about all she'd had going for her her whole life. She wanted this job so badly she ached, even more so now that she'd had the small taste of real professional approval of her ideas.

It was another ten minutes before they called her back in. "It's a deal," John Lansing told her. "But Lesley will go with you as a backup. Okay?"

The request was hardly unreasonable. Even so, the possibility that the art director would learn the whole story about her previous encounter with Jason Halloran made Dana almost as nervous as the prospect of making her first presentation to a man who had little reason to give her a break. Because she had little choice, she nodded. "Okay."

"I'll call you when we have the appointment scheduled," Lesley Bates told her.

John Lansing handed her portfolio back to her and walked her to the door. "You have a bright future, Ms. Roberts. I hope we'll be working together soon."

"I hope so, too."

Outside, Dana clutched her portfolio and made one more thoroughly impulsive decision. Too much was at stake to leave anything about this meeting with Jason Halloran to chance. Drawing in a deep breath of icy air, she straightened her shoulders, walked halfway down the block and caught the next bus to the Halloran Industries building on the outskirts of town.

Inside the lobby she consulted the directory, located the administrative offices and took the elevator to the top floor. She was halfway down the hall when Brandon Halloran stepped into the corridor. Dana's breath caught in her throat as a look of recognition spread across the older man's face.

"Hello, there," he said, a surprising twinkle in his eyes.

Dana regarded him warily. Why wasn't he throwing her out? Hadn't he heard about what had happened on Saturday between her and his grandson?

"Are you here to see Jason?"

"As a matter of fact, I am."

He nodded in satisfaction. "Splendid. Before you do that, though, why don't you and I have a little talk?"

Before she could blink, he'd tucked her arm through his and steered her into a lavish corner office with an incredible view of the Boston skyline in the distance. The view was the only thing impressive about it, however. The large space was thoroughly cluttered. Whatever furniture there was was buried under piles of fabric. Swatches of silk tumbled across the desk in a rainbow of colors. Bolts of wool littered a sofa. Drapes of printed cotton hung over the backs of every chair.

Dana had never seen more beautiful fabrics in her life. Intrigued, she circled the room and impulsively ran her fingers over the material, awed by the various textures. She was more certain than ever that her most innovative logo design was right.

She looked up and realized Brandon Halloran was watching her closely, an expression of approval on his face.

"I can see you appreciate fine quality fabrics," he said.

"They're beautiful. I've never owned anything like them."

"Perhaps one day you will," he said. He swept the bolts of cloth from the sofa and motioned for her to sit down. "What's your name, young lady? My grandson didn't take the time to introduce us properly on Saturday. You seemed to be in a bit of a hurry."

Dana winced. "Actually he didn't know my name."

"Really? How fascinating. I could have sworn the two of you were having a pretty heated argument, too heated for a couple of strangers."

"It was a stupid mistake on my part. I thought he was someone else. When I realized how wrong I was, I came to apologize."

"Carrying a portfolio?"

Dana tried to evade that penetrating gleam in his eyes, but it was unavoidable. Before she could consider the consequences, she was spilling the whole story.

"So you can see why he'd be furious with me. This is the first time I've even come close to getting a job like this. I couldn't risk having him tell the Lansing Agency people what I'd done. I planned on throwing myself at his mercy."

"An interesting tactic, but I have a better idea. Let me take a look at those designs. If they're as innovative as you suggest, Jason will hate them. Then I'll have to overrule him and he'll have even more reason to resent you."

Though this comment echoed what John Lansing and Lesley Bates had suggested earlier, about which man was a risk taker, Dana was puzzled why Brandon Halloran seemed so eager to help her. "Why would you care if he resents me?"

"Let's just say I'm concerned with the future of Halloran Industries and leave it at that, shall we?"

Dana didn't have the vaguest idea what she had to do with the future of this man's company, but she was more than willing to show him the designs. The expression of delight that spread across his face when he saw the final concept was better than any verbal praise, but he said all the right words, too.

"This is perfect. Perfect! Young lady, you are very talented. Why hasn't someone snapped you up long before now?"

"I'm just getting started. To be honest, I was a little unorthodox for some of the companies I applied to."

He grinned. "I can just imagine. Well, you're not too

unorthodox for Halloran Industries. Shall I call John Lansing right now?"

"No!" she said hurriedly. She swallowed hard. "I mean, I wish you wouldn't. I just interviewed with him. He doesn't know I'm here with you. It wouldn't look good."

"I see," he said nodding slowly. "You may have a point. Let's let John and Lesley go ahead and schedule that meeting, then. This conversation will be our secret."

"What about your grandson?"

"You just leave Jason to me."

That worrisome twinkle was back in his eyes when he said it, but Dana was far too grateful about having Brandon Halloran in her corner to question his motives. She realized much later that not finding out about his motives was probably the second major mistake she'd made with the Halloran men.

Jason swiveled his chair around to face the window and stared out at the bleak gray landscape. The snow that had fallen over the weekend had turned to slush, and a new batch of thick clouds kept the Tuesday-morning sky a dull gunmetal shade.

What was wrong with him? Why couldn't he seem to get his life into focus? He needed a goal, a purpose, but he was damned if he could find one. Despite his talk with his grandfather on Saturday, nothing had really changed. Only the unexpected, volatile encounter with the outrageously feisty woman in the bar had shaken the depressing status quo, and that was hardly an experience he cared to repeat.

In fact, he had tried to dismiss the entire incident, but that was easier said than done. Too many people at the symphony gala on Saturday night had heard about it and wanted to know the fascinating details. To his irritation Jason found himself quelling rumors that he was secretly involved with the outrageous woman and that the scene had been a very public lovers' quarrel. Unfortunately his own date had been one of those who'd taken that particular rumor as fact. Marcy Wellington had lifted her aristocratic nose in the air, told him in no uncertain terms what she thought of him and had taken a cab home. He'd been astonishingly unmoved by her departure.

He glanced at his calendar and saw that his secretary had noted a meeting in the boardroom for ten o'clock. He buzzed the outer office.

"Harriet, what's this meeting all about?"

"Your grandfather scheduled it late yesterday afternoon. He said it was essential you be there. He mentioned something about the Lansing Agency and those logo designs you ordered." As if she'd anticipated his next question, she added, "John Lansing had tried to reach you earlier, but you'd already left for the day. I transferred him to your grandfather."

Jason pretended not to notice the censure in her voice. Harriet had very rigid ideas about the length of the workday. He rarely met her standards or those set by his workaholic father and his dedicated grandfather. As near as Jason could tell, he didn't have enough to do to justify sitting in his office for more than the bare minimum of hours it took to complete the few real tasks assigned to him.

"There's not a problem, is there? I didn't see any conflict on your calendar," she said. The latter was meant as a subtle dig about his habit of scheduling things without telling her.

"No, there's no problem." No matter how it got scheduled, at least a ten o'clock meeting would break up the morning's endless tedium.

Jason wasn't surprised to find that he was the first to arrive. His grandfather, a stickler for most things, thought meetings were generally a waste of time. Harriet usually had to track him down in the mill and remind him that he was late. Then he breezed in, ran through whatever was on the agenda and raced back to his beloved fabrics.

Jason paced the boardroom anticipating John Lansing's arrival. He was anxious to see what the agency had come up with based on the suggestions he'd given them. He turned when the door opened. With any luck perhaps he and his grandfather would agree for once.

"Sir, Dana Roberts is here," Harriet said.

The faint note of disapproval in her voice intrigued him. "Does she have an appointment?"

"She's the designer the Lansing people used. Should I send her in or have her wait for the others?"

"By all means, send her in."

The door opened bit by bit. At his first glimpse of the woman framed in the doorway, Jason felt his stomach knot. It couldn't be! Surely fate couldn't be that unkind. Though she'd chosen a more sedate attire—a pencil-slim skirt in disgracefully cheap black wool and a rose-colored sweater that was equally ordinary—there was no mistaking the hellion who'd attacked him on Saturday. For one thing, her hair had been worried into spikes again. For another, his blood was already racing just a little faster. Anger? Sex appeal? He wasn't sure he could tell the difference where she was concerned.

From the start she had aroused all sorts of contradictory feelings in him.

He scowled at her. "*You* work for the Lansing Agency?" he queried, not bothering to keep the note of incredulity from his voice.

"Not yet," she said, looking almost as desperate as he felt. She swallowed nervously. "Where is everyone?"

"You're the first."

She slid into the room, careful to keep her distance. She put her portfolio on the floor, then on a chair, then on the table, then back on the floor again. By the time she was done, Jason was tempted to take it and toss it through a window.

"Am I making you nervous?" he asked instead, taking a certain amount of grim satisfaction in the thought.

"Yes," she said, perching on the edge of a chair as if she were prepared to run at the first sign of trouble.

He nodded and took a seat opposite her, training an unflinching gaze on her. If he'd hoped to further disconcert her, however, the attempt failed miserably. She drew in a deep breath and returned his gaze evenly, then said, "Maybe we should talk about it."

"Oh, no," he said softly, a warning note in his voice. "Believe me, I am in no mood to hear anything you have to say unless it has to do with those designs you brought."

The silence that fell after that was nerve-racking. After another ten minutes of strained quiet, he jumped to his feet, opened the door and shouted down the hall. "Harriet, what the hell is keeping my grandfather?"

At his shout Harriet came running, an expression of alarm on her normally passive face. "He just called, sir. He had an emergency, out of the building. He said you should go ahead without him."

"Out of the building?" His voice again rose to a level he would never have considered using before Saturday. Just being around this Roberts woman seemed to shatter every bit of self-control he had. He lowered his voice. "What kind of emergency would take him away from here?"

"I don't know, sir. He didn't say."

"How about Lansing?"

"Actually his office called, too. He said you and Ms. Roberts should be able to reach a decision without him."

Desperation curled inside him. He did not want to go back into that room with Dana Roberts. He might very well strangle her.

He reminded himself that he was a civilized, sophisticated man. Surely he could contain his anger long enough to look at her designs objectively, then get her out of here. He would never have to see her again, especially if the designs were awful. The prospect of turning them down cheered him considerably.

"Shall I reschedule?" Harriet asked.

"No. As long as Ms. Roberts is here with the designs, we'll go ahead. Tell my grandfather I want him to join us the minute he gets back."

"Of course."

When he walked back into the room, wide blue eyes met his. "If this isn't a good time…" she began.

"No," he said impatiently. "Let's get this over with. Show me what you've brought."

"But your grandfather…"

"Isn't coming."

"But he…" Her voice trailed off in confusion. She cast a panicked glance in the direction of the door and looked as if she'd like to make a run for it.

Jason regarded her oddly. "He what?"

"Nothing." With an expression of grim determination in her eyes, she opened her portfolio. She looked at the stretch of table between them and inched closer. She seemed to be assessing her odds for survival.

Finally she drew in a deep breath. "I can't get into this without at least apologizing first. What I said on Saturday, it was a terrible mistake."

"Yes," he said curtly, "it was." He gestured toward the designs. "Get on with it."

For a minute she looked as if she wanted to say more, but finally she shrugged and began describing her work.

She had just started when Jason interrupted, "You enjoyed slugging me, didn't you?" The words popped out before he could stop them.

Pink stole into her cheeks. "No, really. I mean, if you'd been a thief, I would have enjoyed it, but you're not. Look, I really didn't realize who you are."

"I did try to tell you."

She shrugged. "I wasn't in the mood to listen. It's a bad habit I have. I make up my mind about something or someone and that's it. No second chances."

"Yet you're here, expecting me to forget all about what happened. Why should I?"

"Because I'm genuinely sorry and I really need this break."

"Lucky for you, then, that I'm able to separate my personal feelings from my business decisions." He tried to make it sound noble, but it came out smug. He only hoped it was true. Right this second he wanted very badly to hate her designs. He wanted to tell her she was incompetent. He wanted to make her feel as lousy and humiliated as he'd felt on Saturday.

Unfortunately the logo designs were impossible to dislike. He had to admit he was impressed, his eye immediately drawn to one that was simple and conservative. Elegant. He could see it on some nice gray stationery. Or maybe cream-colored. It would be very businesslike.

"I like this one," he said, quickly settling the matter. "I'll call John."

Dana immediately began shaking her head, no longer the least bit meek or shy. "That one's old-fashioned," she said emphatically.

"We're an old-fashioned company."

"No. Don't you see, the fabrics you create are rich and bold. They're exciting. You need a logo that reflects that. This one," she said, pointing to the one he'd instinctively disliked as being too brash, too much like Dana herself.

Unfortunately he had a hunch Brandon would agree with her. His grandfather was far more daring than he was. His father would only care how much it was going to cost to implement.

"Too expensive," he countered, mouthing what he was certain would be his father's objection.

"Actually, I don't think so. I've costed it out," she said and shoved a piece of paper toward him.

"What do you know about costing out something like this?"

"I work for a printer. We do jobs like this all the time. I figured in all the different ways you'd be likely to use a logo and what it would cost to get a new one implemented."

Disconcerted by her thoroughness, Jason looked over the figures. They looked reasonably accurate. He caught the hopeful glint in her eyes and cursed the day he'd ever met her. She was going to win, though he wasn't about to concede victory too easily. He stood and began to pace, trying to figure out his tactics.

"Okay," he began finally, "if it were up to me alone, I'd consider this one, but…"

Suddenly he found himself enveloped in an impulsive hug. Whisper-soft wool caressed his cheek. The scent of spring flowers teased his senses. Every muscle in his body responded to the lightning-quick roar of his blood.

"Oh, thank you," she said. "Your grandfather said…"

The words had the effect of dashing icy water over him. Jason stepped carefully away from her. His gaze narrowed. "That's the second time you've mentioned my grandfather. When exactly did you speak to him?"

She looked miserable. And guilty. Damn the pair of them, he thought.

"Well, I…" she began.

"Never mind," he said, cutting her off before she could offer him lies. "It's clear that this entire meeting was a set-up. I'm sure the two of you will be very pleased to know that I will go along with your choice. Now, if you don't mind, I have things to do."

Before he could make his exit, the door swung open and his grandfather rushed in, looking harried. "Sorry I'm late. Are you two finished? Jason, what did you think?"

"I think you two are in cahoots," he said bluntly. He glared at his grandfather, then let his furious gaze settle on Dana. "I still don't know how you did it, but let me warn you. Stay the hell out of my way from here on out."

Chapter 3

Stunned by the depth of anger behind Jason Halloran's softly spoken warning, Dana stared after him as he slammed the boardroom door behind him. Her heart pounded wildly as her own temper rose to match his. Of all the arrogant, condescending jerks! She hadn't arranged this meeting. She hadn't conspired with anyone. Didn't he realize that she'd simply been told to show up, just as he had been? Couldn't he see that she'd been every bit as shocked as he at finding them alone?

When her pulse finally slowed, she glanced at Brandon Halloran to see how he was taking his grandson's outburst. Obviously he was the one who'd set them both up, but there wasn't a hint of remorse in his expression. If anything, he looked downright smug.

"I thought it went rather well, didn't you?" he said, sounding pleased.

Dana regarded him as if he were several cards shy of

a full deck. "*Well?* You think it went well?" She shook her head. "Where was Lesley Bates? And where were you anyway? You promised to be here."

"No," he corrected. "I promised to take care of Jason. And I told Lesley not to come."

"And what do you think you accomplished?"

He leaned back in his chair and beamed. "What I wanted to, and quite well, as a matter of fact. Jason almost never loses his temper."

"Oh, really? Well, I have a news flash for you. He seems to make a habit of it around me."

"Exactly," Brandon said.

"Not that I blame him entirely," Dana said before the full impact of Brandon Halloran's comment registered. "You wanted him to lose his temper? Why?"

"The man's bored. He needs a challenge."

Suddenly Dana began to catch on. She didn't like the implication one bit. "Oh, no," she said, shoving designs into her portfolio with little regard to neatness. "Forget it. I'm not hiring on as entertainment for your grandson."

"Of course not," he soothed. "You're an excellent graphic artist. John Lansing will be lucky to have you on staff."

Suddenly the job at the printing company began to look better and better. She could stay on, do a few odd design jobs. Eventually she would find another agency job, one that wouldn't put her into contact with one man who seemed to enjoy yelling at her and another who thought such behavior was tantamount to a mating ritual.

"I'll be in touch," the old man said as she grabbed her purse and headed for the door.

"No, really. Please let it go." There was an edge of desperation in her voice. "If you want the designs, they're yours. I'll leave them at the Lansing Agency. You make whatever arrangements you want with them."

"You don't want the job?"

Dana thought of what it would mean to her to be hired by the small, prestigious agency. She compared that to one more second in the presence of the disconcerting, manipulating Halloran men. "No," she said firmly. "I do not want the job, not if it means seeing that man again." She glared in the direction Jason had gone in case there was any doubt about which man she'd meant.

Even that seemed to bring a smile to Brandon Halloran's lips. Why did she have this terrible feeling in the pit of her stomach that he was likely to have the last word?

"Ms. Roberts? John Lansing. Congratulations!"

Dana sank down on the stool in front of her design table. "Congratulations," she repeated weakly. "For what?"

"Halloran Industries wants the logo design. The job is yours."

Where was the sense of elation? The satisfaction? All she felt was panic.

"I don't think so," she said, forcing herself not to think about the opportunity she was giving up. The future. The money. Was she every bit as crazy as Brandon Halloran and his grandson?

Her response was greeted by silence, then, "I don't understand. You don't want the job? Is it the salary? Have you had a better offer? I'm sure I can come up with a deal that will match anything anyone else in town is likely to give you."

"It's not the money," she said, practically choking on the words.

"What then?"

"I just don't think I'm cut out for that sort of work," she lied.

"Of course you are. I can't tell you how impressed Brandon Halloran is with you."

"I'm sure," she muttered.

"I hate to pressure you, Ms. Roberts, but the truth of the matter is, Brandon wants you on this account very badly," he said. Then he added the clincher: "If you don't agree to join the Lansing Agency, we could lose Halloran Industries."

Dana gasped as she recognized Brandon Halloran's trump card. The man intended to lay a monumental guilt trip on her. "That's ridiculous," she said. "You've had that account forever."

"It's a cutthroat business and it all turns on the quality of the campaign. Brandon Halloran insists he'll take his business to whichever agency you *do* join. It's as simple as that."

"The man is nuts," she said with feeling. "He is certifiably nuts. A fruitcake! Loony tunes!"

"He's one of the smartest businessmen I've ever met and he drives one helluva bargain. He wants you on this account. *I* want you on this account."

"Why me?" she said, but she already knew the answer and it had nothing to do with her designs. Brandon Halloran had handpicked her for that ill-tempered grandson of his. She was sure he hadn't told John Lansing that.

"Maybe I could talk him out of it," she said. Thinking of the stubborn, determined glint she'd seen in his eyes, though, she doubted he'd listen to reason.

"Wouldn't it just be simpler to accept my offer?" Lansing suggested.

Simpler, maybe, Dana agreed. Then images of Jason Halloran popped up. Disconcerting images, the kind that made a woman's pulse race even against her own will. Sure it would be simpler to say yes, but wiser? No way. She and Jason Halloran were like oil and water—they just weren't destined to mix. One or the other of them was always likely to be clinging to a last shred of sanity.

"It's the chance of a lifetime," Lansing reminded her.

Dana sighed. "I'll think about it," she promised as a compromise when she couldn't seem to manage a flat-out no a second time.

"I'll call you tomorrow," he responded. "I'm looking forward to your decision," he said, suddenly sounding every bit as confident as Brandon Halloran that things were going to go his way.

Dana wasted nearly half an hour trying to finish the design she was doing for the next event at the bookstore. Unfortunately all of the children she drew surrounding a storyteller looked like pint-sized versions of Jason Halloran.

He was the crux of the problem, she admitted, not his grandfather. Brandon might be a manipulating, conniving sneak, but her relationship with Jason was the real issue. They'd gotten off on the wrong foot and things had gone from bad to worse.

Leaving Brandon's scheming aside, maybe if she went to Jason, told him how important this job was to her, maybe they could find some way to get along. Bar-

ring that, maybe they could simply agree to avoid each
other. That was, after all, what he'd said he wanted—
rather emphatically, as she recalled. Although it was
beyond her imagination to come up with a way for a
designer to stay out of the path of the head of marketing, she was desperate enough to try anything at this
point. At least she could almost guarantee that their
paths would never cross outside the office.

She looked up the number for Halloran Industries
and called before she could change her mind.

"I'm sorry, Mr. Halloran has left for the day," his
secretary said.

Dana glanced at her watch. "At four-thirty?"

"Yes," she said, her disapproval evident. "May I tell
him who called?"

"It's Dana Roberts. I don't suppose you know where
I could find him?"

"You might try Washington's Tavern."

Dana nearly groaned. The bartender would probably
run her off on sight. "Thanks. I'll try to catch up with
him there," she said.

Why did she have this terrible feeling that returning
to the scene of their original encounter did not bode well
for putting their relationship on an improved footing?

Jason was on his third Scotch. It had clarified his
thinking considerably. He had to get out of Halloran
Industries before he went stark raving mad. He had a
degree in marketing, but it was obvious any important
decisions were still being made by his grandfather. In
fact, judging from the way today had gone, Brandon
had every intention of planning every last detail of his
life. Trying to hook him up with Dana Roberts was the

clincher. Just the thought of what life would be with that brash, impetuous woman made him shudder.

"Mr. Halloran?"

The familiar feminine voice punctured his Scotch-induced serenity. "No," he said firmly without looking up. "Go away."

A knee bumped his as Dana Roberts ignored his plea and slid into the booth. Awareness rocketed through him.

"We need to talk," she said.

Jason groaned. "I thought I told you…"

"I know what you told me. Believe me, if there were any other way, I wouldn't be here, but something has to be done to stop your grandfather."

He glanced up and met her determined gaze. "Now there's something we can agree on. What's the old man done to you?"

"He has some crazy idea that you…that you and I…"

She sounded so thoroughly embarrassed that for once Jason couldn't help a rueful chuckle. "Yeah, I know what you mean."

"He has to be stopped. Now he's told John Lansing that if I don't take this job, he'll take the Halloran Industries account away from them and follow me wherever I go."

Jason blinked and stared. "He what?"

"You heard me. John Lansing shouldn't lose an account just because your grandfather's gotten it into his head to throw us together. Now either you talk him out of that or you and I have to find some other way to put our differences behind us and work together."

"Not damned likely!" At her hurt expression, he mumbled, "Sorry, but you know yourself it would never work."

"We could try."

To his amazement she sounded almost wistful. He
would have thought that the one thing they were never
likely to agree on was staying out of each other's way.
He squinted at her across the table and saw something
vulnerable in her expression. He realized then just how
much she wanted this job. She looked like a kid who'd
awakened on Christmas morning to discover a longed-
for doll under the tree, only to realize it was meant for
someone else. It made his usually impervious heart flip
over. As crazy as it seemed, he was almost envious of
her eagerness.

"This job really means a lot to you, doesn't it?" Jason
said, wondering what it would be like to be embarking
on a career that hadn't been preordained by generations of tradition.

Had he ever felt that kind of excitement and anticipation? He vaguely recalled feeling that way the first
time he'd toured Halloran Industries perched on his
grandfather's shoulders, listening for the first time to
the company's rich history. But that had been long ago.
For too long now his job had seemed nothing more than
an obligation and a misguided one at that. He had only
himself to blame, however, for allowing it to go on so
long, for permitting his talent and allegiance to be taken
for granted. All of that was about to change, though.
He was about to take charge of his own fate. Maybe if
he got a grip on his life, he'd feel a little of that energy
that seemed to drive Dana Roberts.

"I can't begin to tell you how much I would give to
work for a man like John Lansing," Dana admitted with
that candor he found so disconcerting.

None of Jason's friends would have dared to be so
open with their excitement about a mere job. Many, like

him, had had their futures cast in stone from birth. All subscribed to the never-let-them-see-you-sweat school of ambition. By hiding any real feelings, they could protect themselves against the humiliation of rejection. Dana had exposed all of her hopes, trusting him with her vulnerability. For some reason Jason couldn't quite explain, it made him want to do anything to prove himself deserving of her trust. Maybe they could find some way of reaching a truce.

"How about some dinner? Have you eaten?" If they could actually get through an entire meal without arguing, he would consider it a good omen.

"No."

"Then I recommend the clam chowder."

Neither of them seemed quite sure what to do next. They waited in silence for the chowder. When it arrived, Dana ate hers with enthusiasm, but Jason didn't want to touch it.

Under her watchful gaze, he made a pretense of eating, dipping up a spoonful of the chowder. But before he could taste it, he pursued all the answers that had eluded him the last time they'd talked. Maybe if he understood her, she wouldn't get under his skin so. Maybe she wouldn't torment his dreams the way she had the past few nights.

"Why are you so anxious about this particular job? You're good," he conceded grudgingly. "Any agency would be lucky to have you."

"When I was a kid, the place I lived wasn't so terrific," she said in what sounded like it might be a massive understatement. "I'll never forget the first time I went to a museum. All those colors. So much beauty and imagination. After that there weren't enough colors in my box of crayons to satisfy me. Unfortunately my portraits never quite looked like the people I painted and my landscapes were never as good as what I saw in my mind's eye. By the time I was a teenager I'd accepted the fact that I wasn't going to be an artist. I did have an eye for design, though, so I traded in my watercolors and oils for stacks of magazines. I'd clip and paste and create whole new ads."

"Then you went to design school, right?"

She shook her head. "Nope. No money and no time. I took a class or two. I even had an instructor who encouraged me, helped me put together a portfolio, but I couldn't manage any more than that. Since then I've tried to study on my own. I've done a lot of reading. My boss at the print shop has let me build a little side business doing small jobs for his customers, but he takes most of the money I bring in."

Something that felt a lot like guilt crept over Jason. "This job with Lansing would be your first real break, then?"

She nodded. "But I can't take it if it means battling with you every step of the way. We'd both have ulcers inside of a month. No job's worth that."

Jason was surprised by the comment. He'd expected Dana to relish an occasional brawl. She'd struck him as the kind of woman who thrived on doing battle. After all she'd taken him on when she'd perceived him as a threat to her brother.

"You puzzle me," he said finally. "Looking at you, I get the impression of someone with a lot of street smarts, someone who doesn't ever walk away from a fight."

"It's the leather jacket," she said.

"It's true that no one I know would dare to wear one and none of them could carry it off the way you do, but it's more than that. It's an attitude. My guess is that you picked that jacket and the other clothes you were wearing when we met—the boots and jeans—on purpose as a way to defy the world, a way to define who you are, a way to cover up just how sensitive you really are."

"You can tell all that from a jacket?" she said dryly. "Actually, Dr. Freud, I picked the jacket because it was warm and would last through more than one season. It was on special at one of those out-of-season sales at a discount store."

"Right. Would you have picked a cashmere coat if you'd been able to afford it?"

She reached over and touched the topcoat he'd left hanging from a rack at the end of the booth. An expression of near reverence crossed her face. "Is that what this is?"

He nodded.

"It's very soft."

"But would you wear it?"

She stroked it again, the gesture so sensual that Jason could practically feel her touch his flesh. His pulse hammered as her fingers caressed the wool, and his breath seemed to lodge in his throat. If he got this overheated watching her touch a piece of material, what would happen if she ever caressed him with the same level of intense curiosity?

"It doesn't have a lot of flair," she finally admitted.

"Exactly."

"If you hate it so much, why do you wear it?"

"The material comes from Halloran Industries. It would be tacky if the owners of the company didn't wear clothes made from our own fabrics. According to Grandfather, we're all walking advertisements for the company. He keeps a tailor on staff, just to do custom work for us."

"So convention means a lot to you?"

Jason thought about the question. The answer wasn't nearly as simple as it should have been. In his world convention meant everything—and nothing. He tried to explain, as much for his own benefit as hers.

"I've been brought up to believe that the world operates according to certain rules. Some of those rules may seem silly and outdated to me, but I can't deny that they're pretty deeply ingrained. It's only been in the past few weeks that I've ever thought of even questioning them, much less rebelling."

She propped her chin on her hand and regarded him with evident fascination. "And what would a man like you consider rebellious? Trading cashmere for leather? Having dinner with the hired help?"

Jason couldn't miss the edge of cynicism in her voice, even though there was a glimmer of surprisingly tolerant amusement in her eyes. "It's funny," he observed, "I can't tell if it's me you're putting down or yourself."

"Whether I'm dressed like this or in jeans, I know who I am," Dana retorted. "Doesn't sound to me as if you can say the same."

Jason didn't like the fact that this woman seemed capable of reading him so easily. "I suppose there's no denying that. I've been questioning a lot of things about my life lately."

"Why? You have everything a man could want."

"On the surface I suppose that's the way it seems. But don't make the mistake of thinking that just because

I'm a Halloran things automatically run smoothly in my life. It's not true. Haven't you ever heard the expression money can't buy happiness?"

"I've heard it. I just never believed it. Having money sure beats what's second best. I'm an expert at that."

Because she'd opened the door and because he didn't want to delve too deeply into his own admittedly sour attitude, Jason dared to probe. "How much trouble are you in financially?" he said, thinking of her reaction to the loss of the few hundred dollars Sammy had stolen.

"I'm not in trouble. I'm not even in debt." She gave him a wry little smile. "I pay as I go. I learned long ago that credit is a dangerous business. When my father walked out, he left us with a stack of bills that my mother couldn't have paid if she'd worked nonstop until she was eighty. As it was, she just died right then instead. I paid what I could."

Jason felt something constrict in his chest. "How old were you?"

"Sixteen."

He couldn't hide his dismay. "What on earth does a sixteen-year-old do to pay off her father's debts?"

Dana's expression darkened at something in his tone. "I didn't do it on my back, if that's what you're wondering about," she said with ice in her voice. "I've never been *that* desperate."

The angry retort stunned him. Her fury was awfully close to the surface. Why, he wondered. Had too many men assumed she'd be grateful for a little help in exchange for a closer relationship? His own tone softened. "You're very quick to jump to conclusions, aren't you? I never for a moment thought that you did anything like that."

"Not even for a split second?" she countered, her disbelief plain. "I mean what else can some uneducated woman who needs money do, right? Maybe you should tell your grandfather your suspicions. That certainly ought to discourage him."

He leveled a look straight into her eyes. "I have a feeling a woman as determined and remarkable as you are could do a lot besides trade sex for money," he said quietly. "How did you survive?"

Apparently his tone calmed her down. She shrugged. "As a matter of fact there were days when I thought it was going to come to…what we were talking about, but I had Sammy to think about. I didn't want him growing up with a twisted view of what it took to get ahead."

"Is this the same Sammy who stole your savings?" he said wryly.

She nodded, her expression pained at the implied failure. "I've tried so hard with him. He's just going through a rough time right now, like all teenagers," she said with more hope than conviction. "He'll be okay."

"How old was Sammy when all this first happened?"

"Nine."

Jason was appalled. And impressed. This hellion with the fierce pride and the fiery temper had gumption. He'd give her that. It made his own complaints seem petty. Obviously Dana had never been daunted by the task she'd set out to accomplish. Nor did she seem the least bit resentful of the circumstances which had heaped such a burden on her slender young shoulders. She had simply coped. Would any of the women he'd known before have done as well? For all of their strengths and charm, he suspected many of them would have floundered without wealthy daddies to turn to, without deep pockets to finance their fancy colleges and designer wardrobes or to provide seed money for their first businesses. His respect for Dana grew enormously.

"Why didn't you ask for help?" he said. "There are social programs, legal aid, food stamps."

"Sure. And the minute they discovered that we had no adult supervision, they would have split Sammy and me up. I couldn't let that happen. We may not have much of an example, but family counts," she said fiercely. "I wanted Sammy to know that."

"Where did you live? How did you make ends meet?"

"At first I found a rooming house that would take us. This friend of my mom's got us in. Nobody paid much attention to who lived there. I worked two jobs most of the time. I had to lie about my age, which wasn't all that difficult since I was always tall for my age. At the kind of places I worked, no one looked that closely, anyway. They were more interested in whether you'd steal from the cash register. I never touched a dime, I showed up on time and I didn't spill coffee on the customers. Those were the only credentials they seemed to care about."

As if she'd just realized how revealing the conversation was becoming, she began to withdraw. Jason could see the mask shift into place, the struggle to regain the distance she normally kept between herself and the outside world. She took a deliberate drink of her coffee, then another spoonful of soup. Jason waited, wondering whether she'd say more about herself or hide behind a wall of defensiveness.

Again, Jason was struck by the combination of child-like enthusiasm and innocence counterpointed by the tough exterior. He noticed for the first time that the fingers clutching the spoon were short, the nails blunt and unpolished. There were scratches on her knuckles, testimony to her attack on him, perhaps. They were a girl's hands. Yet earlier, as she'd caressed his cashmere topcoat, the gesture had been all woman.

How many other new things could he bring into Dana's life to inspire that same balance of innocent wonder and womanly sensuality? Something told him that sharing those experiences with her would banish his jaded mood. He needed desperately to recapture the sense of awe, the sense of unlimited possibilities that remained unshaken in Dana despite her struggles. Perhaps she could show him the way.

Wide blue eyes, filled with uncertainty, met his gaze at last. "I'm sorry. You didn't come here to listen to my life story."

"No, it's okay. I think I can see now why you jumped all over me on Saturday. If I had been the man who tried to get your brother involved in selling stolen property, I would have deserved it. Have you found out who was responsible?"

"Not yet," she said with a glint of determination in her eyes. "But I haven't given up. Sooner or later, I'll find him."

"Why not just turn what you know over to the police?" He guessed the answer even before she could speak. "Never mind. You don't want to involve your brother, right? Maybe you should. Maybe he should get a taste of the kind of tough questions they ask criminals, the kind of future in store for him if he gets in any deeper with this guy."

"I will not turn my brother in to the police," she said with fierce protectiveness. "We seem to have gotten off the track here. Can you forgive me for what happened on Saturday? Can we try to work together?"

For an instant he actually considered saying yes. Then he saw a future filled with conflict. They were too different. Opposites, in fact. They would clash over everything. And, despite what his grandfather thought, she was all wrong for Halloran Industries and for him.

"Have you ever planned a marketing campaign?" he asked mildly.

"No, but…"

"Do you know anything about advertising?"

"Not exactly, but…"

"Can you buy TV time, magazine space, newspaper ads?"

"That isn't…"

"Tell me, what demographics should Halloran Industries be appealing to?"

Her face was flushed by now and the sparks in her eyes could have started a blaze. He had a hunch she was about to tell him off in no uncertain terms, but he forestalled all of her arguments by saying, "Sorry. I think it's pretty obvious that it just wouldn't work."

She blinked furiously against the tears welling up in her eyes. Jason felt like a heel. He knew that half of those questions he'd thrown at her weren't things she needed to know. An experienced graphic artist might have known the answers, but it was hardly a requirement for doing skillful designs. That's why agency staffs included copy writers, researchers and all the other experts needed to plan a successful marketing strategy.

"I'll help you find something else, though," he promised in a rush of guilt. "I'll even recommend that Lansing take you on and assign you to other accounts."

"I really wouldn't want you to put yourself out," Dana said stiffly, stubborn pride written all over her face. "I'd better be going. I can see this was a mistake."

She scrambled out of the booth, grabbing her jacket and ran from the restaurant. An odd, empty feeling came over Jason when she'd gone.

"It was the only thing to do," he muttered under his breath.

"Sir?" Giles said, his expression concerned as he gathered up the dishes from the table. "Is everything okay?"

"No," Jason said. "Everything is definitely not okay. Bring me another Scotch, will you? In fact, bring me the whole damned bottle."

Chapter 4

All the way home on the bus, through a sleepless night and on into the next day Dana tried to dismiss the trembly feeling in the pit of her stomach as nothing more than the pitch of acid. Jason Halloran had infuriated her. He'd led her on, hinted that perhaps they could find some means to coexist. Then he'd shot her down. No wonder her stomach was churning.

As angry as she was, though, she sensed she had made a very narrow escape. The unexpected effect of those few brief moments of Jason Halloran's warm attention had just about stolen her breath away. No man had ever, *ever* looked at her quite that way, had ever listened so intently, as if she were special and not just another conquest. The guys in the neighborhood had made their crude passes, but she'd fended them off easily enough and forgotten about them in a heartbeat.

None of them had made her tingle inside, though. None of them had stirred the kind of waking, temptation-filled dreams Jason Halloran stirred without even trying. A woman could land in a lot of trouble if she took his kindness seriously. Those warm feelings he inspired had turned to ashes.

Luckily her work at the print shop was piled high. It kept her from remembering the way his gaze had lingered, the way his fingers had curled reassuringly around hers for just an instant, the way his lips had curved into an unforgettable smile.

No, dammit! She would not remember. She had plans and those plans did not include making big mistakes, not when it came to her heart. Besides, she couldn't afford to allow herself to become distracted by a man, especially one as unsuitable as Jason Halloran. With his stuffy, conservative way of thinking, he was the kind of man who could easily turn into a white knight. He would want to do things for her, make her life better. Just look how he'd offered to help her find a job, if only to get himself off the hook. Before she knew it, she would be counting on those little snatches of generosity. She would become weak. And when he lost interest in helping, as everyone who'd ever mattered to her had, this time she might not have the strength to fight back.

Who was she kidding? Jason Halloran didn't want any part of her. He'd made that clear. The last thing she had to worry about was becoming dependent on him in any way. He'd see to that.

"Dana!"

Filled with guilt, she jerked around to meet the impatient gaze of her boss, Henry Keane. "I thought you told me if I gave you yesterday morning off so you could go to your meeting, you'd make up for it today. I don't see that stack of proofreading shrinking."

"Sorry. I'm just a little distracted. Did I have any calls while I was taking those flyers over to Mr. Webster?" she asked, thinking that John Lansing was likely to call at any moment to hear her decision. She was going to force a no past her lips, even if it killed her.

"You were expecting that brother of yours to check in? Is he in trouble again?"

"No, Mr. Keane," she replied dutifully.

"A boyfriend, then?"

His sarcastic tone was meant to remind her about his edict that she not receive or make personal calls except on her break. It meant that Sammy spent too many unsupervised hours after school, but she had little choice in the matter. She doubted a few five-minute phone calls were likely to keep him out of trouble, anyway. The truth of the matter was that he'd been a latchkey kid from the beginning, except on those rare occasions when Rosie had looked after him in her haphazard way.

"No, not a boyfriend, either," she said. "Never mind. I'll catch up on all this by the end of the day. I promise."

He stood behind her until he was apparently reassured that she meant what she'd said. Finally she heard his small, satisfied huff, then the shuffle of his feet as he went back to his own office.

As irritating as she found the man, she knew she owed him. He'd offered her the latitude to expand her duties, to develop a small design business. Even though he took the money, she'd gained in experience. Her portfolio was crammed with top quality flyers and brochures she'd been able to create on shoestring budgets.

Maybe she could even convince him to improve the

terms of the last deal he'd offered her. As cranky as he often was, deep down he was fair. She'd pull together some statistics to show him that his own printing business had improved since having her on board to do occasional designs.

There was a timid tap on her door and she looked up to see Mrs. Finch, who owned the neighborhood bookstore, hovering in the doorway. "Dana, honey? Do you have a minute? I could come back."

Dana smiled. "For you, I always have time. Come in. What's up?"

"I hate to impose, but I wondered if those flyers for the storytelling session are ready. I hate to rush you when I know how busy you are."

Mrs. Finch was a sweet old lady, who'd given Dana a break more than once on books she needed for her classes. Dana liked helping her out now and then by doing the posters for her special events. She also endured the woman's tendency to meddle in her life.

"I have the flyers right here," Dana said, handing her the bundle of bright yellow paper.

"Oh, thank you, dear." She looked at the design and beamed. "They're lovely as usual. By the way, did you apply for that job, like you planned?" Mrs. Finch asked, practically on cue. She hefted her round body up on a stool next to Dana, clearly ready for a nice long chat.

"Yes."

"You'll get it," the old woman said loyally. "Is that Mr. Lansing an attractive man?"

"Very."

"Married?"

"I don't know."

Mrs. Finch sighed with obvious disappointment.

"Dana, it's time you started looking for a nice young man. You can't ignore opportunities that come your way."

"I don't have time for a relationship," she said for probably the hundredth time this month alone. Her social life—or lack of one—was Mrs. Finch's favorite topic. She used inquiries about Dana's job hunting only as an introduction to the more important subject of the men she'd met on the interviews.

"You have to make the time." At Dana's glowering expression, she held up her hands. "Okay. I can see you're busy. You can't talk about this now. You just remember what I said."

"I'll remember," Dana said as dutifully as always. It was no surprise that this time an image of Jason Halloran crept into her mind. There was a predatory gleam in his eyes that would have made Mrs. Finch's romantic fantasies turn downright steamy. Dana tried to banish the image, but Jason's face lingered with the pesky persistence of a man on a mission. She didn't dare to think what that mission might be.

She was still considering the possibilities when the phone rang.

"Dana, it's John Lansing. Can you get over to my office this afternoon?"

She sighed. She could turn him down now or wait and turn him down in person. Waiting could be risky, especially once she saw the inside of that office again and felt those stirrings of creative energy.

"Actually I've reached a decision. I don't think it will be necessary for me to come by. I'm afraid I can't accept your offer."

"Because of the Halloran situation, right?"

She doubted if they were referring to exactly the

same *Halloran situation*, but he was close enough. "Right."

"I think I've found a solution. Can you get over here to discuss it?"

All those dreams she'd had about a career in graphic design combined to overcome her doubts. "I can't get there before five-thirty."

"Then I'll see you at five-thirty."

For the rest of the afternoon and all during the bus ride across town, Dana was torn between anticipation and dread. What sort of solution could he possibly have found? Had he found some way of getting Brandon Halloran to change his mind about taking his business away from the Lansing Agency if he didn't get his way? Brandon didn't strike her as the sort of man to surrender so easily. Besides, would John Lansing even want to hire her if it weren't for Brandon's enthusiasm?

At the agency she was ushered into John Lansing's office immediately. He stood up and held out his hand.

"Congratulations!" he said warmly. "You've got yourself a job and your first account. Jason Halloran has loosened up a bit. He's very anxious to work with you."

She stared at him blankly. "That can't be."

"Excuse me?"

"I spoke with him last night. He said…" She shook her head, trying to clear it. "I'm afraid I don't understand. He wants to work with me directly? You actually spoke to him and he said that?"

Lansing regarded her oddly. "I'll admit I never thought he'd go for those designs, but why does that surprise you so? Your work is good."

"It's a long story," she muttered, not at all sure how she felt about this turn of events. Maybe Jason had simply decided he could put up with her temporarily. Later he would find some way to shift the account to another artist. That way everyone would be happy. Everyone except Dana. She couldn't imagine working with a man who'd made it abundantly clear he couldn't stand the sight of her.

"Tell me something, Mr. Lansing. Is it unusual for a beginner like me to be assigned to an account the size of Halloran Industries?"

John Lansing didn't bat an eye at the question or its implication. "Unusual, yes. Unheard of, no. When an artist is as talented as you are, sometimes career moves happen very quickly."

"But you were surprised by Mr. Halloran's request," she persisted.

"Surprised? Perhaps a little, but not displeased, Ms. Roberts. My goal is always to keep the client satisfied. Clearly Mr. Halloran is more than satisfied by what he's seen so far, as is his grandfather. But you already knew that."

"Yes. So you said," Dana muttered.

"I beg your pardon?"

"Nothing. Shouldn't someone with more experience supervise this account? Lesley, perhaps? I'd be happy to work on smaller jobs at first."

"Absolutely not. As long as the Hallorans are happy with your work, that's all that matters. You will be able to start right away, won't you?"

Dana had no idea what was going on, but she had to take a risk that things would work out. "I'll have to give notice at my current job, but I could begin doing a few things for you in my spare time for the next two weeks if that would be helpful."

"I'll let you work your schedule out directly with Mr. Halloran. I got the impression he wants to work closely with you on this campaign and he wants to get started as soon as possible."

Dana bit back another sarcastic comment. The minute she'd agreed to a starting date and said goodbye, she went straight to the nearest pay phone and called Halloran Industries. Though it was past four o'clock closing time by Jason Halloran's standards, she wasn't surprised to discover that he was still in his office. No doubt he'd been waiting for her to call and bless him for this gift he'd bestowed on her.

"Listen," she said abruptly when he picked up. "I can't begin to understand what made you change your mind, but I think there are one or two things you and I need to get clear."

"What the devil are you talking about now?"

"One, I will do the very best job on the Halloran Industries account that I can."

"What?"

She was too busy warming up to pay much attention to the stunned tone in his voice. "I'm not through. Two, I don't want you to think for one minute that I am so grateful that I will fall into your bed. If I sense even the tiniest hint that you have anything in mind besides business, I will quit and slap you with a harassment suit that will make your head spin. Have I made myself clear?"

"Have you lost your mind?"

"Not yet, but I'm a little concerned that a few weeks around you and I just might."

"Are you finished?" he asked quietly. "I'd like to say something."

"I don't think so," she said, her blood pumping fast

and furiously with righteous outrage. "I'm afraid if I stay on this phone for another second I will tell you what I really think of a man who uses his position and power to control other people's lives, to jerk them around like puppets. I'm not a puppet, Mr. Halloran. Remember that!"

She heard his muttered exclamation just as she slammed the receiver into place. If Jason Halloran thought for one second he was going to play games with her life, he was very sadly mistaken.

With her anger vented, she took a deep breath and allowed herself to think about the fact that she had gotten a job that would be coveted by any design school graduate. Not even Jason Halloran's odd change of heart and questionable motives could take away the pure rush of satisfaction.

"Hot damn!" she said, spinning around in the middle of the sidewalk, oblivious to the smiles of those passing by. For the first time in her life, she really believed that things were going her way.

That notion crashed the minute she got home. She found Sammy in the bathroom trying frantically to disguise the fact that his eyes were black and blue and his jaw bloodied.

"Oh, Sammy," she murmured, gingerly touching the swelling. "What happened to you?"

"I bumped into a door," he muttered, shoving her hand away.

"Did this door have a name?" she asked wryly.

"Stay out of it, sis."

"Did this have anything to do with the VCR? Is that man still bothering you?"

With a glare in her direction, he pushed past her and headed for the front door.

"Sammy!"

"It's nothing, okay. I can handle it."

"Is this your idea of handling it? What about next time?"

For just an instant he looked like a scared kid, then the bravado was back in place. It reminded her all too clearly of her own tendency to mask her fears with false courage.

"I don't think they'll mess with me anymore," he said, sounding hopeful.

"But what if they do?" she asked. "They have to be stopped now, before you wind up really hurt."

He whirled on her furiously. "You know what'll really hurt me? Having my big sister let everyone know that she thinks I'm still a baby, that's what. No wonder these guys think they can push me around. You treat me like a kid."

Dana swallowed the desire to remind him that he was just a kid. Obviously his pride had been almost as battered as his face. He didn't need her to deliver the final blow.

"I'm sorry," she said gently. "It's just that I worry about you. If anything ever happened to you, I really don't know what I'd do."

Sammy's tough facade crumpled the instant he detected the tears welling up in her eyes. "Aw, sis. Don't cry," he pleaded.

"How can I help it?" she said, swiping at the tears. "Seeing you like this scares me. Sammy, if you don't stop hanging around with guys like these you'll end up in more trouble than I can ever bail you out of."

"I can take care of myself," he reminded her.

Dana sighed. She couldn't win this argument. No

matter how badly she wanted to protect him, no matter how hard she tried to steer him on the right course, it was clear that there were some lessons Sammy was just going to have to learn for himself. Letting go, though, was absolute hell.

She drew in another deep breath and forced a smile. "How about pizza for dinner? We can celebrate my new job."

Sammy's responding smile was far more natural than hers. "You got it? I thought you said you weren't gonna take it, that those Halloran guys were nuts."

"I still think that, but I start in two weeks, anyway. The opportunity is too good to pass up. I'll find a way to get along with them."

Sammy's arms came around her waist and he hoisted her into the air, twirling her around until they were both giddy with laughter.

"I knew it!" he whooped. "You've got it made now. Are they payin' you big bucks?"

Dana's laughter faltered. "Oh, my gosh. I never even asked."

Sammy groaned. "Sis, you really gotta toughen up. Want me to go in and negotiate for you?"

Grinning at his change in mood, she said, "No, I really think I can handle this on my own, but thanks for offering. Now how about that pizza? A large one."

"Pepperoni, onions and mushrooms?"

"The works," she countered. "Everything except anchovies."

"You got it. I'll be back in a flash."

It wasn't until Sammy was out the door and thundering down the stairs that she stopped to wonder where he'd gotten enough money to pay for the pizza.

Chapter 5

The impossible woman was going to disrupt his life after all! Jason could have sworn they'd reached a total understanding about steering clear of each other the night before. Now Dana was accusing him of who knew what and seemed to have some crazy notion that the two of them were going to work together despite that agreement. He couldn't allow that to happen. Sooner or later he was likely to abandon all common sense and either kiss her or kill her. He didn't want to lay odds on which it would be.

It had taken a lot of very fast talking, but he had finally convinced John Lansing to give him Dana's home address. She would not have the last word, not this time. The woman had an infuriating knack for jumping to the wrong conclusions, at least where he was concerned. His jaw still ached from the first incident. Once again he didn't know what the hell she was talking about.

That phone call of hers was yet more evidence that she was way too impulsive. So was her decision to slam the phone down in his ear. It had set his teeth on edge, tipping the scales more toward murder than seduction.

He had to admit, though, that for one brief flash he had found it exhilarating to battle wits with a woman who wasn't afraid to offend him. Ironically Dana had more to lose than most women, yet she'd blasted him with both barrels just now on the phone. What she'd said might have irritated him with its unfairness, but the plain speaking had made his blood fairly sizzle with excitement. As Jason drove across town, he realized he could hardly wait to see her. He couldn't help wondering what would happen when all that misguided fury turned to passion.

Now that he was actually in her neighborhood, however, he was so appalled by what he saw that this latest argument faded in importance. Used to Boston's finest old sections, Jason was unprepared for the general air of poverty and neglect he found in this cramped, worn-down area. The buildings were in a sad state of disrepair, some of them clearly deserted. Most worrisome, though, were the young thugs hanging around on street corners obviously looking for trouble.

In some measure the neighborhood explained Dana's fearless nature. But there was no doubt in Jason's mind that a young woman as beautiful and guileless as Dana was in danger here, no matter how hardened she thought she was. A surprising and overwhelming desire to protect her swept through him. Despite her tough exterior, despite the strength he'd seen in her, he'd sensed an underlying vulnerability that aroused all sorts of unexpected and unfamiliar white knight fantasies in him. Dana would probably laugh in his face if he suggested such a thing.

Maybe he should try to talk her into moving, though. He'd find her something safer himself. He'd insist that Lansing pay her a decent salary. Then he could fire her from the Halloran account with a clear conscience, satisfied that her life was in order—or at least in as much order as the life of anyone like Dana was ever likely to be. He would have done his duty, as Hallorans always did.

Despite the evidence all around him, Jason actually hoped to find something nicer once he reached Dana's address. Instead, her building was no better than the rest on the block. He parked his flashy sports car with great reluctance, wondering if it would still be there when he returned. There was a trio of rough-looking characters eyeing it with evident fascination when he set the alarm. He figured they could override the expensive system in less than twenty seconds if they dared to try. No wonder Sammy had developed a larcenous streak, if guys like these had been his playmates.

The downstairs windows in Dana's building were covered with bars. The linoleum in the foyer was yellowed and peeling, though he noticed that someone had recently scrubbed it and the air was scented with a light, flowery fragrance. He climbed the stairs to the third floor and knocked.

He heard footsteps, the cautious rattle of chains, then "Who is it?"

"Jason."

The silence grew thick before she finally said flatly, "We have nothing to discuss."

The stubborn tone was exactly what he'd expected.

"I think we do. I can say what I have to say from out here or you can let me in. Which is it?"

The chained door across the hall opened a discreet crack. Curious eyes watched him. Dana's door remained solidly closed, testimony to her fondness for scenes. Apparently she was just itching for another one.

"Okay, we'll do it your way," he said, unbuttoning his coat and leaning casually against the doorjamb. Fortunately he doubted anyone in this neighborhood had ever heard of the Hallorans. "You seem to have gotten some crazy idea that I want you on the Halloran account, after all. Believe me, nothing could be further from the truth."

There was a long pause while she apparently wrestled with reality, something that obviously eluded her most of the time. Finally she countered, "John Lansing told me point-blank that you wanted to work with me. He said you'd insisted on it."

"I have not spoken to John Lansing in days. Are you absolutely certain he said this was my idea?"

"He said…he implied…" She groaned. "Your grandfather," she said wearily. "Why didn't I think of that? It must have been your grandfather."

Jason rolled his eyes. Now *that* made perfect sense. He should have detected the fine touch of Brandon Halloran himself. "That would be my guess," he agreed.

"Doesn't that man ever take no for an answer?"

"Not that I've noticed."

The door crept open. "I suppose you'd better come in, so we can figure something out."

She sounded resigned. The door across the hall inched open another fraction. Now that he understood what had happened, Jason began to relax. This was a mix-up they could fix. Yet her attitude irked him just a little. Getting involved with him, as his grandfather wanted her to do, was hardly the awful sacrifice she'd painted it to be. Some of Boston's wealthiest, most sophisticated women considered him quite a catch.

"Sure you trust me?" he taunted in a deliberately lazy, seductive tone. A real streak of mischief seemed to creep over him.

The gap in both doorways widened. Dana saw what was happening across the hall and motioned him inside. "Get in here."

"You don't have to let the dude in," a male voice said from behind her. The adolescent tone traveled over several octaves, but it was heavy with animosity. "You want him outta here, I'll take care of it."

Jason caught sight of the skinny young boy with blond hair and blue eyes that matched Dana's. Sammy, no doubt. Jason took an instinctive and immediate dislike to him. If Dana puzzled and disturbed him, this boy was like an alien creature. The kid was in serious need of a decent barber. His expression was filled with hostility and his stance was brotherly protective. On one level Jason admired the attitude; on another he began to realize just exactly what Dana was up against with the little punk.

Dana sighed. "It's okay, Sammy. I can handle Mr. Halloran."

Jason's eyebrows lifted a fraction.

She ignored the implied skepticism. "Do you want some coffee or something? We have a couple slices of pizza left."

Sammy scowled at the invitation. Clearly he would have preferred to slug Jason or, at the very least, escort him forcefully from the apartment. It made him wonder exactly what Dana had told her brother about him. Or if the boy was simply savvy enough to understand the odd chemistry at work between Jason and his sister, a chemistry he didn't begin to understand himself. Now that he was here, he realized he'd been drawn by more than a need to settle some crazy mix-up about a job.

"Coffee would be nice," Jason said.

Sammy took a step closer to his sister. "Sis, you want me to hang around?"

Dana shook her head slowly as if she were reluctant to let him leave, but unwilling to admit to the weakness. "No," she said finally. "It's okay. Mr. Halloran and I need to resolve some business matters."

"I'll be at Joey's if you need me." He glared at Jason. "It's just downstairs."

Jason nodded seriously. "I'll keep that in mind."

When Sammy had gone, Jason observed, "Looks like he's picked up your protective streak."

"We learned a long time ago to stick together."

There was a note of defiance in her voice, a warning that Jason couldn't miss. How many times had Dana put herself on the line to bail out her troublesome brother? He'd figured it for a one-sided avenue, but seeing Sammy just now he realized that the guardian angel activities worked both ways.

"He looks a little the worse for wear. Did he run into a door?"

"So he claims," she said ruefully.

"What happened to the VCR?" he asked, wondering how she'd handled that after she'd foolishly risked her neck to go after the thief who'd sold it to her brother.

"I made him give it to the church down the block."

She grinned. "I was hoping maybe it would make him go down there a little more often, instead of hanging out with those creeps he seems to like so much."

"Has it worked?"

"Not so far, as you can probably tell from the black eyes, but I'm still hopeful."

Dana started to lead the way into the apartment's kitchen. Jason tossed his coat on a chair, then looked around as he followed her. He was hoping for clues that would help him to understand this woman whose personality clashed so with his.

The cracked walls had been painted a shade as bright as whitewashed adobe. A tall basket held paper flowers in poppy red, vibrant orange and sunshine yellow. Throw pillows in similar colors had been tossed on the faded beige sofa that looked uncomfortably lumpy. Clay pots of plants lined the windowsill with shades of green. Despite the frayed condition of the furniture, the room had a cheerful, homey air about it, all achieved on a shoestring. Books were stacked helter-skelter, worn copies of everything from business texts to art books, from history to philosophy. He doubted they were Sammy's.

"You read a lot?" he said. When the question drew her back into the room, he gestured toward the well-dusted, obviously well-used collection.

"Buying books is cheaper than taking classes," she said from the archway leading to the kitchen.

"Looks like some pretty heavy stuff. What made you pick it?"

"I got my hands on the reading lists for some of the courses at Boston College," she admitted with a shrug, as if the act had been no big deal. Once again, though, Jason was impressed by her tenacious desire to improve her lot in life. He had taken so much in his life for granted. Dana would probably have made much better use of a college education than he had thus far.

"You amaze me," he said quietly.

Dana's gaze met his, lingered for a heartbeat, then skittered nervously away. Her cheeks turned pink and she hurriedly took the remaining steps into the kitchen. Jason went after her.

The kitchen held a tiny table for two. The red Formica top was decades old and the chairs didn't match. The stove and refrigerator were so ancient Jason wondered that they worked at all.

Dana was silent as she made the coffee. Jason sat down and watched, surprisingly content for the first time since she'd slammed the phone in his ear an hour earlier.

Odd how little time he'd ever spent in a kitchen, he thought. His mother had been a haphazard cook at best, too busy with her causes to bake cookies or stir homemade soup, though he had a vague recollection of a time when that hadn't been so. On those rare days when a housekeeper hadn't left something warming in the oven for their dinner and his father had stayed late at the office, they had ordered pizza or brought home Chinese take-out. Once in a while they'd even gorged themselves on fast-food hamburgers and fries. Always, though, they'd eaten at the huge mahogany table in the dining room. That table could have seated every Pilgrim at the first Thanksgiving. Jason had always hated it.

Now he discovered there was something cozy and intimate about sitting here while Dana bustled around, putting home-baked cookies on a plate and pouring coffee for the two of them. Another knot of tension eased.

She was dressed as she had been when he'd first seen her, in snug-fitting jeans and a sweater that skimmed past her slender hips. This one was as orange as those fake flowers in the living room and featured an abstract design in electric blue. It took everything in him to refrain from the impulse to trace the design from the V-neckline over the swell of her breasts and on to a waistline he was sure he could span with his hands. Instead he forced his gaze on, focusing finally on her feet. Despite the chill in the air, she was wearing only a pair of orange socks. There was something unexpectedly sexy about the sight.

Face it, he told himself. There was something just plain sexy about Dana. He'd fought it, but there was no denying he'd felt it each time he was around her. His body responded forcefully to the slightest touch, the most fleeting glance. Working with her would be sheer torture. The most exquisite sort of torture, but painful none the less.

"Thank you," he said when she finally sat down opposite him. "I take it you've decided to declare a truce."

"For the moment," she acknowledged. "It's your grandfather I should have yelled at."

"I'll give you the number," he offered with a grin. "In fact, I'll even dial it for you."

"What are we going to do?"

After seeing the way she lived, how badly she needed the money, Jason knew he had no choice. He drew in a deep breath. "You're going to take the job."

Troubled eyes met his. "Are you sure? I know it's not what you want."

"I'm sure I'll survive."

"Could you manage to sound at least a little bit enthusiastic about it?"

"Don't expect miracles overnight."

She nodded, but she no longer met his gaze. "Okay,
so where do we go from here?"

Jason followed her cue. "I suppose you should come
by the plant. I think it would be helpful if you could see
what we're all about. It may give you some ideas. Then
I'd like to go over the timetable I have in mind for the
entire campaign, see if it works for you. I don't want
you to feel pressured to meet an unreasonable deadline
just to prove yourself. Once we're certain everything's
in place, then we'll arrange a meeting with my father
and grandfather."

"I think the less I see of your grandfather the better."

"You may have a point, but there's no escaping it.
Granddad likes to be involved in everything. His father
founded Halloran Industries and handed it down to him.
Of course, at the rate Granddad is going, my father and I
won't get our turns until sometime in the next century."

"He doesn't want to retire?"

"He tosses the idea around every once in a while,
then some new project comes along and he can't bring
himself to let go."

Jason couldn't keep the bitterness out of his voice. He
loved his grandfather dearly, but Brandon's tight grip
on the company's entire operation was keeping both
him and his father from any real sense of ownership.
No wonder he was bored. He hadn't made a significant
decision since he'd joined the firm, at least not without
his grandfather looking over his shoulder.

"When can you start?" he asked.

"It'll be a couple of weeks before I can work full-time, but if you need me for something specific before that, I'll try to work it out."

"How about tomorrow?"

"I'll be working."

"Come over on your lunch hour. I'll show you around. I'll order in lunch."

"It takes a half-hour each way on the bus. That hardly leaves time for lunch and a tour."

"You don't have a car?"

"No."

"Then I'll send one for you. Better yet, why don't you let me finance one through our company credit union? You'll need it if you're going to be running back and forth between Halloran Industries and the Lansing offices. Or would you prefer to have me set up an office over at Halloran? I'm sure John would agree."

Once Jason had accepted the fact that there was no way around working with Dana, he'd actually begun warming to the idea. If his grandfather was so enchanted with Dana, perhaps this was Jason's opportunity to actually impress him with the marketing campaign he'd been trying to implement for months now.

However, Dana's expression grew increasingly distressed as Jason's whirlwind enthusiasm mounted. She held up a hand.

"Whoa! Wait a minute!"

"What?"

"I do not want a car of my own. I can't afford it and you know how I feel about credit. As for any running back and forth, I'll manage. I've been taking public transportation around Boston for years." She ticked off the points on her fingers. "Finally if I am going to be working for the Lansing Agency then I should be based

at the Lansing Agency. You're just one account. John
may have other work for me."

"Not right away," Jason argued. "I'll need you full-
time until we get this off the ground."

"Then John can bill you for the travel time. I'm staying at the agency."

Jason recognized the stubborn finality and decided it
was time to slow down and stop pressuring her. He wasn't
entirely sure himself why his mood had shifted from reluctance to excitement. They could both use a little time
to analyze this new relationship and all of its implications.

"We'll try it your way," he conceded. "At the end of
a month we'll take a look at it and see how it's working
out. Fair enough?"

"Fair enough," she agreed, but without much enthusiasm.

Just then the living room door slammed shut and
seconds later Sammy loomed in the doorway. "You're
still here?" he said, an accusatory note in his voice.
The rudeness immediately made Jason's hackles rise.

"Mr. Halloran and I are just finishing up," Dana told
him.

Looking none to pleased, but staying silent, Sammy
grabbed a handful of cookies, then went to the refrigerator and poured himself a glass of milk. All the while
his distrustful gaze never left Jason.

Jason tried to remember all those lessons in human-
ity his father had preached for years during his social
consciousness phase, but Sammy grated on his nerves.
The kid had trouble written all over his face and an attitude that needed changing. That didn't mean Jason
couldn't be polite to him, though. He fished around
for a neutral topic.

"Dana tells me you're a junior this year," he said. "I remember what that was like."

"Sure," Sammy said skeptically. "At some prep school, right?"

Jason sensed the resentment and countered. "No, as a matter of fact, I went to school right here in the city. What classes are you taking?"

"English, history, the usual stuff."

"Doing okay?"

Sammy looked disgusted by the whole line of questioning. Dana jumped in. "He makes good grades. Mostly Bs."

Sammy shrugged.

"Thinking of college?" Jason asked.

"You've gotta be kiddin'. Where am I gonna get the money for college?"

"There are scholarships. You've still got plenty of time to apply."

"My grades aren't that good and I ain't no athlete superstar."

"Don't say that," Dana said. "You're on the swim team."

"Big deal. I don't see anybody offering big bucks to people because they can swim the length of a pool."

"Plenty of colleges have swim teams and they do offer scholarships," Jason contradicted. Too many years of liberal dinner table conversations prompted him to offer, "Want me to look into it for you?"

Sammy regarded him with blatant suspicion. "Why would you do that? You figure if you get rid of me, you can get my sister into bed?"

Dana turned pale. Infuriated at the kid's insulting audacity, Jason was halfway out of his chair when Dana shot him a quelling look. She leveled a furious gaze on her brother and said quietly, "I think it's time you did your studying."

Sammy looked ready to argue, but Dana's expression stopped him. Finally he shrugged and left the room without a goodbye.

"He owes you an apology," Jason said, keeping a tight rein on his temper. "For that matter, he owes me one, too. Or maybe you should just wash his mouth out with soap."

Dana regarded him levelly. "That's a little outdated, isn't it?"

"It may be old-fashioned, but it's effective when garbage comes out of a kid's mouth."

"Look, he didn't mean anything by it. He's probably just feeling threatened. I don't usually have men coming around. He doesn't understand that this is just business."

Her expression dared him to contradict her. Jason ran his fingers through his hair in a gesture of pure frustration. By now his hair was probably every bit as mussed as hers. He was beginning to see how her style had evolved. Sammy seemed to have that effect on everyone.

"Dana, you can't make excuses for a kid that age. He needs to learn that there are consequences for stepping out of line. Did you punish him when he stole the VCR? I mean did you do something more than make him give it to the church?"

Her hands were shaking when she finally looked at him. "This is none of your business."

"It is when he makes an ugly remark about our relationship."

"Since we don't *have* a relationship, I don't think we need to worry about any more remarks."

"One was too many."

"And I'm telling you it won't happen again. I can handle Sammy."

Dana's tone didn't allow for any more interference from him. Jason bit back the desire to tell her that he'd seen kids like Sammy before. Even in his circle of friends, there had been born troublemakers, kids destined to give their families a rough time. If Sammy wasn't taken in hand now, he was going to cross too far over the line between adolescent pranks and serious criminal activity. He may have already. The VCR deal proved that.

Clearly Sammy was already more troublesome than a caring woman like Dana deserved, Jason thought. Sooner or later she wouldn't be able to bail him out just by running interference for him. He needed firm discipline and he needed it now. Dana, however, would have to reach that conclusion on her own.

Jason sighed. "Just promise that you'll ask if you need some help with him. All boys that age are a handful. I was a terror myself, according to my parents. They like to remind me of that periodically."

"I won't need any help," she said flatly.

Reluctant to leave things on that note, but aware that they'd only end up arguing if he stayed, Jason stood up. "I'll send a car for you tomorrow at noon."

"I told you…"

"I know what you told me, but I need you to look things over as soon as possible. Until you're available full-time, I'll try to make our meetings as convenient for you as possible. Okay?"

Reluctance clearly warred with practicality. "Okay," Dana agreed finally and gave him the address of the print shop where she'd been working.

At the door, Jason's gaze met hers. Confusion filled her eyes.

"I am sorry about Sammy," she said. "What he said was inexcusable."

He touched a fingertip to her lips. "You're not the one who needs to apologize."

She looked so lost that something inside him twisted. Before he could think about what he was doing, Jason leaned down and brushed a gentle kiss across her forehead. As innocent as the kiss was, Dana's breath caught in her throat. Something that might have been panic leaped into her eyes. Jason knew exactly how she felt. He felt as if he'd been slam-dunked by one of the Celtics and was still tangled in the net.

"I'm glad we're going to be working together," he told her, his fingers lingering to caress her cheek. The gentle touch was meant to soothe and tame. "See you tomorrow."

After one last glance, he left hurriedly, before she could see that he was only a scant hairbreadth away from pulling her into his arms and kissing her the way a man kissed a desirable woman who made his senses spin. Who was he kidding? He wasn't running to spare Dana. He was running because in the last five seconds he'd realized he was in water way over his head and sinking fast.

All morning Dana tried to think of some way to avoid going out to Halloran Industries on her lunch hour. She wasn't blind to her own foibles; she recognized that Jason represented a temptation that she couldn't afford in her life. It was getting harder and harder to resist his kisses, more and more difficult to recall why he was all wrong for her, why they were all wrong for each other.

She was not looking for complications, she reminded herself sternly. She was looking to put her foot on the first rung up a tall, professional ladder. Money represented power and, after years of feeling powerless, she wanted that sense of control. She wanted to earn it, though, to know it belonged to her no matter what. Getting involved with Jason would sidetrack that plan. She'd waited too long to lose more time by heading down a dead-end road.

The door to her cramped little office opened. "There's some fellow here for you," Mr. Keane said. "He said you'd be expecting him."

Dana sighed. Obviously she'd hesitated too long to call off Jason's plans. She had a feeling that spoke volumes about her determination to steer as clear of him as was humanly possible under the circumstances.

"You'll be back?" her boss asked, his expression worried. He'd been wearing that same expression since she'd told him this morning that she'd be leaving in two weeks. Though he'd wished her well, he was clearly at a loss about how he'd find anyone to replace her who would do as many extra jobs as she'd done for the same paltry salary. He wanted her fully productive until the last possible second.

"I'll be back," she reassured him. "I'm just going to a lunch meeting with the client I'll be working with when I start my new job."

"Must be some client if he can afford to send a fancy car for you."

"Yeah," she said ruefully. "It's some client."

Chapter 6

Maybe it had been wishful thinking on her part, but Dana had actually expected to find some hired driver waiting for her on the curb outside. She should have known better.

Instead it was Jason himself, his posture relaxed, his golden hair windblown, a smile spreading across his face when she walked out the door. He surveyed the boots, jeans and leather jacket she'd worn in an apparently wasted gesture of defiance and nodded appreciatively, his smile growing. Something about the warmth and approval of that smile heated her insides. Once Jason Halloran decided to make the best of things, obviously he threw over all traces of resentment. She supposed she should have felt grateful. Instead she felt terrified.

No man should have the right to have such a potent effect on a woman, she thought wistfully. Especially on a woman who was trying hard to keep her wits about her.

Jason swept open the door of a low-slung red sports car that was exactly what she would have expected a man like him to drive. It was expensive, impractical and very, very sexy. She barely resisted the urge to run her fingers over the gleaming finish.

Inside she sank into a luxurious bucket seat. She touched the smooth, cream-colored upholstery. The leather was soft as butter. Suddenly she felt as if she were Cinderella on her way to the ball and midnight was still several tantalizing hours away.

"What happened?" she asked, when he was settled behind the wheel. "Couldn't you find a taxi to send for me at this hour?"

"I had an appointment on this side of town, anyway. It was no trouble at all for me to swing by, myself. I figured it would give us longer to talk."

"Very practical," she said. "Why don't I believe you?"

"Because you have this habit of distrusting me?" he suggested without the slightest hint of irritation in his tone. "It's like Pavlov's reflex. I speak, you distrust. Since we've just met, the response can't possibly have anything to do with me. Maybe somebody who looked like me cheated on you in a previous life."

Dana chuckled despite herself and felt a little of her wariness slide away. "I honestly don't recall any cads in my past."

"It's hard to say how many past lives back we're talking about. Can you recall what you were doing in the Middle Ages?"

"Afraid not."

"Any recollections of the French Revolution? The Boston Tea Party? The Civil War?"

"Not a one."

"There, you see? Whatever happened between you and this louse in the past was so awful it's buried in your subconscious. Maybe you ought to see some shrink and dredge it up. Once you've dealt with it, we can get on with things here in the present." He glanced over and grinned at her. "What do you think?"

"I think some of your brain cells froze on the drive over. Did you have the top down?"

"Nope. This is just my lighthearted, accepting-the-inevitable personality."

Dana felt herself responding to Jason's unexpected mood in a way that made her very nervous. It was easy to keep her distance from a man who was stuffy and rigid. This new, relaxed Jason Halloran was devastating. Her defenses were vanishing, even though she didn't trust his declared intentions one bit. She tried to analyze why she distrusted a man she barely knew, but all of a sudden she couldn't think of a single reason more logical than the absurd past-life theory he'd suggested. Which meant there was no reason at all, unless she was willing to admit to the sensual spell he threatened to cast over her.

Maybe she owed the man a chance. If they were going to work together, she really would have to learn to relax just as he had. She couldn't go on questioning his motives for every little action. Then again, if she let down her guard, who knew where things could lead. She bit back the urge to sigh. Her uncomplicated, very focused life suddenly seemed fraught with confusion.

"Tell me about Halloran Industries," she said, hoping to remind both of them that their attention was supposed to be strictly on business. "I know what was in the annual report, but that didn't give me a real feel for the company's history. I think maybe that's what you should be capitalizing on. What do you think?"

To her relief a rare excitement immediately sparked in his light blue eyes. "You mean exploit the fact that this is a family business, that it's been around for four generations, ever since my great-grandfather came over from England at the end of the last century?"

"Exactly. It'll give it a more human image, especially in this age of impersonal conglomerates. Think of a slogan. Four generations of dedication to quality, that sort of thing."

Before Dana realized what he intended, Jason swerved the car to the curb and cut the engine. His hands cupped her cheeks and he kissed her—a quick, impulsive brush of his lips across hers.

Gratitude. That's all it was, she told herself sternly. Like last night's startling goodbye kiss, this one was over almost before the sensation registered. *Almost.* Its swiftness didn't prevent the rise of heat, the lightning flash of desire, but both vanished in a heartbeat, leaving Dana all too readily with the illusion of safety.

"You're fantastic!" he declared, his fingers still warm against her cheeks. "For once Granddad's instincts may have been right. Maybe you will work out. That's the ideal slogan. Everyone will love it, especially my grandfather. Tradition is the only thing that really matters to him."

Dana couldn't help being caught up in his enthusiasm, though a part of her was surprised that he'd embraced the phrase so readily, that he apparently didn't intend to throw up roadblocks at every opportunity. "Are you sure? I mean it was just a suggestion off the top of my head."

"Sometimes the first instincts are the best."

At the exact same instant they both seemed to realize that his hands now rested on her shoulders, that they were still just inches apart.

Talk about first instincts! Suddenly hers had nothing to do with discovering more about textiles. Heat and desire spun through her again, gathering intensity. He was so close that his breath fanned her skin. The exuberant kiss just moments earlier was nothing more than a prelude to this, she realized now. Innocence had been lost to this sparkling awareness. An increasingly familiar, increasingly demanding tension throbbed between them. The lure was irresistible.

"Dana?" It was a soft, questioning plea that matched the confusion in his eyes.

Dana merely sighed, her heart hammering in her chest. Heaven help her, she wanted his mouth to close over hers. She wanted their breath to mingle. She wanted to know the taste of him, the texture of his skin. She could deny it from now until doomsday, but it would be a lie. She wanted to be in his arms. Just for a kiss. Just for this brief moment of discovery.

When she couldn't make herself utter the protest that would have stopped him, he leaned closer, still hesitant, still giving her time to say no. But she couldn't bring herself to do it. With each second that passed, her desire grew. She wanted his lips to caress hers, wanted him to linger long enough for her to savor the unfamiliar sensations that were already exploding inside her.

The first touch was velvet soft and cool. But as if a

fire had been lit somewhere deep inside, the kiss heated. She was aware of the gentle caress of his fingers, of the growing hunger as his mouth claimed hers. With the motor off, the air in the car turned chilly, but Dana felt every bit as hot as if it had been a sunny ninety-five degrees. When the touch of his tongue urged her lips apart, need ripped through her, shaking her with its unexpected intensity.

Why hadn't she known a mere kiss could be like this, that it could awaken astonishing, aching needs? Why did every kiss she'd shared in the past seem as immature and unimportant as those in some silly adolescent game? This one held promise and comfort and danger in an intoxicating blend.

When Jason finally moved away, they were both breathing hard. If she looked half as shaken as she felt, he would know in an instant that he had a power over her that went far beyond his influence with the Lansing Agency. She hoped desperately that he couldn't see that, that the look of triumph and satisfaction on his face had something to do with that crazy slogan she'd come up with and not the few breath-stealing seconds she'd spent in his embrace.

Deep down she knew better, knew that their relationship had shifted onto what for her was uncharted ground. She had gone this far with men before, but never farther. Never had she felt the consuming desire to see where a few kisses might lead.

"I think we ought to be going, don't you?" she said, irritated by the breathless quality of her voice. She knew it would be a waste of what little breath she had to protest that the kiss had been a mistake. They both knew that. She recognized it with dismaying certainty. Jason, for all of his impetuous claiming of her lips, had to know it as well. If anything, he was probably having more second thoughts than she was. It hadn't seemed to matter. That kiss had been as inevitable as a sunrise or the pull of the tides.

"I'm perfectly content to stay right here," he said, his voice low, his gaze lingering in a way that kept her pulse scrambling frantically.

"Jason," she warned, sensing that she was going to have to try those probably futile protests after all.

"Okay, we're going," he said, starting the engine. "But that's not the end of this—not by a long shot."

"It has to be," she retorted quietly.

Serious eyes met hers. "Why?"

"I think that's obvious."

"Not to me."

"Because you're used to getting what you want."

He nodded. "Remember that."

"I don't think I'm likely to forget it," she murmured, grateful that the Halloran Industries building was just ahead.

How was she going to protect herself enough to keep from getting hurt when he remembered that they were all wrong for each other? He was pushy and demanding and powerful. She was struggling to carve a niche in the world. She wouldn't have it handed to her. Power given as a gift could be taken away. How did she make him see that? How did she abstain from the temptation of those potent kisses, the gentle, alluring caresses?

Those questions taunted her as they toured the facility. She was fascinated with everything from the raw wool to the vats of dye, from the giant looms to the finished bolts of cloth. Though it was barely winter, they were already in production on summer fabrics: fine cottons being hand printed with wooden blocks that were centuries old and imported from France. She could have lingered for hours, absorbed by the magic of colorless threads being transformed into rainbows of prints.

Despite her fascination, however, not once could Dana seem to forget that Jason was beside her. One instant his hand was on her back as he guided her through a maze of machinery. Another moment his touch grazed her hand as he held out cloth for her to caress. Nothing, not the coolness of the silks, the soft shimmer of the satins or the richness of the wool blends, could compare with the impact of those seconds when Jason's innocent touch skimmed over her flesh.

By the time they went into his office, Dana felt as if she'd spent six months in the Garden of Eden avoiding the first sinful bite of apple. Her nerves were raw. Desire simmered just below the surface, slamming into her consciousness with the slightest contact.

"How about a glass of wine?" Jason said, forcing her to meet his gaze.

"Wine?"

"With lunch."

Wine was the last thing she needed. She was already too warm, too giddy, deep inside where such reactions were dangerous. Inhibitions flickered too weakly, then disappeared altogether. She mustered one last bit of resolve.

"Just a cup of coffee," she said. "I really should be getting back."

"Not until you've had something to eat. Harriet ordered for us."

Resolved or not, Dana had gone without on too many

occasions to be able to leave food untouched. Reluctantly she sat down at the small table that had been set up by the window in Jason's office. Outside the sun had broken through for the first time in days. It gave the city a silvery cast as it bounced off the windows of the skyscrapers in the distance.

Despite her feelings of guilt over the waste, she found herself merely picking at the lobster salad. She broke off chunks of a croissant and popped them into her mouth without really tasting the delicate, buttery flakiness. The only sensation she was truly aware of was the heat that flared deep inside her each time she met Jason's intense gaze. She tried her best to avoid looking into the blue-gray depths, but again and again her gaze was drawn back.

It irritated the daylights out of her that the man made her so nervous. She'd been on countless dates. Goodness knows, she knew how to carry on a conversation. Most of the time she couldn't seem to shut up. Now, just because she was alone with someone with a little bit of high-class polish, she felt all tongue-tied. No, she corrected. It had nothing to do with Jason's class. The blame belonged on the responses he stirred in her.

Jason was just a man, Dana reminded herself.

Yeah, but what a man! countered a dreamy, feminine voice she'd never heard before.

Oh, grow up, Dana shot right back.

That's the problem, honey. You've just grown up.

Dana was not at all pleased with the way this mental conversation was going. She wasn't much happier with the fascinated expression on Jason's face. He looked as if he could hear every word and was thoroughly enjoying his role in the unexpected awakening of her libido.

"Don't even think about it," she muttered, partly to him, partly to herself.

A knowing grin spread across Jason's face. "Think about what?"

Dana threw down her napkin. "I have to get back to work. Would you call a cab for me?"

"You're running," he observed.

"Will you call the cab or should I do it myself?"

"I'll take you back to work."

When he made no move to get up, she said, "Now."

"As soon as you've eaten your dessert. It's cherry cobbler."

Dana nearly groaned in frustration. How had Jason guessed that cobbler was her favorite? Had he done a background check? He was just the type to leave nothing to chance. Even so, that kind of attention to detail could too easily become addictive. When was the last time anyone had paid attention to what she wanted or needed? Sammy, who knew her better than anyone, couldn't even remember her birthday.

Before Dana could protest that she was full—a blatant lie he'd see through in an instant, anyway—Jason was setting a warm bowl of the rich dessert in front of her. Ice cream melted over the pastry crust, just the way he knew she liked it. He looked so damned pleased with himself, so anxious to please her.

"You don't leave anything to chance, do you?" She didn't mean it as a compliment, but the resentment got lost somewhere between her brain and her voice. Jason heard nothing more than her reluctant gratitude.

"I try my best to please."

"Why?"

"This is your first day with Halloran Industries, after all."

His tone was quietly serious. It was a logical explanation, but she heard the unspoken undercurrents. She put down her spoon and leveled a look at him. "So, Sammy was right. You are aiming to get me into your bed. Or are you trying to scare me off, Mr. Halloran?"

"For some reason, I don't think you scare that easily."

"No, I don't."

He didn't look nearly as embarrassed as she had hoped at having his motives questioned. There was definitely no sign of a quick retreat, just an infuriating, lip-curving hint of amusement.

"I think I liked it better when you were snapping my head off. I don't trust this new act one bit," she said.

"Funny. I would have guessed it was yourself you no longer trusted."

Jason sat back and watched in satisfaction as the full meaning of his remark slowly registered. A blush stole into Dana's cheeks, and the wariness in her eyes increased tenfold. She raked her fingers through her hair.

"Jason, we can't work together if you're going to try to turn this into some sort of seduction every time we have a meeting."

"If you'll recall, I didn't bring it up. You did."

"No, I just..."

"Asked if I wanted to sleep with you."

If anything, Dana looked even more flustered than she had in the car when she had realized that she had kissed him back with every bit as much fervor as he'd displayed. Obviously there was one area in which they could reach an agreement—they both enjoyed playing with fire.

"Okay, you're right. I did say that," she said. "It's best if we get this out in the open and face the fact that it wouldn't work between us."

"I agree," he said, clearly surprising her. "On the other hand, there's something at work here that we can't very well ignore or it will drive us both crazy."

"No, there's not," she denied.

Jason merely regarded her skeptically.

"Okay, so maybe there is this…something. I never expected…"

Jason seized the opening. "What? To get along with me? To want me?"

Dana looked as if she might be grinding her teeth. Finally she said, "I do not want you."

"I could prove just what a liar you are."

Her chin lifted. "How?"

"Don't tempt me."

"How?" she repeated evenly. The dare in her voice belied the doubt in her eyes.

Without allowing himself so much as an instant to consider what he was doing, Jason was around to her side of the table before she could blink. Hands firmly on her waist, he lifted her to her feet and dragged her against him. He looked into the worried blue depths of her eyes and said softly, "Like this."

Then his lips claimed hers, tasting the faint sweetness of cherries, the creaminess of ice cream, the flavor that was uniquely hers. This time Jason abandoned gentle persuasiveness in favor of raw hunger. He had to rid himself of this need that had sprung up seemingly overnight. Those kisses had been like drink for an alcoholic, intoxicating and addictive. It was clear he would never be satisfied until he'd made love to her. Perhaps then he could get back to thinking rationally, the way he always did. This wouldn't be the first time in his life he'd given in to a foolish impulse.

Dana didn't even pretend to fight the kiss. There was the faintest hint of an astonished gasp, and then she was kissing him back, fitting her body to his with an instinctive need every bit as hot and urgent as his own. He could feel the scrambling of her pulse as his fingers curved around her neck. His own heart pounded, the strength of its beat an affirmation of the passion he knew existed between them. Her skin, soft as silk beneath the hem of her sweater, went from shivery cool to searing hot at his touch.

She was still trembling in his arms, her fingers laced together behind his neck, her lips soft and sweet and yielding beneath his, when the door to his office banged open.

"What the devil?" His grandfather's startled reaction was quickly followed by a tolerant chuckle. "Maybe this is a bad time."

"It is," Jason confirmed, holding an obviously embarrassed Dana tight against him. "Go away."

Brandon wasn't about to be turned away so easily. "Not before I say hello to this young woman again," he insisted, striding across the room.

"Save the charm, Granddad. We're both on to you."

Undaunted, Brandon just shrugged. "Just looking out for the company's interests." He grinned at Dana. His gaze lingered on her sweater, a crazy quilt of hot pink, lime green and lemon yellow. His eyes narrowed.

"Interesting," he muttered finally. "Where did you get it?"

Dana was regarding him as if he'd lost his mind. "Get what, sir?"

"The sweater, girl. Cheap yarn, but the design's good. Bold. I like it."

She seemed more confused than offended by the criticism of the wool's quality. "You like it?"

Brandon chuckled. "Sorry. Occupational hazard. Can't resist seeing what the competition's up to."

"I'm afraid I'm not much competition. You have nothing to worry about. It's a very limited edition."

"You designed it?" he said, sounding no more surprised than Jason was himself. Jason regarded the sweater more closely and began to wonder about all the others he'd seen her wear. Had she designed those as well?

"Designed and knit it. I'm afraid you're right about the yarn, but it's the dimestore's best."

She stepped away from Jason. He dragged her back and leaned down to whisper, "Remember, we're in this together."

She glared at him, then tried to stare Brandon Halloran down. "Just for the record, sir, I'm not *dating* your grandson. I don't even *like* your grandson."

Brandon chuckled. "I see. Too bad. Seems to me he could use a woman with a little spunk in his life. The boy doesn't have anyone around to keep him on his toes. Needs to have a little fun."

Dana regarded him with an expression that was both disbelieving and irritated. "Love is a responsibility. It's not some game you play."

"That's true enough," Brandon told her with a gentleness and sensitivity Jason wouldn't have believed his grandfather capable of. Apparently the old man had detected Dana's insecurities and intended to rid her of them.

He went on, "I have a few years on you, young lady, and I'm here to tell you, a relationship works a whole lot better if you can pack a little fun and a lot of sparks into it. Now, you two get back to whatever it was you were—" he hesitated, a twinkle in his eyes "—discussing. Oh, and Jason, I'd like to see you in my office whenever you're free… No rush," he added slyly as he closed the door firmly behind him.

Dana immediately spun out of Jason's arms. "Now, see what you've done! He's going to think because he caught us…"

"Kissing," Jason supplied.

"He's going to think he's winning."

Jason drew her to him. "Well, we'll have the last laugh, won't we?"

She jerked away from him. He sat on the edge of his desk and watched her pace, her agitation mounting with each step. She stopped in front of him.

"I don't think you're taking this seriously."

"Believe me, when it comes to my future, I take everything seriously."

"Well then?" she demanded. "How are you going to convince him he can't manipulate us?"

"Would you suggest I take him out and give him a stern talking to?"

"It wouldn't hurt," she grumbled.

"It wouldn't help, believe me. Granddad's as stubborn as they come."

Her fingers plowed nervously through her hair, setting it on end as she began pacing again. "You're awfully calm about this."

"Dana, he can't make us do anything we don't want to do."

"I'm not so sure about that."

"Well, I am. Relax."

Apparently Dana did not appreciate his matter-of-fact attitude about his grandfather. She looked as if she'd like to strangle the pair of them.

"Jason, what happened just now…"

"And earlier and last night," he reminded her.

She scowled at him. "It is not going to happen again. Ever! We are working together, that's all. If you can't accept that, then I'll arrange to have someone else assigned to your account." She grabbed her jacket and purse from the sofa where she'd dropped them and stormed through the door.

Jason figured it would take about ten seconds for her to realize that she was stranded unless she asked him to arrange for a ride back to her office. He counted on another sixty seconds for her to cool down enough to ask for a lift.

When three minutes had passed without her return, he realized she had every intention of getting back to the print shop on her own. He snatched his coat off the coatrack and took off after her.

"Mr. Halloran," Harriet called after him, "where are you going?"

"I'll be back in an hour."

"But…"

"Take messages, Harriet."

"Your grandfather…"

"He'll understand."

He found Dana halfway to the bus stop. He pulled his car alongside of her. She didn't even look his way. He used the power button to roll down the window.

"Get in."

"Go to hell." She tripped over a mound of icy slush and nearly fell facedown. She grabbed the hood of the car to steady herself.

Teeth clenched, Jason said again, "Get in. I'll take you back to work."

Stubbornly, Dana marched on. There were half a dozen people at the bus stop. Jason wedged his car into the curb, cut the engine and got out.

"Dana, for heaven's sake, don't be an idiot. Let me give you a lift."

She stood behind the other riders and stoically ignored him. He clambered through the slush until he stood face-to-face with her—Italian loafer toe-to-toe with her motorcycle boot.

"Are you more upset over the kiss, or my grandfather catching us or over the fact that you didn't want to be interrupted any more than I did?"

Six faces turned toward the two of them. It was impossible to mistake the amused interest. With the wind whipping down the street, Jason was sure their intimate conversation provided some much-needed heat. How the hell did he wind up in the middle of some scene every time he was with this woman?

"Jason," Dana protested weakly.

"Well, which is it?"

"Do we have to discuss this here?" she demanded in an undertone.

He shook his head. "No. We could discuss it in my car."

She sighed. "Okay, you win." She slogged through the slush and got into the car, leaving the observers thoroughly disappointed. One of the men gave Jason a thumbs-up sign.

"Hey, man, good luck. I have a hunch you're going to need it."

Jason grinned. "I have a hunch you're right," he said, just as a handful of filthy snow landed squarely in the middle of his face. Stunned by her daring, he slowly wiped it away as he rounded the car to the driver's side. As he slid in, he shot Dana a meaningful look.

"You will pay for that, sweetheart," he said quietly.

"Hey, it was your grandfather who said you needed me to bring a little fun into your life. I see what he means. You can't take a joke."

As the remnants of the snowball melted and dripped down his face, Jason found himself chuckling. "I'm not sure this was exactly the fun he had in mind."

"Oh?" she said innocently. "Trust me, *sweetheart*, it's the only kind you and I are likely to have."

"I guess we'll see about that, won't we?" Actually he had discovered in the past twenty-four hours that he could hardly wait for the games to begin.

Dear Lord, he really was losing his mind.

Chapter 7

Jason pulled his car into the first space he could find along the crowded street near the print shop. Before he could cut the engine, Dana had the door open. She swung her long legs out, stepped onto the curb and practically raced down the sidewalk without a backward glance. Jason sat for about sixty seconds admiring the sway of those slender hips, then slowly climbed out to follow. As if she sensed him behind her and actually thought she could elude him, she picked up her pace.

He assumed that sooner or later she would cool off, but for the moment her temper was still steaming mad and her determination to hold him at arm's length was rock solid. It would be fascinating to see how long she could hold out once he launched his full-fledged assault on her senses.

Jason was so busy imagining Dana's eventual passionate capitulation that he nearly missed the fact that she'd paused in her impatient rush back to work. Standing in the middle of the sidewalk, she leaned down to talk to a tiny, white-haired woman, who was bundled up from head to toe in the wildest combination of colors Jason had ever seen besides one of Dana's sweaters. Bright blue sweatpants were topped by a garish green jacket. A plaid scarf in bold squares of bumble bee black and yellow had been wound around her neck. A perky red cap sat jauntily on her head. She looked like a delightful gnome.

Jason was even more enchanted when he overheard her ask in a conspiratorial whisper that carried on the winter wind, "Was that him? Was that handsome man who picked you up earlier your new boss? I couldn't believe that fancy car of his. It must have cost a fortune. You don't suppose he'd take me for a ride in it one of these days, do you?"

Jason couldn't quite hear Dana's murmured response, but it was impossible to miss the sudden stain of color in her cheeks.

The woman patted Dana's hand. "Dear, mind what I say now. You really mustn't let him get away. He looks like the kind of man who would know how to treat a woman like you the way she deserves to be treated."

Dana was almost as red as the woman's cap by the time Jason reached her side. The old woman squinted up at him through lenses as thick as bottle glass.

"Oh my, yes," she murmured without the slightest hint of embarrassment at being overheard. Once she'd examined him thoroughly from head to toe with blatant curiosity, she declared, "I was right. You are a handsome one."

Jason grinned and introduced himself since Dana seemed to be both speechless and mortified.

"And I'm Mrs. Finch," the little woman replied. "I own a small bookstore in the neighborhood. Stop in sometime and I'll give you a cup of tea. We can have a nice long chat." Catching sight of Dana's glare, she added, "About books."

"I'd like that," Jason said.

"Mrs. Finch's favorites are romances," Dana muttered, her expression sour.

Jason grinned. "There's absolutely nothing I'd rather talk about. Maybe you'd like to go for a spin in my car. I've always preferred driving with an appreciative passenger." He glanced pointedly at Dana.

"I have to go to work," Dana said, turning her back on the two of them.

With a final conspiratorial wink at Mrs. Finch and a promise to visit her shop soon, Jason followed Dana inside. She had her jacket off and was seated at a desk piled high with galleys by the time he got to her. Her brow was furrowed in concentration as she stared at the top sheet of type. He might have believed her absorption, if the page hadn't been upside down. He righted it.

She scowled up at him. "Jason, go away. I have work to do. I'm not on your payroll yet."

"Actually, you are. John started billing me for your time as of today."

"I trust you'll let him charge you for the lunch you insisted I eat."

He leaned closer to look over her shoulder, bracing his hands on either side of her. His voice dropped to a seductive purr. "Nope. The lunch and the kiss were definitely not business."

Jason caught the quick, undeniable flare of heat in her eyes at the mention of that kiss. Dana could protest from now until doomsday that there was nothing between them, but her eyes would always give her away. Instead she shook her head and sighed as if she'd grown tired of fighting with him.

"Less than twenty-four hours ago you acted as if you couldn't stand the sight of me. What happened to change your mind?"

"I caved in to my baser instincts."

She gave him a disgusted look. "Is that supposed to make me feel better?"

"Actually I do have a smoother technique. Should I try it out?"

"Can't you give it a rest?"

"I don't think so. Not until you agree to see me again."

"I will see you again," she said, too quickly. "We're going to be working together."

"Not good enough."

"It has to be."

Just then her rotund, balding boss huffed up with a harried expression on his face. "You're back, finally!" he said, his tone more worried than accusing, though Dana seemed to hear only an accusation.

"I'm sorry, Mr. Keane," she apologized at once, her tone uncharacteristically meek. "My lunch hour took longer than I'd planned. I'll stay late to make up the work."

He waved off the offer. "No, no, forget the work. You had a call—emergency, they said."

Dana's face went pale. "Sammy?"

Jason put his arm around her and felt her whole body trembling. When he took her icy hands in his, she instinctively clung to him. He doubted she was even aware of the contact. She was totally focused on her boss, her expression anxious.

"His school," Mr. Keane confirmed, "again. They want you there right away. I told them I couldn't reach you and that I would send you as soon as you got back."

"Is he sick?" she asked, but Jason suspected she already knew that wasn't the problem. He wondered how many calls like this she'd had. Neither she nor her boss appeared as shocked as they might have been.

"They didn't say. Go. I can read any proofs that have to be done today. What I don't finish, you can do tomorrow."

Dana dropped Jason's hand and grabbed her jacket. "Thank you."

"You'll let me know what has happened?" Mr. Keane asked.

Jason sensed that behind the abrupt facade, the man was genuinely fond of Dana and concerned about Sammy. Obviously, though, he didn't want her to know how much.

"I'll call you later," she promised, as she ran through the shop. Outside she headed straight for the bus stop.

"No. I'll drive you," Jason said, surprised that for once she didn't argue. She simply nodded and turned toward the car. Obviously, where Sammy was concerned, she would make a pact with the devil himself if that's what it took to reach her errant brother.

Once she'd given him the directions to the school, though, she clammed up. With her gaze fixed on the passing scenery and her hands clasped tensely in her lap, she looked as if she were struggling against tears. For what seemed the hundredth time since he and Dana

met, Jason wanted to throttle Sammy for putting that
worried crease in her forehead. He searched for some
way to comfort her, but words seemed totally inadequate.
Besides, anything he could think of to say about Sammy
right now would not be a comfort. It would only infuriate her and deepen her pain. Since he couldn't think of a
consoling alternative, he remained as silent as she was.

As they turned the corner in front of the old building, she said stiffly, "Thanks for the lift. You can let
me out here."

He ignored the request, finally pulling into the
school's parking lot. "I'm going with you," he said
blandly, not entirely certain why he felt this need to
stick by her. Maybe it was that flicker of fear in her
eyes that told him her strength was about at its limits.
He told himself if there'd been anyone else she could
have turned to, he would have happily left her, but he
wasn't nearly so sure it was as true today as it might
have been just yesterday.

Afraid or not, her gaze shot to meet his at last. "No."

"Save your breath. I'm going."

"Jason, why? This doesn't concern you."

"It concerns you, doesn't it? If it concerns you, it
concerns me."

"Sammy will just resent your involvement."

His temper flared and he muttered a harsh curse
under his breath. "Frankly, at this point, what Sammy
feels doesn't matter a damn to me."

Alarm filled her eyes. "I won't have you yelling at him."

"He'll be lucky if I don't break his neck."

"You don't even know what he did."

"I know that when you heard the school had called,

you turned absolutely pale. I have to assume you think it's pretty bad."

For an instant she looked as if she was going to argue some more, then her shoulders sagged. "Maybe he just has the flu."

"You don't believe that."

"I want to," she said so wistfully that it wrenched Jason's heart.

His tone softened and he gently brushed away the single tear that had dared to track down her cheek. "I'm sure you do. Let's go see what's going on. There's no point sitting here speculating. Whatever it is, we'll handle it."

"*I'll* handle it."

The words were filled with Dana's usual spunk, but Jason couldn't miss the despair in her eyes, the dejection in the set of her shoulders. For just an instant her lower lip quivered, then as if she'd resolved to tough it out as she always did, she gathered her composure. Clenching her purse so tightly her knuckles turned white, she left the car and stormed off toward the principal's office like some sort of avenging angel, not waiting to see whether Jason followed. He couldn't decide whether he wanted to shake her or kiss her. The woman had so much honor, so damned much loyalty, albeit seriously misguided from what he'd seen of Sammy.

Jason could practically hear his father's voice reminding him that not everyone in the world had it as good as he did and that Hallorans owed it to the less fortunate to give them a helping hand. Up to now his idea of charity had been writing several large checks and putting them in the mail. Maybe it would be good for him to see firsthand what it meant to deal with a troubled kid.

Everyone in the office seemed to recognize Dana the instant she stepped through the door. Gazes met hers and skittered nervously away. Jason did not consider that a good sign. It seemed to confirm his suspicion that these visits happened all too regularly.

"Hi, Ms. Roberts. I'll get Mr. DeRosario," the clerk working at the reception desk said. "He wants to see you before you pick up your brother."

"Is Sammy okay?" Dana asked.

Though the woman looked sympathetic, her only comment was a terse, "Mr. DeRosario will explain."

Jason took an instant liking to the tall, kind-looking man who stepped out of his office and headed toward them. Though the man's expression was serious, his eyes were gentle, suggesting a personality that blended discipline and compassion in equal measures. Jason didn't know much about the education system, but he imagined that the combination was sorely needed in today's overburdened urban schools.

The man greeted Dana with a smile, then glanced curiously at Jason.

"I'm Jason Halloran, a friend of Ms. Roberts," he told the principal. "I came along in case there might be something I can do to help."

"Good."

"Mr. DeRosario, what happened?" Dana asked. "Is my brother all right?"

"Your brother is fine, but I'm afraid I'm going to have to suspend him."

"Suspend him?" Dana echoed. She drew in a deep breath, then asked, "Why?"

"He had a knife, Ms. Roberts. He pulled it during an argument with another student."

"A knife?" she repeated dully. Tears pooled in her eyes, but she managed to keep her voice steady. "Was the other student hurt?"

"No. Thankfully it never went that far. But I cannot tolerate this kind of behavior. We've discussed this before. I've done my best to make allowances for Sammy's circumstances, but I won't allow him to put the other students at risk."

Dana nodded wearily. "I understand. How long will he be suspended?"

"Two weeks this time."

"This time?" Jason questioned, barely controlling his own dismay. "He's done this before?"

The principal nodded. "Sammy seems to feel the solution to his problems is violence. He's instigated several brawls already this school year." He turned to Dana. "I understand that things have been difficult for you, but I strongly urge you to get him some counseling."

"I tried. He won't go."

"He'll go," Jason muttered, daring Dana to contradict him. "Thank you, Mr. DeRosario. I think I understand what's been happening here. If Sammy can go now, we'll take him home."

Mr. DeRosario nodded. "I sincerely hope you can reach him. He's a bright boy, but he's going to have serious problems if his attitude isn't dealt with soon."

"I assure you it will be," Jason said.

As soon as the principal had gone after Sammy, Dana whirled on him. "How dare you interfere like that! This has nothing to do with you."

"It does now." He wondered if he was losing his

mind. Why would a sane man willingly get involved in the salvation of a kid who used a knife to solve his problems? Maybe there was more of Kevin Halloran in him than he'd ever realized. He'd always chalked his father's do-gooder tendencies up to leftover sixties social consciousness.

"Jason!" Dana protested.

"We'll discuss it later," Jason said quietly. "Right now, you and I are going to show your brother a united front."

"Just why are we going to do that?" she snapped, obviously fuming at his intrusion into what she considered a family matter.

He cupped her face in his hands, barely resisting the desire to kiss away the last traces of tears. "Because if we don't, Sammy might never have a chance." He said it slowly and with enough conviction that Dana swallowed whatever she'd been about to say next. She looked thoroughly shaken and, for the first time since he'd met her, she looked defeated. That look touched his soul.

But when Sammy walked out of the principal's office, Dana squared her shoulders and leveled a nononsense look straight at him. Sammy started to protest his innocence, but she glared at him and he fell silent.

"I'll see you back here in two weeks," the principal said, his hand on Sammy's shoulder.

"Whatever," Sammy said, his tone sullen.

"Think about what we discussed."

"Yeah, sure."

Sammy backed toward the door, then whirled and sprinted outside. They caught up with him at the bottom of the steps. No one spoke until they reached the car, then Sammy balked.

"I'm not riding with him," he said to his sister.

"I've had just about all I can take from you for one day. Get in the car. Now!" she said, all of her fury spilling out in that one order.

Sammy took one quick glance at her stormy expression and began to look uncertain for the first time. He climbed in.

When they finally reached Dana's apartment, the tension in the car swirled like a thick, dispiriting fog. Dana started to open the door, but Jason put his hand over hers.

"In a minute," he said. "I have to go back to the office, but I want to say something first." He turned to face Sammy. "I'm sure you love your sister and I'm sure you don't set out to make her unhappy, but you have. I don't want it to happen again, so you and I are going to make an effort not only to get along, but to fix that lousy attitude of yours. We're starting tonight. I'll pick you up at eight."

"Not a chance," Sammy said. "I didn't commit no crime. I don't need a probation officer."

"Actually you *did* commit a crime. You'll be very lucky if the other student doesn't press charges, so don't smart-mouth me on that score. It's me or a counselor. Take your pick," Jason said, his voice clipped. Where the hell was his father when he needed him? Was he going about this the right way? All he had to guide him were his instincts and that faint glimmer of hope that was finally sparking in Dana's eyes.

Sammy turned pale. He studied Jason closely, as if measuring the chances for a reprieve, then glanced at Dana. Whatever she was thinking about Jason's plans, she didn't contradict him. Apparently Sammy decided that his choices truly were limited to those two. "I'll be ready," he said resentfully.

Jason nodded. "Good. Bring your gym clothes and sneakers."

Sammy looked startled. "Why?"

"Just bring them." He squeezed Dana's hand. "I'll talk to you later, okay?"

She nodded. All the way back to the office, Jason had to fight the image of the fearful expression in her eyes when he'd mentioned the possibility of assault charges. How many times had she walked into that school dreading such an outcome? How much longer could Sammy escape serious jail time? If it took being pals with a juvenile delinquent to wipe away Dana's fears, then that's what he was going to do.

For one fleeting instant Jason wished like crazy that he'd had the good sense to override his grandfather's manipulating moves and refused to work with Dana. What he knew about dealing with a kid as troubled as Sammy would fit on the head of a pin. As for what he knew about a woman like Dana, his expertise failed him there as well, but he was definitely learning fast.

"Cute girl," Brandon Halloran observed when Jason finally got to his office. "Reminds me of someone I used to know."

"I'm surprised you lived to tell about it," Jason muttered.

Brandon chuckled. "I think you'll be surprised at just how easily you adapt."

"I don't want to adapt."

"But you will," Brandon said with confidence. "You will. By the way, I've been thinking it's time to bring your father up to speed on this whole marketing thing we've got working. You know how he gets if he thinks one of us is keeping secrets from him. He's been meaner than a tied-up pit bull these last few weeks. Any idea what's going on with him?"

"I think he and Mom had some sort of disagreement. Neither one of them is saying much, but the last time I dropped by their house the tension was pretty awful."

"Think we ought to have a man's night out at my club and get to the bottom of things?"

"I think if we try, Dad will just clam up or tell us to mind our own damned business."

Brandon grinned. "Never let that stop me before. No need to stop now. You free tonight?"

"Not really," he began, then caught sight of the expression on his grandfather's face. He forgot all too often how lonely things must be for his grandfather since his wife of nearly fifty years, Jason's grandmother, had died in the spring. Though Brandon put on a good front most of the time, there were times, like now, when his sorrow was unmistakable.

"Tonight would be great, if we can make it early."

"Early is best for me, too," Brandon said. "Say six-thirty. You tell your father. Hog-tie him if you have to."

Jason chuckled at the idea of making Kevin Halloran do anything he'd set his mind against. Of all of them, his father was the most stubborn. "I'll do my best," he said.

It looked to Jason as if his entire evening was likely to be spent with men who, with the exception of his grandfather, weren't particularly interested in sharing his company.

Chapter 8

Dinner was not a success. Kevin Halloran maintained a stoic silence throughout the meal, responding to questions in terse monosyllables whenever he could get away with it. He barely touched his prime rib, but steadily sipped the cabernet sauvignon. Jason's frustration matched that of his grandfather's tone when Brandon finally snapped, "Son, what the hell is wrong with you?"

Raking his hand through blond hair shot with silver, Kevin glared at his father. "Nothing I care to talk about."

"Well, you've made that clear enough. Since when can't you open up with family?"

His expression utterly exhausted, Kevin rubbed his hand across his eyes. "Dad, please. Drop it. Let's talk about anything else—the weather, sports—I don't give a damn. Just leave my state of mind out of the conversation."

"Granddad's just worried about you," Jason reminded

him. "So am I. You've been like this for weeks now. Are you feeling okay? Have you seen a doctor lately?"

Kevin threw down his napkin and shoved his chair back. "If I'd wanted to be psychoanalyzed, I could have gone home," he snapped. As if horrified by what he'd revealed as well as the uncharacteristic display of raw anger, he mumbled, "I'm sorry, Dad. Jason. I have things to do. I'll see you both at the office tomorrow."

He stalked off, leaving Jason and Brandon to stare at each other in open-mouthed astonishment.

"What do you suppose that was all about?" Brandon said finally. "Kevin's not a man to lose control."

"You don't suppose he and Mom are really having problems, do you? That crack about being psychoanalyzed at home sounded pretty bitter."

Jason had never been more shaken. The thought that his parents' marriage might be in serious trouble threw him for a loop. He'd always viewed them as a perfect example of marital harmony. They'd been married nearly thirty years, had known each other since childhood. When he'd been growing up, his home had been filled with laughter and genuine affection. He'd considered himself one of the luckiest kids around. Had something gone terribly wrong in these last two months, something that in his absorption with his own life he had failed to notice?

"Damned if I know what to think," Brandon responded, his expression bewildered. "I do know that it won't do us a bit of good to try to pry any more information out of him, while he's in this mood. Your father's a proud man. Never was one to share his problems. Never did like anyone to catch him down."

Brandon suddenly looked weary, every one of his

sixty-eight years showing. "Guess I made a mistake in pressing for answers."

"You were just trying to help. We both were."

"Maybe so, but I should have known better. It looks like we just made things worse."

"I'll talk to Mom," Jason promised. "Maybe she'll tell me what's going on."

Brandon sighed. "I wish I were closer to your mother. She's a good woman."

Jason stared at him in astonishment. "I've always thought the two of you got along just fine."

"We've done pretty well at maintaining a truce, but there was a time when she didn't owe me the time of day. I suspect you know I tried to keep your father away from her. It's one of my real regrets."

Jason had heard bits of the story before. He knew that Lacey Grainger Halloran had long since forgiven his grandfather for his interference, that family had always been every bit as important to her as it was to his grandfather and she'd worked hard at mending fences. He'd always thought his grandfather recognized that bond.

"Granddad, she doesn't hold that against you. Not after all this time."

"Wouldn't blame her if she did." He met Jason's gaze. "You run along. I know you have plans."

"I don't want to leave you."

"Don't worry about me. I think I'll stay here and have a brandy. I saw some of my friends go into the card room a while back. Maybe I'll join them. Haven't played bridge since your grandmother died."

Jason felt torn. He didn't want to leave his grandfather alone when he was in this strange melancholy mood, but he didn't dare cancel the plans with Sammy, either. The idea of asking his grandfather along crossed his mind, but he dismissed it at once. If his grandfather had tried to keep his father and a woman as sweet as Lacey Grainger apart, who knew what he would do if he met Sammy while he was at his rebellious worst. It might forever change the way he felt toward Dana and, for some reason he couldn't entirely explain, Jason didn't want that to happen.

He squeezed his grandfather's shoulder. "Try not to worry. Dad will be okay."

Brandon placed a hand over his. "At my age worrying about family just comes naturally."

As Jason drove across town to Dana's, he knew exactly what his grandfather meant. All through dinner Dana and Sammy had never been far from his mind. Family. His family. The thought brought him up short. Where the hell had that come from?

When he got to the apartment, he bounded up the stairs and rapped lightly on the door, wondering if he shouldn't be taking the first flight out of town instead.

Dana looked surprised to see him. "I thought you were going to call first."

"I said I'd be here at eight. Is Sammy ready?"

"He's not here."

Jason's gaze narrowed. "What do you mean he's not here?" he asked slowly, fighting to keep a lid on his temper.

She held up a hand. "Don't get angry. He's just downstairs. He'll be back in a minute. I want to talk to you before you leave, anyway."

He shoved his hands in his pockets and waited for the explosion of outrage over his arrogant interference. Dana watched him for a minute, then said, "I'm sorry."

He blinked. "Sorry?"

Her smile was rueful. "Don't sound so shocked. You know perfectly well I owed you an apology. I overreacted at the school this afternoon. You were just trying to help. I don't know why you'd want to get mixed up in this, but I'm grateful."

He brushed an errant hair away from her face. "Why did my wanting to help upset you so much in the first place?"

As if to escape his touch, she began to pace. "I thought you were convinced I couldn't handle it myself. Since I was already feeling like a failure, it was like rubbing salt in a wound. I've done a lot of thinking since then. If you can accomplish something with Sammy that I can't, then that has to be my first priority. I won't interfere."

Jason heard the stoic resolve and sensed the deep hurt behind it. "Dana," he said, stepping in front of her and taking her hands, "you have not failed anyone, least of all your brother."

She regarded him anxiously. "Then why does it feel that way?"

"Because parents—and for all intents and purposes that's what you are—parents always seem to blame themselves when things go wrong for their kids. I just spent a couple of hours with my grandfather, who's feeling guilty for mistakes he made years ago with my father. Sammy isn't a child anymore. He's making choices for himself, choices you can't control."

"But they're such bad choices."

"Yes," he agreed, seeing no reason to sugarcoat the obvious. "And between us, we are going to make him see that."

Uncertain whose need was greater, he pulled her into his arms and simply held her. At first she was stiff, but then she melted against him, her arms tightening around his waist, her cheek resting against his chest. Jason felt the distinct stirring of desire at the press of her breasts, the warm brush of her thighs. As if he was no longer in control, his hands slid down her back to cup her bottom more tightly against him. He felt an immediate rush of heat and drew in a ragged breath. This felt far too right. What would happen when he could no longer get his common sense to outweigh this attraction that was growing day by day? What worried him most was that it was deepening on all levels, not just the physical. As he became more and more entangled in Dana's life, he saw her strengths more clearly. She was beginning to bring out traits in him that he hadn't even known existed. Just being here tonight was a perfect example, but spending an evening with Sammy was the last thing on his mind at the moment.

Jason tilted Dana's chin up and gazed into her eyes. "I want you," he said bluntly, so there could be no mistaking his intentions.

Her eyes widened. "Where did that come from?"

Though his body ached for her, he tried to laugh off the desire. He loosened his hold, but he couldn't quite bring himself to release her. "I'll be damned if I know," he admitted. "Sometimes I'm just as stunned by it as you are. Something tells me that sooner or later we're going to have to deal with these feelings, though. We can't go on denying them."

Dana wasn't sure whether her heart was hammering from Jason's nearness or from his promise. It was something she wasn't likely to discover tonight, either.

Jason stepped away just as the door opened and Sammy burst in. His glance went from Jason to Dana and back again. For an instant he looked as if he wanted to make an issue out of the embrace he'd interrupted, but apparently he read something in Jason's expression that stopped him. Dana was grateful for that. She didn't think she could stand another outburst on a day that had been filled with emotional peaks and valleys.

Though he kept one hand on her waist, Jason focused his attention on Sammy. "You ready, pal?"

"Where are we going?"

"To the gym. If you feel like fighting, I'm going to show you a way to do it that will keep you out of trouble."

Dana saw the reluctant spark of interest in Sammy's eyes and heard the eagerness in his tone when he asked, "You and me are gonna fight?"

"That's right," Jason said.

Somehow the prospect of her brother and Jason going at it tooth and nail did not strike Dana as a wildly terrific idea. Jason would expect to play by the rules. Sammy would not. "I'm coming, too," she announced, grabbing her jacket.

Both men stared at her. "Why?" Sammy asked. "You don't like it when I fight."

"That's right. Besides, I will not have either of you knowing moves that I can't counter," she said, giving Jason a meaningful look.

"Dana," he protested.

"Don't even try to stop me. I've made up my mind. I'll get my things."

As she left the room, Jason and Sammy exchanged a *what-do-you-expect-from-a-woman* sort of look.

"Okay," Jason said with obvious reluctance. "Let's go."

At the sight of the seedy gym, Dana began to have second thoughts. For some reason she'd been hoping for some fancy health club, maybe a sterile martial arts studio with mirrors and mats. She had not been expecting a place with punching bags that looked as if they'd been through a half century of practice, a decrepit barn of a building where the smell of sweat and the sound of painful grunts were clearly commonplace. What startled her even more than the grime and low-class atmosphere was the fact that Jason seemed perfectly at home.

Half a dozen men in boxing shorts, their bare chests gleaming with perspiration, greeted him and stared at her with open curiosity. She halted just inside the door. "Maybe this was a bad idea," she said, though she had to admit to a certain fascination.

"Oh, no, you don't," Jason said with a grin. "You're not backing out on us now. Just try to keep your eyes off all the other men." He turned toward the grizzled old man who was working with a gigantic black man. "Hey, Johnny, since we're short on ladies' dressing rooms around here, do you mind if my friend uses your office to change?"

"It's okay with me, as long as she doesn't try to tidy up."

"I wouldn't dream of it," Dana declared, though she had cause to reconsider when she saw the mess the office was in.

Apparently paperwork was not Johnny's forte. Stacks of it, most with yellowed corners and faded type, were piled on what was most likely a dining room table. Nothing that looked remotely like a file cabinet existed, though there were a dozen or so boxes scattered on the floor. It seemed as though someone had once made a haphazard attempt to turn those boxes into a filing system. They were lettered A-F, G-I and so on. Most contained boxing gloves and what looked to be bottles of liniment. Dana itched to make order out of chaos, but settled for changing into shorts and a T-shirt.

It took a certain amount of courage to step back out into a room filled with sweaty, macho men in what suddenly seemed to be fairly revealing attire. She quickly realized, though, that Jason seemed to be the only one paying much attention to her legs. The look in his eyes made her pulse race. At this rate she wouldn't have to bother with aerobics to get her heart rate up—the sight of Jason's bare chest, with its whorl of golden blond hairs, was enough to do that. She'd never expected to discover such well-developed muscles under those sedate clothes he seemed born to wear.

He provided her and Sammy with boxing gloves, then led them to a punching bag. He demonstrated in slow motion, then gestured for them to try it. Dana drew back and slammed her fist into the bag. She felt the shock all the way up her arm. Determinedly she punched again.

"Get a rhythm going," Jason suggested to Sammy, who seemed intent on knocking the bag from its mooring in the ceiling. "This is all about finesse, not just brute strength."

Sammy's attention kept straying toward the ring in the center of the room. "When do you and me get to fight?" he asked Jason with what Dana thought was an entirely too bloodthirsty tone.

"When you know what you're doing," Jason said. "You haven't even worked up a good sweat yet."

Dana, however, was dripping from the effort. She'd had no idea how out of shape she was. With her schedule there was no time for running, much less the money for an expensive health club and the forms of exercise available there.

Breathless, she grabbed a towel and sank down onto a chair just outside of Johnny's office. Jason followed her.

"You okay?"

"I'm okay now. Something tells me tomorrow will be a different story."

"A nice hot shower will do you good."

Something in his tone brought her head up. "Here?"

"You'll catch cold if you go back outside without changing into dry clothes."

"But you said there wasn't a women's dressing room."

"I could come in and keep the place clear for a few minutes."

"Why don't I think that's an entirely benevolent offer?"

He grinned. "Because you understand me too well. However, I'm unlikely to try to ravish you or even join you in the shower with so many witnesses, including your brother. You'll be safe enough."

Dana had to admit that a steaming shower sounded like heaven. "Are you sure the guys won't mind?"

"They'll wait."

"I'll get my clothes," she said.

At the door to the locker room, she experienced another moment of doubt. Going into a male domain struck her as being on the cutting edge of a danger she wasn't sure she wanted to experience. Then again, Jason was going to be there to see that no one bothered her. For all of his teasing and innuendoes, she knew from his support at the school today and from what he was now doing for Sammy, that she could trust him with her life. She'd never before known a man who could inspire that kind of trust.

"Five minutes," she promised.

"Take your time." He stationed himself protectively in the doorway.

"You did check inside, right? No one's in there?"

"I guarantee it. Believe me, if I'm stuck out here, no one else is going to share that shower with you."

Dana couldn't resist patting his cheek. "You are so noble."

"No," he said softly, "I'm not. Remember that."

The low warning with its hint of intimacy doubled the temperature in the shower. Dana wasn't sure whether the steam arose from the water or her thoughts. Whichever it was, she decided she didn't dare linger. The sooner she got outside, where the cold air could snap her back to reality, the better off she'd be.

She toweled herself dry, tugged on her clothes and exited the locker room to discover that Johnny was posted as guard.

"Where's Jason?" she asked the old man, who grinned at her.

"Over there." He pointed toward the ring.

Jason was in the center squared off with a man who had a good twenty pounds and six inches in height on him. Sammy was standing ringside, his gaze fastened on Jason with something akin to awe on his face as Jason's blows landed with speed and obvious cunning. Dana winced as his opponent directed a punch straight at Jason's jaw, then followed with one to his midsection. Jason countered with a hit that rocked the other man back on his heels. He staggered and sank to the mat.

Grinning, Jason held out his hand and gave the other man a boost up.

"That was awesome," Sammy said, when Jason left the ring. "How'd you learn to fight like that?"

"My father and his father before him. We were all on the boxing teams at our colleges."

"How long before I can be that good?"

Jason shrugged. "Depends on how hard you're willing to practice."

"Could I come back here, maybe after school sometimes?"

Though Dana wasn't really certain how she felt about boxing as a sport for Sammy, she was more than ready to give anything a try that would keep him off the streets and away from his old friends. "It's okay with me," she said. "Jason, is it possible?"

Jason nodded. "Let's go talk to Johnny. Maybe he'll work with you when I can't be here."

Dana watched as they crossed the gym. The two men who meant the most to her, she thought as her breath seemed to catch in her throat. Her brother, who'd been everything to her from the day he was born. And the man who, unwillingly or not, seemed destined to become an integral part of her life.

Sammy was standing just a little taller than usual, and for the first time in weeks the note of hostility in his voice had vanished. He actually seemed excited about something. She owed Jason for that. She wasn't entirely sure why he had done it, but the reason mattered far less than the outcome. The motivation worried her, but she couldn't deny that the gift was precious.

What would he expect in return, though? There was every indication that he was beginning to want her in his bed. A man as virile and attractive as Jason would have a healthy love life. Undoubtedly he wasn't used to a woman saying no. Despite all of her qualms about deepening the bond between them, Dana couldn't deny that they appeared destined to make love sooner or later unless they stopped seeing each other altogether. The attraction grew hotter with each meeting. She was beginning to experience this odd, aching emptiness each time his kisses ended, an emptiness she suspected only Jason could fill. And the look in his eyes told her he wanted her every bit as badly. It was a turn of events she definitely hadn't counted on.

She couldn't allow herself to confuse wanting with love, though. Unexpected attractions sprang up between all sorts of mismatched people. That didn't mean they had to break their hearts by falling in love. If she kept her eyes wide open, if she experienced the wild sensations promised by Jason's touches just once, she could walk away with her heart unscathed.

Rot! She was deluding herself and she knew it. But because of Sammy, she couldn't walk away now, while the damage would be minimal. Jason was proving to be a good influence, and she wouldn't rob her brother of a chance to get his life in order. She would just have to be strong enough to withstand Jason's best efforts to woo her.

That was easier said than done, she decided an hour later as they sat in a tiny Italian restaurant that smelled of garlic and tomato sauce. A huge pizza loaded with everything sat in the center of the table. Sammy was greedily eating his fourth or fifth slice. Her first slice sat half-eaten on the plate in front of her. Jason's eyes were on her, as if he found her far more tempting than anything the restaurant had to offer.

Fortunately Sammy kept up a non-stop stream of questions that diverted Jason's attention for five- and ten-minute spurts, just long enough for her to catch her breath. He answered distractedly, but his gaze never wavered from her. That avid attention was enough to give a woman wild ideas about her attractiveness, yet Dana knew she couldn't look all that great after a workout and a shower that had soaked her hair.

As if he'd read her mind, Jason leaned close and murmured, "You look gorgeous with your cheeks all flushed like that. Throwing a few punches obviously agrees with you."

She thought of the punch she'd thrown the day they'd met and grinned. "I can think of some occasions when that's been true."

Obviously following her thoughts, he grinned back. "Maybe teaching you the rudiments of boxing is not such a hot idea, after all. As I recall, you packed a pretty good punch without it."

Sammy looked intrigued. "You hit him?"

"She did," Jason answered for her. "I was just standing there minding my own business and your sister came up and slugged me. Apparently starting brawls is a family trait."

Sammy's gaze narrowed. "Why'd she hit you? Were you coming on to her?"

"Actually she was defending your honor. She thought I was the creep who sold you that stolen VCR."

Her brother squirmed uncomfortably. "You know about that?"

"Yes. I assume that you've seen the last of that guy."

"Yeah, I guess."

"You guess?" Jason repeated, his voice rising ominously.

"I haven't seen him for a while now," Sammy said quickly to Dana's relief.

Jason nodded. "Look, although I think the guy ought to be turned in, I'm not going to force you to rat on him. However, if I find that you've been within a mile of him again, you and I will go a few rounds and I guarantee you won't like the way your face looks when I've rearranged it."

Dana waited for a rebellious outburst and was stunned when Sammy struggled against a giggle and lost.

"You heard that in some old movie, right?" he demanded. "James Cagney, Edward G. Robinson, one of those guys."

Jason shook his head. "Nope. That was pure Jason Halloran and I meant every word. If you doubt that, just try me."

Sammy's grin faded.

"So," Dana began hurriedly. "It's probably time we got home."

After one last measuring look, Jason and Sammy nodded.

When they reached the apartment, Sammy took off for his room without another word. Jason dropped his coat over the back of a chair and headed straight for the kitchen. "Do you have any coffee?" he called over his shoulder.

"Make yourself at home, why don't you?" Dana muttered as she trailed after him.

In the kitchen she took the can of coffee from his hands and scooped some into the pot. When she'd turned it on to perk, she faced Jason. "Thank you for everything you're trying to do, but be careful, Jason. Don't push him too hard. He'll just rebel."

"If I let up on him for even a second, I'll lose the edge. Right now he's giving me a sort of grudging respect because no one has ever been this tough with him before. I want him to understand the ground rules."

She regarded him oddly. "Is that how you were raised?"

"Hardly. My parents were just one step away from being the kind who thought a child should be allowed to express himself, even if that included tearing down the house. There were a few times when I really wished someone would set down a few rules, so I'd know what the hell was expected of me. Fortunately my grandfather wasn't shy about doing just that. I used to love to visit him because I always knew exactly what I could and couldn't do. And I always knew he and my grandmother loved me, even when I crossed the line."

"You think I've been too lenient with Sammy," Dana said.

"Maybe. Maybe not. I just see a kid now who's crying out for someone to point him in some direction. If it's not you, then it'll be those thugs he considers his friends."

Dana poured the coffee, then sank down across from Jason. "Sometimes I get so damned tired of being responsible," she said wearily.

Jason reached for her hand. "You're not in this alone

anymore," he said softly. "From now on we'll share the responsibility."

Although everything in her screamed that she had to remain strong, had to remain independent, she couldn't bring herself to voice the words that would keep him at bay. She felt his strength pouring into her, felt the warmth and concern that surrounded her like a velvet cloak and wanted with all her might to draw it closer.

When he raised her hand to his lips and pressed a kiss against her knuckles, she felt like the most cherished woman on the face of the earth. The sensation was too intoxicating by far to turn away. She would indulge herself, just for tonight, in the fantasy that Jason would always be around to protect her.

Chapter 9

Feeling an unfamiliar need for a long, friendly chat that might help her to put things with Jason into perspective, Dana walked over to Mrs. Finch's bookstore on her way home from work at the print shop a week later. Although she didn't really need an excuse for dropping by, she had one all prepared. She'd finished the bookstore's latest flyers. Mr. Keane had run them off on the copying machine just before closing.

Glancing in the shop's window before entering, her mouth dropped open. Wearing slacks and a dress shirt, Jason was scrunched down in one of the faded chintz chairs that were placed here and there for browsing customers. His tie was loose, his collar open. He was holding a china cup of tea that looked completely out of place in his big hands, but his expression was rapt as he listened to Mrs. Finch. Dana couldn't imagine what the two of them had to talk about.

Except her, she thought with horror, rushing inside.

"Agatha Christie is the very best mystery writer ever," Mrs. Finch was declaring to Dana's relief.

"John D. MacDonald," Jason countered. He glanced up and shot Dana a warm look. "And there's Dashiell Hammett. What do you think, Dana?"

She regarded the two of them warily, not entirely convinced of the innocence of the conversation. "I don't have time to read mysteries."

"I've tried," Mrs. Finch said apologetically as if Dana were one of her failures. "I sneaked one of Christie's best into her sack last time. She brought the book back the next day. Said I'd mixed it in with her books by mistake."

"Didn't you even peek?" Jason teased.

"No," Dana said, then amended, "Okay, I peeked. I read the first few lines…and a little bit at the end."

Mrs. Finch looked delighted. "Oh, my, I'll have you hooked yet."

"Don't count on it," Dana warned. "And don't even think about trying to get me addicted to those romances you love so much. They're frivolous."

"Only if you don't happen to care about human relationships," Mrs. Finch informed her.

"Interesting how she keeps bringing those romances up, isn't it?" Jason observed, giving the bookstore owner a deliberate wink. "Do you suppose she's developed an obsession with romance lately?"

Dana looked from one to the other, scowling, then muttered something about looking for a new design book. This visit was doing absolutely nothing to ease her mind. If anything, she felt more ganged up on than ever. Obviously her friend had chosen sides. What puzzled her was that there were even sides to choose. A week ago Jason Halloran hadn't even wanted to spend a few hours in an office with her. Now he was popping up every time she turned around. Was the man trying to drive her nuts?

"Certainly, dear. Look all you want," Mrs. Finch said, clearly already distracted by her handsome visitor. "You know where they are."

Jason didn't even bother to comment. He jumped right back into the mystery discussion they'd been in the midst of before her arrival.

Suddenly feeling thoroughly out of sorts, Dana went down the narrow aisle to the back of the store. She plucked books off the shelves, scanned them without seeing the words, then put them back. After she'd been through half a dozen books, she realized she was straining to listen to Jason and Mrs. Finch. They seemed to be having a grand time without her.

Dana edged closer, then sat in an old armchair that invited customers to curl up. She'd spent hours in this chair on other occasions, lost in the design books that she suspected Mrs. Finch had started to stock just for her. Though she held one of the newest books now, all of her attention was riveted on the chattering pair at the front of the store. They were just out of view, though occasionally she glimpsed Jason's blond hair when he leaned forward to make a point.

She supposed it was nice that a man as busy as Jason would take the time to visit a sweet little old lady. No, there was no supposing about it. It *was* nice. So why did she seem to resent it? Why was she so suspicious of this sudden change of heart?

Actually she'd been increasingly disgruntled this

whole week when Jason had ignored her and spent his
spare time with Sammy. Her brother had come home
filled with stories about Jason's excellent left hook, his
fancy footwork in the ring, his awesome sucker punch.
Dana wondered idly where those punches had been
when she'd slugged him at Washington's Tavern. She
should probably consider herself lucky that she'd escaped that day without a scratch.

At any rate it seemed that Jason was slowly but surely
winning Sammy over. She couldn't very well begrudge
her brother the male attention he so badly needed, but
she was beginning to wonder exactly where she fit in.
It bothered the daylights out of her that it seemed to
matter.

The truth, she finally admitted with a sigh, was that
she was feeling left out. Downright lonely, in fact. In
a life that had been crowded with work and school and
raising Sammy, it was a totally new and not particularly welcome sensation. Mrs. Finch was the closest
thing she'd ever had to a grandmother. Sammy was *her*
brother. For reasons that escaped her, Jason seemed intent on adopting both of them.

As for Jason's plans where she was concerned, his
precise role in her life seemed to defy description. In
another era, he would have been described as a beau,
one who'd already made his intentions perfectly clear.
In this bolder day and age, he might have been her lover
by now, if both of them hadn't had serious reservations
about such a drastic move. For the past week he'd been
virtually ignoring her. Had he lost interest? Wasn't that
what she'd wanted? Since she wasn't able to put him—
or her own emotions—into a nice, neat little compart-
ment, he was troublesome.

She glanced wistfully toward the front of the store. She could just walk up and join them. They hadn't deliberately shut her out of the conversation earlier. In fact, the expression in Jason's eyes had been warmly welcoming. In a way, she supposed, she envied them their uncomplicated conversation, their free and easy laughter. Whenever she was with Jason the conversation always took a dangerously intimate turn, and the laughter had a wickedly provocative edge to it that set off fireworks deep inside her, even when they were arguing. Sometimes *especially* when they were arguing.

"Where did you go?" Jason asked softly, coming up and hunkering down in front of her. He braced his hands on her thighs, sending a jolt of awareness through her. Those fireworks exploded in fiery splendor.

Dana's pulse scrambled at the probing look in his eyes.

"I've been right here," she said.

"Maybe physically, but your mind must have been a million miles away. You looked, I don't know, a little sad, I guess."

Dana wasn't about to admit to the oddly jealous turn her thoughts had taken. Instead, she said, "Who won the battle over the mystery writers, you or Mrs. Finch?"

"We agreed to disagree. I promised to read old Agatha with a more open mind and she's going to reconsider MacDonald's Travis McGee series." A spark of pure devilment lit his eyes. "I was hoping she'd offer me one of those romances with the sexy covers."

Dana chuckled at his disappointed expression. "I'll just bet you were. Carrying one of those around would have done astonishing things to your image."

"Think it would counteract the stodgy coat?"

Without thinking about what she was doing, Dana reached over and fingered the hair that had fallen over his eyes. As she smoothed it back into place, she felt his skin heat beneath her touch, detected the sudden leap of his pulse. Knowing that she could stir him so readily gave her an unexpected sensation of power. Why was it Jason who made her feel so much like a woman? What quality did he have that wreaked havoc with her best intentions? Compassion? Gentleness? Strength? He had them all.

And that terrified her.

"There's nothing wrong with the image that coat projects," she told him, tracing the line of his jaw with her fingertips.

"Oh?" he said, his voice suddenly whisper rough. "I was under the impression you considered me and my coat deadly dull."

"A week ago I might have," she admitted.

"And now?"

"I don't know what to think of you anymore," she said, sounding bemused. "Sometimes...sometimes I can't even think when I'm around you."

Jason looked every bit as bewildered as she felt. He captured her hand and drew it to his chest. She'd never touched material as soft as the fine cotton of his shirt. Beneath it she could feel the powerful thunder of his heart as his gaze held hers.

"But you feel things when you're with me, don't you?" he asked quietly. "Tell the truth, Dana. Aren't you the least bit tempted?"

Something in his tone pleaded for honesty. She owed him that much, even knowing she couldn't commit to more than this one costly admission.

"Tempted to go to bed with you? Yes," she confessed.

He shook his head. "No, to fall in love with me."

"Oh, Jason," she whispered, wishing she could admit this truth as readily: she wasn't just tempted, she was already falling. And it scared her silly.

All of these tantalizing glimpses and teasing remarks were beginning to torment Jason. He'd deliberately kept his distance from Dana for the past week, hoping that this craziness would go away, that he'd awake in the morning and Dana would no longer appeal to him. He had a sinking feeling that changing the color of his eyes or the rhythm of his heart would be easier.

Last night in the bookstore he'd sensed that she was on the edge, struggling with deep emotions that were clearly as foreign to her as they were to him—emotions neither of them were ready to accept.

She'd looked so lost and alone that he'd wanted to take her into his arms and swear to her that she would never be lonely again, that he would always be there to offer comfort and strength and love. He wasn't sure, though, that it was a promise he could keep. He had no track record with commitment and responsibility. As for handling the implications of love—not just sex—between a man and a woman, he was every bit as inexperienced as she.

And then there was Sammy. His respect for the boy's intelligence was growing, even as his frustration mounted. For all the progress the two of them had made in recent days, the kid was hardly ready for sainthood. Jason suspected that their outings to the gym might only be giving Sammy the skills he would need to tough it out on the streets. Jason doubted the teen actually saw boxing as an alternative to the thrill of real violence. Every time Jason tried to speak to Sammy about making a serious change in his attitude and his companions, the youngster's overt hostility returned.

Faced with the least attractive side of Sammy's personality, Jason continually had to remind himself that he was doing this to prove to himself that he was capable of being totally unselfish for once in his life. Maybe it would be a sign that he'd finally grown up.

The bonus, of course, was the approval and relief that shone in Dana's eyes with each tiny bit of progress he made with her brother. It made him feel ten feet tall. He hadn't realized how badly his self-confidence needed such a boost.

He had started doubting his own common sense. Maybe he'd misjudged how wrong Dana was for him. He'd felt revitalized the past couple of weeks. Maybe it wouldn't be so terrible to risk deepening their relationship.

Convinced of that, Jason left work early with his blood pumping just a little harder as he contemplated a very romantic evening ahead. He found a florist who'd managed to rush the season with an abundant assortment of spring flowers. Jason filled his arms with red tulips and golden daffodils, picked up a bottle of wine, then stopped at a meat market that dealt only in the choicest steaks and chops.

It occurred to him to call ahead to be sure Dana would be home. But he felt certain she'd find a dozen excuses for turning him down. He skirted the most obvious one by buying a third steak. He figured there was no escaping Sammy's presence. Jason appreciated the irony in having the kid as a chaperon.

It was dusk when he reached the neighborhood. The nearest parking place was an unsavory two blocks away. Jason gathered his purchases from the back seat, then started toward Dana's. He had just started to cross the entrance to an alley, when he heard a commotion and sensed a violent undertone. One glance into the gloomy alley brought his heart to his throat.

Dana was pressed against a brick wall. A trio of unkempt youths were taunting her. A fourth, his back to Jason, was hanging back, oddly silent. From where Jason stood at the entrance to the alley, there was no question at all about their intentions—they were going to rob her or worse.

Jason was filled with such a murderous rage, his hands shook. Every instinct shouted at him to rush to her rescue. His muscles ached from the tension of listening to his head, which warned him that rushing in against these odds wouldn't help Dana and might even get her hurt.

As he considered what to do, his heart pounded so hard he was sure they would hear it. Anger rushed through him with raw, primitive force. If they laid one finger on her, one finger, he would delight in taking them apart.

"You don't want to do this," Dana said. She was pale, but there wasn't the slightest quaver in her voice. Jason winced at the spunky declaration. Didn't she know she was just daring them to contradict her? Didn't she have enough good sense to recognize the very real danger she was in? Maybe it was just as well. He was terrified enough for the two of them.

He'd never felt more helpless in his life, trying to cling to reason when all he wanted was to strike out blindly, to pay them back for threatening her. In that instant he realized with a sense of shock that he was falling in love with her.

And, with horrifying clarity, that he could lose her.

"Hey, did you hear that, Rocky? We don't want to do nothin' to the lady." The punk who said it leered at her and inched closer as if to contradict her statement. His fingers swept down her cheek. Jason felt sick to his stomach as he thought of how easily the boy could have wielded a knife instead.

Finally, his hands knotting into fists, the boy hovering in the background spoke. "Leave her alone, Vinnie."

Vinnie didn't look inclined to take his advice. "Kid, stay out of this."

At the hint of a split in their ranks, Jason took heart. Maybe the odds weren't so uneven after all. Suddenly, with a move so swift it took both Vinnie and Jason by surprise, the boy leaped. He began pummeling the ringleader, obviously fearless or determined to pretend to be. Jason recognized the attitude even before he picked up on the slim build and blond hair. Sammy, coming to his sister's defense without regard to the consequences to himself—or to her, for that matter.

With Vinnie occupied, Dana flew at the one called Rocky. Just as the remaining youth prepared to come to the assistance of the gang leaders, Jason tore down the alley and slammed the guy into the wall. The boy managed one glancing blow to Jason's head that drew blood. Then Jason grabbed the boy's arm and twisted it behind his back until he heard a satisfying grunt of pain.

"I think maybe you should plan on sitting this one out," he said as he wound his tie around the youth's wrists, then looped it around a drainpipe. Satisfied that this one was out of commission, Jason went to Dana's assistance. He decked Rocky with a blow that the kid didn't even see coming. The crunching shot gave him a mild sense of satisfaction.

Even before the thug crashed to the ground, and with barely a glance at Jason, Dana moved on to help Sammy. The two of them were all over Vinnie. They didn't look as if they needed any help from him in winding things up. In fact, Dana actually looked as if she was enjoying her moment of revenge on the scum who'd threatened her. Jason had no intention of denying her the pleasure. He figured the punk had it coming.

With blood dripping from the gash above his eye, Jason settled on a garbage can to watch. He pressed a clean handkerchief to the scrape and admired the upper-cut that Sammy delivered to Vinnie's jaw, while Dana held his arms pinned behind him. Vinnie sank slowly facedown into a bank of gray slush. Apparently out of some misguided concern for the punk's life, they rolled him over before walking over to Jason, whose temper was kicking in at full steam now that the danger was past.

"My heroes," Dana declared, looking downright invigorated by the success of the brawl. She had a scrape down one cheek and scratches on her hands. Other than that she looked none the worse for wear. It took everything in Jason to keep from crushing her in an embrace.

Instead, he glared at her. "Heroes, hell. Sammy, what were you doing here in the alley with those guys when they went after your sister?" he demanded.

Dana looked shocked by Jason's implication. "He wasn't with them."

"Oh, wasn't he?" He leveled a look at Sammy, who

had the good sense to look uneasy. "You were right in the thick of things until you realized it was Dana they'd dragged back here, weren't you?"

"No. I saw 'em and followed," he swore unconvincingly. His gaze never met Jason's directly. "That's all."

"You don't know these boys?" Jason pressed.

Dana regarded him oddly, her expression puzzled. "Sammy is not on trial here. He threw the first punch to protect me."

"The police might think otherwise. Sammy, you haven't answered my question. Do you know these guys or not?"

"I've seen 'em around."

"Are they part of a gang?"

"I guess."

"What about you?"

Sammy looked from his sister to Jason and back again. "I'm not in any gang."

"But you want to be."

"Dammit, Jason, leave him alone," Dana said protectively. "I'm telling you he came to my rescue. You were here. You must have seen it."

"In the end, yes, he did," Jason admitted, then sighed. "We'll talk about it later."

"There is nothing to discuss," Dana declared. "Sammy, go call 911 and get a policeman over here so I can file assault charges."

Sammy's expression went from hostile to scared in an instant. "Sis, can't you forget about it?" he pleaded, confirming Jason's belief that he'd been up to his skinny little neck in the activities of this gang of hoodlums.

"No, I cannot forget about it. If I don't press charges, they could do this to someone else. Get the police now."

Sammy ran off. As soon as he'd gone, Jason said mildly, "I seriously doubt that the police will show up here anytime soon."

"Of course they will," Dana said. "Why wouldn't they?"

"Because Sammy won't call them, not if he expects to hang out with his friends ever again. These guys don't rat on each other."

Fury flashed in Dana's eyes. "And I'm telling you that you're wrong about that. Just because a kid's had it tough in life, doesn't mean he automatically turns into some criminal. I thought you were his friend."

"I'm trying to be. That doesn't mean I turn a blind eye to his faults."

"The way I do?" she asked resentfully.

"I didn't say that, but yes, the way you do."

Dana's lower lip trembled. "I see his faults. I've told him…"

"Telling him isn't enough." He reached for her hand, but she stiffened. "Dammit, Dana," he said impatiently. "There have to be consequences. Can't you see that, even after this?"

"What kind of consequences did you have in mind? Jail? Beating him with a belt? What?"

Jason raked his fingers through his hair. "No," he said wearily.

"What then?" She perched on the lid of the garbage can next to him. "Take tonight. He came to my rescue. Am I supposed to punish him for that?"

"No, but you'd better make darned sure you know who his friends are from now on."

"And just how am I supposed to do that? I work two jobs at the moment. I can't stick around all afternoon and do background checks on the kids he spends time with after school."

Jason sighed. There was no denying the complexity of the problem. "You're right," he admitted. "I don't know what the answer is. I just know that he's headed for trouble."

"I thought the time he was spending with you was helping."

Jason grinned ruefully. "Sure. Didn't you see those punches he threw? The kid's a natural. On one hand, I'm damned proud of him. On the other, I want to shake him until his teeth rattle." He glanced sideways. "There may be one thing you could do to improve things."

"What's that? I'll try anything."

"Move. This neighborhood's not safe for you, and it sure as hell isn't doing Sammy any good to associate with the kids around here."

For a fleeting instant Dana's expression brightened, then her face fell. "I can't afford to move."

Before Jason could open his mouth to offer to help, she held up her hand. "I won't take a cent from you."

"Do you really have a choice? If you don't do something, Sammy's likely to end up in jail. Let me help. If you won't take money, then move into my place."

Her eyes widened. "You have to be kidding."

Actually Jason thought he might be slightly insane, but the longer he toyed with the idea, the more he saw it as the only solution. Once Sammy was removed from these surroundings, the kid might actually have a chance. As for Dana, at least she would be out of danger. Of all of them, he was the one most likely to be endangered by such a move. The feelings that had slammed into his gut when he'd faced the prospect of losing her would be on the line if she were in close proximity. He had to risk it, though. For her sake. And Sammy's.

"Just temporarily," he said, giving both of them a needed out. "Just until you save enough to get a better place in a better neighborhood. There are plenty of bedrooms. You and Sammy can both have your privacy."

He allowed his gaze to linger until he saw the rise of desire in her eyes. He dropped his voice. "If you want it."

Dana seemed to shake off the spell she'd clearly been succumbing to. "Not a good idea," she said, but there was a breathlessness to her voice that contradicted the declaration. She was tempted. He would just have to make her see the logic of it.

At the first stirring of Vinnie and his cohorts, Jason glanced toward them and asked pointedly, "Do you have a better idea?"

"No, but…"

"Just promise me you'll think about it."

With her gaze locked with his, she finally sighed and nodded. "I'll think about it."

"By the way, are you ready to concede that the police are not headed our way? If so, I suggest we take off before these guys decide they'd like to go another round. If they ask for more, I'm not at all sure I won't be the one in jail with a murder rap hanging over my head. With any luck, we can make that call ourselves and get the cops down here before these jerks vanish."

Dana's chin inched up. "I'll wait. You call the police."

"Oh, no," Jason said. "You're not staying here another minute. And since we've already established that there are very valid reasons for not leaving me within a mile of these guys without witnesses, we're going together."

"What if they escape?"

"Then we'll just have to convince Sammy to tell us who they are. Now let's go." He groaned as he leaned down to pick up the bag with the steaks in it. They were about the only thing he could salvage from his romantic offerings. The bottle of wine had broken when he dropped it to go after Vinnie. The bouquet of flowers had been trampled. Dana stared around at the mess, seeing it for the first time.

"Flowers?"

"For you. Sorry they didn't make it."

She picked up one spunky daffodil that was less bruised than the rest and held it gently. "They're beautiful," she said. "Thank you."

"I'll buy you more."

"No. I like this one. It's a survivor."

Jason shook his head wearily and admitted with grudging admiration, "Like you."

Sometimes Dana's fight-to-the-end philosophy scared the daylights out of him. Protecting a woman like that took more ingenuity than most mortal men possessed. He was trying, though.

And with a little divine intervention and a whole lot of patience, maybe he'd survive Dana's stubborn determination to fight him every step of the way.

Chapter 10

After the incident in the alley, Jason could barely bring himself to let Dana out of his sight. He was astounded by the deep feeling of protectiveness she aroused in him. Again and again he tried to tell himself it wasn't because he was falling in love with her. He couldn't be. He was a man who always used his head, and his head had warned him from the outset to steer clear of her. His heart, though, was another matter. He couldn't seem to control it the way he could his thoughts.

The only thing keeping him from forcing the issue of a move was the knowledge that Dana's reaction to pressure was likely to be withdrawal. She didn't seem to trust simple generosity. It had taken him a long time to understand that. It was Halloran tradition to reach out, to give something back to the community, to help those in need. In Dana's world, though, she'd learned to look for the ulterior motive.

Jason had no idea how to break through that kind of instinctive self-protection except to give her time. Since she was about to start working full-time for the Lansing Agency, and thus for him, on Monday, he didn't want to do anything that would scare her off. Once they were locked into a day-in, day-out pattern, he could look after her the way he wanted to without arousing her fiery streak of independence.

That didn't keep him from calling as many times each day as he could justify. It was astonishing the number of excuses he could manufacture. If Dana suspected his motives on this too, she never let on. On most occasions, she actually sounded glad to hear from him, at least until he tried to delve into anything personal. She dodged those questions with the skill of a shady politician. When he brought up Sammy, who'd refused any more boxing lessons, she turned downright testy. Jason wondered if they would ever be able to agree on anything having to do with her brother.

That didn't stop him from trying, though he was rapidly reaching his wit's end. Not even the lure of tickets to a Celtics game had improved Sammy's mood, which seemed surlier than ever. He'd refused the invitation. As a result, Dana had begged off, too. Jason had gone to the game with his father, hoping that the night out would lead to confidences that would help him understand what was going on with his parents.

To his frustration, he'd struck out on that as well. The only thing his father seemed remotely inclined to discuss was the basketball game, and even then he'd kept his comments terse. Jason was more convinced than ever that things weren't right between his parents.

On one level he realized he was no more ready to deal with that aloud than his father was.

It was after midnight when Jason finally got home, too late to call Dana. After the tense standoff with his father and the close Celtics' victory, he was too wired to sleep. Disgruntled as well by his lack of progress with Dana, he tried to read over the marketing and advertising plan he'd been finalizing in preparation for Dana's first day on the job.

No matter how hard he tried, though, he couldn't seem to concentrate. For some reason he felt this odd sense that Dana needed him, that she was in trouble. He tried valiantly to ignore it, but time and again he glanced at the phone, debating with himself. He'd finally convinced himself to call and was already reaching for the phone, when it rang.

"Yes, hello," he said, instantly convinced that his instincts had been accurate. No one ever called him this late unless there was a problem.

"Jason," Dana said in a voice that sounded sandpaper husky from crying.

His heart slammed against his ribs. "What's wrong?"

"It's Sammy. I know I shouldn't call you after the way he's acted, after the way I've acted, but I didn't know what else to do. There isn't anyone else who could help."

"What's he done?" To his regret, his antagonistic tone sounded as if he were anticipating the worst.

"He hasn't *done* anything," she said, clearly bristling. "He's just gone. I came home earlier and he was out. I didn't think much about it until a couple of hours ago. He knows he has an eleven-o'clock curfew on weekends unless we discuss a later one. He always calls if he's going to be late," she said staunchly, as if to defend him from an attack she knew Jason was likely to make.

"I'll be right there," Jason said, already reaching for his clothes.

"Thank you."

Dana sounded so tired, so vulnerable. Jason felt something tear lose inside his chest as he considered the state of panic she must be in. This time he was going to shake Sammy until his teeth rattled. Dana didn't deserve this kind of treatment from a kid she'd spent years protecting and nurturing, a boy whose needs she'd always put above her own. If Jason had anything to say about it, Dana was through making sacrifices that went unappreciated.

He reached her apartment in record time and raced inside. At the sound of his footsteps pounding up the stairs, she had the door open before he reached the top. Her expression wavered between relief and disappointment when she saw it was him. Jason could understand the ambivalence. Obviously she'd been praying it was Sammy. Jason's help came in at a distant second best.

Jason took one look at the tears tracking down her cheeks and swept her into his arms. For some reason she felt almost fragile, as if fear alone had robbed her of her usual strength. There was no hint of the famed Dana Roberts spunk.

"Any news?" he asked gently.

He felt the subtle shake of her head, the sigh that shuddered through her.

"Let's go inside and think this through."

"I want to go look for him," she insisted stubbornly.

"Running around the streets at this hour won't accomplish anything unless we have a plan. Come on.

Make some coffee and tell me every single place you think he might be."

In the kitchen she scooped up the coffee, then spilled it from a spoon that shook uncontrollably. Jason retrieved the spoon, urged her into a chair, then wiped up the coffee and started over. When the pot was on the stove, he pulled a chair close to her and enfolded her trembling, icy hands in his.

Looking downright miserable, Dana met his gaze and said, "He's never done anything like this before— never. What if he's hurt?"

"Don't worry. We'll call the hospitals and the police. We'll find him."

She looked thunderstruck. "The police?"

"To see about reported accidents."

She nodded reluctantly. "Okay. Wouldn't they have called me, though? He has ID with my name and number for emergencies."

Jason could think of several reasons, all of them bad, that no one had called Dana. He evaded. "Not necessarily."

She started to get up. "Shouldn't we be doing that now?"

"As soon as you drink a little coffee. Have you eaten anything tonight?"

"A sandwich." At his skeptical glance, she added, "Honest. I really didn't start worrying until eleven when he was due in."

"Okay, then. Drink the coffee and let me make a few calls. Where's the phone book?"

"In the living room by the phone."

"You stay here and try to relax. I'll be right back."

Naturally she didn't stay put. Though Jason worried

that listening to question after question would only add to her stress, she weathered the next hour fairly well. In fact, she seemed to grow calmer, more determined. That strength in a crisis was an admirable trait, but Jason almost wished she would cry or scream—anything to wipe away that increasingly bleak, stoic expression.

The police had no record of Sammy either being picked up or in an accident. After the last futile call to a hospital, Jason sighed. "No luck."

Dana's expression did brighten slightly then. "That's good, though, isn't it? It means he's not hurt and we already know he hasn't been arrested."

What it meant to Jason's way of thinking was the kid had absolutely no excuse for not calling. None. If he did turn out to be okay and just exercising his selfish independent streak, Jason very well might put him in the hospital himself.

"You're right. I'm sure there's no reason to worry," he found himself saying, hoping to put a little color back into Dana's pale, drawn face.

She wasn't quite that easily consoled, however. The next thing he knew, she was on her feet and reaching for her jacket. "I'm going to look for him. He has to be someplace."

"Dana, no."

"I can't just sit here."

"You can." When she continued toward the door, her expression defiant, he said, "Stay. I'll go look. He could come back or call and you should be here."

Only when he'd promised to search the neighborhood thoroughly did she remove her coat and sit back down, drawing her knees up to her chin and circling them with her arms. He squeezed her hands and dropped a feather-light kiss on her cheek. "Try not to worry. I'll check in every half hour and let you know what area I've covered. See if you can think of any place he might go, some friend he might visit."

He left her staring at the phone.

As the hours wore on toward morning with no sign of Sammy, Jason grew almost as alarmed as Dana. Sammy might infuriate him, and Dana's blind, unwavering defense of the boy might drive him to distraction, but he wouldn't want anything to happen to him. The kid had so much untapped potential. It was that waste more than anything that caused Jason to lose patience with Sammy so readily. How could he so casually throw away not only his own natural gifts, but the opportunities Dana struggled to offer him? What in God's name would it take to reach him?

Each time Jason called with no news, he could hear the mounting fear in Dana's voice. By the time he got back to the apartment at dawn, she was in a state of near panic. He was nearly as frazzled himself.

"He probably spent the night with one of his friends," he said, though somehow Sammy didn't strike him as the type to go on some innocent sleep-over at a friend's house.

Dana didn't seem to buy the explanation any more than he did. She tried her best to look hopeful, but the effort fell discouragingly short. Jason would have dragged home moonbeams, if they would have cheered her up. He doubted it would have mattered.

"Are you hungry?" she asked dutifully. "I have some eggs."

He shook his head. "No, just give me some more coffee, so I can warm up a little. Then I'll go out again."

"You don't think we're going to find him, do you?" Dana said, her voice flat.

Jason considered lying to her, but couldn't do it. Pulling her close, he said as gently as he could, "Not unless he wants to be found. He's sixteen and pretty ingenious. My guess is he'll come home when he's good and ready."

"Why would he have left in the first place? We didn't have a fight. Everything was just fine when I went out."

"Sweetheart, it may have absolutely nothing to do with you. Maybe he had a run-in with that gang of his and figured he needed to hide out. It's hard to tell how a teenager's mind works. Maybe he did something he knew would upset you and was too ashamed to admit it. When he gets hungry enough and lonely enough, he'll figure out that running's not the answer."

"I wish I could be as sure of that as you are."

Jason wasn't sure of much of anything, just that he would have given his life to save Dana this kind of heartache.

"You don't suppose he would call *you*," she said, a sudden spark of excitement in her eyes. "I mean if he were in trouble, he might think you could get him out of it."

"I think I'd be the last person he'd call."

"But he might," Dana insisted. "Is your answering machine on?"

"Yes."

"Check it for messages. Please, Jason."

Jason thought it was a waste of time, but he called, then punched in his security code. The tape rewound through one lengthy message and began to play.

"Jason, it's Johnny. You know, over at the gym. I know it's early, man, but I found that friend of yours, you know the kid, over here. He was asleep in the locker room. I'm trying to get him to hang loose, but he's jumpy as a cat. Get over here as soon as possible. I figure you're with his sister, but the kid won't tell me how to reach her. Make tracks, buddy. I have a feeling the kid's in some kind of trouble."

Jason closed his eyes in relief.

"What is it?" Dana demanded. "He called, didn't he?"

"No, but Johnny from the gym called. He found Sammy when he went in this morning. He's trying to get him to stick around, but we'd better get over there. If Sammy figures out that Johnny called me, Johnny's afraid he'll split."

Dana already had her coat and was sprinting for the door. As Jason followed, he wondered if he'd been right about Sammy's reaction to Johnny's call. Maybe there was a significance to the fact that he'd chosen the gym to run to, knowing that Johnny *would* call Jason. If so, maybe Sammy was finally beginning to trust him, beginning to reach out to him. He had a feeling this was a turning point. No matter what, he had to control his temper long enough to give Sammy the chance to open up.

At the gym they found Johnny pacing out front, looking grim. His expression brightened the minute he spotted them. "Thank goodness. I was beginning to think I was going to have to tie him up."

"Is he okay?" Dana asked, her brow creased with worry.

"Looks okay to me, but if everything were peachy, he wouldn't have been conked out in the back room, would he?"

"I want to see him. Where is he?"

"In my office. I talked him into eating. I brought him back some eggs and pancakes from the fast-food place down the block."

"Dana, let me talk to him," Jason said.

"No. Sammy's my brother. It's my problem."

"You made it mine the minute you called me. Now let me see if I can find out why he's hiding out. It may be something he doesn't want to involve you in."

Even as the words came out of his mouth, Jason knew that he'd hit on the answer. But what could possibly be so bad that Sammy would fear telling Dana? Like his sister, the boy tended to think he was invincible, that he could handle anything.

Dana looked reluctant, but she finally nodded. "Jason, please don't yell at him."

Yelling at the kid was the least of what he had in mind, but he nodded. "Get Johnny to teach you a few punches. It'll work off the frustration," he suggested, squeezing her hand before he went inside.

The door to Johnny's office was wide open and for an instant Jason panicked. What if he'd been wrong? What if Sammy had spotted them and gone out the back while they were outside? Dana would never forgive him for letting him get away. He crossed the gym in a dozen strides, then quietly stepped into the office.

Sammy was still there, the empty breakfast container shoved aside, his head on Johnny's desk. He'd fallen asleep again. He was snoring softly. In sleep, with that crazy hank of blond hair falling over his eyes, he had the look of an innocent kid. Jason found it almost possible to believe that it really wasn't too late to turn his life around.

He shut the door softly, then pulled up a chair and sat

down between Sammy and the only escape route. He reached over and shook his shoulder. "Wake up, son."

Sammy mumbled something, then lifted his head and stared at Jason through groggy, sleep-filled eyes. Instantly alarm filled those blue depths. He slid his chair back, glancing around frantically for a way out.

"You might as well sit back down. You're not going anywhere."

"That no-good, lyin' so…" The words were tough, but the tone was halfhearted.

"Cut the crap," Jason said. "You knew Johnny would call me. That's why you came here, isn't it?"

Sammy's mouth clamped shut and his defiant expression faltered.

"What kind of trouble are you in?"

"I can handle it," he said with one last bit of bravado.

Jason nodded and softened his tone. What was it with these Roberts siblings? Both of them had to do everything on their own. "Maybe so," he said to Sammy. "But why not let me help if I can."

"I don't need help," he insisted, then amended, "Not for me, anyway. It's Dana."

Jason felt his heartbeat slow. "What about Dana?" he questioned very quietly, his hands slowly clenching into fists.

"The guys who attacked her in that alley, they threatened to come after her again. They wanted to know where we lived. I got away, but I think they wanted me to. They thought I'd go home, but I saw them followin' me. That's why I came here. I couldn't go back to the apartment. I was afraid they'd hurt her and I wouldn't be able to stop them."

Suddenly Sammy's expression grew even more worried. "She's okay, isn't she? They didn't find her?"

"She's okay," Jason reassured him, keeping a tight leash on his fury. This was the last straw. "She's right outside with Johnny."

"What are we gonna do?"

Jason had to give him credit. He sounded genuinely distressed. Maybe Sammy had grown up a little tonight, realized that there were consequences to his actions not just for him, but for his sister.

"We're going to convince your sister that it's time to move. With any luck we'll have the two of you out of that apartment by the end of the day and neither of you will have to worry about those thugs again."

Sammy looked skeptical. "I don't think Dana's gonna go for it. Moving costs money."

"Money's the least of our problem."

Sammy managed a little half smile. "Maybe for you. But Dana worries about it a lot."

"She won't have to, not anymore."

"What are you gonna do? Give her a loan? I don't think she'll take it."

Jason nodded. "You're probably right. She's turned me down before. Think we can talk her into moving the two of you into my place?"

Sammy's mouth dropped open. "You want us to move in with you?" His gaze narrowed speculatively. "Both of us?"

Jason chuckled. "You don't think she's likely to come without you, do you?"

"No, but I just can't imagine you and me in the same house. We don't exactly see eye to eye."

"We both care about your sister, don't we? Maybe

we should concentrate on that. It would make your sister happy if we got along."

"What's your real scam?" Sammy suddenly looked very grown up. In a sober tone he demanded, "You plannin' to marry her or somethin'?"

"The thought has crossed my mind," Jason admitted, as much to his own astonishment as Sammy's. "Think she'd go for it?"

Sammy seemed to consider the idea, then shook his head. "Not a chance. It doesn't make much sense to me, but she's got this crazy idea that she has to do everything the hard way. I don't think marriage is in her plans."

"Then I guess I'll just have to change her mind," he said, knowing that Sammy was right on target with his analysis. "First things first, though. We've got to convince her that this move is for your good. It's the only way she'll go for it."

"Isn't that like lyin' or something?" Sammy asked, his expression too knowing, in Jason's opinion.

The kid had certainly picked a fine time to develop scruples, Jason thought. "It's not entirely a lie," he informed Sammy. "After all it won't hurt you to find some new friends."

"Right," Sammy said skeptically, then opened the door and went to find his sister.

Jason followed slowly, trying to figure out the right way to phrase the decision he and Sammy had reached.

"Oh, no!"

Dana's voice echoed throughout the gym and Jason realized the phrasing had been taken out of his hands. Obviously Sammy had already told his sister about their plan. She didn't seem to be taking it well. She was marching across the gym with fire in her eyes.

"What kind of hogwash were you filling his head with in there?" she demanded, backing Jason into a corner.

"Hogwash?"

"You are not going to use my brother to get to me. We are perfectly safe living where we are—a lot safer than I would be living with you."

There was safety and then there was *safety*. Jason refrained from trying to explain the difference to her. "Dana, my house could accommodate a dozen people. You'll have all the privacy you want. You have to admit, it would be better for Sammy to get away from the influence of those creeps."

Admittedly the prospect of having the kid under his roof gave him pause, but it was a sacrifice he was prepared to make to keep them both safe. It was way too soon to think much beyond that.

"It's happening, isn't it?" she demanded. "You've got some crazy idea about rescuing me. Well, I won't have it. I can stand on my own two feet. I always have."

Jason could see her reasoning, at once, and she was right. She had awakened some white-knight fantasy in him. That didn't mean the idea was a bad one. "I'm not trying to rob you of your independence," he said tightly. "Think about your brother, dammit. He's the only person in the whole blessed world who matters to you, and you seem willing to throw away his chances out of some stubborn need to handle everything on your own. Talk about selfish!"

Dana stared at him, obviously stung by his outburst. Slowly the fight seemed to drain out of her. "You're probably right about moving," she conceded grudgingly. "But we'll find an apartment in another neighborhood. I'll pick up today's paper on the way home and check out the ads."

"That takes time. Stay with me until you find another place. I don't like the idea of those guys tracking you down. They won't give up easily." An idea flashed through his mind and he added determinedly, "If you don't come to my place, I'll have to move into yours and then we really will be in close quarters."

There was a flash of defiance in her eyes, but apparently she recognized that he wasn't budging on this one. She finally nodded. "Okay. You're probably right. That would be the sensible thing to do."

Jason's pulse leaped.

"But it will only be temporary, just until I find a new apartment."

"Absolutely," he agreed.

With any luck he could keep her so busy she wouldn't have time to look for weeks.

Dana couldn't imagine what had possessed her to think that living in the same house with Jason would work. Even as a stopgap measure to protect her brother, it struck her as a dramatic, foolhardy move. The whole time she was packing enough things to get them through the first few days, she practiced excuses for backing out. Every time she started to say one out loud, Jason shot her a forbidding look that caused the words to lodge in her throat.

Okay, so she could make the best of anything for a few days. That's all it would be. She would find a new apartment no later than Friday. She and Sammy could move next weekend, her sanity intact. She would thank Jason profusely for his trouble and run like crazy. No problem.

That was before she saw the house.

Settled on a block of gracious old town houses, there was a wide bay window in front which guaranteed the window seat she'd always wanted inside. There were fireplaces not only in the living room, but in all of the bedrooms. The high ceilings would welcome the tallest Christmas tree. She stood in the living room after touring the house and tried to hide the delight that spilled through her. It wouldn't do for Jason to ever discover that he owned her dream house, the one she'd spent countless hours fantasizing about while sitting on her own graffiti-decorated front steps.

Fortunately he seemed unaware of her speechlessness. Sammy was keeping Jason occupied with a series of awed questions. He'd gaped in astonishment when Mrs. Willis, the smiling housekeeper, had shown them a kitchen that was almost the size of their entire apartment. She'd taken one look at Sammy's skinny physique and immediately gone to work. She'd shooed them all into the living room with a promise of sandwiches and pie.

As she looked at the obviously pricey antiques, Dana worried that her rambunctious brother, who was just growing comfortable with his new height, would clumsily destroy something valuable.

"Well, what do you think?" Jason asked quietly, his hands resting on her shoulders as she gazed longingly at the window seat that was just as she'd always imagined.

"It's lovely," she said honestly.

"Think you'll be comfortable here?"

She shook her head at the anxious note in his voice. "Jason, you saw the way we've been living. How could we not be comfortable?" Determined to make it clear, though, that this was a temporary measure, she added firmly, "We'll try to stay out of your way. There's no need to change your routine for us."

"Dana," he said, his voice a low warning. "What's wrong with you? Why do you look so edgy? We even have chaperons. There's Sammy, and Mrs. Willis lives in."

"You didn't mention her before."

"I didn't think of her as a selling point. Of course, she and Mrs. Finch do share a fascination with romances."

"Terrific," Dana muttered. She glanced around and realized they were alone. "Where's Sammy?"

"Back in the kitchen. I believe he wanted to be sure the sandwiches weren't anything sissy like watercress."

Despite her nervousness, Dana chuckled. "Sammy's never even heard of watercress sandwiches. Why on earth would he think they might be?"

Jason looked guilty. "I believe I might have planted the possibility in his head."

She scanned his face. "Why?"

"So I could be alone with you. Come on. Let's sit over here."

He drew her to the window seat which was wide enough for both of them to sit with their backs to the sides, their legs brushing as they faced each other. Outside, rain had started to fall with the promise of snow by night. Dana felt a rare warmth and coziness steal through her. Living in a place like this would make her soft. She would grow too complacent.

"Why did you want to sit here?" she asked, wondering at his perfect choice in a room filled with comfortable-looking chairs.

"Because you haven't taken your eyes off it since you came in."

Unwilling to admit to the fascination with the window seat, she asked, "How long have you had this house?"

"Forever, it seems. It's the home my parents had when they first married. When we moved into a bigger place, they kept this one. For years it was rented, but I insisted on having it when I got out of college. I bought it from them. Some of my best memories come from the years we spent here. I used to sit in this window seat and read on rainy days. I'd read adventure stories and imagine that I was the hero. You have no idea the number of dragons I slayed in this very place."

Dana smiled. "And you're still slaying them, aren't you?"

"I'm trying," he admitted.

"Why?"

"I think you know the answer to that. Do you want me to say it out loud?"

"No," she said hurriedly. Somehow she knew what he'd say. And hearing him say aloud that he loved her here in this wonderful house, in this perfect setting would distract her from her goals. It would make her dreams actually seem within her grasp.

And anyone from her neighborhood knew all too well that dreams didn't come true, not unless you made them happen yourself. If Jason gave them to her, she would lose something, though exactly what was beginning to elude her.

Chapter 11

Dana had every intention of starting her new job as scheduled on Monday. Jason had other ideas. In fact, he had the perfect ruse. He convinced John Lansing to let her complete a project for him before filling out all the necessary paperwork at the Lansing Agency. That left her free to spend the entire day Monday making arrangements for Sammy to transfer to a new school. Last night she and Jason had devoted long hours to arguing about the transfer. She'd insisted that there was no point in pulling him out of his old school until she knew where they were going to be moving. Jason had countered that leaving her brother where he was would defeat the whole purpose of getting them out of the old neighborhood.

Even though they'd disagreed, Dana had felt an odd sense of relief at being able to share the burden of decision making. It frightened her how easily Jason was weaving himself into the fabric of her life, how readily she was willing to relinquish her responsibilities. It just proved what she'd known all along: she didn't dare let a man like Jason into her life. It would make her weak.

As it turned out, Sammy's suspension complicated matters. The new school didn't want to take him until he'd completed the punishment. Overhearing Dana's dilemma, Mrs. Willis offered to tutor Sammy until he could start classes again. Since she also offered to reward him with chocolate chip cookies, Sammy readily agreed to continue his lessons at home.

Dana watched in astonishment as Sammy and the housekeeper immediately disappeared into the kitchen. Sammy had his arm draped around the older woman's shoulders as he tried to convince her that he needed food first if he was to study properly. Chuckling, Mrs. Willis agreed. She seemed destined to play the same grandmotherly role in his life that Mrs. Finch played in Dana's.

With Sammy settled for the moment, Dana spent the remainder of the afternoon at loose ends, wandering through the house. It was the first time she could recall when she didn't have a dozen things that had to be done. She found a leather-bound copy of *Treasure Island* in one of the living room shelves and settled into the window seat to read. Caught up in the adventure, and imagining Jason reading the story in the very same place as a boy, made her feel closer to him than ever. It was a dangerous allure.

Jason didn't arrive home until after six. From her place on the window seat, Dana watched him, feeling unexpectedly shy as he came into the living room looking for her. As if they were an old married couple, he dropped a kiss on her brow, then handed Sammy a bag filled with the latest computer games.

Sammy emptied them onto the sofa, his eyes widening. "Hey, these are radical! Are they for me?"

Jason grinned. "They're yours. Maybe you can teach me to play them after dinner."

"Sure. Hey, sis, did you see?"

"I saw." She shot him a pointed glance. Sammy responded with a puzzled expression, then jumped up.

"Oh, yeah." He held out his hand to Jason. "Thanks, man."

"You're welcome. I thought maybe they'd keep you busy until it's time to go back to school."

Sammy groaned. "Who's got spare time? Did you know Mrs. W. used to be a teacher? She gave me more assignments than I ever had in school. I'll be up till midnight."

Anxious to get to the computer games, neither man seemed inclined to waste much time lingering over the housekeeper's beef stew. Amused that Jason seemed every bit as excited as Sammy, Dana went back to her place in the window seat to watch the two of them as they hunched over the computer. Sammy couldn't believe that Jason had never played a computer game before. He delighted in patiently explaining the rules, then beating the daylights out of Jason. Listening to their heated exchanges, she decided it was a toss-up which one was influencing the other.

Curious about the games, she got up and took a closer look. The game they were so intent on masked a geography lesson, one of Sammy's poorest subjects.

"Pretty sly," she told Jason, when Sammy finally went to his room, leaving the two of them alone.

Jason came over and nudged her legs aside, so he could sit across from her. Dana was all too aware of the way their knees intimately bumped, her faded jeans a sharp contrast to his expensive wool slacks.

"I haven't the foggiest idea what you're talking about," Jason said.

"Oh, really? I suppose it was just an accident that the game focused on geography."

"True," he said, his expression all innocence. "It looked like fun. I'd seen a lot about it in magazines and on public television. I'd just never gotten around to trying it."

"You're a crummy liar, but thank you. For the first time, I think Sammy realized learning could be fun. He's never loved books the way I have. He's just wanted to experience things, to see them firsthand."

Jason tucked her sock-clad feet in his lap and began massaging them. The deep strokes were both soothing and oddly exciting. Tingles shot from her toes straight to her midsection.

"There are some who say that his way is right, that people who get all their education from books never really learn about living," he said as if it were no more than an idle thought. His caresses said otherwise.

Dana's breath had gone perfectly still. "Is that what you think? Do you think I've been missing out on life?"

His gaze met hers. "It doesn't really matter what I think. What do you think?"

Dana had to try very hard to stay focused on the train of the conversation. "Maybe I've missed out on some things, but not the important ones."

Jason's hands slid beyond her feet and began a hypnotic caress of the bare skin just above her socks. She'd had no idea just how shivery sensitive that part of her anatomy was.

"What about love?" he said as matter-of-factly as if he'd asked about the likelihood of snow. "Isn't that one of the most important things?"

"I suppose. What about it?" she asked, her voice suddenly choked. That increasingly familiar ache was back again, that deep-down need that was aroused in her by Jason's most casual touches.

"Don't you think that's one of those things you have to experience to understand? You can read about it, but until you've felt your heart open up to another person, you don't really know what it is. I'm just beginning to realize that myself. How about you?"

"Maybe." Her voice was a near whisper as she succumbed to the delicious warmth spreading through her. With the fire crackling in the fireplace and Jason's intoxicating touches, she felt as if she'd discovered paradise. If ever she was going to allow herself to love a man, it would be this one. He could be exasperating and arrogant and stuffy, but his heart and his touch were gentle.

His fingers came to rest just above her knee. Her stomach quivered in anticipation. Yet nothing more happened.

Why wasn't he finishing what he started? she wondered, filled with a frustration she couldn't quite explain. Why, for the first time in her life, wasn't she afraid of what might happen next? Could it be that she was actually ready to admit she needed another person in her life and that Jason Halloran was that person?

Fending off male advances had become second nature to her by the time she was twelve. The guys in her neighborhood hadn't been respectful of age or innocence. Dana had known intuitively that the first time she gave any one of them the slightest encouragement, she would become fair game for them all. That's when she'd learned exactly where to hit to prove that no meant *no*.

To her confusion, she wasn't the least bit interested in saying no now. On some level she couldn't explain, it was as if she'd waited her whole life for this moment, yet Jason was holding back. His touches teased, inflamed, then left her wanting. Agitated by the sensations and her own unexpected response to them, she dared to meet Jason's gaze. At once she saw the turmoil, saw her own turbulent desire reflected there.

"Jason?"

"What?"

"I think I need you to kiss me."

A half smile came and went, then his mouth slowly covered hers with exquisite tenderness. His tongue coaxed her lips apart, and Dana's senses went spinning. It was a response she'd come to expect and, again, she wasn't afraid.

Nor was she satisfied. There was a sweetness to the kiss, a gentle persuasiveness, but she knew there had to be more, and she wanted it, desired it with a fierce intensity that shook her to her very core. She wasn't ready to label the wanting love, wasn't ready to think at all beyond tonight. Tonight, though, she wanted to be held in Jason's arms.

The daring prospect was fraught with obstacles. Sammy, for one. She couldn't make love to Jason with her brother in the same house. And what would Mrs. Willis think if she discovered that Dana's bed hadn't been slept in?

Those were just excuses, she told herself. Jason's

master suite was at the opposite end of the house from the rooms she and Sammy had taken. As for the house-keeper, Mrs. Willis wouldn't see anything out of the ordinary if Dana's room was tidy when she first entered it tomorrow. Dana was too used to making her own bed to leave it for someone else to do. Even this morning everything had been neatly in place before she'd ever walked out the door. Though Mrs. Willis was clearly inclined to pamper her while she was there, Dana had explained that she was used to doing things for herself.

There was nothing, then, to stand in the way of her spending the night with Jason. Except maybe Jason himself. She gazed at him and saw the banked desire still lingering in his eyes, felt the hesitation in his touch. He was every bit as troubled by the prospect of taking this next step as she was. Maybe it was his willingness to hold back that touched that part of her heart that had always said no in the past. She would never find a man who cared more about her feelings than Jason.

Sliding toward him, she took his face in her hands and slanted her mouth across his. She felt the heat climb in his cheeks, felt the urgency mount in his kiss as he matched her hunger.

Then his hands covered hers and he pulled back, no more than an inch, but the separation was too much. She felt bereft. She tried to close the gap, but he held back. "What do you want, Dana?"

"You know," she said, lost in the first whisper of a smoldering sensuality she was just beginning to discover. "Can't you tell?"

"I want you to say it. I need to know that you mean it."

She swallowed hard. "I want you to make love to

me." She began faintly, but by the end she managed to sound bold and convincing.

Against her hands, Jason's fingers trembled. "You're sure?"

"Very sure."

"You aren't doing this out of some misguided sense of obligation because you're staying here?"

"I'm doing it because I think I'll fly apart if I don't experience what it's like to have you love me."

The words had come from her heart—her poor, misguided and probably soon-to-be-broken heart. Apparently they were enough. Jason scooped her into his arms and carried her up the steps. "You can back out anytime," he said, but the look in his eyes pleaded with her not to.

There was no chance she was going to change her mind now, anyway. Dana felt a shimmering feminine awareness that pulled like a magnet. It was all she could do to keep her hands from roaming down Jason's shoulders to explore his chest. Curiosity mixed with desire made her bold. Whatever shyness she might have been expected to feel had long since vanished, swept away by wave after wave of deep longing. All of the warnings she'd given herself just this morning seemed unimportant when compared to the discoveries she was about to make—about herself, about Jason, about making love.

With the door to Jason's room firmly locked behind them, she stood on tiptoe to draw him into a kiss from which there could be no retreat. She was desperate to know where passion led, where this tantalizing spiral of white-hot sensation peaked.

Lifting Dana gently and putting her on the bed, Jason scanned her face, his gaze intent. "No regrets?"

"Not now. Not later," she promised. And if there

were, she would keep them to herself, knowing instinctively that there would be worse regrets if they never shared this moment.

His fingers looped under the hem of her sweater, then slowly drew it over her head. The casual brush of his fingers against her bare midriff left a trail of heat. He traced the swell of her breasts, teasing until she was sure she would die if his touch didn't reach the sensitized nipples. With one deft movement, he unhooked her bra and for a moment he simply stared, his expression rapt. If Dana had ever worried about her attractiveness, that look put her worries to rest. Fascinated, he touched one swollen, rosy peak, first with the pad of his thumb, then with his tongue. Dana's back arched as a riot of new sensations shimmered through her.

But for every feathered touch and every deep caress, satisfaction was followed too quickly by a rising sense of need. Like the climber who always discovers new peaks the instant the last has been attained, Dana discovered that each glorious, thrilling sensation only hinted at one even more spectacular.

She lost track of where one stroke ended and the next began, caught up instead in a never-ending wave that crested, then eased gently away before building again, higher than ever. Still there was this emptiness that she didn't understand.

Jason's flesh burned every bit as hot as her own. His desire was written on his face, but he seemed determined to take his time, determined to tease and taunt until neither of them could wait an instant longer for fulfillment. That time was fast approaching.

Up until the last possible second, Dana waited for the fear to ruin what was happening between them. She was so sure that her conscience and common sense would kick in and rob her of Jason's tenderness, of his love. As her body lifted toward his, seeking the elusive fulfillment he withheld, she realized that behind the desire in his eyes there was worry. He, too, was waiting for her to change her mind, giving her time for thought to overrule sensation.

She reached for him then, boldly caressing, telling him without words that there would be no retreat. He couldn't hold back a low moan as her strokes became more insistent. And then he was chuckling.

"I get the message," he murmured as he held himself above her.

"I certainly hope so," she said. "There's a lot to be said for anticipation, but I think it's time you make a commitment."

The word with its multitude of meanings crept out before she realized how Jason would interpret it. Satisfaction flared in his eyes as he eased into her at last. There was one brief, searing instant of unexpected pain, then Dana was filled with that sense of completion that had eluded her for so long. Lost to the sensations, she forgot all about her foolish slip of the tongue, forgot everything except the wild racing of her heart, the rush of heat and, finally, the most incredible release—as if she'd just discovered a way to catapult over rainbows.

The night was all about giving—and learning to accept. It was morning before her last teasing remark came back to haunt her. She woke to find Jason propped up on his elbow, staring at her. His sleepy, sensual smile made her stomach flip over.

"So, let's talk about commitment," he said, drawing a fingertip over her breast.

"I can't talk about anything when you're doing that," she said.

To her regret he opted for talking over touching. "How do you feel about commitment?"

Suddenly all too aware of the silver-framed family photographs that lined his dresser, she was shaking her head before the first words were out of his mouth. "Are we talking in general? I think it's a fine idea... for some people."

"But not for you?"

"Not for me."

"Then why are we here?" he demanded mildly. "Why did you make the choice to make love last night, when it's a choice you've obviously never made before?"

"Because I..." She saw the expectant look on his face, but she couldn't bring herself to say the words she knew he wanted to hear. "Because I trust you. Isn't that enough for now?" she said wistfully.

For a minute his gaze clashed with hers, but then he sighed. "For now," he agreed. "But I want more than an occasional night in bed with you, Dana."

"It wasn't all that long ago that you dismissed me as a flake. Why the abrupt change?"

"I wish I could explain it," he said. "All I know is that for the past few weeks I've felt alive for the first time in months. You've brought out a side of me I never even knew existed. I may be a lot of things, Dana, but I'm not stupid. I recognize a good thing when I have it within my grasp. I will give you anything you ask, do anything you want, but I'm not known for my patience."

"Tell me about it," she muttered.

He scowled at her. "All I'm trying to say is that I can wait only so long."

Dana was shaken by the unspoken threat underlying his words, but she put on her bravest front and resorted to teasing. "You'll do anything, huh?"

"Anything," he vowed.

"Well, that presents some intriguing possibilities."

There was just enough time for him to show her one of them before they left for work.

The expression on Dana's face made Jason very nervous.

"Okay, spill it," he said finally, sensing that he was about to pay for his impetuous early-morning promise to give her anything she wanted. "What's up?"

"I was talking to Harriet just now," she began slowly.

"Harriet?" he repeated blankly. "You've been conspiring with my secretary?"

"I wouldn't call it conspiring and don't look so stunned. She's really very nice."

"Harriet?"

"Will you stop it and listen? She told me about this part-time job, in the mailroom."

"You have a job," he said tightly. He was not going to encourage her to take a second job, just so she could afford to move into a fancier place of her own that much sooner. Besides, she barely had enough time to sleep as it was—especially when she was occupying his bed, which was where he intended she stay.

"Not for me," she said patiently.

Suddenly he realized why she looked so nervous. "Oh, no," he said, coming out from behind his desk. "I will not give your brother a job."

She laced her hands behind his neck and gave him an imploring look. "It's just a part-time messenger job.

He could come in after school, earn a little of his own money, learn about accepting responsibility—it would be perfect. How much trouble could he possibly get into?"

Jason eased away from her and raked his fingers through his hair. He couldn't think straight when she had her arms around him like that, and this situation definitely called for straight thinking.

"You're asking this about a boy who a few short weeks ago was ready to go into business selling stolen goods. The same boy who was thrown out of school last week for pulling a knife on a classmate. The same kid who's this close—" he held up fingers a scant inch apart "—this close to getting into a gang that mugs people for kicks."

Dana remained undaunted by the facts. It was one of her more endearing and infuriating qualities.

"Just look how he's blossoming now that he's out of that environment. He's already taking his studies more seriously with Mrs. Willis there to tutor him. Haven't you ever made a mistake?" she demanded. "Or is the difference that Hallorans have enough money to cover up any little indiscretions they might make?"

"This isn't about money or family."

"No. It's about second chances."

The whisper-soft tone of her voice was persuasive. The look in her eyes could have converted sinner to saint. Jason sighed.

"He won't do it."

"He will," she said, throwing her arms around him. She gave him a tantalizing peck on the cheek. "I'll call and tell him to come over this afternoon. Thank you, Jason. You won't regret it."

He already did. The mere thought of that little punk

on the loose at Halloran Industries made him shudder. It was one thing to have Sammy living in his house, where Mrs. Willis could keep her stern eye on him and only Jason would have to pay for any of his royal screw-ups. It was another thing entirely to inflict him on the family business. What sort of magic was this woman working, Jason wondered, that would make him even consider such an idea?

On the other hand, he thought slowly, maybe Dana was right. Maybe this was an opportunity, a challenge. The one thing he and Dana argued about more than anything else was her brother. Maybe by taking one giant leap of faith in Sammy, he could eliminate the bone of contention between them and further cement a relationship that was coming to mean everything to him.

One look at Sammy's sullen expression a few hours later and Jason wasn't so sure. Whatever progress they'd made at home seemed to have been lost. He wondered if Sammy viewed this as punishment, rather than a chance.

After a cursory nod, Sammy sprawled in the chair across from Jason and regarded him with open hostility. His attitude improved only slightly when he turned his attention to the computer, the fax machine and the calculator. Jason could practically see the larcenous wheels spinning in his head.

"Don't even think about it," he warned in a low voice.

Sammy looked startled. "Hey, I was just checkin' the place out."

"I'm sure you were. However, if one item in this office moves by so much as an inch, I will know where to look. Do we understand each other?"

Sammy shrugged. "You're the boss."

"That's right."

"What am I gonna do?"

"It's a messenger job. You'll see that the mail is picked up from the offices, sorted and distributed. Once in a while you might be asked to take something into town."

"How? You plannin' to loan me your car?"

"No. I'm planning to give you bus fare."

"What's this job pay?"

Jason named the minimum wage figure.

"You're kiddin' me, right?"

"I'm not kidding you."

"I could make more than that busing tables in some dive."

"Maybe. Is that something you're interested in doing? I have a couple of friends who own restaurants."

Sammy seemed startled by Jason's willingness to give him a choice. "I thought this was a done deal. Now I get it. You're just doing my sister a favor—again. The minute I screw up, I'm out, right? If you can pawn me off on one of your friends, you won't need to mess with me at all and you'll still be square with Dana."

It was a long speech for Sammy. To Jason's surprise, he realized that there was an edge of real hurt in the boy's voice. Jason wondered how many times people had made snap decisions about Sammy, had promised him something only to yank it away again.

"Sammy, let's back up a minute. Do you really want a job?"

Sammy shrugged. "Dana works too hard. I should help out."

"That's an admirable attitude. Now, if you really had a choice, if you could do anything in the world you wanted to, what would it be?"

Sammy rolled his eyes. "I'm just a kid."

"You're sixteen years old. You're almost a man. Surely you've thought about what you'd like to do when you get out of school."

"Not really."

"What is your best subject?"

"Math, I guess. I like English, too. I get good grades on all my essays."

There was no mistaking the faint spark of enthusiasm. Sammy tried hard to maintain his distant, nonchalant attitude, but Jason detected the slight shift in his mood from boredom to interest.

"What if we rethink this job situation a little, then? How about working three hours after school? You spend the first two hours taking care of the mail. Then during the last hour each day we'll let you spend some time in different departments around here. You could start in accounting, maybe spend some time with me in marketing, helping me with some writing I have to do. If you're interested, I'm sure my grandfather would be happy to teach you about the manufacturing process, too."

"We're still talkin' that minimum-wage stuff, though, right?"

Jason grinned. "At first. But if you catch on quickly in any of the departments and want to move up, we'll talk about a salary increase then."

"I suppose that would be okay."

His tone was lukewarm, but there was a rare spark of excitement in Sammy's eyes.

"You'll start tomorrow?"

"Why not," Sammy said, then added with studied nonchalance, "I got an hour to kill now, if there's somethin' you want me to do."

"I'll have Harriet take you down to personnel and

you can fill out some forms. Then, if you still have some time, I'll show you around."

He buzzed for Harriet, then watched Sammy leave with her. To his astonishment, the boy actually seemed to be walking a little taller. Jason heard Dana's greeting in the outer office, then the quick rush of questions about how the interview went.

"No problem," Sammy said, his tone cocky. "I'm a tough negotiator, sis. You're lookin' at one top-notch executive trainee."

Jason was still chuckling when Dana stepped into his office, her eyes sparkling.

"Executive trainee?" she said. "I thought you were having trouble with the concept of messenger."

"Actually Sammy was having more trouble with that than I was. Minimum wage did not appeal to him. We compromised. He still gets minimum wage, but he'll rotate through the departments so he'll get a little experience in various things. Who knows, maybe he'll find his niche." He regarded her hopefully. "Do you suppose there's any chance we could talk him into a more normal haircut before my father sees him?"

Dana chuckled at the wistfulness in his voice. "I doubt it. You know, Jason Halloran, you're not nearly as tough as you like to pretend to be."

"Oh, but I am," he said. "I intend to make the person who got me into this pay."

"Pay how?"

He reached for her hand and tugged her closer. "Like this," he said softly and pulled her into his arms. "I think for a few more kisses like this, I might be willing to make Sammy head of marketing."

Chapter 12

For a man who'd always been determinedly grounded in reality, Jason had developed a surprisingly fanciful habit of imagining Dana's voice whenever he started feeling lonely. This morning, however, he was certain that for once it was not his imagination playing tricks on him. They didn't have an appointment, but he was willing to swear she was in his outer office. He poked his head out and discovered her in the midst of what looked like a very conspiratorial group—Sammy, an astonishingly lighthearted Harriet and his grandfather. Brandon looked like the sassy cat who'd just swallowed the canary.

"What kind of trouble are you all getting into out here?" Jason demanded. "And why wasn't I included?"

Four moderately guilty faces turned in his direction. Brandon was quickest on his feet. He'd had years of experience twisting tricky situations to his own advantage.

"You can't possibly begrudge an old man a little time with your girl," he said. "However, if you're jealous, you can come along. We're about to go on a tour of the plant."

"Harriet has worked here for the past twenty years. She's seen every nook and cranny of the place," Jason reminded him. "And Dana saw the plant from top to bottom just a couple of weeks ago."

"Not through *my* eyes. You probably did one of those wham-bang tours that barely touched the tip of the iceberg."

"I did leave out all the nostalgia," Jason admitted, grinning at him. His grandfather was clearly in his element, relishing the prospect of an attentive audience. Jason turned to Dana and her brother, who was slouched on a corner of Harriet's desk twisting paper clips out of shape. "I hope you know what you're in for. His version could take hours."

"You could come along," Dana coaxed. "Maybe it would improve your skills as a tour guide—add a little color. Tours could become a great marketing device. Dozens of little fifth-graders parading through here every day. Just imagine."

Jason shuddered at the thought. But he'd discovered lately that when Dana got that impish look on her face, he found it impossible to refuse her anything. His intentions to reform and become a dutiful company official flew out the window. He forgot all about the stack of work on his desk. Maybe, if he got lucky, he could sneak a kiss behind one of the giant looms.

"Yes," he murmured. "Just imagine."

Draping an arm around Dana's shoulder, he gestured to Brandon. "Lead on, Granddad."

Jason listened with tolerant amusement as his grand-father launched into a family history that started back in England before the turn of the century. Dana and even Sammy listened raptly as Brandon talked about his grandfather's textile mill in England and his struggle to build a name for himself.

"His son, my father, had bigger dreams. He'd heard there was newer, faster equipment to be had in America and he had a spirit of adventure. He came to this country with little money in his pocket and a lot of desire. His uncles had been here for years, working for one of the mills that had been around for decades. It was founded by a competitor of Francis Cabot Lowell right around 1816, 1820. In those early years most of the country's wholesale wool trade was handled right out of Boston.

"Anyway, James and the uncles pooled their money and bought the plant. The equipment wasn't as up-to-date as some, but they knew where to go in England and Scotland for the best wool, and pretty soon they developed a reputation for the finest fabric. That was the start of Halloran Industries.

"Nowadays, this place is something of a dinosaur. Most of the big mills from before the turn of the century went south. We decided to stay right here. We were never interested in quantity or in producing cheap material. We've concentrated on making the best."

He plucked up a handful of soft gray hairs and showed them to Sammy. "You know what this is?"

"Looks like a bunch of old hairs to me."

"Expensive old hairs. Here, feel them. Feel how soft they are. That's cashmere, son. It comes from Himalayan goats in Tibet. We blend this with wool to make some of the winter fabric."

He led Sammy to another loom. "Now you watch this. It used to be done completely by hand. Just imagine that. All that spinning and weaving took days just to get enough material to make a coat or a dress."

Jason watched in astonishment as Sammy's expression turned from boredom to fascination. He seemed to be hanging on Brandon's words. Brandon seemed equally delighted to find someone who'd actually listen to all his old stories with rapt attention. How had they so easily found the rapport he'd had to struggle for? Maybe it was because his grandfather was genuinely accepting of other people, flaws and all.

"I thought most textile manufacturers specialized," Dana said. "Halloran Industries does woolen fabrics, silks and cottons. Isn't that more expensive?"

"Sure," Brandon agreed. "But remember what I said. We wanted to do quality, not quantity. The decision to diversify goes back to my father. The truth of the matter was he was fascinated by the techniques. Every time he'd see a piece of fabric that intrigued him, he'd set out to learn how it was made. He even traveled to the Far East to learn more about silkworms."

"I've been trying to convince Granddad and Dad for ages that we ought to concentrate on one specialty," Jason said. "Then Granddad goes off on one of his vacation trips and, just like his father, he comes home with some ancient French woodblocks for printing cotton and we add a new line. It's not cost-effective."

Brandon shrugged. "If I wanted to manufacture the material for cheap bed linens, I'd have gone south years ago and set up shop near a cotton field. Top designers and decorators come here when they want something rare and spectacular for their finest customers. We'll work to order, match a dye to suit the customer. Few places can afford to do that."

"*We* can't afford to do that," Jason countered.

Brandon chuckled. "You sound more like your father every day."

Jason couldn't help grinning back at him. "Now that is a depressing thought."

Sammy had wandered over to a bale of Sea Island cotton waiting to be processed. "This stuff actually turns into material?" he asked, his expression incredulous. "Like my shirt or somethin'?"

Brandon studied Sammy's faded plaid shirt and said, "Maybe not that shirt, but you've got the idea. First it's carded, then it goes through three more steps before we spin it." He showed him the stages, leading up to the final woven material. "Feel the difference between ours and yours. It's all in the thread count." He scowled at Jason. "Can't seem to make *some people* understand the importance of that."

He moved across an aisle. "Now look over here. We're handprinting it. I found these woodblocks at a mill that was closing in France last year after four centuries. What do you think of that?"

"Awesome," Sammy said. "Tell me again about the wool. Where's that place the sheep come from?"

The two of them went off together, Brandon responding animatedly to Sammy's rapid-fire questions.

Jason watched them go with something akin to wonder spreading through him. "I think Granddad has finally met a soul mate. Dad and I have always been more fascinated with the business end of things. Granddad just loves the product. He inherited that obsession with the textiles themselves from his father and who knows how many generations before him."

Suddenly he realized that Dana was barely listening. She was scribbling rapidly on the notepad she'd carried during the tour.

"What are you doing?" he asked.

"Some of this information might be helpful when we design that new campaign, don't you think?"

"You're probably right, but this minute I'm much more fascinated with these silk threads you've got caught in your hair." He reached up to brush away strands of pale pink silk. "Did you tangle with a silkworm somewhere along the way?"

"Actually I was peeking under something to see how the machinery worked."

"Can I see your notes?" he said, holding out his hand. "They must be fascinating."

Dana handed him the notebook. A half dozen pages had scrawled notes on them, but what Jason found incredible were the sketches. "These are amazing."

"You really think so?"

"I can't believe you did them in just the little bit of time Granddad spent in each area. We could use these in the next brochure instead of photographs. Let's go back to my office and rough out an overall design, while the idea's still fresh."

As they walked back to his office, Jason was astounded at his mounting excitement. He couldn't help but be struck by the change in his attitude, the sense of fulfillment he suddenly felt. Whether it was having Dana at the office or simply having her in his life, those days of boredom and dissatisfaction seemed like a distant nightmare. Maybe it was simply a matter of seeing his world through fresh, unjaded eyes. Or perhaps it was simply finding a focus. At any rate, for the first time in his life he truly felt a part of something bigger than his own selfish interests.

They were bent over Dana's sketchbook an hour later, when the door to his office burst open. Jason glanced up and caught his father's agitated expression, the quick head-to-toe examination to which he subjected Dana before mentally dismissing her.

"Hey, Dad, come on in. I want you to meet the new artist who's working with us. Dana Roberts, this is my father, Kevin Halloran."

Kevin's fierce expression softened slightly as he shook Dana's hand. "Son, if you've got a minute, I think you and I need to talk."

There was an edge to his father's tone that worried Jason. Kevin rudely turned his back on Dana and went to stare out the window as he waited for Jason to create the sort of privacy he'd requested.

Jason bit back a furious retort and said quietly, "Sure. Dana, we can finish this later. I think you've got the right idea now, anyway."

When she was gone, Kevin turned back. Before Jason could say a word about his father's rudeness, Kevin snapped, "What's this I hear about some woman moving in with you?"

Jason froze. "Where did you hear that?"

"Actually I believe your mother heard it from one of her friends, Marcy Wellington's mother."

Jason recalled the visit he'd had the previous evening from Marcy. Always more aggressively interested in him than he'd been in her, she'd stopped by hoping to spend the evening, perhaps even the night, with him.

She'd even expressed a willingness to forgive him for what she described as that humiliating evening at the symphony gala. Discovering Dana on the premises had brought out her cattiest nature. He wasn't surprised that the news had traveled this fast.

"How could you take a step like this without informing us?" Kevin demanded. "Your mother's distraught."

"I doubt that," Jason countered. It was his father, not his mother, who tended to worry about appearances. "Don't you think I'm a little old to be called on the carpet about my living arrangements?"

"Not when they reflect on this family. Not when you're living in our house."

"It's not your house. I bought it, remember? And having Dana and her brother living under my roof is hardly likely to damage the Halloran reputation."

Kevin stared at him in astonishment. "That's the one? That girl who just left here is living with you?"

Jason bristled at the demeaning tone, but managed to keep his own tone even. "She needed to get out of her old apartment. She's staying with me until she can find her own place in a better neighborhood. If I have my way, she'll stay on indefinitely. I'm planning to ask her to marry me, Dad."

Kevin regarded him as if he'd lost his mind. "You're *what*?"

Jason wasn't sure exactly when he'd made up his mind. Maybe it was simply hearing his father's demeaning tone that had formalized the decision. "I'm asking her to marry me. She'll probably turn me down, but I intend to keep on trying until she says yes."

"Well, thank goodness one of you is displaying some sense. Are you determined to ruin your life?"

Jason's voice dropped to a low, ominous tone. "If I recall, there was a time when Granddad said the same thing about Mother. You of all people should understand what kind of havoc an outdated attitude like that can wreak. Are you planning to follow in his footsteps, anyway?"

The charge had the desired effect. Kevin's face fell. He rubbed a hand across his eyes and sank into a chair across from Jason's desk. When he finally met Jason's gaze again, he looked genuinely contrite. "I'm sorry. I don't know what's gotten into me lately."

Worried at the gray cast to his father's complexion, Jason pulled a chair up opposite his father and sat down. "Dad, can't you talk to me about what's going on?"

His father shook his head. "No. I'm not sure I even understand it myself."

"Why don't you and Mom come to dinner tomorrow night? You can spend some time with Dana and her brother. I want you to see how truly special she is. I'll ask Granddad, too. He's out in the plant with her brother now. He and Sammy have really hit it off."

His father didn't look thrilled with the prospect of a family dinner, but he said, "I'll talk to your mother and let you know, okay?"

"Please try, Dad. It's important to me."

Kevin stood up and squeezed his shoulder. "I'll do what I can."

As he left Jason's office, though, Jason couldn't help wondering if his father had any intention at all of passing along the invitation. To make sure that the dinner came off, if for no other reason than to provide an opportunity to see his parents together and get a sense of what was troubling them, Jason dialed his parents' number.

"Mom, I was just talking to Dad about a family dinner at my place tomorrow night. There's someone I want you to meet."

"The woman who's living there?" she said, though her tone was far less judgmental than his father's had been.

"Yes. You'll really like her. Her brother's a little—" he searched for a word "—unexpected. So is Dana, for that matter. You'll come, won't you?"

"If it's important to you, we'll be there," she promised, though he could tell her heart wasn't in it.

Still, that was two down and three more to go. His grandfather would probably be delighted to have the opportunity to spend more time with Dana and Sammy. And Sammy could be persuaded to do anything that involved Mrs. Willis's cooking. Dana, however, was another story. He had a hunch she was going to take one look at the Halloran clan gathering and head for the hills. For a woman who craved family the way she obviously did, she seemed deadly earnest about avoiding any personal connection with his.

He debated telling her at all, then decided she'd never forgive him if she turned up for dinner in jeans and discovered his whole family at the table.

He broached the subject at the dinner table that night, after Sammy had left to spend an hour playing computer games before doing the assignments Mrs. Willis continued to heap on him.

Dana listened to the plans, then repeated, "They're all coming here? Tomorrow?"

"Yes. You already know Dad and my grandfather, right? And you'll love my mother."

"I don't think so. Sammy and I will go out for the evening."

"The whole point of this dinner is to have everyone get to know you."

Her gaze narrowed. "Why?"

Sensing that he'd made a tactical blunder, Jason tried to backtrack. "I want you to meet my family. It'll help you understand what Hallorans are all about."

"Professionally?" she inquired hopefully.

"Exactly."

"I suppose that does make sense, but…"

For the first time since he'd known her, she suddenly looked totally at a loss. "But what?" he prodded.

"Nothing," she said finally.

Jason suspected he knew what *nothing* meant. He'd seen her one dressy outfit and suspected she was already finding fault with it, trying to imagine how she could possibly fit in with his family, wearing discounted clothes. He vowed then and there to find her something special first thing in the morning. What good was manufacturing the finest fabric, if you couldn't call in a favor from a designer every now and then?

Dana imagined she knew what it felt like to be walking toward a guillotine. Despite Jason's reassurances that this family dinner was nothing more than an opportunity for her to understand the Hallorans, she knew she was the one being trotted out for inspection. Not even Sammy was under the kind of unspoken pressure she was facing. He'd greeted news of the dinner with blasé indifference, then had gone back to one of the books Brandon had loaned him about the history of the textile industry.

Determined to strive for the same kind of nonchalance that Sammy was affecting, Dana didn't even bother to go home from work early. What was the point? She had one decent skirt, one reasonably fashionable sweater, one pair of high-heeled shoes. With no feminine dawdling over choices to factor in, it would take her about twenty minutes to shower and dress.

That was her thinking right up until the minute she walked into her room and discovered the boxes stacked in the middle of her bed—a bed she'd slept in only once since moving in with Jason. She stared at the assortment of packages in wonder.

Never, not once in her life had she received this many presents at one time. What was she supposed to do about them? She couldn't take gifts from Jason. She might not have been to finishing school, but she knew what was proper. Even in her neighborhood, a woman took presents like this only when she was willing to have her reputation compromised. Hers might be shaky at the moment, but so far she hadn't done anything she might regret later. These packages represented regrets.

She scooped them up in her arms and marched down the hall to Jason's suite. Since her hands were full, she kicked the door until Jason came to open it.

"What's all this?" he questioned, feigning innocence.

"I might ask you the same thing."

"Haven't you opened them?"

"No. I can't accept them."

"You don't even know what's inside."

"I can guess," she said stubbornly. She dumped the boxes onto the bed, then turned to glare at him. "If I'm not good enough for your family the way I am, then I don't need to be at this dinner tonight. And if you're ashamed of me, then you'd better say so now, because I will not allow you to try to pretty me up just so I'll fit in."

Her point made—rather emphatically she thought—she stalked toward the door.

"Whoa!" Jason said, putting his hands on her shoulders and spinning her around. "Let's get one thing straight right now. I am not ashamed of you. I want you to like my family and vice versa, but if that doesn't happen, so be it. I bought these things for you because I want you to feel comfortable, because you deserve to have beautiful things. If you'd rather wear something else—if you want to wear your jeans and one of your sweaters—it's okay with me. I love those jeans. They do great things for your legs."

The sincerity in his voice reached her. Her temper slowed to a simmer, then finally cooled altogether. "Maybe I could at least look in the boxes," she said cautiously.

Sammy at his most indifferent couldn't have been any more casual than Jason when he shrugged. "It's up to you."

"I'll look."

She opened what appeared to be a shoebox first. Folded inside layers of tissue paper were the slinkiest, highest silver sandals she'd ever seen. She recognized the label from one of the city's swankiest shoe stores.

"Ohmigosh," she murmured, trying to imagine wearing the shoes without feeling a little like Cinderella in her glass slippers. If the shoes were this incredible, what on earth did the rest of the boxes contain?

"More?" Jason inquired lazily. He'd sprawled in a chair to watch. His posture was relaxed, but there was a tension beneath the surface that suggested he couldn't wait for her reaction to the rest.

Suddenly Dana grinned and gave in to temptation.

How often did fairy-tale extravagances happen to a woman like her? "Oh, what the hell? Let's go for it."

She tugged open the biggest box and discovered a slinky black dress that shimmered with silver beads on the shoulders. She held it up and moved in front of the full-length mirror. She swallowed hard when she saw her reflection. She looked glamorous. She turned slowly back to Jason. "If this is what you had in mind for a simple family dinner, I would never have forgiven you if you'd let me go downstairs in jeans."

"I had my own jeans out, just in case."

The remaining boxes contained the sheerest, laciest lingerie Dana had ever seen. She tried to picture Jason shopping for it, but her imagination failed her. "You bought these?" she asked holding up one of several pairs of virtually nonexistent panties. The pair dangling from her finger was black. There were others in the sexiest red, the richest cream, the most virginal white.

He grinned. "Had the time of my life doing it, too. You just have to promise you'll wear them under your jeans. The image will drive me wild. In fact, if you don't get them out of here this very instant, you and I are going to be very late for dinner and that will really take some explaining."

Dana gathered the clothes up from the bed and started out the door. At the next instant she looked back and caught the pleased expression on Jason's face. "Thank you," she said softly. "I feel like Cinderella."

"There's a difference, sweetheart. You're already home."

Dana couldn't get Jason's words out of her head all through dinner. She barely noticed that Sammy was wearing new slacks, a dress shirt and a tie that he kept

trying to tug loose. There was a new confidence about
him that even in her distracted state was impossible
to miss. He watched Brandon Halloran and mimicked
every move the older man made. Brandon was careful
to include Sammy in the conversation, for which Dana
was grateful.

Everything about the evening was perfect. Everyone
admired her dress. Mrs. Willis's menu was superb, even
if Dana didn't know what half the things were. Lacey
Halloran went out of her way to be gracious to both
Dana and Sammy. After his initial reserve, even Kevin
Halloran opened up. It had taken several glasses of wine
to accomplish that, but whatever the cause, Dana was
grateful. After his behavior in Jason's office, she'd been
prepared for open disapproval.

Jason sat back and watched the byplay with the satisfaction of a man who'd put all of his chess pieces
into motion and was waiting for certain victory. When
they moved into the living room after dinner, he poured
brandy for everyone—even Sammy, who choked on the
first sip and asked for a soda.

Lacey Halloran set her own snifter of brandy on an
end table and leaned toward Dana. "Jason tells me you
had to leave your old apartment."

"That's 'cause these guys I knew said they were
gonna come after her," Sammy piped up. "Jason and I
figured it wasn't so safe for her to be there anymore."

Jason's mother looked nonplussed for an instant.
"That must have been very frightening," she said finally.

"You get used to the violence in a neighborhood like
that," Dana responded.

"I'm sure living here is a vast improvement," Kevin

said. It sounded to Dana as if he were accusing her of something, though his expression was perfectly bland.

"Actually I don't expect to be here all that long. Sammy and I will find a place of our own."

Lacey Halloran looked confused. "But I thought…"

"There's no rush," Jason said, interrupting his mother.

Dana had a terrible hunch she knew exactly what the woman had been about to say. Apparently Brandon Halloran was not the only one with a mistaken understanding of where her relationship with Jason was headed. They'd probably taken one look at this fancy dress she was wearing tonight and leaped to all sorts of wrong conclusions. They probably thought she intended to take Jason for everything she could get. Unfortunately there was no way she could correct their impressions without embarrassing Jason and making matters worse.

It was one of those rare times when retreat seemed the most prudent course.

She stood up. "If you'll excuse me, I really should be going up. I have work to do and I'm sure you all would like to spend some time together without an outsider around. Sammy, I know you have homework."

Jason was on his feet at once. "Dana…"

"No, really. I have to get those sketches finished tonight. It was very nice meeting all of you."

She was halfway up the stairs before Sammy caught up with her, his expression puzzled. "Are you mad about somethin', sis?"

Dana sighed. "No. I'm not mad."

"Then why'd you run out like that?"

"We're not Hallorans, Sammy. We can't let ourselves forget that."

"But…"

She hugged him tight. "I don't think I mentioned it earlier, but you look very handsome."

His eyes lit up. "You really think so?"

"I really think so. Good night, Sammy. I'll see you in the morning. Don't stay up too late."

Unfortunately she wasn't able to take her own advice. She changed into an oversized T-shirt, climbed into bed, than stared at the ceiling for what seemed like hours. When sleep continued to elude her, she got up and, dragging a blanket with her, curled up in a chair by the window.

She was still sitting there, staring out at the inky darkness when she heard the faint tap on her door, then saw it inch open. Jason didn't wait for a response before sliding inside. Dana's breath lodged in her throat.

It was an instant before his eyes adjusted to the darkness, before he spotted her in the chair. When he did, he crossed the room in three angry strides, then hauled her up against him and slanted a bruising kiss across her mouth. Dana was so stunned by the onslaught of sensations, by the rough demand, that it was an instant before she fought to free herself.

Breathing hard, she stepped away from him and demanded, "What the hell was that all about?"

"Just a reminder," he said in a low, warning tone.

"Of what?"

"A reminder that you're not some stray border in this house. You're here because I love you and want to marry you. That gives you every right to be here."

Her heart hammering, she held up a hand. "Jason, please. You have to slow down. Where did all this talk of marriage come from?"

He looked every bit as startled as she felt. "Okay, it didn't come out quite the way it should have, but I meant every word. I want to marry you. I won't have you acting like some second-class citizen around here."

Since the thought of marriage was too troubling to deal with, she murmured, "I'm sorry if I was rude."

He plunged his fingers through his hair. "Dammit, Dana, this is not about being rude. It's about understanding that you belong. No matter what anyone thinks, what anyone says, you belong."

She sighed and rested a hand against his cheek. "I wish that were true, Jason. I really wish it were true." And for the first time since she'd met him, she admitted to herself that she'd done the unforgivable: she had fallen head over heels in love.

Chapter 13

Dana had taken a real liking to Brandon Halloran. She would have been grateful to him for no other reason than the way he treated Sammy, but there was more to it. He was a lot like Jason. Impetuous on the surface, but rock solid underneath. There was something comforting in thinking that Jason would be just like him in another forty or so years.

She thought of his lively humor, his loving meddling, his sage advice, and she wished she had a grandfather like that. Since she didn't, she wished she could adopt the man sitting across from her, who was regarding her so pensively.

She'd been surprised when he'd invited her to lunch. No, invited was the wrong word. He'd insisted on it, latching on to her coat and her elbow with a determination that had left her with little choice. She couldn't say she was sorry to be with him, though, even if he had brought her back to Washington's Tavern where her relationship with the Hallorans had begun so inauspiciously.

"Okay," Brandon said finally, pinning her with one of his no-nonsense gazes. "Let's talk turkey, young lady. What was that little speech all about last night?"

Dana's spoon fell from her fingers, splattering clam chowder in every direction. Cleaning up the mess gave her time to think. Even with the extra time, the best she could manage was, "What speech?"

"Don't play dumb with me. Your exit lines. All that garbage about leaving us Hallorans alone."

"It was obvious to me that there were things you wanted to talk about, personal things. There was no room for strangers." The same argument hadn't worked on Jason, but perhaps Brandon would be more gullible.

He gave a rough hoot. "Young lady, who are you trying to kid? You're hardly a stranger. Looks to me as if my grandson is intent on marrying you. And if I know Jason, he'll have his way."

"That's wishful thinking on your part," she countered.

He regarded her intently. "You trying to tell me you're not interested?"

Dana tried. She gathered up all the appropriate denials and tried to force them past her lips, but the lies wouldn't come. "I wish I weren't," she said finally.

"Why?"

Dana ignored the question in favor of asking, "Did he put you up to this?"

"Up to what?" he inquired innocently. "So far all I've asked is a simple question. Are you in love with the man or not? I'll admit I'm biased, but he seems like a fine catch to me. No real faults, unless you count that stubbornness he gets from me. Actually, I see that as a beneficial quality."

"He is a fine catch, as you put it. My reasons are between Jason and me."

"Not entirely," he said. "In this family we all care what happens to one another. Haven't you noticed how much meddling has gone on trying to figure out this mess between Lacey and Kevin? We still don't have a clue. It's a damned shame, too. There was a time they were so much in love, they lit up a room just by coming into it. I was blind to it then, but I'm not blind to what's going on between you and Jason. You have the same effect on each other."

Dana settled for agreeing with his observation about Kevin and Lacey Halloran. Even if Jason hadn't told her how worried he was about his parents, she would have sensed the undercurrents last night. Even so, it was none of her business. Or theirs. She reminded Brandon of that.

"I've also noticed that they're telling everyone to butt out," she said.

"True, but that doesn't mean we won't go on trying. Now let's get back to you and Jason, a subject you seem determined to avoid, I might add. Only explanation I can think of is that I'm hitting too close to the truth. You are in love with the boy, but something's holding you back from saying it."

Dana really wished he'd drop the subject, but she couldn't see any way of avoiding the discussion short of getting up and walking out of the restaurant. So, even though the conversation was likely to make her miserable, she would sit here and listen while he extolled his grandson's virtues. She doubted he even knew half of them. She knew them all. One of the most important was his family loyalty. She also understood Brandon's need to protect his own. They were two of a kind on that count.

"Well, girl, what do you have to say for yourself?" he was demanding again. "What's wrong with marrying into this family?"

"It seems to me you're the one with all the answers," she retorted. "You tell me."

"My guess is you're scared."

She nodded reluctantly. "On the mark so far."

"Of what, for goodness' sake?"

"You've seen how Jason is. He gets all caught up in being protective."

"What's so terrible about having a man cherish you like that?"

"What if I forget how to take care of myself?"

There was a twinkle in his eyes. "You aiming to give up your career and stay home and eat bonbons?"

"Of course not."

"You planning to cut out that razor-sharp tongue of yours? I've heard you've given my grandson what for more than once."

"I usually say what's on my mind. I guess that wouldn't change," she conceded grudgingly.

"Then it must be that you think you're not good enough to be part of this highfalutin Boston clan. Let me straighten you out on that right now. We've always been a family of scramblers. Ain't nothing ever been handed to us. I think you'd fit right in."

He regarded her slyly. "Besides, if you love my grandson, that's all it takes. I learned my lesson long ago, when it comes to making hasty judgments and interfering in other people's lives. I walked away from love once in my own life. I know how that can change a person forever. I don't want to see you and my grandson waking up one day with regrets the way I do."

Dana's eyebrows rose a fraction.

"Don't you smart mouth me," he said.

"I never said a word."

He nodded, his expression turning complacent. "Okay, then. Here's the deal. You think you need to make a contribution, something beyond the fact that you're making Jason happy, something more important than giving our old company a spruced-up image. Am I right?"

Though she wanted to argue just on principle, Dana had no ready comeback for the truth. She folded her hands and waited. Whatever this sneaky old man had in mind was bound to be a doozy.

He grinned at her stubborn silence. "I'll take that for a yes. So, that being the case, I'm going to let you buy into Halloran Industries. You'll be a partner right along with the rest of us."

Dana couldn't help it. She laughed. "With what, pray tell?"

"With the money you're going to make designing a whole new line of sweaters."

She stared at him incredulously. "Sweaters?"

"That's right. You've got an eye for what young people like and a flair for the dramatic. Take the one you have on now. Cheers the whole place up. I've snapped a few photos over the past few weeks. Showed them to a friend of mine. He'll make you an offer to carry the line, if you're interested. You can do whatever you want with the money, but if it'll make you feel more like a part of the family to invest in Halloran Industries, we'll work it out."

His gaze pinned her. "Or you can make Jason the happiest man in the world and accomplish exactly the same thing by marrying him."

"You can't bribe me into becoming a Halloran."

Brandon regarded her indignantly. "Who's bribing you? It's a fair deal. If you think about it, you'll realize that. This is one time you shouldn't let bullheadedness get in the way of what's best for your future. Those sweaters would give you and that brother of yours a mighty fine stake."

It was only later, when she'd mentally stripped the scene of her emotional reaction, that she realized how much faith Brandon Halloran had in her—and in Jason's love for her. Granted, Brandon was somewhat biased, but it was probably the most objective opinion she was likely to get from someone who knew all the parties involved.

Yet it still wasn't enough.

"So how was lunch with my grandfather?" Jason wanted to know the minute Dana got back to his office. "Why did he want to see you?"

She regarded him closely. "You don't know?"

"Know what?"

"He made me an offer. He wants Halloran Industries to produce a line of sweaters that I will design. He figures if he gives me a stake in the company, I'll feel like I belong. I think he was proposing on your behalf."

After an initial spark of excitement, Jason's expression faltered. "You turned him down, didn't you?"

"No," she said, still feeling pressured. "I told him I'd think about it. I'm not blind to the opportunity he's offering me. I'm just worried about the strings."

"There are none, Dana. My grandfather doesn't operate that way and neither do I. He obviously sees this line as an excellent way of expanding our presence in the marketplace. He's been itching to tackle something new for a long time now. I've had a hunch from the day he saw that first sweater of yours that he was plotting something like this."

Dana began to pace. "It's ridiculous. I don't know a thing about designing sweaters."

"Oh, really?"

She noticed him glance over at the one she was wearing, the one his grandfather told her cheered up a room. It was bright red with yellow accents and one bold streak of blue. She had to admit her spirits had risen when she'd been making it. She'd used the yellow yarn simply because it had been left over from another project. The instant she'd begun knitting it in, though, she'd known it was right.

"Who came up with that one?" Jason asked.

"I did."

"And the other half dozen or so I've seen you wear?"

"I did."

"Ever get any compliments on them?"

"Yes," she said slowly. "Quite a few people have asked where I bought them."

Jason nodded. "What did my grandfather suggest? A limited line, sold in exclusive boutiques?"

"Actually I didn't let him get that far. He did say he knew someone who was interested in the line."

Jason picked up his phone and rang his grandfather's

office. Dana was so busy trying to imagine seeing her sweater designs in some fancy boutique, she barely heard his end of the conversation. What would it be like to have unlimited resources at her command? To be able to select a color and create a dye that matched exactly what she saw in her mind's eye? To choose yarns that felt soft, rather than those on sale? She was surprised to discover that the idea tempted.

Jason whistled softly at something his grandfather said. "I see," he said. "Yeah, I will definitely tell her that."

She glanced at him as he hung up.

"Granddad told me who he showed your sweaters to."

"And?"

Jason named a designer whose clothes were sold in the most exclusive shops in the world. Dana's mouth dropped open. "You're kidding, right?"

"I'm not kidding. He'll take any one-of-a-kind design you make by hand as exclusives for his private customers. He thinks the ski crowd will flip over them. Then he'd like at least four other designs in limited production for his ready-to-wear line that's going into department stores for the first time next year."

Dana couldn't even grasp the fact that this man wanted to sell a few of her sweaters, much less the fact that Brandon Halloran was willing to commit his company to producing four designs in quantity. She shot Jason a puzzled look.

"Won't it be incredibly expensive just to set up the equipment to make these sweaters? It's not the same as making a bolt of cloth, is it?"

Jason grinned. "As Granddad sees it, that's just part of the fun. We'll be doing something new and exciting."

"You'd probably prefer that he stick to weaving woolens."

Jason sighed. "A month ago, maybe even a few days ago, I would have said yes. I'm starting to look at things differently now. Sure, Halloran Industries is a business and we want it to be profitable, but if you're going to spend your life doing something, you'd really better like it as well. It won't kill us if we make a little less. And at the kind of prices Granddad intends to charge, we definitely won't go broke."

"What kind of money are we talking about?"

"I'd say your share ought to enable you to do just about anything you'd like to do," he said, naming a figure that would have seemed beyond the realm of possibility just a few short months ago.

Dazed, Dana nodded. "I've got to go," she said. "I'll see you at home later."

Jason's expression grew puzzled. "Are you okay?"

"For a woman who feels as if she's been hit over the head with a baseball bat, I'm doing just fine."

She walked for hours, oblivious to the cold, oblivious to the snow that swirled in the air. What Brandon Halloran was offering to her was total financial independence for the first time in her life. She would truly be free to make choices, to give Sammy the kind of life she'd wanted for herself growing up, including a college education. They'd be able to live almost anyplace they wanted. Maybe not in a house as fine as Jason's, but certainly in one that was comfortable, that had its own fireplace and maybe even a bay window.

So, why wasn't she shouting for joy? Why wasn't she racing to look through the classified ads for apartments? Why wasn't she picking up a sketch pad to draw sweater designs, rather than brochure layouts? Was it because the thought of walking away from Jason left this lonely emptiness deep inside her?

When she finally went home, still with no answers, she slowly climbed the steps to her room. Inside, she pulled out all of the sweaters she'd made over the years and spread them on the bed. She studied each one, recalling the exact moment when she'd come up with the idea, the hunt for the right yarn in some discount store, the frustration when she couldn't find the exact shade she'd had in mind. She rubbed her fingers over uneven stitches and careless seams in her first faltering attempts.

Somewhere along the way these bold sweaters had become a part of her, an expression of all of her bright dreams for the future. How could she bear to give away—even for a bundle of money—something that was her? Wouldn't she lose herself in the process?

There was no question, though, that an opportunity like this knocked once in a lifetime. Only a fool would turn it down. It would give her options she'd never even imagined. She could leave the Lansing Agency. Or stay. She could leave this house.

Or, she realized with a start, she could stay. If she stayed, she could pay her own way and Sammy's. She would have the financial independence she'd always craved, even here in Jason's home. As for emotional independence, that didn't look nearly as attractive to her as it once had.

The freedom to choose. Wasn't that all she had ever really wanted? And given the choice, wasn't Jason the only man she could imagine loving? It kept coming back to Jason and the depth of the feelings that had flourished despite her best attempts to fight them.

For a woman who had left the house this morning convinced that there was no way for her to have a future with a man like Jason, a few hours had made an undeniable difference. She had hope now. She could finally see that letting Jason into her heart was not the same as losing a part of herself. For the first time in her life, she could see that love gave people strength. It didn't rob them of it.

Chapter 14

When his mother called and asked him to lunch, Jason didn't know what to think. She wasn't in the habit of meeting him in the city. On top of that, it had been less than forty-eight hours since he'd last seen her. Although he was having a horrible day, with no promise of improvement even if he were to put in sixteen hours straight, something in her tone told him to make the time for her.

"Could we do it here? I'll have something sent in," he suggested, reluctant to alter his new routine now that he was finally energized about work.

"I'd rather not," she said. "This won't take long, but it is important, and I'd prefer a little privacy. What about that little French restaurant up the street. We won't be interrupted there, will we?"

Jason sensed she was asking about more than the size of the restaurant's crowd at noon. Was she truly trying to avoid his father? "No one from here goes there, if that's what you're asking."

"I'll see you there, then."

Now that Jason was sitting across from her, he felt an ominous sense of foreboding. Lacey Halloran looked uncomfortable. No, Jason thought, studying her more closely. She looked miserable. Though she was dressed cheerfully enough in a becoming rose-colored wool dress with her mane of caramel-colored hair falling in loose waves to her shoulders, there was an air of despair that was unmistakable. There was no hint of the usual sparkle in her blue eyes. He had a hunch that skillful makeup hid dark shadows under those eyes as well.

"Mom," he began quietly, "what's bothering you? You aren't worried about Dana and me, are you?"

She glanced up from the consommé she'd been idly stirring for the past five minutes. For the first time since he'd arrived there was a spark of animation in her eyes. "No, absolutely not. I like her. She has a lot of spirit. I used to be like that once."

She sounded so melancholy and sad, as if she'd lost something precious and didn't know how to get it back. Jason felt his stomach knot. He laid a hand on hers. Hers was like ice. "Are you okay?"

She closed her eyes for an instant, and Jason's worry mounted. When she opened her eyes, that unmistakable sadness was there again.

"I really don't know how to get into this with you," she said finally. "I told your father I wanted to be the one to tell you, but now that the time has come, I can't seem to find the words."

Jason's heart thudded. "What is it? Are you ill?"

She shook her head, reaching over to squeeze his hand. "No, it's nothing like that."

"Is it Dad, then? He's okay, isn't he?"

She drew in a deep breath. "I've moved out," she blurted finally. "Yesterday."

Jason felt as if she'd slammed a fist into his midsection. If she'd declared that she'd burned the place down, he would have been no more shocked. Even after that awful dinner with his father a few weeks earlier and the tension in his own dining room just two days earlier, he wasn't prepared for this announcement.

"What?" he said blankly, praying he'd misunderstood. "I don't understand."

"I've moved out of the house. I just wanted you to know so you wouldn't go over there looking for me. Not that you drop in unannounced," she murmured. "Oh, who am I kidding? I was terrified you'd see it in some gossip column. I'm sure there are a few people who won't be able to wait to share the news of a split in the Halloran clan."

The prospect of publicity was the least of Jason's concerns. "Why did you move?" he asked weakly, thinking of all the signs he'd seen that things weren't right between his parents. He'd blinded himself to them because he didn't want to believe there was anything seriously wrong. "What did Dad do?"

He tried to imagine his father having an affair and couldn't. Kevin Halloran was not a philanderer. Jason would have staked his last dime on that. Kevin did spend too many hours at the office. Maybe that was it. His father had turned into a workaholic and his mother was lonely.

Funny how he'd always thought his parents' marriage so solid, so free from the kinds of problems and pressures that split other families apart. He could see now that they were only human and it shook him more than he could say.

"Your father didn't do anything, not really. It's complicated," she said.

"That's not good enough, Mom," he snapped in frustration. At her startled, hurt look, he said, "I'm sorry, but there has to be a reason."

"I would explain it to you if I could, but I can't. Not entirely." She gazed at him apologetically. "I'm sorry to spring this on you now, when you've just met someone you really care about. This should be the happiest time in your life. I'm sorry for spoiling it. I would have waited until, I don't know, after you were engaged, maybe even married, but there's no telling just when that would happen. I decided postponing the move wouldn't change anything. The longer it went on, the more I felt as if I were suffocating."

"I'll talk to Dad," he said, ignoring the denial she'd made too easily. "Whatever he's done, he can fix it."

Lacey smiled sadly. "No. I've told you this is not his fault. Not entirely, anyway. At any rate, it's between your father and me. Promise me you'll let it be. This is the right thing for both of us."

"How can moving out be the right thing?" Jason exploded in frustration. "Isn't that just running away? Or are you filing for divorce? Have things gone that far?"

"Not yet."

It suddenly occurred to him that perhaps he'd been trying to cast blame in the wrong direction. What if his mother…? Dear Lord, it wasn't possible that she had found someone to fill the lonely hours when her husband was at work. "Mom, is it…you haven't…there's not…"

No matter how he tried to phrase it, he couldn't get the words out. It was clear, though, that his mother understood. Suddenly she was reaching into her purse. "I really have to go."

Jason spotted the tears welling up in her eyes and felt more helpless than he'd ever felt in his entire life. "Mom?"

She brushed a kiss against his cheek, then hurried from the restaurant. She hadn't even told him how he could get in touch with her.

He spent the afternoon closeted in his office with the door shut, trying to make sense of what had happened. It took everything in him to keep from going down the hall and slugging his father. Unfortunately he couldn't seem to make up his mind whether or not he deserved it. His mother had never once said that his father was to blame for anything. But no matter how hard he tried, he couldn't imagine his mother walking away from the family that had always meant everything to her, unless his father had committed some terrible sin.

He barely looked up at the tap on the door. He didn't bother responding. Harriet would send whoever it was away. He'd told her he didn't want to be disturbed.

The door opened a crack. "Jason?" Dana said softly, then added more anxiously, "What are you doing sitting in here in the dark?"

He glanced around and realized the room was filled with shadows. He hadn't even noticed. "What time is it?" he asked wearily.

"Past six. Are you okay?"

"No," he said. "I am definitely not okay."

"What's wrong?"

"I had lunch with my mother today. She's moved out of the house." He looked at Dana and astonishment filled his voice. "She's actually left my father."

The startled expression on Dana's face reflected his own feelings exactly.

"I don't understand," she said.

"Neither do I. She didn't see fit to explain it." He shook his head. "No. That's not fair. I think she was too upset to talk about it."

"What does your father say?"

"I haven't talked to him. I was afraid I'd hit first and talk later."

"Maybe it's not his fault."

"It has to be somebody's fault," he said, itching to cast blame and unwilling still to pin it on his gentle, sensitive mother. The fact that she hadn't denied the suggestion that she was having an affair nagged at him like a hangnail. He toyed with the idea until the pain was nearly unbearable.

"Maybe it really is no one's fault," Dana said, coming up behind his chair and beginning to massage away the tension in his shoulders.

The brush of her fingers against his neck had his pulse bucking. Though he was certain she meant to relax him with the kneading strokes, the effect was anything but soothing. Every nerve in his body craved the magic of her touch.

When he could stand the tantalizing, innocent caresses no longer, he swiveled his chair around and pulled her down onto his lap. Before it even registered what he intended, his mouth was covering hers with a desperation that might have frightened him if he'd recognized it. Instead he was just acting on his feelings, hungry for the taste of her.

The kiss was bruising, needy and it wasn't nearly enough. He shoved her sweater up until he unhooked her bra. Her breasts spilled into his hands. He took the rosy tip of one into his mouth, urging it into a hard bud, then did the same with the other. The silk of her skin burned hot beneath his touch.

As if she sensed his need, Dana unbuttoned his shirt with matching urgency, her hands stroking and teasing with renewed purpose, this time to inflame. Her mouth found his masculine nipples and teased with the same desperate intensity. Jason had never before been aroused so fast. He felt as if he were going to explode if he couldn't bury himself inside her.

He gathered her into his arms and carried her to the sofa. With hands that shook with emotion, he stripped away her jeans, then his own slacks, until he was able to enter her with a quick, powerful thrust.

With each desperate stroke some of his anger and confusion began to fade. With each caress he thought less and less about his parents' failure and more about his own future, here in Dana's arms. How could emotions this powerful ever die? Surely this kind of intensity couldn't be lost.

With one last shred of sanity, he slowed, only to have Dana quicken the pace again, luring him over the edge with an instinctive understanding of his need.

When they were both spent, tangled in rumpled clothes and slick with perspiration, he cradled her in his arms. The peace he'd craved hadn't come. If anything, he felt worse than before because he'd used a woman he loved without regard for her feelings.

"I'm sorry," he whispered, distraught by the uncaring way he'd treated her. He tried to find the words to explain, settling finally for the simple, raw truth. "I needed you so much."

"I know," she said gently.

"That's no excuse for being so thoughtless, so rough."

"You weren't rough. Just demanding." She gave a little half smile, the kind which Mona Lisa had been enchanting people with for years. "You always are, you know. I think that's what I love about you. You don't hold anything back. I always know how much you want me."

"I gotta tell you, Dana, right now that scares the hell out of me."

"Because of what's going on with your parents."

"Exactly. If they can't make it after all these years, after so damned much history, nobody can. Nobody."

There was a bleak finality in his tone, a weariness. If his well-suited parents couldn't hold on to their marriage, how could he possibly expect to have a future with someone so much his opposite? Perhaps in the end his first instincts had been right. The only future he and Dana were likely to have would be whatever days they could grab before their differences inevitably caught up with them.

After that evening in his office, Jason never even hinted about wanting to marry Dana. She had no doubts about his love for her, no doubts that he still wanted her. Each night in his bed proved the depth of his hunger for what they had found together. But it was as if a switch had been turned and he no longer saw marriage as an option.

She had absolutely no idea what to do about it. Her sense of helplessness was all the worse because she had finally admitted to herself that she loved him, that she wanted a life with him. At least she was ready to take the risk, because for the first time she had realized that Jason needed her every bit as much as she needed him.

That's what love was all about, she had realized with astonishing clarity that evening in his office when he'd come to her with all of his insecurities and desperate yearnings on the line. That moment had solidified all the emotions she had recognized over the past days. There would always be times when one person needed and the other person gave, and times when they would reverse roles. Right now it was critical for her to find some way to make Jason see that what was happening to his parents was not an indictment of marriage, but proof that love wasn't something ever to be taken for granted.

Troubled, she found herself turning to Brandon Halloran for advice. "I think he's going to walk away from what we have," she told him, her expression bleak.

"Because of this nonsense between Kevin and Lacey?"

"It's shaken his faith in love."

"But not in you," Brandon reminded her. "You're still sharing that house with him. You ready to make it permanent?"

Dana smiled ruefully. "Yes. My timing's lousy, isn't it?"

"I don't think it could get much better actually. He needs you now. The fact that you haven't abandoned him ought to tell him what he needs to hear."

"He's not listening. I don't think he's comfortable

with needing anything from me. He's used to being the one needed."

"Seems to me the real test of love is surviving the crises."

"And this is one of those crises, right?"

"Looks like it to me."

Dana gave him a swift hug on her way out. "I'll let you know how it turns out."

"Just tell me when to show up at the church. What this family needs all the way around is a good wedding."

"You're an old romantic."

"Damn right, I am. I want some great-grandchildren before I'm too old to enjoy 'em, too."

Dana groaned. "Let's take this one step at a time, okay?"

She could think of only one sure way to snap Jason out of his mood, a way that would only work if he loved her as much as she thought he did. That night she sent Sammy to a movie with Mrs. Willis, set the table with the finest china and candles, and wore the slinky black dress Jason had given her.

He glanced around, took in the seductive setting and regarded her warily. "What's this all about?"

"I need to talk to you about something."

"If you're serving prime rib, I'm really going to start worrying."

Dana carried two plates of medium-rare prime rib in from the kitchen.

"Okay. Spill it," he said. "What's going on?"

"Actually, I've been thinking about getting my own place."

Jason's fork clattered to the table. "You've what?" His voice rose ominously.

"It's clear I'm just in the way here. You can't be expected to put up with Sammy and me indefinitely. I've picked out a couple of apartments. I was hoping you'd agree to go with me tomorrow to take a look at them. I could use your advice."

"No. Absolutely not."

"Why not? Don't you have the time?"

"This has nothing to do with time." His gaze narrowed. "I thought you were happy here. I thought we had something."

Dana shrugged. "I thought so, too, but lately..." She allowed her voice to trail off.

"Lately I haven't been paying enough attention to you."

"That's not it."

"What then?"

She studied him regretfully. "If you can't figure it out, then I'm not going to explain it. Look, if you don't want to go with me to look at apartments, it's okay. Sammy and I will go in the morning. We should be able to move in a week or two."

Jason threw his napkin on the table and stormed from the room. A minute later the front door slammed. Fortunately he left before he caught the smile of satisfaction on Dana's lips.

She cleaned up the dishes, then went into the living room. She sat in the window seat, her legs tucked under her and watched for Jason to come home. It was nearly an hour later before she saw him coming up the front walk. When he caught sight of her in the window, he paused and squared his shoulders. His step became even more determined.

The front door shook on its hinges, when he closed it

behind him. He strode into the living room and straight over to her. Hands on hips, he faced her with a familiar stubborn spark in his eyes.

"You are not moving out of here tomorrow or any other time and that's final."

"Excuse me?"

"You may think you'll be better off someplace else, but I'm not letting you out of my sight. I love you. If you're not ready to marry me, that's fine. I'll wait. But I will not let you run off."

He was still ranting when Dana rose from the window seat and shut him up by covering his mouth with her own. After one startled instant, his arms circled her waist. He leaned back with an unexpected glint of amused understanding in his eyes.

"Who won that battle?" he inquired.

"We did," she said. "I finally got you to admit that you still loved me."

"There's never been any doubt in my mind about that."

Dana shook her head. "Oh, I think you've been questioning a lot lately. I just wanted you to see that the most important thing in loving someone is not ever taking them for granted."

Jason chuckled. "How could I ever take a woman like you for granted? There's not a day that goes by when I don't realize how lucky I am to have found you."

"It's possible then that given time your parents will remember they once felt that way, too. We'll just have to help them."

"So, now that you've brought me into line, you're ready to take on my parents. I suspect Granddad will want to have a hand in that, too."

"Last time I saw him he was more worried about having great-grandchildren."

A slow smile spread across Jason's face. "I think we can accommodate him on that score, don't you?"

Dana took his hand and led him toward the stairs. "Frankly, I thought you'd never ask."

* * * * *

PLAIN ADMIRER

Patricia Davids

This book is lovingly dedicated to my father, Clarence—a man who can look at any stretch of water and tell just where the fish are. Thanks for teaching me, my daughter and my grandchildren to bait our own hooks. Love you.
Let's go fishing soon.

And God blessed them, and God said unto them, Be fruitful, and multiply, and replenish the earth, and subdue it: and have dominion over the fish of the sea, and over the fowl of the air, and over every living thing that moveth upon the earth.
—*Genesis* 1:28

Chapter 1

"This isn't easy to say, but I have to let you go, Joann. I'm sure you understand."

"You're firing me?" Joann Yoder faced her boss across the cluttered desk in his office. For once, she wasn't tempted to straighten up for him. And she didn't understand.

"*Ja.* I'm sorry."

Otis Miller didn't look the least bit sorry. Certainly not as sorry as she was to be losing a job she really needed. A job she loved. Why was this happening? Why now, when she was so close to realizing her dream?

She'd only been at Miller Press for five months, but working as an assistant editor and office manager at the Amish-owned publishing house was everything she'd ever wanted. How could it end so quickly? If she knew what she had done wrong, she could fix it. "At least tell me why."

He sighed heavily, as if disappointed she hadn't accepted her dismissal without question. "You knew when you came over from the bookstore that this might not be a permanent position."

Joann had moved from a part-time job at the bookstore next door to help at the printing shop after Otis's elder brother suffered a heart attack. When he passed away a few weeks later, Joann had assumed she would be able to keep his job. She loved gathering articles for their monthly magazine and weekly newspaper, as well as making sure the office ran smoothly and customers received the best possible attention. She dropped her gaze to her hands clenched tightly in her lap and struggled to hang on to her dignity. Tears pricked the back of her eyelids, but she refused to cry. "You told me I was doing a good job."

"You have been. Better than I expected, but I'm giving Roman Weaver your position. I don't need to tell you why."

"*Nee,* you don't." Like everyone in the Amish community of Hope Springs, Ohio, she was aware of the trouble that had visited the Weaver family. She hated that her compassion struggled so mightily with her desire to support herself. This job was proof that her intelligence mattered. She might be the "bookworm" her brothers had often called her, but here she had a chance to put her learning to good use. Now it was all being taken away.

She couldn't let it go without a fight. She looked up and blurted, "Does he really need the job more than I do?"

Otis didn't like conflict. He leaned back in his chair

and folded his arms across his broad chest. "Roman has large medical bills to pay."

"But the church held an auction to help raise money for him."

"He and his family are grateful for all the help they received, but they are still struggling."

She'd lost, and she knew it. Only a hint of the bitterness she felt slipped through in her words. "Plus, he's your nephew."

"That, too," Otis admitted without any sign of embarrassment. Family came only after God in their Amish way of life.

Roman Weaver had had it rough, there was no denying that. It was a blessing that he hadn't lost his arm after a pickup truck smashed into his buggy. Unfortunately, his damaged left arm was now paralyzed and useless. She'd seen him at the church meetings wearing a heavy sling and heard her brothers say the physical therapy he needed was expensive and draining his family's resources.

Her heart went out to him and his family, but why should she be the one to lose her job? There were others who worked for Miller Press.

She didn't bother to voice that thought. She already knew why she had been chosen. Because she was a woman.

Joann had no illusions about the male-dominated society she lived in. Unmarried Amish women could hold a job, but they gave it up when they married to make a home for their husband and children. A married woman could work outside the home, but only if her husband agreed to it.

Amish marriage was a partnership where each man

and woman knew and respected their roles within the *Ordnung,* the laws of their Amish church. Men were the head of the household. Joann didn't disagree with any of it. At least, not very much.

It was just that she had no desire to spend the rest of her life living with her brothers, moving from one house to another and being an unwanted burden to their families. She'd never had a come-calling boyfriend, although she'd accepted a ride home from the singings with a few fellas in her youth. She'd never received an offer of marriage. And at the advanced age of twenty-six, it wasn't likely she would.

Besides, there wasn't anyone in Hope Springs she would consider spending the rest of her life with. As the years had gone by, she'd begun to accept that she would always be a maiden aunt. Maybe she'd get a cat one day.

Otis folded his hands together on his desk. "I am sorry, Joann. Roman needs the job. He can't work in the sawmill with only one good arm. It's too dangerous."

"I must work, too. My brothers have many children. I don't wish to burden them by having them take care of me, as well."

"Come now, you're being unreasonable. Your brothers do not begrudge you room and board."

"They would never say it, but I think they do." She knew her three brothers had taken her in out of a strong sense of duty after their parents died and not because of brotherly love. Hadn't they decided her living arrangements among themselves without consulting her? She stayed with each brother for four months. At the end of that time, she moved to the next brother's home. By the end of the year, she was back where she had started. She always had a roof over her head, but she didn't have a home.

She wanted a home of her own, but that wasn't going to happen without a good-paying job.

"Joann, think of Roman. Where is your Christian compassion?"

"I left it at home in a jar."

Otis scowled at her flippancy. She blushed at her own audacity. Modesty and humility were the aspirations of every Amish woman, but sometimes things slipped out of her mouth before she had time to think.

Why couldn't someone else give Roman a job he could manage? She dreamed of having a home of her own, a small house at the edge of the woods where she could keep her books and compile her nature notes and observations unhindered by her nieces and nephews. Best of all, she'd be able to go fishing whenever she wanted without her family's sarcastic comments about wasting her time. The only way she could accomplish that was by earning her own money.

She was so close to realizing her dream. The very house she wanted was coming up for sale. The owners, her friends Sarah and Levi Beachy, were willing to sell to her and finance her if she could come up with the down payment by the end of September. If she couldn't raise the agreed-upon amount, they would have to sell to another Amish family. They needed the money to make improvements to their business before winter.

What only a week ago had seemed like a sure thing, a gift from God, was now slipping out of her grasp. Joann didn't want to beg, but she would. "Can't you do anything for me, Otis? You know I'm a hard worker."

"All I can offer you is a part-time position—"

"I'll take it."

"One day a week on the cleaning staff."

"Oh." Her last bit of hope vanished. Her book learning wouldn't be needed while she swept the floors and emptied wastepaper baskets.

Otis leaned back in his chair. "Of course, your part-time position at the bookstore is yours if you want it."

A part-time salary would be far less than she needed. Still, it was better than nothing. She wasn't proud. She'd do a good job for him. In time, she might even get a chance at an editorial position again. Only God knew what the future held.

She nodded once. "I would be grateful for such work."

Otis rose to his feet. "*Goot.* You'll work afternoons Monday through Wednesday at the bookstore, and here on Saturdays. But there is something I need you to do for me before you switch jobs."

"What is that?"

"I need you to show Roman how we do things here. He's only worked in the sawmill and on the farm. The publishing business is foreign to him. I'm sure it won't take you more than two weeks to show him the ropes. He's a bright fellow. He'll catch on quickly. You can do that, can't you?"

He gets my job, but I have to show him how to do it? Where is the justice in that? She kept her face carefully blank.

Otis scowled again. "Well?"

"I'll be glad to show Roman all I've learned." It wasn't a complete lie, but it was close. She would do it, but she wouldn't be happy about it.

Otis nodded and came around the desk. "Fine. I hope

my nephew can start on Monday morning. After you get him up to speed, you can return to the bookstore. That's all, you can go home now."

"Danki." She rose from her seat and headed for the door. Pulling it open, she saw the man who was taking her job sitting quietly in a chair across the room. Did he know or care that she was being cast aside for him? They had attended the same school, but he had been a year behind her.

After their school years, she saw him and his family at Sunday services, but their paths rarely crossed. He'd run with the fast crowd during their *rumspringa,* their running-around teenage years. She had chosen baptism at the age of nineteen while he hadn't joined the faith until two years ago. His circle of friends didn't include her or her family. She studied him covertly as she would one of her woodland creatures.

Roman Weaver was a good-looking fellow with a head of curly blond hair that bore the imprint of the hat he normally wore. His cheeks were lean, his chin chiseled and firm. He was clean-shaven, denoting his single status. His years of hard physical work showed in the muscular width of his shoulders crisscrossed by his suspenders. He wore a black sling on his left arm. It stood out in stark contrast to his short-sleeved white shirt. His straw hat rested on the chair arm beside him.

Compassion touched her heart when she noticed the fine lines that bracketed his mouth. Was he in pain?

He looked up as she came out of the office. His piercing blue eyes, rimmed with thick lashes, brightened. He smiled. An unfamiliar thrill fluttered in the pit of her stomach. No one had ever smiled at her with such warmth.

His dazzling gaze slid past her to settle on Otis, and Joann realized she'd been a fool to think Roman Weaver was smiling at her. She doubted he even saw her.

"Hello, *Onkel,*" Roman said, rising from his chair.

"It's *goot* to see you, nephew." Otis stepped back to give him room to enter his office. Roman walked past her without a glance.

She kept her eyes downcast as an odd stab of disappointment hit her. Why should it matter that his smile hadn't been for her? She was used to being invisible. She'd long ago given up the hope that she'd become attractive and witty. She wasn't ugly, but she had no illusions about her plain looks. She was as God had made her.

She consoled herself with the knowledge that what the Lord had held back in looks He'd more than made up for in intelligence. She was smarter than her brothers and her few friends. It wasn't anything special that she had done. She was smart the way some people were tall, because that was the way God fashioned them.

For a long time, she thought of her intellect as a burden. Then, an elderly teacher told her she was smarter than anyone he'd ever met and that God must surely have something special in mind for her. That single statement had enabled Joann to see herself in a completely new light.

Being smart wasn't a bad thing, even if some others thought it was. When she landed this job, she knew being smart was indeed a blessing.

As Roman Weaver closed the door behind him, old feelings of being left out, of being overlooked and unvalued wormed their way into her heart. They left a painful bruise she couldn't dismiss.

Crossing to her desk, she lifted her green-and-white quilted bag from the back of her chair and settled the strap on her shoulder. Roman Weaver might look past her today, but come Monday morning, he was going to find he needed her. He wouldn't look through her then.

Roman forced a bright smile to his lips in order to hide his nervousness. The summons from his uncle had come out of the blue. He had no idea what his mother's brother wanted with him, but the look on her face when she relayed the message had Roman worried. What was going on? What was wrong?

The better question might have been: What was right? He had the answer to that one: not much in his life at the moment. The gnawing pain he endured from his injury was constant proof of that.

Otis indicated a chair. "Have a seat."

Roman did so, holding his injured arm against his chest, more from habit than a need to protect it. "I've often wondered what it is that you do here."

He glanced around the room filled with filing cabinets, books and stacks of papers. The smell of solvents and ink gave the air a harsh, sharp quality that stung his nostrils. Roman preferred the clean scent of fresh-cut wood.

His uncle was the owner of a small publishing business whose target audience was Old Order Plain People, Amish, Mennonites and Hutterites. A small bookstore next door housed a number of books he published as well as a small library. Although Roman occasionally read the magazine his uncle put out each month, he'd only visited the office and bookstore a few times. He wasn't a reader.

"How's the arm?" Otis asked.

"It's getting better." Much too slowly for Roman's liking.

"Are you in pain?"

"Some." He didn't elaborate. It was his burden to bear.

"I'm sure you're wondering why I've asked you here. Your parents came to see me last Sunday," Otis said, looking vaguely uncomfortable.

"Did they?" This was the first Roman had heard of it.

"Your father asked me for a business loan. Of course, I was happy to help. I know things have been difficult for all of you."

Roman's medical bills had already cost his family nearly all their savings. His inability to do his job in the sawmill was cutting their productivity, making his father and his brother work even harder. If his father had come to Otis for a loan, things must be dire.

"You have my gratitude and my thanks. We will repay you as soon as we can."

"I know. I'm not worried about that. Before they left, your mother spoke privately with me. My sister is very dear to me, but I will admit to being surprised when she asked if I would offer you a job here at my office."

The muscles in Roman's jaw clenched. "I work at my father's side in the sawmill. I don't need a job. I have one," he said.

Sympathy flashed in his uncle's eyes. "You have one that you can't continue."

"My arm is better. I'm making progress." He concentrated on his fingers protruding from the sling. He was able to move his index and middle finger ever so slightly.

He could tell from the look on his uncle's face that he wasn't impressed. If only he knew how much effort it took to move any part of his hand.

"I give thanks to God for His mercy and pray for your recovery daily," Otis said. "As do your parents, but your father needs a man with two strong arms to work in the mill if he is to earn a profit and meet his obligations."

"He hasn't said this to me."

"I don't imagine he would. I'm asking you to consider what is best for your family. I have work, worthy work, for you to do that requires a good mind but not two strong arms. Besides, your mother will rest easier knowing you aren't trying to do too much."

A sick sensation settled in Roman's stomach. "She told you about the incident last week?"

"Ja."

"It was a freak accident. My sling got snagged on a log going into the saw. The strap broke and freed me." He tried to make it sound less dire than it had been. He would relive the memory of those horrible, helpless moments in his nightmares for a long time. His confidence in his ability to do the job he'd always considered his birthright had suffered a harsh blow.

"I understand you were jerked off your feet and dragged toward the saw," Otis said.

"I was never in danger of being pulled into the blade." He was sure he could have freed himself.

Maybe.

"That's not how your mother saw it."

No, it wasn't. Roman's humiliation had been made all the worse by his mother's fright. She had come into the mill to deliver his lunch and witnessed the entire thing. Her screams had alerted his father and younger brother, but no one had been close enough to help. God had answered her frantic plea and freed him in time.

"I'm sorry *Mamm* was frightened, but sawmill work is all I know. I don't see how I can be of use to you in this business," Roman said.

"I fully expect you to give me a fair day's work for your wage. Joann Yoder will teach you all you need to know about being a manager and an editor."

Roman barely heard his uncle's words. He stared at his useless arm resting in the sling. It was dead weight around his neck. He didn't want to be dead weight around his family's neck. Could he accept the humiliation of being unable to do a man's job? He wasn't sure. All his life he'd been certain of his future. Now, he had no idea what God wanted from him.

"Say you will at least think about it, nephew. Who knows, you may find the work suits you. It would please me to think my sister's son might carry on the business my brother and I built after I'm gone."

Roman glanced at his uncle's hopeful face. He and his wife were childless, and his recently deceased older brother had never married, but Roman had no intention of giving up his eventual ownership of the sawmill. If he did accept his uncle's offer, it would only be a temporary job. "Who did you say would train me?"

"The woman you saw leaving just as you came in."

"I'm sorry, I wasn't paying attention. Is she someone I know?"

"Joann Yoder. The sister of Hebron, Ezekiel and William Yoder. I'm sure you know her."

Roman's eyebrows shot up. "The bookworm?"

Otis laughed. "I had no idea that was her nickname, but it fits."

"It was something we used to call her when we were kids in school." She was a plain, shy woman who always stayed in the background.

"Joann can teach you what you need to know about this work."

Roman clamped his lips shut and stared down at his paralyzed arm. He had trouble dressing himself. He couldn't tie his own shoes without help. He couldn't do a man's job, a job that he'd done since he was ten years old. Now, he was going to have a woman telling him how to do this job, if he took it. How much more humiliation would God ask him to bear?

He looked at his uncle. "Why can't you show me how the business is run?"

"I'll be around to answer your questions, but Joann knows the day-to-day running of the business almost as well as I do."

So, he would be stuck with Joann Yoder as a mentor if he accepted. Was she still the quiet, studious loner who chose books over games and sports?

Otis hooked his thumbs under his suspenders and rocked back on his heels. "What do you say, Roman? Will you come work for me?"

Chapter 2

Joann trudged along the quiet, tree-lined streets of Hope Springs with her head down and her carefully laid plans in shambles. Early May sunshine streamed through the branches overhead, making lace patterns on the sidewalk that danced as the wind stirred the leaves. The smell of freshly mowed grass and lilacs scented the late afternoon air.

At any other time, she would have delighted in the glorious weather, the cool breeze and the fragrant flowers blooming in profusion beside the neatly tended houses of the village. At the moment, all she could see was more years of shuffling from one house to another stretching in front of her.

If only I hadn't dared dream that I could change my life.

A small brown-and-white dog raced past her, yipping furiously. His quarry, a yellow tabby, had crossed the street just ahead of him. The cat shot up the nearest tree. From the safety of a thick branch, it growled at the dog barking and leaping below. The mutt circled the tree several times and then sat down to keep an eye on his intended victim.

As Joann came up beside the terrier mix, he looked her way. She stopped to pat his head. "I know just how you feel. So close and yet so far. Take my word for it, you wouldn't have liked the outcome if you had caught him." The cat was almost as big as the dog.

Joann walked on, wondering if there was a similar reason why she couldn't obtain the prize she had been working so hard to secure. Would the outcome have been worse than what she had now? Only the Lord knew. She had to trust in His will, but it was hard to see the good through her disappointment.

After a few more minutes, she reached the buggy shop of Levi Beachy at the edge of town. She passed it every day on her way to and from work. Across the street from the shop stood the house that had almost been hers.

Sarah Wyse, a young Amish widow, had lived there until shortly after Christmas when she married Levi. For a time they had rented the house to a young Amish couple, but they had moved away a month ago and the small, two-story house was vacant again.

Vacant and waiting for someone to move in who would love and cherish it.

Joann stopped with her hands on the gate. The picket fence needed a coat of paint. She itched to take a paintbrush to it. The lawn was well-kept, but if the home belonged to her, she would plant a row of pansies below the front porch railing and add a birdhouse in the corner of the yard. She loved to watch birds. They always seemed so happy.

She would be happy, too, if all it took to build a snug home for herself was bits of straw and twigs. However, it took more. Much more.

She gazed at the windows of the upper story. She'd been a guest in Sarah's home several times. She knew the upstairs held two bedrooms. One for her and one for visitors. Downstairs there was a cozy sitting room with a wide brick fireplace. Off the kitchen was a room just the right size to set up a quilt frame. Joann longed for a quilt frame of her own, but she didn't have a place to keep one.

"Joann, how nice to see you," Sarah Beachy said as she came out of the shop with her arms full of upholstery material. She did all the sewing for the business, covering the buggy seats and door panels her husband made in whatever fabric the customer ordered.

"Hello, Sarah," Joann returned the greeting but couldn't manage a cheerful face for her friend.

"Joann, what's wrong?" Sarah laid her bundle on a bench outside the door and quickly crossed the narrow roadway.

Unexpected tears blurred Joann's vision. She didn't cry. She never cried. She rubbed the moisture away with her hands and folded her arms across her chest. "Nothing," she said, gazing at the ground.

"Something is definitely wrong. You're scaring me." Sarah cupped Joann's chin, lifting gently until Joann had no choice but to meet her gaze.

She swallowed and said, "I've come to tell you that you don't have to wait until September to put your house on the market. You can do it right away."

"You mean you've decided that you don't want it?"

"I'm afraid I can't afford it now."

"I don't understand. Just two weeks ago you told us you were sure you could earn the amount we agreed upon by that time."

"I was fired today."

"Fired? Why on earth would Otis Miller do that?"

"To give the job to someone who needs it more. He's keeping me on as a part-time cleaning woman, and I can have my old job at the bookstore back, but I won't earn nearly enough to pay you what you need by the end of the summer. It was really nice of you and Levi to offer to let me make payments over time, but I know how much you want to make improvements to the business before winter."

"Levi would like to get the holes in the roof fixed and a new generator for the lathe, but I would rather see you happy. If you want, I can talk to him about giving you more time. Perhaps, instead of selling it we could rent it to you. We would both be delighted to have you as our neighbor."

"*Danki,* but that isn't fair to you. Selling your house outright makes much more sense. Besides, with only a part-time job, I wouldn't be able to afford the rent, either. There will be another house for me when the time is right."

She said as much, but she wasn't sure she believed it. Her brothers didn't feel she should live alone and they weren't willing to cover the cost of another house. The local bank had already turned her down for a home loan. She didn't have enough money saved to make a substantial down payment and her employment record wasn't long enough. Only Levi and Sarah had been willing to take a chance on her.

Another home might come along in the distant future, but would it have such a sunny kitchen? Or such an ample back porch with a well-tended garden that backed up to the woods, and a fine sturdy barn for a horse and buggy? This house was perfect. It wasn't too large or too small, and it was close to work.

To the job she didn't have anymore. Her shoulders slumped.

"Come in and have a cup of tea," Sarah said. "There must be something we can do. Perhaps you can find a different job."

The wind kicked up and blew the ribbons of Joann's white prayer *kapp* across her face. She glanced toward the west. "*Danki,* but I should get going. It looks like rain is coming this way."

"I'll have one of the boys hitch up the cart and drive you."

Joann managed to smile at that. "I'm not about to get in a cart with Atlee or Moses. People still talk about how they rigged the seats to tip over backward in Daniel Hershberger's buggy and sent him and his new wife down the street, bottoms up."

Sarah tried not to laugh but lost the struggle. She giggled and pressed her hand to her lips. "It was funny, but my poor Levi was so upset. You will be safe with either one of the twins. Levi's mischief-making brothers have been a changed pair since our wedding."

"How did you manage that?"

Sarah leaned close. "I only feed them when they behave. They do like my cooking."

Joann laughed and felt better. "Ah, Sarah, your friendship is good for my soul."

"I cherish your friendship, as well. Who did Otis give your job to?"

"Roman Weaver. I'm to teach him everything I know about the business."

"I see." A thoughtful expression came over Sarah's face. "So you will be working with Roman. Interesting."

"Only until he has learned enough to do my job. What's so interesting about it?"

A gleam entered Sarah's eyes. "Roman is single. You are single."

Joann held up her hand and shook her head. "Oh, no! Don't start matchmaking for me. Roman doesn't know I exist, and it wouldn't matter if he did. I'm not the marrying kind."

"You will be when God sends the right man your way. I'm the perfect example of that. I didn't think I would marry again after my first husband died, but Levi changed my mind. Roman's a nice fellow. Don't let the disappointment of losing your job color your opinion of him."

"I'll try. Just promise me you won't try any of your matchmaking tricks on me."

"No tricks, I promise."

After refusing a ride once more, Joann bid Sarah farewell and glanced again at the lovely little house on the edge of town before heading toward her brother's farm two miles away. Her steps were quicker, but her heart was still heavy.

Roman left his uncle's publishing house and stopped on the narrow sidewalk outside. The realization that he couldn't do the job he loved left him hollow and angry.

He'd never once wanted to work anywhere except in

the sawmill alongside his father. The business had been handed down in his family for generations. His mother used to say that he and his father had sawdust in their veins instead of blood. It was close to the truth. Now he was being asked to give it up. The thought was unbearable. He'd already lost so much. He tried not to be bitter, but it was hard.

He wouldn't accept his uncle's offer until he'd had a chance to talk things over with his father. Roman had to know if his father wished this. It hurt to think that he might. The gray clouds gathering overhead matched Roman's mood. Thunder rumbled in the distance.

"What did *Onkel* Otis want?" The question came from Roman's fifteen-year-old brother, Andrew, as he approached from up the street. His arms were full of packages.

"He wanted to see how I'm getting along. Did you find all that *Daed* needed at the hardware store?" He held open the door so his brother could put the parcels on the backseat. The job offer was something he wanted to discuss with his father before he shared the information with Andrew.

"I checked on our order for the new bearings, but they haven't come in yet. I have everything else on Father's list."

When Andrew climbed in the front, Roman moved to untie his mother's placid mare from the hitching post. Meg was slow but steady and unlike his spirited gelding, she wouldn't bolt if he lost control of the reins. Managing his high-stepping buggy horse with one arm was just one more thing that he couldn't do anymore.

Maybe his uncle was right. Maybe he should move

aside so his father could hire a more able man. It wouldn't be forever.

His parents and Bishop Zook had counseled him to pray for acceptance, but he couldn't find it in his heart to do so. He was angry that God had brought him low in this manner. And for what reason? What had he done to deserve this? Nothing. He climbed awkwardly into the buggy.

"Do you want me to drive?" Andrew asked.

"*Nee,* I can manage." Earlier, Roman had tied the lines together so he could slip them over his neck and shoulder as he often did when he worked behind a team in the fields. That way he couldn't accidently drop the reins. By pulling on first one and then the other, he was able to guide Meg along the street without hitting any of the cars lining the block. Driving still made him nervous. He cringed each time an *Englisch* car sped by, but he was determined to return to a normal life.

Just beyond the edge of town, they passed a woman walking along the road. She carried a green-and-white quilted bag slung over her shoulder. He recognized it as the one that had been hanging from a chair in his uncle's office. This had to be Joann Yoder. He glanced at her face as he passed her and was surprised by the look of dislike that flashed in her green eyes before she dropped her gaze.

What reason did she have to dislike him? The notion disturbed his concentration. He tried to ignore it, but he couldn't.

Dark gray clouds moved across the sky, threatening rain at any moment. Lightning flashed in the distance. The thunder grew louder. He pulled Meg to a stop.

Andrew gave him a quizzical look. "What are you doing?"

"A good deed." He waited.

When the woman came alongside, he touched the brim of his hat. "Would you like a lift?"

"Nee, danki," she replied coldly as she walked past without looking at him.

He studied her straight back and determined walk. If she were this unfriendly, it wouldn't be a joy working with her. Why was she upset with him? He'd rarely even spoken to her.

Roman looked at his brother. "What do you know about Joann Yoder?"

"What is there to know? She's an old *maedel*. She does whatever old maids do. Can we get home? I have chores to do yet this evening, and I'd rather not do them in the dark."

The road ahead was empty. The next farm was over a mile away. A few drops of rain splattered against the buggy top. Roman clicked his tongue to get Meg moving. She plodded down the road until she came even with Joann and then slowed to match the woman's steps. They traveled that way for a few dozen yards. Finally, Joann stopped. The mare did, too.

She smiled as she patted the animal's neck. When she turned toward Roman, her smile vanished. She kept her eyes lowered. He was surprised by a sharp desire to make her look at him again. He wanted to see if her eyes were as green as he thought.

"Did you need something?" she asked.

"Nee. We are just on our way home."

"At a snail's pace," Andrew added under his breath.

Roman ignored him. "Allow us to give you a ride.

We are obviously going in the same direction. It looks like rain."

"I won't melt."

"But you will be uncomfortable."

"I'll be fine."

"Won't your books get wet?"

She looked down at her bag and back at him. A wary expression flashed across her face. It had been a guess on his part but it appeared he was right about the contents of her bag.

As she stared at him, he saw her eyes *were* an unusual shade of gray-green. They seemed to shift colors according to the light or perhaps her mood. Why hadn't he noticed that about her before now? Maybe because she was always looking down or away. A raindrop struck her cheek and slipped downward like a tear.

For a moment, she didn't say anything, then she nodded and wiped her face. "A lift would be most welcome."

"*Goot.* Where can we take you?" He was ashamed to admit he didn't know where she lived.

"I'm staying with my brother, Hebron Yoder. His farm is just beyond the second hill up ahead."

"We don't go that far," Andrew said under his breath.

"It won't hurt us to go a little out of our way." Roman ignored Andrew's put-upon sigh and waited as Joann rounded the buggy and opened the door on the passenger's side. Maybe he could find out why she disliked him.

Joann wasn't sure what to make of Roman's unusually kind gesture. He'd passed her dozens of times when she was walking along this road without offering her a lift. What was different about today? Did he know she was being fired in order to give him a job? She didn't believe Otis would share that information, but perhaps he had.

Was Roman feeling guilty? If so, then it was up to her to grant forgiveness and get their working relationship off to a good start.

She leaned forward to look around his brother, determined to overcome the shyness that had gotten ahold of her tongue. "Congratulations on your new position."

"What new position?" Andrew demanded.

She caught the annoyed glance Roman flashed at her. She sat back and looked straight ahead. So much for a good start.

"*Onkel* Otis offered me a job at his publishing office," Roman admitted reluctantly.

"Why?" Andrew looked incredulous.

Roman didn't reply. Joann immediately felt sorry for him. The answer was so obvious.

The reason finally dawned on Andrew. "Oh, because of your arm. You didn't take it, did you?"

Joann hadn't considered that possibility. Hope sprang to life in her heart. Was her job safe after all? She waited anxiously for his reply.

"I'm considering it," he said.

Considering meant he hadn't said yes. Was there some way she could convince him to turn down the offer? She had to try. "I'm sure the job wouldn't be to your liking."

"Why do you say that?" he asked.

She racked her mind for a reason. "The work is mostly indoors."

"Not working in the hot sun this summer sounds nice."

She chewed the corner of her lip as she tried to think of another reason he wouldn't want the best job in the world. "It's very noisy when the presses are running."

"I seriously doubt it's noisier than a sawmill." His amusement brought a flush of heat to her face. How silly of her.

All that was left was the truth. She took a deep breath. "It requires hours of reading, excellent comprehension and a firm grasp of writing mechanics as well as an inquisitive mind," she said.

He pulled the mare to a halt and turned to face her. Andrew looked from his brother to Joann and then leaned back out of their way. Roman's brow held a thunderous expression that rivaled the approaching storm. "You don't think I possess those skills?"

She swallowed hard. The truth was the truth. Just because he was upset was no reason to change tactics now. Her chin came up. "I doubt that you do."

"Is that so?"

Joann was tempted to tell him his uncle only offered the job out of pity, but she wisely held her tongue. Nothing good could come from speaking out of spite. She tried to match his stare, but her courage failed. She dropped her gaze to her clenched hands. Why had she started this conversation? It was up to God to decide which one of them was best suited for the job.

In the growing silence, she chanced a glance at Roman's face. His dark expression lightened. Suddenly, he burst out laughing.

"What's so funny?" Andrew asked.

"She's right. I'm not a fellow who enjoys reading or writing."

Joann's hopes rose. "So you don't intend to take the job?"

Roman slapped the reins to get the horse moving. "We'll see. I can learn a new thing if I set my mind to it. Do you always speak so frankly, Joann Yoder?"

Embarrassed, she muttered, "I try not to."

"And why is that?" he asked.

Did he care, or was he trying to make her feel worse? She repeated the phrase her brothers often quoted. "Silence is more attractive than chatter in a woman."

"Says who?" he asked.

"A lot of people."

He wasn't satisfied with her vague answer. "Who, specifically?"

"My brothers," she admitted.

Andrew nodded sagely. "I have to agree."

"I think it depends on the woman," Roman replied.

She glanced at him and thought she caught a glimpse of humor shimmering in his eyes, but she couldn't be sure. Was he laughing at her? Most likely he was. He held her gaze for a long moment before staring ahead again.

Raindrops began splattering against the windshield and roof of the buggy. Joann was every bit as uncomfortable inside as she would've been out in the rain but for a very different reason. Being near Roman made her feel fidgety and on edge, as if something important were about to happen. Thunder cracked overhead and she jumped.

"How long have you worked for our uncle?" Roman asked, looking up at the sky.

"About five months."

"He said that you'll be my teacher if I take the job."

"That's what he told me, too."

"What kind of things would you teach me?"

Andrew interrupted. "I don't know why you're considering it. *Daed* and I need your help in the sawmill. We can't do it all alone."

"I didn't say I was taking it, but I need to know enough to make an informed decision. What things would I have to learn?"

"Many things, like how to set type and run the presses and how to use the binding machines. Eventually, you will have to write articles for the magazine. Many people send us stories to be printed. You'll have to learn how to check any facts that they contain. We don't want to hand out the wrong advice."

"Give me an example."

She thought a moment, and then said, "People send in home remedies for us to publish in our magazine all the time. Sometimes they are helpful, but sometimes they can be harmful to the wrong person, such as a child. When in doubt, we check with Dr. White or Dr. Zook at the Hope Springs Clinic."

He glanced her way. "Have you written any articles?"

"A few."

"What were they about?"

"I wrote a piece about our history in Hope Springs. I've submitted several tips for the Homemaker Hints section that were published. I've even done a number of poems."

"Interesting. What else would my job entail?"

Andrew rolled his eyes. "I can just see you writing homemaker tips and poetry, *bruder.*"

Roman paused a moment, then said, "Roses are red, violets are blue, pine is the cheapest wood, oak is straight and true."

Roman chuckled and smiled at his brother. Andrew grinned and said, "That's not bad. Maybe uncle will use it."

The affection between the two brothers was evident. Joann wished for a moment that she could joke and laugh with her brothers that way. They were all much older than she was. She had come along as a surprise late in her parents' lives. Hebron, the youngest of her brothers, had been fifteen when she was born. They were all married and starting their own families by the time she went to school. Her brothers pretty much ignored her while she was growing up. It was only after their parents died that they decided they knew what was best for her.

Roman clicked his tongue to get Meg to pick up the pace. "Tell me what else I would have to learn."

"You would have to proofread the articles that Otis writes or that others send in to be published. You'll have to attend special meetings in the community in order to report on them, such as the town council meetings and school board meetings. We report the news weekly as well as publish a monthly magazine."

"Sounds like a piece of cake."

"Do you think so?" If he didn't value what they did, how could he do the job well?

When he didn't say more, she leaned forward to glance at him. His face held a pensive look. Was he thinking about taking the job or rejecting it? If only she could tell.

Finally, her brother's lane came into view. By the

time they reached the turnoff, the rain had slowed to a few sprinkles. "I'll get out here," she said. "Thanks for the lift."

Roman stopped the buggy. Joann bolted out the door into the gentle rain and hurried toward the house. Once she gained the cover of the front porch, she watched as he turned the buggy around and drove away. At least she could draw a full breath now that she wasn't shut in with him.

What was it about being near him that set her nerves on edge? And how would she be able to work with him day in and day out if he did take the job?

"Please, Lord, let him say no."

Chapter 3

Roman sat at the kitchen table that evening with his parents after supper was done. His conversation with green-eyed Joann earlier that day hadn't helped him come to a decision. He wasn't sure what to do. What would be best for him? What would be best for his family?

Although he lived in the *dawdy-haus,* a small home built next to his parent's home for his grandparents before their passing, he normally took his meals with his family. He waited until his younger brother left the kitchen and his mother was busy at the sink before he cleared his throat and said, "*Daed,* I need to speak to you."

"So speak," his father replied and took another sip of the black coffee in his cup. Menlo Weaver was a man of few words. Roman's mother, Marie Rose, turned away from the sink, dried her hands on a dish towel and joined them at the table. Roman realized as he gazed at her worried face that she had aged in the past months, and he knew he was the reason why.

He took a sip of his own strong, dark coffee. "I spoke with *Onkel* Otis today," he said.

"And?" his mother prompted.

"He offered me a job."

There was no mistaking his father's surprise. Menlo glanced at his wife. She kept her gaze down. Roman knew then that it hadn't been his father's idea. That eased some of his pain. At least his father wasn't pushing to be rid of him.

As always, Menlo spoke slowly, weighing his words carefully. "What was your answer, *sohn?*"

Roman knew his father well. He read the inner struggle going on behind his father's eyes. Menlo didn't want his son to accept the job, but he also wanted what was best for Roman. "I told him I'd think it over."

His mother folded her dish towel on her lap, smoothing each edge repeatedly. "And have you?"

"Of course he's not going to take it," Menlo said.

Roman knew then that he had little choice. His father would keep him on, but the cost to the business would slowly sink it. If Roman had an outside job and brought in additional money for the family, they could afford to hire a strong fellow with two good arms to take his place and make the sawmill profitable again.

He looked his father square in the eye. "I've decided to accept his offer. I hope you understand."

Menlo frowned. "Are you sure this is what you want?"

Roman didn't answer. He couldn't.

"You'll come back to work with me when your arm is better, *ja?*"

Roman smiled to reassure him. "*Ja,* Papa, when my arm gets better."

Menlo nodded. "Then I pray it is a good decision and that you will be healed and working beside me soon."

Roman broached the subject weighing heavily on his mind. "You will have to hire someone to take my place. Andrew and you can't do it all alone."

"We can manage," his father argued.

"You'll manage better with more help. Ben Lapp is looking for work. He's a fine, strong young man from a good family," his mother countered.

Menlo glanced between his son and his wife. He nodded slowly. "I will speak to him. I thought you were going to tell us you had decided to wed Esta Barkman."

Roman had been dating Esta before the accident. He'd started thinking she might be the one. Since the accident, he'd only taken her home from church a few times. It felt awkward, and he wasn't sure how to act. He didn't feel like a whole man. He avoided looking at his father. "I'm not ready to settle down."

"You're not getting any younger," his mother said. "I'd like grandchildren while I'm still young enough to enjoy them."

"Leave the boy alone. He'll marry soon enough. The supper was *goot.*"

"*Danki.*" She smiled at her husband, a warm smile that let Roman know they were still in love. Would Esta smile at him that way after thirty years together? He liked her smile. Her eyes were pale blue, not changeable green, but it didn't matter what color a woman's eyes were. What mattered was how much she cared for him.

He wanted to wait until his arm was healed before asking her to go steady, but his mother was right. He wasn't getting any younger. Now, more than ever, he felt the need to form a normal life.

Menlo finished his coffee and left the room. Roman stayed at the table. His mother rose and came to stand behind him. She wrapped her arms around him and whispered, "I know this is hard for you, but it will all turn out for the best. You'll see."

If only he could believe that. Ever since he was old enough to follow his father into the mill, Roman had known what life held for him. At the moment, it felt as if his life had become a runaway horse and he'd lost the reins. He had no idea where it was taking him. He hated the feeling.

"Are you worried about working for my brother? Otis is a fair man."

"It's not *Onkel* Otis I'm worried about working with. It's his employee, Joann Yoder. She's taken a dislike to me for some reason." It was easier to talk about her than about his self-doubts.

"Nonsense. I can't imagine Joann disliking anyone. She's a nice woman. It's sad that no man has offered for her. She has a fine hand at quilting and a sweet disposition."

"Not so sweet that I've seen."

"She is a little different. According to her sister-in-law, she spends all her time with her nose in a book or out roaming the woods, but it can't be easy for her. Be kind to her, my son."

"What do you mean it can't be easy for her?"

"Joann gets shuffled from one house to another by

her brothers. I just meant it can't be easy never having a place to call home."

"I don't understand."

"She's much younger than her brothers. When her parents died, her brothers decided she would spend four months with each of them so as not to burden one family over the other. I honestly believe they think they are being fair and kind. I'm sure they thought she would marry when she was of age, but she hasn't. She's very plain compared to most of our young women."

"She's not that plain." She had remarkable eyes and a pert nose that matched her tart comments earlier that day. Why hadn't he noticed her before? Perhaps because she seldom looked up.

His mother patted his arm. "She's not as pretty as Esta."

"*Nee,* she's not." He rose from the table determined to put Joann Yoder out of his mind. He had much more important things to think about.

"Joann, we're going fishing. Come with us."

Looking up from her book, Joann saw her nieces come sailing through the doorway of the bedroom they shared. Ten-year-old Salome was followed closely by six-year-old Louise.

Joann didn't feel like going out. Truth be told, all she wanted was to sit in her room and pout. Tomorrow they would all travel to Sunday services at the home of Eli Imhoff, and she was sure to see Roman Weaver there. She had no intention of speaking to him.

On Monday, she would learn if she still had her job or if she had lost her chance to buy a home of her own. Last night she prayed to follow God's will, but she really hoped the Lord didn't want Roman to take the job any more than she did. She had tried to find pity in her heart, but the more she thought about him, the less pity entered into the picture. He seemed so strong, so sure of himself. She'd made a fool of herself trying to talk him out of working for Otis.

Why couldn't she stop thinking about him?

Because he was infuriating, that was why. And when he turned his fierce scowl on her, she wanted to sink through the floor.

"Come on, Papa is waiting for us." Louise pulled at Joann's hand.

She shook her head and said, "I don't think I'll come fishing today, girls."

"You love fishing, *Aenti* Joann. Please come with us," Salome begged.

Louise leaned on the arm of the chair. "What are you reading?"

Joann turned her attention back to her book. She'd read the same page three times now. "It's a wonderful story about an Amish girl who falls in love with the Amish boy next door."

"Does she marry him?" Louise asked.

Joann patted the child's head. "I don't know. I haven't finished the book. I hope she does."

Louise looked up with solemn eyes. "Because you don't want her to be an old *maedel* like you are?"

Joann winced. Out of the mouths of babes.

"That's not nice, Louise," Salome scolded. "You shouldn't call *Aenti* Joann an old maid."

Louise stuck out her bottom lip. "But Papa says she was born to be a *maedel*."

Joann was well aware of her brother's views on the

subject of her single status. Perhaps it was time to admit that he was right. A few months ago, she had cherished a secret hope that Levi Beachy would one day notice her. However, Levi only had eyes for Sarah Wyse. The two had wed last Christmas. Joann was happy for them. Clearly, God had chosen them for each other.

Only, it left her without even the faintest prospect for romance. There was no one in Hope Springs that made her heart beat faster.

She closed her book and laid it aside. "Salome, do not scold your sister for speaking the truth."

Joann wanted to know love, to marry and to have children, but if it wasn't to be, she would try hard to accept her lot in life. When did a woman know it was time to give up that dream?

Salome scowled at Louise. Louise stuck her tongue out at her sister and then ran from the room.

Salome turned back to Joann. "It was still a rude thing to say. Never mind that baby. Come fishing with us."

Joann shook her head. "I don't think so."

"But your new fishing pole came. Don't you want to try it out?"

Joann sat up. "It came? When?"

"The mailman brought it yesterday."

"Where is it?"

Salome pointed to the cot in the corner of the upstairs bedroom. "I put it on your bed."

"It's not there now. It wasn't there when I went to bed last night."

"Maybe Louise was playing with it. I told her not to," Salome said, shaking her head.

Joann cringed at the thought. If the younger girl had

damaged it, she wouldn't be able to get her money back. She'd foolishly spent an entire week's wages on the graphite rod and open-faced spinning reel combo. In hindsight, it was much too expensive.

Oh, but when she'd tried it out in the store, it cast like a dream. Maybe she should keep it.

No, she gave herself a firm mental shake. She couldn't afford it now. If her hours were cut, she would have to make sacrifices in order to keep putting money in her savings account. Otherwise, she faced a lifetime of moving her cot from one household to another.

Salome dropped to the floor to check under the other beds in the room. Finally, she found it. "Here it is."

Joann breathed a sigh of relief when Salome emerged with the long package intact. Taking the box from her niece, Joann checked it over. It bore several big dents.

"Did she break it?"

"I don't think so." Joann carefully opened one end and slid out the slender black pole. The cork handle felt as light and balanced in her hand now as it had in the sporting goods store. She unpacked the reel. It was in perfect shape.

From the bottom of the stairs, Joann heard her brother call out, "Salome, are you coming?"

"Yes, Papa. Joann is coming, too." She ran out the door and down the stairs.

Joann stared at the pole in her hands. Why not try it out once before sending it back? What could it hurt? It might be ages before she had a chance to use such a fine piece of fishing equipment again. She bundled it into the box, grabbed her small tackle box from beneath her cot, exchanged her white prayer *kapp* for a large black kerchief to cover her head and hurried after her niece.

On her way out of the house, Joann paused long enough to grab an apple from the bowl on the kitchen table. Outside, she joined the others in the back of the farm wagon for the jolting ride along the rough track to a local lake. It wasn't far. Joann walked there frequently, but she enjoyed sitting in the back of the wagon with the giggling and excited girls at her side.

The land surrounding the small lake belonged to an Amish neighbor who didn't care if people fished there as long as they left his sheep alone and closed the gates behind them. Joann had been coming to the lake since she was a child. Joseph Shetler, the landowner, had been friends with her grandfather. The two men often took a lonely little girl fishing with them. Occasionally, Joann still caught sight of Joseph, but he avoided people these days. She never knew why he had become a recluse. He still came to church services, but he didn't stay to visit or to eat.

The wagon bounced and rumbled along the faint wheel tracks that led to the south end of the lake. It had once been a stone quarry that had filled with water nearly a century ago. When they reached the shore, everyone piled out of the back of the wagon and spread out along the water's edge. The remote area was Joann's favorite fishing place. She knew exactly where the large-mouth bass, bluegill and walleye hung out.

She'd spent many happy hours fishing here peacefully by herself, but each time served to remind her of the wonderful days she'd spent there with her grandfather. He had been the one person who always had time for her.

If she closed her eyes, she could still hear his craggy voice. "See that old log sticking out of the bank, child?

There's a big bass right at the bottom end of it. Mr. Bass likes to hole up in the roots and dart out to catch unwary minnows swimming by. Make your cast right in front of that log. You'll get him."

Joann smiled at the memory. It had taken many tries and more than a few lost lures before she gained the skill needed to put her hook right where she wanted it. Her *daadi* had been right. She caught a dandy at that spot.

She was always happy when she came to the lake. She kept a small journal in the bottom of her tackle box and made notes about all of her trips. She used the information on weather conditions, insect activity and water temperature to compile information that made her a better angler.

Normally, she released the fish if she was alone. Today, she would keep what she caught and the family would enjoy a fish fry for supper.

When everyone was spreading out along the lakeshore, she said, "I haven't had much success fishing on this end of the lake. The east shore is a better place."

"Looks *goot* to me." Hebron threw in his line.

Joann shrugged and headed away from the lake on a narrow path that wound through the trees for a few hundred yards before it came out at the shore again near a small waterfall. This was where the fishing was the best.

Carefully, she unpacked her pole and assembled it. From her small tackle box, she selected a lure that she knew the walleye would find irresistible and began to cast her line. Within half an hour, she had five nice fish on her stringer.

She pulled the apple from her pocket and bit into

the firm, sweet flesh. The sounds of her crunch and of the waterfall covered approaching footsteps. She didn't know she wasn't alone until her brother said, "Joann, I've been calling for you."

Startled, she turned to face him. "I'm sorry, Hebron, I didn't hear you. What do you need?"

"We're getting ready to go. The fish aren't biting today."

"I've been catching lots of walleye. Have you tried a bottom-bouncing lure?" She set her apple beside her on a fallen tree trunk and opened her tackle box to find him a lure like the one she was using.

He waved aside her offering. "I've tried everything. What's that you're fishing with?"

"An orange hopper."

"I meant the rod. Where did you get that?"

She extended her pole for him to see. "I ordered it from the sporting goods store in Millersburg."

"Mighty fancy pole, sister."

"It works wonderfully well. Try casting it, you'll see. You'll be wanting one next."

"My old rod and reel are good enough."

She turned back to the water. "Okay, but I'm the one catching fish."

"Be careful of pride, sister. The *Englisch* world has many things to tempt us away from the true path."

"I hardly think a new fishing pole will make my faith weaker."

"May I see it?" he asked.

"Of course. You can cast twice as far with it as your old one. Give it a try." She handed it over, delighted to show him how well-made it was and how nicely it worked. She picked up her apple and took a second bite.

Hebron turned her rod first one way and then another. "A flashy thing such as this has no place in your life, sister."

"It does if I catch fish for you and your children to eat."

"Are you saying I can't provide for my family?"

"Of course not." She dropped her gaze. Hebron was upset. She could tell by the steely tone creeping into his voice.

He balanced the rod in his hand, nodded and drew back his arm to cast.

Eagerly, she sought his opinion. "Isn't it light? It really is better than any pole I've owned."

He scowled at her, and then threw the rod with all his might. Her beautiful pole spun through the air and splashed into the lake.

"No!" she cried in dismay and took a step toward the water. The apple dropped from her hand.

"False pride goes before a fall, sister," Hebron said. "I would be remiss in my duty if I allowed you to keep such a fancy *Englisch* toy. Already, I see how it has turned your mind from the humble ways an Amish woman should follow. Now, come. We are going home. I will carry your fish. It looks as if God has given us enough to feed everyone after all." With her stringer of fish in his hand, he headed toward the wagon.

She stood for a moment watching the widening ripples where her rod had vanished. Now she had nothing to return and nothing to show for her hard-earned money. Like the chance to own a home, her beautiful rod was gone.

Tears pricked against the back of her eyes, but she refused to let them fall.

* * *

Late in the afternoon on Saturday, Roman took off his sling and began the stretching exercises he did every day, four times a day. His arm remained a dead lump, but he could feel an itching sensation near the ball of his shoulder that the doctors assured him was a good sign. As he rubbed the area, the uncomfortable sensation of needles and pins proved that the nerves were beginning to recover. He had been struck by a pickup truck while standing at the side of his buggy on a dark road just before Christmas. The impact sent him flying through the air and tore the nerves in his left shoulder, leaving him with almost complete paralysis in that arm.

Dr. White and Dr. Zook, the local physicians he saw, were hopeful that he would regain more use of his arm, but they cautioned him that the process would be slow. Unlike a broken bone that would mend in six or eight weeks, the torn nerves in his arm would take months to repair themselves. Even then, there was no guarantee that he would regain the full use of his extremity.

Roman tried to be optimistic. He would work for his uncle until his arm was better. When it was, he would return to working with his father in the sawmill as he had always planned. He held tight to that hope. He had to.

The outside door opened and his brother Andrew came in. He held a pair of fishing poles in one hand. "I'm meeting some of the fellows down at the river for some fishing and a campout. Do you want to come along?"

Roman put his sling back on. He didn't like people seeing the way his arm hung useless at his side. "I don't think so."

"Come on. It will do you good. You used to like fishing."

"I like hunting, I like baseball, I like splitting wood with an ax, but I can't do any of those things. In case you haven't noticed, I've only got one good arm." The bitterness he tried so hard to disguise leaked out in his voice.

"You don't need to bite my head off." Andrew turned away and started to leave.

"Wait. I'm sorry. I didn't mean to snap at you."

Andrew's eyes brightened. "Then you'll come? There's no reason you can't fish with one arm."

"I'm not sure I can even cast a line. Besides, how would I reel in a fish? That takes two hands."

"I've been thinking about that and I have an idea. It only takes one hand to crank a reel. What you need is a way to hold the rod while you crank. I think this might work."

Andrew opened his coat to reveal a length of plastic pipe hooked to a wide belt and tied down with a strap around his leg.

Roman frowned. "What's that?"

"A rod holder. You cast your line and then put the handle of your pole in this. The inside of the pipe is lined with foam to help hold the rod steady. This way it won't twist while you're cranking. See? I fixed it at an angle to keep the tip of the rod up. All you have to do is step forward or backward to keep tension on the line."

Roman looked at the rig in amazement. "You thought of this yourself?"

It was a clever idea. It might look funny, but the length of pipe held the rod at the perfect angle. "It just might work, little brother," Roman said.

"I know it will. With a little practice, you'll be as good as ever. Come with us." Andrew unbuckled his invention and held it out.

Roman took it, but then laid it on the counter. "Maybe next time."

He didn't want his first efforts to be in front of Andrew and his friends. A child could cast a fishing pole but Roman wasn't sure he could.

Andrew nodded, clearly disappointed. "Yeah, next time," he said.

He left Roman's pole leaning in the corner and walked out. After his brother was gone, Roman stood staring at the rod holder. He picked up his brother's invention. Surely, he could master a simple thing like fishing, even with one arm.

There was only one way to find out. After checking to make sure no one was about, he gathered his rod and left the house. Since he knew Andrew and his friends were going to the river, Roman set off across the cornfield. Beyond the edge of his father's property lay a pasture belonging to Joseph Shetler. Wooly Joe, as he was called, was an elderly and reclusive Amish man who raised sheep.

It took Roman half an hour to reach his destination. As he approached the lake, he saw Carl King, Woolly Joe's hired man, driving the sheep toward the barns. Roman knew Carl wasn't a member of the Amish faith. Like his boss, he kept to himself. The two occasionally came to the mill for wood for fencing or shed repairs, but Roman didn't know them well. When Carl was out of sight, Roman had the lake to himself.

He glanced around once more to make sure he was unobserved. In the fading twilight, he faced the glass-like water that reflected the gold and pink sunset. Lifting his rod, he depressed the button on the reel and cast it out. He hadn't bothered adding bait. He wasn't ready to land a fish and get it off the hook with one hand. Not yet.

He slipped the handle of his rod into the holder his brother had made. It was then he discovered that actually reeling it in wasn't as difficult as he had feared. When he had all the line cranked in, he pulled the rod from the holder and flipped another cast.

This wasn't so bad. Maybe he should have brought some bait. He'd only reeled in a few feet when he felt his hook snag and hang up. He yanked, and it moved a few feet but it wouldn't come free. What was he snagged on?

Chapter 4

Roman discovered just how hard it was to crank his rod with something on the other end. It wasn't a fish, just deadweight. Suddenly, it gave a little more. He half hoped the line would break, but it held. Whatever snagged his hook was being pulled across the bottom of the lake. When he finally managed to wrestle it in, he stared at his prize in amazement. It was someone's fishing pole.

When he stepped down to the water's edge, he noticed a half-eaten apple bobbing at the shoreline. There were fresh footprints in the mud at the edge of the water, too. He'd stumbled upon someone's fishing spot, and they hadn't been gone more than an hour or two.

It was easy to tell that the pole hadn't been in the water long, either. There wasn't a speck of rust on the beautiful spinning reel. The rod and handle were smooth and free of slime.

Whoever had lost the nice tackle had done so recently. Had Carl been fishing before Roman showed up? Was this his pole? It wasn't a run-of-the-mill fishing pole. This was an expensive piece of equipment. Far better than the one Roman owned.

He'd found it. Should he keep it?

He carried his prize to a fallen tree and sat down. It didn't seem right to keep such a high-priced rod and reel. How had it come to be in the lake? Maybe the unfortunate angler had hooked a fish big enough to pull his unattended gear into the water. Whatever happened, Roman was sure the unknown fisherman regretted the loss. He certainly would.

He debated what to do. If he left it here, would the owner return to fish at this spot, or would another angler chance upon it?

He decided on a course of action. From his pocket, he pulled the pencil and small notebook he normally carried to jot down wood measurements. Keeping it handy was a habit.

He wrote: *Fished this nice pole from the lake. Take it if it's yours or you know who owns it.*

That should suffice. He left the pole leaning against the log and weighted his note down with a stone. If the owner returned, it would be here for him. He'd done the right thing. He would check back later in the week. If the rod was still here, then the good Lord wanted him to have it.

Gathering up his old pole, Roman tucked it under his arm and headed for home, content that he'd be able to enjoy an evening of fishing with his brother in the future without embarrassment. At least one thing in his life was looking up. Hopefully, his new job would be just as easy to master.

* * *

Joann followed her sister-in-law and her nieces into the home of Eli Imhoff on Sunday morning. She took her place among the unmarried women on the long wooden benches arranged in two rows down the length of the living room. Her cousin, Sally Yoder, sat down beside her.

Sally was a pretty girl with bright red hair, fair skin and a dusting of freckles across her nose. While many thought she was too forward and outspoken, Joann considered her a dear friend. She often wished she could be more like her outgoing cousin. Just behind Sally came Sarah and Levi with Levi's younger sister, Grace. Sarah sat up front with the married women. Grace took a seat on the other side of Joann. Levi crossed the aisle to sit with the men.

Joann's eyes were drawn to the benches near the back on the men's side where the single men and boys sat. She didn't see Roman.

"Are you looking for someone?" Grace asked.

Joann quickly faced the front of the room. "No one special."

"Is Ben Lapp back there?" Sally asked with studied indifference. She picked up a songbook and opened it.

Joann wasn't fooled. Sally was head over heels for the handsome young farmer. Ben was the only one who didn't seem to know it.

Joann glanced back and saw where Ben was sitting just as Roman came in and took a seat. Their eyes met, and she quickly looked forward again. She whispered to Sally, "Ben is here."

"Is he looking at me?"

"How should I know?"

"Check and see if he's looking this way."

Joann glanced back. Ben wasn't looking their way, but Roman was. Joann quickly faced forward and opened her songbook.

Sally nudged her with her elbow. "Well? Is he?"

"No."

"Oh." Disappointed, Sally snapped her book closed. After a moment, she leaned close to Joann. "Is he looking now?"

"I'm not going to keep twisting my head around like a curious turkey. If he's looking, he's looking. If he isn't, he isn't."

"Fine. What's wrong with you today?"

"I'm sorry. I'm just upset because I may lose my job."

"Why? What happened?" Grace asked.

"Otis wants his nephew to take over my position."

Sally gave up trying to see what Ben was doing. "Which nephew?"

"Roman Weaver."

Grace shot her a puzzled look. "What does Roman know about the printing business?"

"Whatever I can teach him in two weeks. After that, I go back to my old job at the bookstore. Oh, I'm the cleaning lady now, too."

"That's not fair," Sally declared. "You do a wonderful job for the paper. My mother says the *Family Hour* magazine has been much more interesting since you started working for Otis."

Joann sighed. "I love the job, but what can I do?"

"Quit," Sally stated as if that solved everything. "Tell Otis he can train his own help and clean his own floors."

"You know I can't do that. I need whatever work I can get."

Esta Bowman came in with her family. Grace nodded slightly to acknowledge her. Esta moved forward to sit on a bench several rows in front of Sally. The two women had been cool toward each other for months.

According to gossip, Esta had tried to come between Grace and her come-calling friend, Henry Zook. Happily, she had failed. Grace confided to Sally that she and Henry would marry in the fall. Although Amish betrothals were normally kept secret, Sally shared the news with Sarah and Joann. Joann hadn't told anyone else.

Grace whispered to her. "Esta has been at it again. Everyone knows she's walking out with Roman Weaver, but according to her sister, she's just doing it to make Faron Martin jealous. Two weeks ago, Henry saw her kissing Ben Lapp."

"Ben wouldn't do that," Sally snapped.

Grace waved aside Sally's objection. "I think she was only trying to make Faron notice her. Anyway, it worked. She left the barn party last Saturday with Faron, and I saw them kissing. I noticed he drove his courting buggy today. Mark my words, she'll ride home with him this evening and not with Roman."

Joann discovered she wanted to hear more about Roman's romantic attachment, but she knew church wasn't the place to engage in gossip. She softly reminded Grace of that fact. Grace rolled her eyes but fell silent.

Joann resisted the urge to look back and see if Roman's gaze rested tenderly on Esta. It was none of her business if he was about to be dumped by a fickle woman.

Joann turned her heart and mind toward listening to God's word.

After the church service, the families gathered for the noon meal and clustered together in groups to catch up on the latest news. There were two new babies to admire and newlyweds to tease. Then Moses and Atlee Beachy got up a game of volleyball for the young people that kept everyone entertained. It was pleasant to visit with the friends she didn't see often. Joann was sorry when it came time to leave. She found herself searching for Roman in the groups of men still clustered near the barn but didn't see him. Nor did she see Esta among the women.

Hebron walked up to her, a scowl on his face. "Have you seen the girls?"

She looked around for her nieces. "I think they were playing hide-and-seek in the barn with some of the other children."

"See if you can find them. I'm ready to go."

Joann walked into the barn in search of her nieces. It wouldn't be the first time the girls had stayed hidden to keep from having to go home when they were having fun. They often played this game. After calling them several times, Joann accepted that she would have to join the game and find them herself. She climbed the ladder to the hayloft. A quick check around convinced her they weren't hiding there. So where were they?

Joann returned to the ground level and began checking in each of the stalls. She didn't believe the girls would be hiding with any of the horses, but she didn't know where else to look. One stall was empty. A rustling sound from within caught Joann's attention. She stepped inside but her search only turned up a cat with a litter of kittens curled up in a pile of straw in the far corner. She took a moment to reassure the new mother.

Stepping closer, she stooped to pet the cat and admire the five small balls of black-and-white fur curled together at her side. It was then she heard Roman's voice. "Esta, I wish to speak to you alone."

"You sound so serious, Roman. What's the matter?"

"May I speak frankly?" Something in his voice held Joann rooted to the spot.

"Of course. We're friends, aren't we?"

"I hope that we have become more than friends. That's what I wish to talk about."

"Why, Roman, I'm not sure I know what you mean." Esta's coy reply sent Joann's heart to her feet. She needed to let them know she was present, but she dreaded facing Roman. Maybe if she stayed quiet, they would leave and she wouldn't be discovered. She held her breath and prayed. To her dismay, they stopped right outside the stall where she crouched beside the kittens.

"Can I take you home tonight?" Roman asked.

"Did you bring your courting buggy? I thought you came with your family."

"I did come with my family, but it would make me very happy if you would walk out with me this evening."

"I've already told Faron Martin that he could take me home. He brought his courting buggy."

"Tell him you've changed your mind."

"But I haven't."

"Esta, don't do this to me."

"Don't do what? I want to ride in Faron's buggy. He's got a radio in it, and his horse is a mighty flashy stepper. Almost as pretty as your horse, but of course, you can't drive him anymore, can you?"

Joann heard the teasing in Esta's voice. She was toying with Roman. Did she care who took her home as long as they had a tricked-out buggy? Joann wanted to shake her. How could a woman be so fickle?

"Esta, I'm ready to settle down. Aren't you?"

"Are you serious?"

"Very serious."

Joann wished she was anywhere else but eavesdropping on a private conversation. She shouldn't be listening. She covered her ears with her hands and took a step back. She didn't know the mother cat had moved behind her until she stepped on her paw.

The cat yowled and sank her teeth into Joann's leg. She shrieked and shook the cat loose as she stumbled backward. She lost her balance and hit the stall door. The unlatched gate flew open and Joann found herself sprawled on her backside at Roman's feet.

Esta began laughing, but there was no mirth on Roman's face.

"What do you think you're doing?" he demanded.

"I'm sorry," she sputtered, struggling to her feet.

Esta crossed her arms. "She's making a fool of herself, as usual."

"I was looking for my nieces, if you must know." Joann said as she dusted off her skirt and straightened her *kapp*.

A smug smile curved Esta's lips. "She's just eavesdropping on us because she can't get a boyfriend of her own."

Joann's chin came up. "At least I don't go around kissing everyone who walks out with me."

Shock replaced Esta's grin. "How dare you."

Growing bolder, Joann took a step closer. "Which one is a better kisser? Ben Lapp or Faron Martin?"

"Oh!" Esta's face grew beet red. She covered her cheeks with her hands and fled.

It was Joann's turn to sport a smug grin. It died the second she caught sight of Roman's face. The thunderous expression she dreaded was back.

"What have I ever done to you?" he asked in a voice that was dead calm.

She looked down, unable to meet his gaze. "Nothing."

"Then why your spiteful behavior?"

"You call the truth spiteful?" She glanced up, trying to judge his reaction.

"What truth is that?"

"Esta Barkman is a flirt, and she's using you."

"I won't listen to you speak ill of her."

"Suit yourself." She swept past him, wishing that she had kept her mouth closed. What did she care if Esta was leading him on? It was none of her business what woman he cared for. Joann only hoped she had opened his eyes to Esta's less-than-sterling behavior even if it cost his good opinion of her.

On Monday morning, a faint hope still flickered in Joann's heart as she walked up to the front door of the publishing office. She didn't see Roman's buggy on the street. Perhaps he wouldn't come, and she could continue with her job as if nothing had happened. Oh, how she prayed that was God's will.

She paused with her hand on the doorknob. "Please, Lord, don't make me work with that man," she whispered.

She pushed open the door and came face-to-face with the object of her prayers. Roman Weaver stood behind the front counter. He scowled at her and glanced over his shoulder at the clock on the wall. It showed five minutes past nine. Looking back at her, he said, "You're late."

Great. Just great. He was here in spite of her prayers. This was going to be a long day.

Joann hung her bag on the row of pegs beside the door as she struggled to hide her disappointment. "I'm not late. That clock is ten minutes fast. I've been meaning to reset it. Welcome to Miller Press. We publish a monthly correspondent magazine with reports from scribes in a number of Amish settlements, plus other news and stories. We also publish a weekly paper that has sections on weddings, births, deaths, accidents and other special columns. Besides those two, we also do custom print jobs."

Two straw hats hung on the pegs. That meant only Otis and Roman had come in. Gerald Troyer and Leonard Jenks would be in anytime now. Hopefully they would come quickly. She was running out of things to say.

The thought no sooner crossed her mind than the outside door opened and Gerald walked in. A tall and lanky young man, his short, fuzzy red-brown beard proclaimed him a newlywed. "Morning, Joann. Did you have a nice weekend?"

"Well enough. And you?" She refused to look at Roman. She would need to apologize at some point for her behavior yesterday.

Although he was Amish, Gerald belonged to a congregation from a neighboring town. He sighed heavily. "My wife's family came for a surprise visit."

"And how did that go?" Joann asked.

"Her mother is nice enough, but I don't think her father likes me. He didn't say more than four words to me the entire weekend."

She saw him glance pointedly at Roman. She couldn't delay the moment any longer. She gestured toward Roman. "Gerald, this is Roman Weaver. Roman is going to be working with us."

"Excellent. Are you a pressman, reporter or typesetter?" Gerald asked as he held out his hand.

Roman shook it. "None of those, I'm afraid, but I'm willing to learn."

Joann said, "Otis wants Roman to learn all aspects of the business. Gerald is our typesetter and helps with local news reporting."

"Minding my p's and q's, that's me," Gerald said with a wide grin.

Joann noticed the puzzled look Roman gave him. He really didn't know anything about the business. She explained. "All type is set in reverse so that when it's printed it's in the correct position. The p and the q look so much alike that it is easy to mix them up. Typesetters have to mind their p's and q's. It's a very old joke."

Roman didn't look amused. "I see. Minding my p's and q's is my first lesson. What's next, teacher?"

He stressed the last word. To Joann's ears it almost sounded like an insult. Any hope of a good working relationship between them was fading fast.

"I guess we'll start with the layout of the building."

She indicated the high front counter with a tall chair behind it. "The business consists of six separate spaces. Here in the front office, we take orders for printing jobs, accept information and announcements for the paper and take payments for completed orders."

Otis had his office door closed so she knew not to disturb him. "To the left is your uncle's office. Otis oversees all aspects of the business. Any questions I can't answer, he'll be able to."

The front door opened again and a small, elderly gray-haired man entered. He wore faded blue jeans and a red plaid shirt with the sleeves rolled up. His fingernails were stained with ink. He nodded to Joann.

"Leonard Jenks, I'd like you to meet Roman Weaver," she said.

"You're Otis's nephew, aren't you? He told me he offered you a job. Don't expect special treatment."

"I don't," Roman replied, meeting the man's gaze with a steady one of his own.

Leonard nodded, and then said, "Once I get the generator started, we can run those auction handbills. You have them ready, right Joann?"

"I need to put one through the proof press before we get started. I wanted to wait and show Roman how that's done."

"Then you'd best get to it. Make sure he knows I won't waste my time and my eyesight trying to read his chicken scratching. Block print every order," Leonard said, then crossed to a door at the back of the room and went out.

"Friendly fellow," Roman said.

"You have to give him a chance to get to know you. As he mentioned, no one uses cursive writing here. Everything must be printed legibly. Anything you've written that you want to go into print must be typed up. Can you type?"

He arched one eyebrow. "No."

Joann could have kicked herself. Of course he

couldn't type with just one hand. She rushed on to cover her mistake. "Leonard's wife will type up your work. Just let Otis know when you need her."

"I'll learn how to do it. I'm surprised to see an *Englisch* fellow working here. I thought they all went in for computer printing these days."

"Leonard worked for fifty years at a printing company in Cleveland. When they upgraded to more modern presses, he found himself out of a job. Your uncle purchased their old equipment. When Leonard learned where the equipment was going, he asked Otis for a job and moved to Hope Springs. He's invaluable. He knows the equipment inside and out and he can fix anything that goes wrong."

"Is that why his unsociable behavior is tolerated?"

"In part. As I was saying, these are the front offices. Through this door is the makeup room and the table where the type is kept along with our proof press."

She opened the door and went in. Gerald was putting on a large leather apron. "I'll show you how type setup works when Joann is finished with you," he said to Roman.

The sooner she was finished with him the better. Having Roman following her was like having a surly dog at her back. She expected him to snap at her at any second. Her nerves were stretched to the breaking point.

Should she apologize for her comments yesterday or should she go on as if nothing had happened? She certainly wasn't about to mention their meeting in front of Gerald.

"Next door to this building is a bookshop where our books are available to the public," she said. "The store is run by Mabel Jenks, Leonard's wife."

"My uncle hired the wife, too? That's surprising."

"She isn't an employee. He sold half the bookstore to her. Your uncle's business needed to expand beyond the borders of this town. He had books and pamphlets for sale in the store as well as a library of important Amish works. Many are quite rare. Selling part of the bookstore to Mabel, an *Englisch* partner, allowed Otis to expand to the internet so that people from all over the world could find information about the Amish and search for our books. Mabel runs our website, too."

"I had no idea this was such a big operation."

At least he finally seemed impressed with something she was showing him. "Beyond this setup room are the presses. We have four. You'll learn to run each one."

"Leonard will show me that?"

"Ja."

"I can hardly wait."

She ignored his sarcasm. "In keeping with the *Ordnung* of our Amish congregation, we don't use electricity. The lamps are gas. A diesel generator that sits behind the building runs the equipment that isn't hand-operated. It's Leonard's baby, but he'll show you what to do in case you have to run it in a pinch."

"I took a look at them earlier. They're the same type we use at our sawmill."

"I'm glad you're familiar with them." At least he was qualified to do something at his uncle's business.

She wasn't sure why he had accepted the position. She'd never met anyone less suited to become an editor and office manager, a job that fit her like a glove. Somehow, she was going to have to get him up to speed and quickly. If she couldn't, would Otis let her stay? She doubted it. He was getting on in years. Was he thinking about who would take over after he was gone? If he wanted it to be his nephew, well, she understood, but she didn't have to like it.

She kept walking with Roman close on her heels as they passed between the presses. Hopefully, Otis would want Roman to spend the rest of the day with him or with Leonard. She was going to be a nervous wreck if he was breathing down her neck all day.

"Back here is our storage room." She opened the door and stepped inside. Roman followed.

She'd never noticed how small the room was until he took up all the available space and air. "We keep paper, solvents for cleaning ink off the type and such in here along with rolls of wire for our binder," she said breathlessly. "I'll give you a list of what we stock and how to find it."

"All right."

She turned to face him and gathered her courage. "That's the grand tour. Any questions?"

"Not really." He leaned casually against the door-jamb blocking her only exit.

Now what should she do?

Chapter 5

Her voice held a funny quality that Roman couldn't quite identify. Was it resentment, fear or something else? Before he could decide, she clasped her hands together and said, "About yesterday."

He wondered if she would bring it up. She had spoiled more than his opportunity to take Esta home. He had doubts now that hadn't existed before. What if she was telling the truth? Did he want to know?

"What about yesterday?"

"I want to apologize."

"For what?"

She stared at the floor. "You know."

"I'm not sure I do. Why don't you explain." He couldn't help the amusement that crept into his voice. It wouldn't hurt her to squirm a little before he forgave her. She had been rude to Esta. Although, he had to admit Esta shared part of the blame for the exchange.

He almost missed the baleful glare Joann flashed at him before she looked down at her hands. No wonder she didn't look up often. She gave herself away when she did. Those green eyes of hers reflected her emotions the way still waters reflected the sky and clouds overhead.

"I'm sorry I didn't announce myself when I realized you were having a private conversation," she said. "I should have."

"And?" he prompted.

"And I shouldn't have said those things to Esta," she added in a rush. She tried to move past him, but he continued blocking the doorway.

"And?"

The color rose in her cheeks, making them glow bright pink. He wanted to see how far he could push before that outspoken streak she tried so hard to curtail came out. He didn't have to wait long.

Her gaze snapped up and locked with his. Sparks glittered in the depths of her eyes. "And I'm sorry it was all true!"

He struggled not to smile, having gotten the reaction he wanted. "That's hardly an apology."

Her eyes narrowed as she glared at him. "It's all you're going to get. Your uncle hired you to work here. Don't you think you should get started?"

Roman stepped out of the door and swept his arm aside to indicate she should go first. She hesitated, then squeezed past him. He caught a whiff of a pleasing floral scent. Roses maybe. It had to be from her shampoo or soap. Amish women didn't wear perfumes. Whatever it was, he liked it.

She marched ahead of him to the front of the office.

His uncle was behind the front counter waiting on a customer. He called Roman over and showed him the price list they used for ads and single-page flyers and posters. It was easy enough to understand. When the customer left, Otis asked, "How is your first day going?"

Roman lowered his voice. "Joann doesn't seem happy to have me here."

Otis frowned as he looked around Roman to where Joann was gathering a stack of papers from her desk. "Has she said something to that effect? I'll speak to her if she has been rude."

"No, it's probably just me."

"All right, but let me know if she or anyone makes you feel unwelcome. This is my shop, and I say who works here."

Joann crossed the room to join them with several letters clutched to her chest. Her smile was stiff. "Are you ready to learn how to use the proof press?"

"Absolutely, teacher. Lead on."

Her smile stayed in place, but he knew she was annoyed by his pet name for her. All she said was, "Please follow me."

Her instructions were precise and to the point. She quickly showed him how to operate the small press that made a single copy of the handbill they were doing. She handed the first printed page to him. "Read it over and look for mistakes. If you have set the type, get someone else to read it. Errors can slip by because you read it knowing what it should say instead of what is actually on paper."

He scanned the paper carefully and immediately spotted a misspelling. "This should be 'working baler' not 'woking baler,' unless someone does bale woks, whatever that would be."

She frowned at him and leaned close to examine the paper in his hand. Again, he caught the fresh scent of flowers. She glanced up at him and quickly moved a step away. "You're right. I'll let Gerald know. Once he has corrected the letters in the composition stick, we'll turn the project over to Leonard. He'll print the size and number of handbills that were ordered."

"Okay, teacher, what's next?"

He caught a glimpse of the sparks that flashed in her green eyes again before she looked away. With deliberate calm, she said, "The mail. We'll go through it and sort it into letters for the newspaper, ones that might go in the magazine and those that need Otis's attention."

She strode toward the front of the building, and he followed, amused by the square set of her shoulders and intrigued by the gentle sway of her hips.

That thought brought him up short. She had done nothing but cause trouble for him. The last thing he expected was to find her attractive in any way. He quickly dismissed his reaction and focused on what she was saying.

She indicated a stack of mail and offered him a letter opener. She read the first letter. "Alma Stroltzfus is going to be one hundred years old on the twenty-fifth of this month. Her family is hosting a get-together in honor of the day. Family from all across the state will be there. This should go in the weekly paper. Our magazine doesn't come out until after the date, but we could mention it there, too."

He opened his first letter. "This is from a farmer on

Bent Tree Road. He is offering forgiveness to the youth who set fire to his haystacks. Magazine or newspaper?"

"Newspaper, I think." She opened the next letter. "This is a poem about losing a child and dealing with that grief. Definitely a piece for the magazine."

They both reached for the stack of mail at the same time. Their hands touched. She jerked away as if he were a hot stove, her eyes wide with shock. "We can finish this later. Let's have Gerald show you how to set type."

As she hurried away, he noticed again the soft curve of her hips beneath her faded dress. There was definitely more to Joann Yoder than met the eye.

By noon, Roman's head was spinning with all the information Joann poured onto him like syrup over a stack of hotcakes. Some of it was soaking in, but a great deal of it slid off his brain and pooled around his feet. He had no idea there was so much to his uncle's business. He hated to admit it, but he was impressed by Joann's scope of knowledge.

There had been a steady stream of customers into the shop all morning. Some placed orders, but many stopped in simply to leave notices and announcements to run in the paper. Joann took care of the customers, accepted payments, filed the notes and continued to serve him a steady diet of information about what his work would entail.

This wasn't going to be an easy job to master. It wasn't one job. There were dozens of new skills he'd have to learn. He clung tight to the thought that if a woman could manage the place so easily after only five months, then so could he.

Otis came out of his office and said, "Time for lunch."

Joann went to the front door and turned the open sign to closed. Below it, she hung a second sign that said they would return at one o'clock.

"Roman, you are welcome to come home with me. My wife would be delighted to feed you," Otis said.

"I'm sorry, I can't join you today. I have an appointment with Doctor Zook. Please tell *Aenti* Velda I'll be happy to eat with you tomorrow."

"I'll do that. I go right by the clinic on my way home. I'll walk with you." He settled his hat on his head and held open the door. Roman grabbed his own straw hat from the peg and stepped out ahead of him.

As they walked side by side on the narrow sidewalk, they passed a few buggies and cars parked alike in front of the various businesses. It was Monday, and quiet in the small village that nestled amid the farms and pastures of rural Ohio. The main activity seemed to be near the end of the street. Roman noticed his mother's cart parked outside a shop.

Otis asked, "Well, what do you think?"

"I think there is a lot to know."

Otis chuckled. "I do more than shuffle papers all day."

"I'm learning that. It's sure not what I expected."

They stepped aside to let a group of women pass in front of them. They were headed into the fabric shop. Roman caught sight of his mother through the window. Otis saw her, too, and waved. She smiled brightly and waved back.

Otis said, "I see the ad and flyers I printed for the big sale today at Needles and Pins are bringing in customers. That's good. That will mean repeat business."

Roman looked at his uncle. "What made you start a printing shop? Your father ran a dairy farm, didn't he?"

"*Ja.* I worked on the farm with my brothers, but I saw a need among our people for decent things to read. There was a series of articles in one of the local newspapers by an unhappy ex-Amish fellow who believed his new ways were better, and he urged others to follow them."

"We face that all the time. Our life is not for everyone."

"True, but a man must be careful what he reads. Without meaning to, he can allow unholy thoughts to take root in his mind. I started thinking about getting a small press because of those writings and because a friend told me about an old Amish book he wanted to see reprinted. My brother and I printed the book in our barn. It was no thing of beauty, but people bought copies. Not long after that, a woman I knew wrote a manuscript and she asked our Bishop how she might get it published. The Bishop sent her to me. I soon realized the Lord was nudging me to start a business where good Amish folks could find appropriate reading material."

"You print more than books now."

Otis smiled and nodded. "That we do. The magazine grew out of letters people wrote to us after reading some of our books. Once the magazine became popular, people wanted to read the news about their Amish neighbors every week instead of once a month. I bought a bigger press and hired people to help me. Running the press only one day each week wasn't cost-efficient so we started printing flyers, pamphlets and advertisements."

"Not everyone who came in today was Amish."

"We do work for *Englisch* customers as long as the content is acceptable according to our ways. We now print schoolbooks and cookbooks, too. Tourists love our Amish cookbooks. I truly believe the good Lord has caused my business to prosper because I stayed true to His teachings."

"You have created a fine thing, Uncle."

"No more than your father has done. Men need good solid wood to build strong houses and barns. I believe we also need good solid books to build strong minds."

They had come to the corner in front of the Hope Springs Medical Clinic. Otis walked on toward his home and a hot lunch while Roman entered the waiting room of the clinic. His uncle's words about good books stayed in his mind. Roman had always considered reading to be something he needed to get by in business and for church. He'd never thought of it as a way to improve his mind.

His father led the family in prayers and Bible reading each morning and evening. Roman read the Bible sometimes at night, but not as often as he should. He wondered what books his uncle would suggest he read. He would make a point to ask him. The thought of books brought Joann to mind. What did she like to read?

He shook his head. Why was he thinking about her, again? She was like a cocklebur stuck to his sock. Not exactly painful, but irritating and difficult to get rid of.

Fortunately, his name was called, and Roman followed the nurse back to a small exam room. Dr. Zook came in a few moments later. Roman waited quietly as he read his chart.

He looked up at last. "I received a letter from the

neurosurgeon that did your surgery," Dr. Zook said. "He's optimistic about your recovery."

"I'm glad one of us is."

Dr. Zook closed the chart. "He believes with therapy you should recover some of your hand functions."

"Some, but not all?"

"Are you doing your exercises regularly?"

"*Ja,* but I still can't move my arm."

"I'm not surprised. Brachial plexus injuries such as the one you sustained take a long time to heal. Nerves grow very slowly. Only a fraction of an inch in a month. It may be a few months to a few years before your recovery is complete."

"No one will tell me if I'll be able to use my arm again. Will I?"

"We simply don't know. The brachial plexus, the network of nerves that carry signals from your spine to your shoulder, arm and hand, was badly damaged. Two of your nerves were torn apart. While the surgeon was able to repair them, we're not sure they will function as they once did. Other nerves were stretched drastically when that pickup hit you. It was a blessing you weren't killed."

"Somehow, this doesn't feel like a blessing."

Dr. Zook rose and helped Roman remove his sling. He examined the arm, moving it gently. "Have you noticed any changes at all?"

"I've had some twitches in my forearm."

"That's good. As the nerves start to regrow, you'll feel twitching in the muscles they supply. We can start specific exercises to improve those muscles when it happens. Keep up with your stretches. It's important to keep your joints limber. Once they freeze, there isn't much that can be done for them. How is the pain?"

"Always there."

"Have the pills I've given you helped at all?"

"Some. Keeping my mind occupied helps, too."

"I wish there was more I could do to help, but it is going to take time and it's going to be painful."

"So I've been told."

"I want you to be very careful at work. You could injure your arm badly and never feel it. A sawmill can be a dangerous place at the best of times."

Roman slipped his arm back in the sling. "I'm not working at the mill right now."

"Oh?"

"I'm working at my uncle's print shop."

"That's good. While it may be less physically demanding there, it has its own set of dangers. I've bandaged a few crushed fingers and put some stitches in your uncle, too. Just remember to pay attention."

"I will."

"This injury was life-changing for you, Roman. It can't be easy making the adjustments you've had to make. How are the flashbacks?"

"Less frequent."

"Are you sleeping okay?"

"Sometimes."

"Nightmares?"

"Sometimes."

"Roman, depression is natural after an injury like yours. Anger and sadness are symptoms that can be treated if they persist. Don't be afraid to tell me if you have that kind of trouble."

"It was God's will. I must accept that."

"I believe everything happens for a reason, and that God has a plan for everyone, but He invented doctors to help people along the way. So let me do my job, okay? I'll see you in two weeks or sooner if you need me." The young doctor smiled and left the room.

Roman saw no reason to smile. He was crippled, and no one could tell him when, or if, he would recover.

Joann jumped when the front door banged open, but it wasn't Roman returning. It was only her cousin, Sally.

"Hi, Joann. I brought the sketches that Otis wanted. Is he here?" Sally's cheerful face never failed to brighten Joann's day. Her talent as an artist was well known in the community, and she often supplied the black-and-white line drawings that were the only graphics used in the *Family Hour* magazine. Otis would give her a list of things he wanted for the next month's layout and what size they should be. Her beautifully drawn images of ordinary Amish life never failed to amaze Joann.

"Otis isn't back from lunch yet. Can you wait for him?"

"Sure. I've already done my shopping. I got the prettiest lilac material at Needles and Pins for half off. You should get over there and get some. It's going fast."

"I don't have need of a new dress. Mine are fine."

"They may be fine as you see it, but they are getting a little threadbare and stained. Besides, that gray isn't your best color."

Joann looked down at her dress and matching apron. It was an old dress, but it was comfortable. "I like it because it doesn't show the ink stains so readily."

"I'm just saying it wouldn't hurt to take a little more care with your appearance. You might have the chance

to impress a fine fellow who comes in to place an ad,"
Sally said.

What did Roman think of her attire? Why should he
think of her at all? Deciding it was time to change the
subject, Joann reached for the folder her cousin held.
"May I see your sketches?"

Sally beamed. "I was hoping you'd ask."

After laying the sketches side by side on the countertop, Sally shifted her gaze to Joann. "Do you think
these are what Otis had in mind?"

The outside door opened, and Roman entered the
shop with a deep frown creasing his forehead. Had the
doctor given him bad news? "I hope he feels bad about
taking your job," Sally whispered to Joann as she gave
him a cool stare.

Joann gripped Sally's arm and said under her breath,
"Please don't say anything."

Fortunately, Gerald came out of the typesetting room
at that moment. "Sally, have you brought us some more
of your artwork?"

"I brought in four pieces to see if this is what Otis
wanted."

"He should be back any minute. Let's see what you
have. Roman, Sally is our artist. She can draw almost
anything."

Sally blushed. "I have a small talent."

Gerald moved to stand beside the women. Roman
hesitated, as if unsure what to do. Joann said, "Come
look at these, Roman, and tell us what you think."

He came forward and studied the array. "They're
nice. I like this one best."

"I do, too." Joann held up the sketch of a small girl
handing her mother jars from a basket.

"It reminds me of my mother's storeroom in the cellar," he said. "She has hundreds of jars on her shelves."

Sally nodded. "I sketched it while my mother was helping my sister put up green beans last summer. The little girl was inspired by my niece."

"It's darling, Sally," Joann said. "I hope Otis will use it on the cover of the next issue. He's writing a series of articles about stewardship. What a great way to show people how being good stewards is really a part of everyday life."

"I didn't know if he would object to the partial view of the child's face. I know some of your customers belong to more conservative churches."

Joann studied the picture closely. Sally had been careful to draw the woman's figure from the back so that her face wasn't seen, but the child had been sketched in profile.

"I think it's fine. What do you men think?"

"Looks good to me," Gerald said.

"If it's controversial, I say don't use it," Roman added his two cents.

Joann saw the joy go out of Sally's eyes. Roman didn't realize how much Sally's artwork meant to her. She never signed her work or took credit for doing it, but she wanted to use the talent God had given her to glorify Him. This was her way of doing that.

"Otis has the final say," Joann said. "It's up to him."

Otis returned a few minutes later. He looked over Sally's sketches and agreed with Joann's assessment. Thankfully, he kept Roman with him the rest of the afternoon, and Joann had a chance to relax. Roman left a few minutes before five. Joann stayed behind to tidy up the shop.

When she left the building, she was surprised to see Roman come out of the bookstore next door. He had two novels tucked inside his sling. He paused when he caught sight of her. After a moment of hesitation, he said, "My buggy is just around the corner. Would you care to share a ride?"

There wasn't a cloud in the sky. He had no reason to offer her a lift today. "It doesn't look like rain."

"I thought since we were going the same way…" His voice trailed off. He cocked an eyebrow and waited.

It was a long walk after a long day, but she'd rather crawl home on her hands and knees than spend another minute in his company. Thankfully, she managed not to blurt out her opinion. "I have errands to run. I'll see you tomorrow."

Tomorrow would arrive all too quickly.

"Suit yourself." Without another word, he walked away and turned the corner.

Had he actually sounded disappointed? She couldn't imagine why unless he'd come up with a new way to torment her and wanted to test it out.

She started walking, determined not to look back. She was being unkind, but the thought of spending the next two weeks showing him how to do her job was almost more than she could bear. She wasn't herself when he was near. She had to be careful not to trip on her words or run into a desk. He made her feel awkward and jumpy and she had no idea why.

The sad part was that her two weeks with him wouldn't be the end of it. She'd still be coming in to clean. Would he ask why she'd changed jobs? Or why she was cleaning when she knew so much about print-ing? What would she say?

The answer to those questions would have to wait. There was no sense worrying about it before it happened.

She did have an errand to run. It hadn't been just an excuse. She stopped at the public library to inquire if the latest copy of *Ohio Angler* had come in. It hadn't.

The *Angler* was the one *Englisch* magazine that she read cover to cover. She suspected that her brothers wouldn't approve, so she never checked it out. She simply read it at the library. It was from those glossy pages that she had gleaned much of her knowledge about fishing. That and spending hours and hours with a pole in her hand.

Disappointed, she left the library and walked through town toward her brother's home. She passed Sarah's house without stopping. That dream was over. She would just have to learn to accept it. When she reached the lane to her brother's farm, she stopped. She didn't feel like going home yet. She needed to be alone and think. She needed the solace of the lake.

Chapter 6

Roman's spirits lifted when he walked into his mother's kitchen. The wonderful aromas of baking ham, scalloped potatoes and hot dinner rolls promised a delicious meal would soon be ready. His mother, with beads of sweat on her upper lip, was stirring applesauce in a large pan on the stove.

She looked over at him and smiled. "You're just in time. Your papa has gone to wash up. How was it? Was Otis kind to you?"

"It was fine. I'll go wash up, too. Where is Andrew?" His bottomless pit of a brother was always in the kitchen trying to sneak a bite of this or that before his mother got it on the table.

A worried frown creased her brow. "He said he wasn't hungry."

Roman stared at her in shock. "Andrew said that? He must be sick."

Roman's father came into the room. "He's not sick. He just doesn't like change. Can't say that I do, either."

"We change when we must," Marie Rose stated quickly. "It's ready. Have a seat." She opened the door of the oven and pulled out the ham.

Roman could tell his father wanted to say more, but he simply took his place at the head of the table.

Marie Rose scowled at Roman. "Go wash up. Don't make your father wait on you."

Joann rounded the bend in the narrow path that led to her favorite spot at the lake and stopped dead in her tracks. A fishing pole, exactly like her new one her brother had thrown into the water, was leaning against a log where she liked to sit. She glanced around expecting to see another angler, but there was no one in sight. She called out, but no one answered.

The breeze off the water caused a bit of paper on the log to flutter. She moved closer and saw the paper had been weighted down with the stone. Picking it up, she read the note and her heart gave a happy leap. It wasn't a pole like hers. It was hers.

By the grace of God, someone had snagged her pole and pulled it from the depths of the lake. She hugged the note to her chest as she spun around with joy.

"Oh, thank you, thank you, thank you," she shouted. If only the unknown angler were present, she would thank him or her in person.

As quickly as her elation bubbled up, it ebbed away. She had her pole back, but she could hardly return it to the store after letting it soak in the lake. Nor could she take it to her brother's home. Hebron would never allow her to keep it after he had made such an issue of her owning it. So what now?

Hebron rarely came to the lake. If she kept the pole here, he would never know. The fallen log she normally sat on was hollow on one end. She knelt down to check and see if it would work as a storage locker. The rotted-out area was almost big enough to hold the rod. Looking around, she found a long pointed branch and worked at making the cavity bigger. After five minutes, she had an adequate space. If she stuffed a little grass into the hollow, she would have a perfect hiding spot.

Dusting off her hands, she sat back on her heels. Somehow, she had to thank the person who'd rescued her rod. Surely, he would return to check on his find. She quickly opened her tackle box and took out her journal. She tore off a sheet of paper. After searching through her lures, she found the blue and green rattle-trap she was looking for. It was a homemade lure, but she'd caught plenty of bass with it. She pondered what to say for a few minutes, then wrote a brief letter. She folded the paper over with the lure inside it and laid the note on the log. She put the same stone on top of it, took a step back and smiled.

At least one thing had improved in her life. She had her pole back. She jotted a few quick notes in her journal about the wind direction and the temperature, then she tied a spinner on her new rod and cast it out into the water. The lure landed exactly where she had aimed. A second later, she had a hard strike and she spent the next half hour happily catching and releasing fish. Her one regret was that the friendly fisherman wasn't here to enjoy the evening, too.

When she judged it to be about suppertime, she put

her rod back inside the hollow log and headed for home. During the long walk, thoughts about the kind fisherman who had given her back her pole kept going around and around in her mind.

Was it someone she knew? Joseph Shetler, perhaps, or his hired man? She thought his name was Carl King, but he wasn't Amish. There was speculation that he had been once but had left the faith.

Who else could her friend be? She couldn't tell from the brief note if he was *Englisch* or one of the Plain people. Maybe it was a woman. That didn't seem likely. The handwriting had been bold, strong and to the point.

Whoever it was, she hoped one day she would have the chance to thank him or her face to face.

Roman stepped off his parents' front porch into the cool evening air. The days were getting longer. It wouldn't be dark for another hour. Supper had been an awkward meal. His father didn't ask about his day. Roman wouldn't have known what to say if he did ask. Andrew had remained absent from the table. Roman didn't want his new working arrangement to put a strain on his relationship with his brother.

He went in search of Andrew and found him sweeping the sawmill floor. The boy was attacking the accumulated sawdust with a vengeance. "I should go get *Mamm,*" Roman said. "She would be impressed. She's never seen you intent on getting this place so clean. It would do her heart good."

Andrew stopped sweeping but didn't look at Roman. "I'm not doing it to impress anyone."

"I know. I'm just trying to make conversation, but I'm not doing such a good job. This is awkward for me, too. I realize you're upset with me for taking the job in town."

He looked at the stacks of new two-by-fours sitting against the wall. They'd had a productive day without him. He'd made the right decision.

Andrew started sweeping again. "So how is your new job?"

"Complicated. *Daed* said he hired Faron Martin to work here. Do you think he'll work out?"

"It's too soon to tell. I guess he is all right, but it's not like working with you."

"Yeah, he has two good arms."

"But he doesn't know up from down about our business."

Roman chuckled. "I'm pretty sure the people at our uncle's office feel the same way about me."

"I don't believe that. You're twice as smart as they are."

Roman pulled a whisk broom from its hook on the wall and began cleaning wood chips off the counter near the doorway. "Thanks for the vote of confidence, but I'm like a babe in the woods. Everything is new. It's not like this place where I know every nook and cranny and every piece of equipment as well as I know the back of my hand."

"So come back." Andrew didn't look up, but Roman didn't need to see the tenuous hope in his eyes, he heard it in his voice.

"If only it were that simple, Andy."

"I miss having you around."

Roman stepped close to his brother and ruffled his hair. "I miss you, too."

"It's not the same. I've worked beside you since I was old enough to hold a handsaw."

"Andy. I've been meaning to thank you for your gift."

Andy stopped sweeping and looked up with a puzzled expression. "What gift?"

"Your fishing rod holder. It works pretty well."

"It does? You tried it out? When? Did you catch anything?"

"I tried it the other evening when you went fishing with your friends, and I did catch something."

"Wait a minute. You went fishing by yourself? Why didn't you come with me?"

"I wasn't eager to embarrass myself in front of others."

"I didn't think about that. I'm sorry."

"The fault lies with me, little brother, not with you. Anyway, I wanted to thank you."

Andrew brightened. "Hey, do you want to go fishing this evening? We caught some nice catfish below the bridge at the river."

"Sure, but let's go over to Woolly Joe's lake. I caught a new rod and reel there."

"What?"

"Honest. I pulled a brand new rod with an open-faced reel out of the water. It was a beauty."

"What did you do with it?"

"I left it there with a note in case the owner came back. I'm curious to see if someone claimed it, so I'm going over there now. Want to come with me?"

Andrew tossed his broom in the corner. "Sure. Can I get my rod? We've got time to get in a little fishing, don't we?"

Roman smiled at his excitement. "Get your rod and

go get a sandwich from mother. I know you missed supper."

"Good idea. I'm starving." He took off toward the house at a run. He reappeared with a sandwich in one hand and a second one in a plastic bag sticking out of his pocket.

It was nearly dusk by the time Roman and Andrew reached the north end of the lakeshore. "Is this the place you left the pole?" Andrew asked.

"*Nee,* it's farther along on the east side."

Roman nearly missed the path, but he managed to locate the fallen log after a brief search.

Andrew turned around once in the small clearing. "I don't see it. Looks like somebody took it home."

"But they left my note." He picked up the piece of paper weighted down with a rock. Once he had it in his hand, he realized it was a larger sheet of paper than the one he'd left the other day. It had been folded in half. When he opened it, something fell out. It was a fishing lure in the shape of a small fish, a plug, obviously hand-carved and painted with iridescent blue and green colors.

He held the page to catch the fading light from the setting sun.

Dear Friendly Fisherman,
You have no idea how happy I was to see my new rod and reel resting against this log today. I knew when I read your note that a true sportsman had recovered my possession. At a time when everything seems to be going wrong in my life, you have created a bright spot with your kindness. As a small token of my thanks, I'm leaving this jig. It

isn't much, but if you cast it along the rocky out-cropping to the west, you should land a nice bass or two with it. Thank you again.

A Happy Angler

Roman grinned. He'd managed to make someone happy. He was glad that he'd left the fishing pole behind. The good Lord had used him to comfort a stranger.

"What's that?" Andrew asked.

"A note of thanks and a fishing lure for my trouble." The pole had done more than make a stranger happy. It had given Roman a reason to come to the lake with his brother. How strange to think a lost rod and reel was God's tool to mend the rift between them.

"That's cool. Why don't you give it a try?"

Roman hesitated. He didn't want to look like a fool in front of Andrew. He couldn't tie on the lure. Besides, what if he hooked a fish and couldn't reel it in? He almost said no, but something in his brother's eyes stopped him.

Instead, he said, "I believe I will if you rig it for me. I'm not very good at knots with one hand yet." It was the first time he had asked Andrew for any kind of help.

"Not a problem." Andrew grinned from ear to ear. He soon had the iridescent fish secured to the end of Roman's line. When he stepped back, Roman approached the shore and located the spot the thank-you note had mentioned. On his fourth cast, he felt a strike. "I've got one."

"Do you need me to help?" Andrew put his own pole down and moved to Roman's side.

"I think I can manage." It was hard to crank the reel

one-handed with a fighting fish on the other end, but Roman realized he was enjoying the challenge.

"Lean back and keep your rod tip up. Giving him a little more line." Andrew continued to call out instructions until Roman landed the fish. At that point, he raced to the water to grab their prize.

Roman realized he was grinning from ear to ear now, too. If he could do this, he could do other things. He sat down on the log and laughed aloud. "Did you see that? I did it."

Even in the fading twilight, he could see Andrew's happy smile as he held the fish aloft. "You did it, all right. It's a beauty of a bigmouth bass. Must be four pounds if it's an ounce. If we catch a few more, *Mamm* can fry them up for supper tomorrow."

"I'm game if you are, but you know you're going to have to clean them all. I don't think I can manage that with one hand just yet."

Andrew's grin faded and then quickly returned. "That's a deal."

Later, when Andrew had walked a little farther along the shore, Roman took a moment to admire the colors of the sunset reflected perfectly on the still surface of the water. The sun rose and the sun set, no matter what troubled him. The world unfolded as God willed. Roman pulled the note from his pocket and read it again.

At a time when everything seems to be going wrong in my life, you have created a bright spot with your kindness.

He knew exactly how it felt to have everything going wrong. Yes, he had recovered the pole and left it here. It had been a simple thing to do, not really a kindness on his part, but he was glad that he had brightened someone's day in much the same way as the letter and the lure had brightened his.

The Happy Angler had more than repaid Roman's offhand kindness with a true gift. The lure was home-made. The maker had surely spent hours carving and painting the piece. Its value was much more than wood and paint. Using it had shown Roman he could ask for help without feeling helpless. He could do the things he used to do. He just had to learn to do them in a dif-ferent way.

He turned the piece of paper over and wrote a note of his own on the back. Hopefully, the happy angler would return to the spot and learn that the small gift was greatly appreciated and it was so much more than a fishing lure. When he finished the note, he hesitated to sign it.

It was possible the happy angler was someone he knew. Like Roman, the anonymous writer wasn't look-ing for praise for what he'd done and had chosen not to sign his own name. Perhaps he had a reason for want-ing to remain unknown. Roman decided to close the letter with the name the happy angler had given him.

"Andrew, did you save your sandwich bag?"

"*Ja,* mother likes to reuse them, you know."

"Do you think she'll mind if I keep it?"

"I doubt she'll notice. Why?"

"I'm going to write a note thanking this fellow for the plug. I thought I should put it in a plastic bag in case it rains."

"Good thinking. And tell him how well it worked."

Joann was on her way to town the next morning when Roman passed her in his buggy. He stopped the horse a few yards ahead of her and waited. When she came alongside, he said, "Good morning. I'm going your way."

It wasn't exactly a warm invitation. She thought she would have another two miles to mentally prepare herself to spend the day with him. That hadn't happened. She tried to find an excuse, but none came to her. Oh, well, she could hardly refuse a lift this morning without appearing rude.

"Danki." She climbed into the passenger's side, and he set the horse in motion. She wished she had taken more time with her appearance that morning. She had picked her oldest work dress, determined not to think about what Roman Weaver thought of her. Now, she was sorry she hadn't chosen a newer dress. She felt dowdy and small next to him.

The silence stretched uncomfortably as the horse clipped along at a good pace. The steady hoofbeats and jingling harness supplied the only sounds. Joann racked her mind for something to say. She wasn't much good at small talk, especially with men. Finally, she said, "It's a nice morning."

"Ja."

She waited, but he didn't say anything else. Apparently, he wasn't one for small talk, either. As he concentrated on his driving, Joann had a chance to study him.

He seemed more at ease today, although he glanced frequently in the rearview mirror that was mounted on his side of the buggy. He held the reins in one hand. He hadn't looped them over his neck as he had the first time she'd ridden with him. He was dressed as usual in dark pants with black suspenders over a short-sleeved pale blue shirt. It looked new. She couldn't help noticing that he had missed two buttons in the middle of his chest.

She didn't realize she had been staring until he said, "What?"

She jumped and looked straight ahead. "Nothing."

He glanced down and gave a low growl of annoyance. "I was trying to hurry."

He attempted to do up the buttons and hold the reins, but the horse veered to the left into the oncoming lane. He quickly guided the mare back to the proper side of the road.

Joann held out her hand. "I'll drive for you."

He hesitated, then finally handed over the lines. From the corner of her eye, she watched as he struggled with the buttons for several long seconds without success. Another low growl rumbled in his throat. "I'm as helpless as a toddling *kind.*"

Roman didn't remind her of a child. Just the opposite. To her, he seemed powerful and sure of himself in spite of his injury. She'd never been more aware of being a woman. He gave up fumbling with his shirt with a sigh of exasperation.

She said, "Let me get them for you."

He took the reins from her and raised his chin as he half-turned toward her. Joann felt the heat in her face and knew she was blushing bright red. This was the kind of thing a wife did for a husband, not a casual acquaintance. Her fingers fumbled with the buttons much longer than she would've liked. When she had them closed at last, she jerked her hands away from his broad chest. "Got it," she said breathlessly.

"Danki." His gruff reply held little gratitude.

"You're welcome. Have your mother cut open the

buttonholes a little more. It will make it easier to get the buttons through them."

"I don't need my mother to do it for me."

It was impossible for her to say the right thing to him. They rode the rest of the way in silence. Joann thought the ride would never end.

The awkwardness between them persisted throughout the morning. Joann tried to show him how to use the saddle binder but quickly realized it took two hands to position the pages and then remove them even though the actual staples were driven in by pressing a lever with her foot.

She pulled the pamphlet off the machine. "I'm sure Gerald can do any of the binding work that's needed."

Roman said, "I'll find a way to make it work."

"Of course." Determined to get past the awkward moment, she said, "Over here we have the Addressograph and our address files. One set of cards is for the newspaper, the other is for our magazine."

"This looks like something a one-handed fellow can manage," he drawled.

Thankfully, she heard the jingle of the bell over the front door and went out to greet their customer. A middle-aged man in a fancy *Englisch* suit stood waiting at the counter with a briefcase in his hand. His black hair was swept back from his forehead. He wore a heavy gold ring on one hand.

"Good morning. How can we be of service?" she asked. He wasn't someone she recognized.

"I was told that Roman Weaver works here. I'd like a few words with him."

The man's serious tone sent a prickle of fear down her spine. "He's in the back. I'll get him."

She turned around, but Roman had followed her and was standing a few feet away. "I am Roman Weaver," he said.

"Good morning, sir. Your father told me that I might find you here. I'm Robert Nelson. I'm an attorney. I represent Brendan Smith. Is there somewhere we can talk privately?"

Otis had taken a carton of books to the bookstore next door. "We may use my uncle's office if this won't take long," Roman said.

"Not long at all," the *Englischer* assured him.

Joann had trouble stifling her curiosity as the two men went into the empty office.

Chapter 7

Roman closed the door and turned to face the attorney representing the man responsible for the accident that had altered his life forever. He didn't invite him to sit down.

Mr. Nelson opened his briefcase on top of the desk. "As I'm sure you are aware, the trial for my client is under way. The jury has heard closing arguments, and we expect a verdict tomorrow or the next day."

"Your *Englisch* law is of no consequence to me. I follow God's laws."

"Yes, that's very admirable. I've heard the Amish offer forgiveness to those who have wronged them. Is that true?"

"I have forgiven Brendan Smith. I have already told your partner this."

The junior attorney had come to Roman's hospital room with a letter from Mr. Smith's insurance company.

They offered money to pay Roman's hospital bill and repair his carriage. Roman rejected their offer.

"Yes, I was informed of the conversation. As you were told then, if you change your mind, the insurance company is still willing to make a settlement."

"That is not our way. It would not be right to profit from this misfortune. It was God's will."

Mr. Nelson smiled. "If everyone felt the same way, attorneys such as myself would soon be out of business."

"I am not responsible for how other people feel. Have you come to discuss something else? If not, I must get back to work."

"Actually, I have come for a different reason. It is possible the jury will find my client guilty of vehicular assault. If they do, it will mean jail time for Brendan. As you know, he has had several run-ins with the law, minor things."

"He deliberately destroyed Amish property. He and several of his friends beat an Amish man for no reason."

"Bad judgment, bad company and too much alcohol. He has paid for those crimes according to the law. Hitting your buggy was nothing but an accident. Pure and simple."

Roman wasn't so sure. He remained silent.

"My client also has a family. He has a wife and a small child. He has parents and a younger brother who depend on him. If the judge gives him the maximum allowable sentence, it will be a hardship for more than Brendan."

"I am sorry for his family. I will pray for them."

"I was hoping that you could do more than that. We, Brendan and I, would like to ask you to come to the sentencing hearing if he is found guilty. We're hoping for an acquittal, of course."

"I have no wish to become involved with your *Englisch* court."

"I can understand that, but if you come and speak on Brendan's behalf, ask for leniency for him, the judge might be persuaded to hand down a lighter sentence."

Roman remained silent as anger boiled inside him. He saw no reason to beg for mercy when Brendan had shown no remorse.

The attorney rushed on. "The Amish are well-known for their generous and forgiving nature. I'm asking you, I'm begging you, to speak on this young man's behalf. Enough grief has already been caused by what was a terrible accident. We'll be happy to reimburse you for any expenses involved. We realize you would have to hire a driver to take you to Millersburg, take time off from work, that sort of thing."

This man had no idea of the damage that had been done to Roman's life, yet he stood there offering to pay for his help. To buy forgiveness. In the *Englisch* world, money solved everything, but it couldn't give Roman back a useful arm.

"Is he sorry for the pain he caused? I have not heard him say so."

"I'm sure he is sorry, but we entered a plea of not guilty. You must shoulder some of the blame for the accident. You were parked in a poorly lit location. You didn't have hazard lights out."

Bitterness swelled up inside Roman. He barely managed to keep his voice level. "I have said I have no wish to become involved with your *Englisch* court."

He turned around, jerked open the door and left the room.

* * *

Joann watched as Roman stormed out the front door. A few moments later, Mr. Nelson came out of the office. He stopped at the counter, opened his briefcase and held out a card. "Tell Mr. Weaver if he changes his mind he can contact me at the phone number on the back of this. It's my cell phone. He can reach me day or night."

Joann took the card. "I'll give him the message."

"I thought you Amish were a forgiving people. That's the way you're portrayed on television."

She didn't care for his snide tone. "We are commanded to forgive others as we have been forgiven."

"You might want to remind Mr. Weaver of that." Mr. Nelson snapped his briefcase closed and left.

Roman returned fifteen minutes later. He didn't say anything when she handed him the card. He simply tore it in two and threw it into the trash.

For Joann, the rest of the week passed with agonizing slowness. She constantly managed to irritate Roman while he seemed to delight in irritating her. It got to the point that even Gerald and Leonard noticed the friction.

Gerald approached her when Roman had gone out with his uncle to purchase supplies they were running low on. He stood in front of her as she sat at the front counter. "Joann, what's going on?"

"What do you mean?" She continued working.

"I've never known you to be so on edge. What's going on between you and Roman?"

"For some reason we rub each other the wrong way. I'll make more of an effort to be nice."

Leonard came in wiping his stained hands on an equally stained rag. He scowled at her. "Joann, my wife told me this morning that you're going back to the book-store."

"I am."

"Why?" the two men asked at the same time.

Sighing, she propped her hands on the countertop. "Because that's the way Otis wants it."

Gerald crossed his arms over his chest. "We thought Roman was here as added help, not to replace you."

Leonard grunted his annoyance. "He doesn't know enough to replace her. Although, he does know the generator inside and out."

She said, "He will learn what he needs to know. We just have to give him time. Please don't tell him that he's taken my job or hold it against him. I was here on a temporary basis, and now I'm going back to my old job."

"It ain't right," Leonard grumbled as he turned away.

Gerald gave her a sympathetic half-smile. "Well, that explains a lot. I know you like what you've been doing here. It's got to be hard giving it up."

"It is, but all good things must come to an end, right?"

"So they say." Gerald went back to his typesetting table.

Joann waited for Roman to return, determined to be kinder and more helpful. If only he didn't insist on calling her teacher in that snide way.

No matter what had been said between them, each evening when she went out the door, Roman was waiting in his buggy to drive her home. Each morning, he was waiting at the end of her lane to give her a lift into town. When Friday evening rolled around, he was there as usual. She was delighted to have a real excuse not to ride with him.

"I'm staying in town this evening. I'm having supper with Sarah and Levi Beachy."

Was that a look of disappointment in his eyes? It was gone before she could be sure. He said, "I reckon I will see you on Monday, then."

"Actually, I'm driving my cart in on Monday so you won't have to pick me up."

"I see."

He nodded toward her and then drove away, leaving Joann feeling oddly bereft. She watched until his buggy rounded a bend in the road and vanished from sight.

At Sarah's home, Joann found her friend tending her garden. Long rows of green sprouts promised a bountiful harvest in the fall. Sarah was busy making sure the occasional weed that dared to sprout didn't stand a chance of growing to maturity.

"Why don't you put the boys to work doing that?" Joann called from the fence.

Sarah looked up from her work and leaned on her hoe. "Because I want my garden to flourish and not be chopped to pieces."

"Are you saying the twins can't tell a tomato plant from a dandelion?"

"I'm sure they can but it's safer if I do this myself. I'm so glad you could come for supper. Sally and Leah are coming, too."

"Wonderful." The women had all become close friends after Sarah's aborted attempt at playing matchmaker for Levi. The whole thing had been the brainchild of Grace, his sister. In spite of all the women Sarah had put in his path, he only had eyes for her.

Sarah chopped one last weed and then walked toward Joann. "How are you and Roman getting along?"

Joann sighed and shook her head. "Like oil and water. Like cats and dogs. Like salt and ice."

Sarah grinned. "In other words, just fine."

"Please, can we talk about something else?"

Sarah's grin faded. "Is it really that bad?"

"Every time I open my mouth, I manage to say something stupid."

"I always thought you would make a nice couple." Sarah carried her tools to a small shed at the side of the barn and hung them up.

Joann was sure she hadn't heard correctly. "You thought Roman and I would make a good couple? We barely knew each other. Why would you think that?"

From behind them a man's voice said, "It's just a feeling she gets. She can't explain it. It comes over her like a mist. She sees two people groping their way toward each other."

Sarah turned around and fisted her hands on her hips. "Do not make fun of my matchmaking skills, Levi Beachy. I found a wife for you, didn't I?"

He moved to stand close beside her. "If I remember right, I'm the one who found a husband for you," he said softly.

Joann chuckled. "If you two are gonna start kissing, I'm going to leave. However, I would like to point out that I knew before you did, Sarah, that Levi was in love with you. And I told you that, didn't I?"

Levi slipped his arms around his wife. "I remember all the effort she put into convincing me that she loved fishing. It was a ploy to get you and me together on a fishing trip, Joann. She hates fishing."

Sarah cupped his cheek with one hand. "I don't mind fishing. As long as I don't have to touch them, clean them or take them off the hook. If you wanted a fishing buddy instead of a wife you should've asked Joann to marry you."

Levi looked at Joann. "If I had only known, I would've given you much more serious consideration."

Joann giggled. "I'm afraid Sarah is the only one brave enough to take on you and the twins. I wouldn't have the heart for it."

"Speaking of the twins," Levi said as he looked around, "where are they?"

"They went to a singing party at David and Martha Nissley's place." She whispered to Joann, "The Miller twins are going to be there."

Levi scowled. "Those girls are too young to be going out."

Sarah patted his arm. "They're old enough to catch our boys' attention. Get used to it, Levi. Once Grace is married, the boys will soon follow suit."

"Hey, that will leave us all alone, my love. Nice."

"Until the babies start arriving," Joann added with a chuckle.

Sarah took Levi's hand and began walking toward the house. "We should go in. I'm sure Grace has supper about ready."

He stopped in his tracks. "Grace is cooking supper?"

Sarah blew a strand of blond hair off her face. *"Ja."*

He turned to Joann. "If we hurry, we can beat the crowd to the Shoofly Pie Café."

Sarah yanked him toward the house. "Stop it. Grace's cooking has gotten much better."

He gave her a quick peck on the cheek. "She'll never make a peach pie better than yours, *liebchen.* Remem-

ber that, Joann. The way to a man's heart is through his
stomach. Good looks fade, good cooking never does."

Joann followed her friends to the house. Finding a
way to a man's heart wasn't an issue for her. Her looks
were nothing special, so it wouldn't matter if they faded.
Her last thought before she stepped into the house was
to wonder what type of pie Roman liked best.

It wasn't until early Saturday morning that Joann had
a chance to get away and go fishing again. She packed
a couple of pieces of cold fried chicken left over from
lunch, a few carrots and an apple along with a pint jar
filled with lemonade into her quilted bag. She left a note
for her brother and his family telling them she wouldn't
be home for the noon meal. When she arrived at the hollow log, she wasn't surprised, but she was disappointed
when there was no message waiting for her.

She left her pole in its hiding place. She didn't really feel like fishing. She just needed to be by herself.
The day had been warm, so she slipped off her shoes,
gathered up her skirt and waded knee-deep into the
cold water.

The muck and moss squished between her toes.
When she stood still, she could see tiny minnows swimming around her feet, eager to investigate the new in-
truder in their watery domain. She looked over the calm
surface of the lake and blew out a deep breath. It was
such a good place. She always felt happy when she was
here.

A splash off to the left made her look that way. She
didn't see the fish, but something white caught her attention. She waded toward a stand of cattails. Nestled
among the reeds at the edge of the water was a plastic
bag. She picked it up and recognized her letter tucked

inside. With growing excitement, she opened the bag and pulled out her note. On the back, she saw her unknown friend had written another letter. Quickly, she waded back to shore and sat down to read it.

Dear Happy Angler,
I'm glad the pole has been returned to its rightful owner. Strange how things work out sometimes. You don't owe me any thanks, but I appreciate the lure. I caught two nice four-pounders with it in the spot you suggested. Your gift brought me much more than a pair of fish. It brought me closer to someone I care about. Thank you for that. Like you, little seems to be going right in my life. I won't bore you with the details. I will say that something about this peaceful spot makes my troubles seem smaller. Perhaps it's only that I've gained some perspective while enjoying the quiet stillness of this lake. It's a good place to sit and refresh my soul. I hope it has refreshed yours. The sunset tonight leaves me in awe of the beauty God creates for us. It is a reminder for me that He is in charge and I am not. Sometimes, it is hard to accept that.
    Have you caught anything good lately?
A Friendly Fisherman

Joann hugged the letter to her chest. How strange and yet how wonderful that this person had found the lake was a place to soothe away the problems of life. What problems did her unknown friend face? She wished she knew. She wished she could help.
Joann smoothed the letter on her lap as she consid-

ered what to do next. Her first impulse was to write a note to the Friendly Fisherman, but was that wise? Was she really going to start a correspondence with someone she knew nothing about? Her innate good sense said it would be foolish.

Yet something in the letter she held called to her. Someone else faced troubles and was still able to appreciate the beauty of the natural world.

She read the letter again. There was nothing to tell her if the author was Amish or *Englisch,* single or married. She strongly suspected it was a man. He'd signed it the Friendly Fisherman, not Fisherwoman. Joann had encountered few of her gender who enjoyed fishing as much as she did. And there was the rub.

The unknown writer probably assumed she was a man, too.

What would he think if he learned she was an Amish maiden? Would he laugh at the thought that she spent her free time making fishing lures and studying the lakes and ponds around Hope Springs? Would he even reply to her note if he knew the truth?

She wrestled with her conscience. It was wonderful to find someone who saw this place the way she saw it: as a God-given gift that refreshed her soul.

On the other hand, exchanging letters with a stranger would be frowned upon by her family. If he were *Englisch,* her brothers might forbid it outright. Joann realized she had started down a slippery slope. First, by hiding the pole her brother had tossed in the lake. Now, she was considering a secret correspondence, as well. The thought of doing something forbidden was romantic and exciting. When would something exciting come into her life again? Quite likely, never.

She read the letter for a third time. This fisherman, whoever he was, wasn't eager to be known. Otherwise, he would've signed his true name. He might be someone she knew who was troubled. Didn't she have an obligation to help in her own small way?

The smart thing to do would be to toss the note away and not write another one.

Joann, who had long accepted that she was a smart woman, chose the unwise course. She pulled out her journal and wrote another letter.

When she was finished, she read it over. Nothing hinted that she was a female. She'd taken pains to make her writing dark and bold. Nothing hinted that she was Amish, either, only that she had faith in the healing power of God's love. She hoped it would find its way into the Friendly Fisherman's possession and cheer him.

With that in mind, she drank the rest of her lemonade, then rinsed and dried the jar with a corner of her apron. She tore the page out of her journal, put the letter inside the jar and screwed on the lid. The log had a knothole in its side where a branch had broken off the tree long ago. The jar fit perfectly inside the cavity.

Would the Friendly Fisherman find it? It wasn't apparent to the casual observer and that was the way she wanted it. She gathered a handful of small pebbles from the shore and laid them on the ground in the shape of an arrow pointing to the knothole. It was a subtle clue, but if the other fisherman was looking for a reply, he would see it.

Joann ate the remains of her lunch and enjoyed a pleasant few hours watching a family of ducks paddle and dunk for food in the lake. Glancing at her note's hiding place one last time, she realized she couldn't do it. She couldn't continue the correspondence unless she was completely truthful. She didn't have to add her name, but her unknown friend deserved to know he was writing to a single, Amish woman. If he was a married man, his wife might take a dim view of their perfectly innocent letters. She took out her note and added a postscript. Then, she started for home with a new and profound sense of excitement bubbling through her. She'd come as often as she could to check her make-shift mailbox.

Perhaps she might even meet her Friendly Fisherman.

Chapter 8

"What's the lesson for today, teacher?"

Joann kept her temper in check by praying for patience. It was finally Wednesday morning. Only two more days of his constant company. She could hardly wait.

Roman leaned on the counter in front of her with that annoying grin on his face. He knew she hated it when he called her teacher in that mocking tone. Oh yes, he knew, and he made a point of calling her that every day since he'd started.

"What's the matter, teacher? Has the cat got your tongue?"

She was determined to be pleasant in spite of his taunts. "We're going to the Walnut Valley school board meeting."

Walnut Valley was one of several Amish schools that dotted the county. Leah Belier was the teacher there.

The school stood a few miles west of Hope Springs, on Pleasant View Road.

He grinned. "So my teacher is taking me to school."

"*Ja.* Be careful, or you'll learn something," she snapped as she walked out the door. He followed close behind her.

She had driven her pony and cart to work that day, so she wouldn't waste as much time getting to and from the school. She unhitched Barney and climbed into the cart. Roman climbed in beside her and reached for the reins. "I'll drive."

"I'm quite capable of driving my own cart to Walnut Valley without any assistance from you."

His hand closed over her wrist in a firm grip. "No point in taking two vehicles. I may only have the use of one arm, but I can handle a pony cart. I drive or we sit here all day."

"Okay." She quickly relinquished her hold and tried to rub away the tingling sensation his touch caused.

He frowned at her. "Did I hurt you?"

"*Nee,* I'm fine." She folded her arms tightly across her chest and scooted to the far edge of the seat. She'd never admit his touch did funny things to her insides. It wasn't that she liked him. It had to be something else.

Roman glanced at the woman seated beside him. She looked as jumpy as a cricket in a henhouse. Why was she so nervous? Surely, she wasn't afraid to be alone with him. Her tongue was sharp enough to fend off any man.

She noticed his gaze. "It would be nice if we weren't late," she said tartly.

No, she wasn't afraid. He backed the tawny-brown

pony into the street and sent him trotting down the road. After traveling in silence for a mile, he asked, "What kind of things will you report from this meeting and others like it?"

She began to relax. "Not me. You'll be writing up this report. Did you get a notebook as I suggested? If not, I have one you can use."

"I brought a notebook and two pens, teacher. I'm prepared."

She bristled. "Basically, you should take note of things that are important to the community. People want to know if the school has enough funds for the coming year. They want to know who the new school board officials are and if there are any needs among the children."

"What kind of needs?"

"Well, last year one of the children starting in the first grade was in a wheelchair. The school needed to install ramps and make all areas of the school wheelchair accessible. Your uncle ran the story in his paper and a large number of people, including your father, showed up to help remodel the building."

"I remember the day. He took a load of wood with him to donate."

"Were you there?" she asked.

"I stayed to work in the sawmill, but my mother and brother went to help."

She fell silent for a while. He concentrated on driving. "I haven't asked what your father thinks of you working for Otis," she said.

"My father looks forward to the day I can return and work with him."

"So you see this job as a temporary one. I get it now."

"You get what?"

"Why you don't seem interested in learning the business."

"Maybe I don't seem interested because I don't have a good teacher."

That silenced her. She clamped her lips closed and looked off to her side of the road. He regretted the harsh remark almost instantly, but before he could apologize, a red sports car whizzed past as they were cresting a hill. It narrowly missed an oncoming car and had to swerve back quickly in front of them. Roman closed his eyes.

He heard the crack of splintering wood a split second before the truck hit him. He heard squealing tires as he flew through the air. He landed with a sickening impact and tumbled along the asphalt. There was blood in his mouth. He couldn't get up.

"Roman, watch out!"

He opened his eyes to see the pony had swerved dangerously close to the edge of the deep ditch. He managed to bring the animal back into the roadway without upsetting them. As soon as he could, he pulled to a stop.

He drew a ragged breath. "I'm sorry."

Joann didn't make the snide remark he expected. "Are you all right?" she asked quietly instead.

It was too late to disguise how shaken he was. He wiped the cold sweat from his face with his sleeve. "I think so."

She took a deep breath and sat back. "Take your time. We can go when you're ready."

"I thought you didn't want to be late."

She didn't reply. He couldn't bring himself to look at her. He didn't want to see pity in her eyes. "I expect you'll insist on driving now."

"There's nothing wrong with your driving. Barney can get skittish when traffic is heavy."

The placid pony was standing with his head down and one hip cocked. He could have been asleep on his feet except his tail swished from side to side occasionally.

Roman had to smile. "I think you're maligning your horse's character to make me feel better."

"Do you feel better?" she asked softly.

"I'm getting there." His pounding pulse was settling to a normal rate.

"Then Barney is glad he could help. Does it happen often?"

Did he really want to talk about it? Something in her quiet acceptance of the situation made it possible. "*Nee,* and I'm thankful for that. The doctor calls them flashbacks. It feels as if I'm caught in the accident all over again."

"I never knew exactly what happened. Would it help to talk about it, or would that make it worse?"

"I don't know. I've never talked about it before."

"Maybe you should. It happened at night, didn't it?"

"It was dusk, but not full dark."

"Were you going someplace special?"

"I was coming home from seeing Esta." He clicked his tongue to get Barney moving.

"So you were alone when it happened."

"*Ja.*"

"I imagine you were thankful she wasn't with you."

"It wasn't a pretty sight, that's for sure." He stopped talking as he thought back to that evening. Some of it was a blur. Some of it was painfully clear.

"My horse had started limping. I thought that maybe

he'd picked up a stone in his shoe. I pulled over to the side of the road and got out. It was a cold and windy winter evening. I left the door open. I don't know why I did that."

"Maybe to block the wind off you while you checked the horse."

"Maybe. I don't remember. The man said he didn't see me. He went around thinking he had left enough room. Only, he hit the door and then me. It happened so fast. One second I'm standing by the side of the road and the next second I'm lying face down, and I can't get up."

"It must have been terrible."

"I could taste blood in my mouth but couldn't get any air into my lungs. I thought I was dying. We're supposed to think about God when we're dying. I didn't. I just wanted to get up and take a breath." He was ashamed of that. It was a betrayal of his faith. Why had he told her that?

She was quiet for a time, then she said, "You may not have been thinking about God, but He was thinking about you. We really are His children, you know. Children sometimes get frightened. That doesn't make them bad children. Our Father understands that."

She had managed to hit the nail on the head. He had been terrified of dying. The fear still lingered.

The sound of a siren startled them both. They turned to look behind them. The sheriff's cruiser, with red lights flashing, swept past them. He turned off the roadway a quarter of a mile ahead of them.

Joann stood to get a better look. "I think he's going to the school. I wonder what's wrong."

"Sit down and I'll get us there a little faster." He slapped the reins against the pony's rump. Barney responded with a burst of speed. Within a few minutes, they were turning into the schoolyard. A dozen buggies were already there. Men were clustered in a group at the side of the building. Some of the women and children were weeping openly. The smell of smoke lingered in the air from a charred hole in the side of the schoolhouse.

Joann looked frantically for Leah and was relieved to see her being comforted by Nettie Imhoff and Katie Sutter. Sheriff Nick Bradley stood talking to them, a notebook in his hand. Joann jumped down from the cart and raced toward them. "What has happened?"

Leah looked up. Her eyes were red and there were streaks of tears on her face. "Someone tried to burn down the school."

"Who would do such a thing?" Joann was shocked.

"We don't know, but we must pray for them, whoever they are," Nettie said. Everyone nodded in agreement.

"Tell me exactly what you saw when you arrived, Leah," the sheriff said.

She wiped her face on her sleeve, and then stretched her arm toward the building. "I came early to get ready for the school board meeting, and I found it like this. Someone had piled the school's books and papers against the building and set it on fire. All the children's artwork, all my grade books and papers, all gone." She broke down and started crying again.

Nettie enfolded her in a hug. "God was merciful. The rain last night must have put out the fire before the whole building went up."

"Have you noticed anything suspicious in the last few days or weeks?" Sheriff Bradley asked.

Leah shook her head. "Why would they burn our children's books?"

"I don't have anything but speculation at this point. Maybe it was a group of kids horsing around and things got out of hand. Maybe it was something more sinister. Not everyone loves the Amish." Nick Bradley had family members who were Amish. He understood the prejudices they sometimes faced.

"You think this was a hate crime?" Joann asked in disbelief.

"It's my job to find out." He walked to where the men were gathered at the front of the building.

Leah gave a shaky laugh. "I've been complaining that we need new schoolbooks. I hope no one thinks this was my way of getting them."

Joann managed a smile. "No one would possibly think that."

"At least we'll have time to get the damage repaired before school starts again in the fall."

Roman, along with Nettie's husband Eli Imhoff, the new school board president for the coming year, joined the women. "This is not how I expected to start my term," Eli said. "Do not worry, Leah. We'll have our school back together in no time. Roman, please tell Otis I'll be in to see him about ordering new textbooks."

Roman glanced back to where Sheriff Bradley was speaking to the men. "I'm surprised to see the sheriff involved in this."

"None of us sent for him," Leah said.

Eli stroked the whiskers on his chin. "I wonder how he knew about it."

The Amish rarely involved outsiders in their troubles. What happened in the community normally stayed in the community. Their ancestors had learned through years of persecution to be distrustful of outsiders. It was a lesson that had not been forgotten. "I'll see what I can find out," Joann said.

The sheriff had left the men and moved to examine the charred side of the school. He squatted on his heels and used his pen to move aside the remains of partially burned book covers and bindings. He lifted an aluminum can out of the ashes. Joann stopped beside him and withdrew her pen and notebook from her pocket. She flipped it open. "Sheriff, have there been other attacks on Amish property?"

The moment she asked the question, she remembered the letter they had received from an Amish farmer whose hay crop had been burned.

The sheriff stood and pushed his trooper's hat back with one finger. "Nothing that I've heard about."

He glanced toward the group of men clustered at the far end of the school where Bishop Zook had just arrived. "You're more likely than I am to hear about something like this. The Amish don't usually call in the law. Makes my job harder sometimes, but I accept that your ways are your own."

"We appreciate that, Sheriff." Should she mention the letter? Like many of the notes they received, it hadn't included a name or return address.

"Could you run a reminder in the paper that people should report anything suspicious to the law? It's part of being a good neighbor to watch out for each other."

Perhaps the man would read the notice and contact the sheriff himself and she needn't say anything about it. "I'm sure Otis will agree to that. How did you know about today's incident?"

"I received an anonymous tip. It was a woman's voice. She said to hurry or someone was going to get hurt out here." He placed the can in a plastic bag.

"That sounds like a threat." She glanced around, reassured by the presence of only her Amish friends and their families.

"I thought so, too. I took it seriously."

Roman came to stand beside Joann. "Sheriff, the men want to know if they can start cleaning up."

"Tell them I need them to hold off until I have my crime scene people out to look this over. They should be finished by the end of the day. Have there been any problems in your local church group? Any disagreement between members?"

Joann spoke up quickly. "Our brethren would not do this no matter what kind of disagreements they were having."

Nick shrugged. "People are people. I won't rule out anyone. How are you doing, Roman?"

"Goot."

"Is the arm better?"

Roman looked at his sling. "Not much."

"I'm sorry to hear that. The jury found Brendan Smith guilty of vehicular assault yesterday. His attorney told me that he asked you to speak at the sentencing next month, but you declined."

A cold look came over Roman's face. His voice shook as he spoke. "I have forgiven him. It is your law that seeks to punish him. His fate is in God's hands."

Joann had never seen Roman so angry. "Who is Brendan Smith?"

"He's the young man who struck Roman with his pickup. His attorney was hoping that Roman would speak on Brendan's behalf, talk about Amish forgiveness and all that. He was hoping it might persuade the judge to go easy on Smith. He's facing jail time."

The sheriff rubbed a hand over his jaw as he looked at the scorched building. "Quite a coincidence that we have a fire at an Amish school the next night, isn't it?"

Joann glanced from Roman to the sheriff. "What are you saying?"

"That I'm not a big believer in coincidences." He touched the brim of his hat. "Take care, Roman, Miss Yoder. I'll be in touch."

As the sheriff walked away, Joann turned to Roman. "Why would you refuse such a request?"

"I don't want to talk about it." He stalked off, leaving her wondering just how much hurt and anger he still carried inside. Forgiveness was the only way to heal such sorrow.

Roman couldn't help wondering if this was somehow his fault. Was it retaliation by the friends of Brendan Smith? If he had agreed to speak on Brendan's behalf, would the school have been spared? He was deeply troubled by the idea.

As the sheriff marked off the school with yellow tape, Eli Imhoff stood on the back of his wagon to address the crowd. Bishop Zook stood at his side along with several men who were also members of the school board. Eli said, "We will hold our meeting here. It will not take long."

The people moved to gather around them. The Bishop spoke first. "Let us give thanks to our heavenly Father that no one was injured, and let us pray for those who tried to carry out this grievous deed. May God show them mercy and the error of their ways. Amen."

The crowd, standing with their heads bowed, muttered, "Amen."

"The first order of business is to clean up the building and assess what needs to be torn down and what can be repaired," Eli said. "The sheriff will let us know how soon we can do that. Once we know what needs to be done to make the school safe, we will set a date to start rebuilding."

"We can put an announcement in the paper," Joann said. "We will need it by Thursday morning in order to make Friday's edition."

Bishop Zook nodded. "That can be done. I will send notices to our neighboring churches so that they may make a plea for donations at this coming Sunday's preaching. Please spread the word about our need. And do not worry, Leah, the school will be as good as new come the first day of class in the fall."

Eli looked at Roman. "Please tell your uncle that I will be in to see him as soon as we know what books must be replaced."

They went on to discuss other issues. Roman took careful notes. This was a story everyone needed to know about.

On the drive home, Joann sat quietly beside him. Roman wasn't up to making small talk or teasing her. She seemed to feel the same way. About a half-mile out of town, she finally spoke. "Did you tell the sheriff about the letter we received?"

The fact that there had been two fires on Amish property had struck him as odd, too. "*Nee,* did you?"

"I was afraid to, but now I wonder if I was wrong."

"What's done is done. The school will be repaired."

"I know, but what if this happens again and we could have prevented it?"

"Romans 12:19, Dearly beloved, avenge not yourselves, but rather give place unto wrath: for it is written, Vengeance is mine; I will repay, saith the Lord."

"You're right. We must leave it in God's hands." She didn't say anything else, but he could see she was troubled.

Back at the office, he told Otis what had happened. Otis shook his head sadly. "We shall do what we can for the school. I would like to see your notes when you're finished with them. I will want to add something about this to our magazine this month."

Roman struggled through the afternoon to type up his notes for Otis to review. Typing with one hand was a laborious process that he was sure he would never master. Across the room, Joann made quick work of her notes and handed them to Otis before Roman had finished a single page.

She came and stood in front of Roman's desk. She reached for his notebook. "I can help."

He slapped his hand down on it to prevent her taking it.

Annoyance flashed across her face. "I was only offering to type your notes for you."

"I can do my own work."

"I can do it faster."

Like he needed to be reminded of that. "I must learn to do it myself. You won't always be around to help."

"That's for certain," she said cryptically. She left and went back to work at her desk. When it was time to leave, Roman was glad she had her cart to drive. He wasn't up for company.

He learned when he arrived home that evening that news of the fire had preceded him. When he entered his father's house, he found his father and brother seated at the kitchen table. Faron Martin sat with them.

Roman's mother stood by the sink dabbing the corner of her eye with her apron. "Who would do this terrible thing?"

"Only God knows," his father said with a sad shake of his head.

Andrew looked at Roman. "Is it true the sheriff questioned you?"

"He spoke to everyone who was there."

"Nick Bradley is a good man. He will get to the bottom of this," Marie Rose declared.

Roman poured himself a cup of coffee and took a seat at the table. "*Daed,* do you know of a fellow on Bent Tree Road that had his haystacks burned recently?"

"I heard something about it from Rueben Beachy just yesterday. Why?"

"Did the fella know who started the fire?"

Menlo shook his head. "If he did, he didn't mention it."

"It seems like an odd coincidence, don't you think?"

"*Ja,* it does. Andrew, Faron, I reckon we can get a few more board cuts before supper." Menlo set his coffee cup in the sink, put on his hat and walked out the door. Andrew followed him.

Faron said, "Roman, could I speak to you outside?"

"Sure." Now what? Was this about Esta? Roman took a last sip of his coffee and got to his feet even though this was a conversation he was sure he didn't want to have.

When the two men were out of earshot of the house,

Faron said, "I reckon you should know that I've been stepping out with Esta."

So Joann had been telling the truth. "I heard something like that."

"I didn't mean to go behind your back while you were laid up. Esta said there's nothing serious between you. If that isn't the case, you should tell me now and I'll stop seeing her."

Roman was surprised by how little it hurt to know Esta didn't see him as a serious suitor. He'd been foolish to think she would find a one-armed man a good catch. "*Danki,* Faron, I reckon Esta is the one to decide that."

"All right then. Just wanted to set that straight. Didn't want any bad blood between us, what with my working for your dad and all." He held out his hand.

Roman shook it. "How's the job going?"

"It's the best work I could have asked for. Your father is a good teacher and a patient man, but I don't think your brother is very happy that he took me on."

"Andrew will get over it. Give him time."

"I hope that's true. What about you? How do you like working for your uncle?"

"It's not what I expected, but I'm starting to like it." To his amazement, he realized his words were the truth. He was starting to enjoy the job. Reporting and sharing information with the Amish community was important if they were to stay connected and strong in their commitment to care for each other.

As Faron went to finish his work, Roman began walking down the lane thinking about Esta and Faron. Were they meant for each other? If so, who was the woman God had in mind for him? He couldn't think of anyone. Before long, his thoughts turned to Joann and her conflicting feelings about reporting another fire to the sheriff. He shared the same feelings. What was the right thing to do?

It was a fundamental part of his faith to live separate from the world. Yet, like Joann, he remained uncertain in his heart as to what he should do.

He didn't realize until he was at the fence to Woolly Joe's pasture that he had been headed toward the lake. Well, why not? It was a good place to ponder the rights and wrongs of life. Maybe the Happy Angler had written him another note.

Cheered by the thought, he made his way into the woods and down to the small clearing on the shore. To his disappointment, there wasn't a message on the log. He wondered if his last letter had been found. He wanted the Happy Angler to know his gift had been appreciated.

Roman sat down and stared out at the placid lake. High cliffs topped with lush trees made up the north shore. He caught sight of a lone doe walking along the rim briefly before vanishing into the trees. Barn swallows swooped across the surface of the water catching insects and taking drinks while zipping past the surface. Their agility was amazing.

"Little swallows you fly away but return each spring on the very same day."

With a start, he realized he'd just spoken the beginning of a poem. He took out his notebook and balanced it on the log. "Where do you go when you leave this home? What draws you afar, what makes you roam?"

While he was groping for his pen, his notebook fell off the log. The calm peacefulness that the evening brought his soul vanished. Frustration hit him like the kick of a mule. Would he ever learn to manage with just one arm?

Why him? Why had he been crippled? Because some foolish *Englischer* had one too many beers before getting behind the wheel of his truck? Where was the justice in that?

He looked to heaven and shouted, "Why me? What am I to learn from this?" The birds he'd been watching scattered.

He closed his eyes and listened, but only the croaking of frogs and the drone of insects answered him.

God wasn't speaking to him tonight. He'd just have to muddle on. He leaned down to pick up the notebook and noticed a row of pebbles on the ground. They had been laid in the shape of an arrow. It pointed toward the log. He stood and looked over the gray bark. There was a knothole in the side of the log he hadn't noticed before. Something shiny caught his eye.

He reached in and pulled out a glass canning jar. Inside, he saw a folded piece of notebook paper. He smiled, opened the jar and took out the note to read it.

Chapter 9

Dear Friendly Fisherman,
If you are reading this, you have found my make-shift mailbox. The last letter you left had blown into the water. If you hadn't been wise enough to put it in a plastic bag, it would have been gone for-ever. I didn't want to risk losing one of your notes again, so I came up with this idea.

I'm humbled and happy that my small gift has been of value. You won't bore me if you'd like to talk about your troubles. I've been told that troubles shared are troubles halved. Here in this beautiful spot, they do seem less important. I'll share my story with you and hope you feel free to return the favor.

I had plans to buy a house of my own soon. It's been a longtime dream of mine, but recently I lost my job. I can't afford the house now. The new job I accepted doesn't pay as well. To top it off, I have to work with someone I don't much care for. He has made it plain that he doesn't care for me, either.

I'm determined to make the best of it, and I hope I can one day call him a friend. Until that time, I shall come here often to refresh my soul and regain some perspective. If I can't do that, I can sit here and imagine tossing him headfirst into the cold water. What a scare that would give the poor fish.

I shouldn't complain about my circumstances. My troubles are small compared to some. After all, how bad can it be if I have time for fishing? They only seem big because I can't see beyond them.

There, I've unburdened myself to you. I expect your troubles are worse than mine and you're laughing at me. Actually, I do feel better for having shared them with you.

The sky is overcast this morning, but I can imagine the colors of the sunset you saw. Were there clouds in the west? Were they fiery gold and rose pink? From this spot, all the colors must have been reflected in the lake. Two sunsets for the price of one. That's a good bargain in anyone's book.

I didn't fish today. The wind was in the north. Another reminder that we are not in charge, God is. I hope the fishing is good for you. You might want to try an orange, bottom-bouncing hopper to tempt a big old walleye that lives in the deep part of the lake. I had him once, but he broke my line.

I must close now, I've run out of paper.
P.S. I must add that I'm a single woman. (I almost

didn't.) I'll understand if you choose not to write again. Please know that I have enjoyed your letters, and thank you again for returning my pole. Your Happy Amish Angler

A woman!

Roman certainly hadn't expected that. A single Amish woman, to boot. Who was she? Did he know her? Was she a grandmother or someone's little sister?

No, the note said she had planned to buy a house. That was an uncommon thing for an Amish maid. Single women past marrying age sometimes lived alone, but most often, they lived with family members the way Joann did. If they desired to live by themselves, their father or other male members of the family would see to it that they were given a suitable dwelling such as a *dawdy-haus* as he lived in. He didn't know of any woman who had purchased her own house. His letter-writing friend was one very unusual woman.

Oddly, it did feel as if she were a friend, as if she were offering kind advice and gently steering him toward a better path. What would she think of him if she knew who he was?

"She would probably think I'm a poor, pitiful excuse for a man," he muttered as a wave of self-pity hit him.

He glanced at the letter again. No, she'd likely toss him headfirst into the lake and tell him to quit feeling sorry for himself.

Roman folded the letter in half and tucked it in the pocket of his shirt. To own a house was a fine dream. It was a shame she had to give it up. It took a good person to make the best of a bad situation and work toward creating friendship where none existed. Roman knew a moment of shame for his treatment of Joann. He hadn't tried to make friends with her. He gained delight in teasing her, in making her snap back at him. It wasn't well done on his part.

Tomorrow, he would turn over a new leaf and be kinder to her. She was only trying to do her job. It wasn't her fault that he was ill-suited to the work and found it so difficult.

Roman considered what he should do. Finally, he brought out his notepad and started a letter of his own. Before he realized it, the note was two pages long, and he felt better for having unburdened himself. The Happy Angler was right. A burden shared was a burden halved.

He sealed the letter inside the jar and returned it to the knothole in the log as the evening light faded. He headed for home determined to do better at the job his uncle had given him and treat everyone there with fairness. Including Joann Yoder.

When he reached the house, he saw his mother weeding in her garden. He opened the gate and joined her. Stooping, he pulled a dandelion that had sprouted among the peas.

His mother paused and leaned on her hoe with a heavy sigh. "*Danki,* Roman. I appreciate the help. I declare, these weeds grow faster every year. I can hardly keep up with them."

"I'll take over the weeding from you this summer. My town job leaves me with extra time on my hands."

"Oh, that's sweet of you, but I enjoy being out here. I like the smell of growing things. I feel closer to God in my garden. It would be a blessing if you could do it once in a while."

"Whenever you want, *Mamm.*"

"Where have you been?" She started hoeing again.

"Over to Woolly Joe's lake."

"Ach, that's a pretty place."

"*Mamm,* do you know any Amish women who like to fish?"

She laughed. "Goodness, I know plenty of women who like to fish. Your grandmother loved to sit on the riverbank with a pole in the water. Sometimes, I think she didn't even put a worm on the hook, she just sat there and enjoyed the day. Why?"

"No reason. I heard a local Amish woman was trying to buy her own house but lost her job. Do you know who it was?"

His mother frowned as she concentrated. "*Nee,* I know of no one like that."

"Then I must have heard wrong." He took the hoe from his mother and set to work.

It seemed that the identity of his pen pal would remain a mystery. Maybe it was for the best this way. He hadn't revealed his name, either.

Joann stepped off her brother's front porch and scowled. She could see the end of the lane from the house. Roman wasn't waiting for her this morning. Now she was going to be late.

She'd grown accustomed to accepting a ride from him. She made a point of telling him when she would drive herself and she hadn't mentioned anything like that yesterday.

She didn't have enough time to walk all the way to town by nine o'clock. She started running. Oh, she could just see Roman standing behind the counter and glancing pointedly at the clock when she finally got there. He'd be happy to tell her she was late. She could hardly point out that it was his fault. Odious man.

She reached the road just as a horse and buggy came into view. She slowed to a walk. Roman pulled up beside her. "Sorry I'm late. I had trouble getting Meg hitched up. My brother normally does it for me, but he was sick in bed with a fever so I had to do it myself."

"That's okay. I hope he feels better soon." She was a little winded as she climbed in beside him.

"Why were you running?"

"I thought you'd decided not to come for me today. I didn't want to be late."

His brow darkened. "I'm sorry you thought I would deliberately make you late for work. That was never my intention."

Joann hugged her book bag to her chest and remained silent as he set off down the road. That was exactly what she had been thinking. Who was the odious one now?

She gathered her courage and said meekly, "I'm sorry for thinking poorly of you. Please forgive me."

"I reckon I've given you some cause."

"Still, I was in the wrong."

A smile twitched at the corner of his mouth. A touch of humor slipped into his voice. "I never expected to hear you say that."

She sat up straighter. "I can admit when I'm wrong. It just doesn't happen very often."

He chuckled, but then cleared his throat. "What's on our agenda for today?"

He hadn't called her "teacher" in that annoying tone. Perhaps her goal of eventual friendship was possible, after all.

"We'll be putting together the magazine. They need

to be finished before five o'clock tomorrow night so we can get them to the post office."

"How many copies do we print?"

"Twelve hundred."

"Are you serious? We don't even have twelve hundred families in Hope Springs."

"The *Family Hour* goes all across the county to Amish and Plain folk and even some *Englisch* subscribers."

"There's still so much I don't know."

"You're doing okay. It takes time to learn it all. On Friday, we'll get out the newspaper as usual."

"That sounds like a lot of work for the week."

"I thought you found our work easy." Oh, why did she have to say that? Just when things were getting better. She could have cheerfully bitten her tongue.

He glanced at her and then laughed. "I have seen it is not as easy as I once thought. When I'm wrong, I say so."

She managed a slight smile. "I don't imagine that happens very often."

"More often than you might think, Joann Yoder. More often than you might think." He grinned at her, and she blushed with delight.

They rode the rest of the way into town in companionable silence. Joann's high hopes for a pleasant day vanished when they turned the corner and saw an ambulance in front of the office with its red lights flashing. Leonard and his wife, Mabel, were standing outside. The front window had been broken.

Joann jumped out of the buggy before it rolled to a stop. "Leonard, what happened?"

"Someone threw a brick through our window. Otis was standing just inside. The brick hit him in the head. He was knocked unconscious."

Leonard's wife Mabel said, "We called an ambulance right away."

Roman rushed past them and into the building. Joann tried to follow him, but Mabel held her back. "There's broken glass and blood everywhere, dear. He's being taken care of. They said we should stay out of the way until the sheriff arrives."

A crowd was gathering around them. Leonard said, "Did anyone see who did this? Did the brick come from a car or from a buggy?"

Everyone shook his or her head. Mabel said, "It was early, businesses aren't open, there weren't many people on the street, but someone must have seen something."

Joann glanced over the crowd. No one stepped forward. The ambulance crew came out of the building with Otis on a stretcher. Roman came right behind them. As they put the stretcher in the back of the ambulance, Roman spoke to Leonard. "Will you drive me to my uncle's house to get his wife and take her to the hospital?" The nearest hospital was more than thirty miles away. Too far for a buggy.

"Of course."

Mabel said, "I'll go and get her. Leonard, you should stay and talk to the sheriff. You were inside when it happened. Roman, would you like to come with me?"

"*Ja,* I would. I should tell my mother what has happened."

Joann spoke up to reassure him. "I will take your buggy and let your mother know where Otis has been taken. Leonard, will you call Samuel Carter, the van driver, and see if he can take her to the hospital as well?"

Leonard pulled a cell phone from his pocket. His hand shook as he tried to dial the number. "I can't believe this. Otis is such a fine man. He wouldn't hurt a flea."

Mabel put her arms around him. "It's going to be all right."

Leonard wiped at his eyes. "He gave me a job when everyone else said I was through. I don't know what I'll do if anything happens to him."

Roman laid a hand on Leonard's shoulder. "We will keep the paper and the magazine running just as he would want."

Leonard looked at him, his eyes bright with unshed tears. "You're right. Just as he would want. I'm sorry now that I wasn't nicer to you."

"We will start anew, you and me."

Gerald came jogging down the street as the ambulance was pulling away. "What's going on?"

Roman said, "My uncle was hurt when someone threw a brick through the window. They're taking him to the hospital now. The sheriff will be here soon. When he is done, I want you to get some plywood to board up the window. Mabel, we should go before my aunt hears about this from someone else."

She kissed her husband on the cheek and hurried toward her car with Roman at her side. Joann and Gerald ventured as far as the doorway and looked in. There was broken glass everywhere. In the center of the mess was a pool of blood. A bloody towel had been discarded on the counter.

"What is happening to our town?" Gerald asked sadly.

Joann understood his sense of loss. First the school and now this. Was it a coincidence that it had happened during Brendan Smith's trial or was something more sinister at work?

Joann said, "I must go and tell Roman's family what has happened. I'll be back as soon as I can."

Gerald shook his head. "Don't hurry. I doubt we'll get any work done today."

"We'll get it all done. We have a magazine to get out and a business to run. That's the best thing we can do for Otis."

"It'll take twice as long without him."

"Then we must work twice as hard."

She made the trip out to Roman's home as quickly as she could. Poor Meg was covered with flecks of sweat and foam by the time they reached the mill.

Marie Rose and Menlo were grateful that she had brought the news and had thought to send for Samuel Carter. It wasn't long before his gray van pulled into the yard. The retired *Englischer* earned extra money as a taxi driver for his Amish friends.

Joann helped Marie Rose bundle together what they might need and saw them off. Andrew and Faron stood beside her as the dust from the vehicle settled. "I'll hitch up another horse for you, Joann. Meg is getting a little old to be making so many trips to town," Andrew said.

He led the mare away and returned a short time later with a piebald pony hitched to a two-wheeled cart. "This is Cricket. He'll get you there and back."

"*Danki,* Andrew. I'll take good care of him. I must let my family and Bishop Zook know what has happened."

"I'll see that the bishop knows," Faron said.

"*Danki,* that will save me many miles of travel," Joann said.

She stopped by her brother's farm. Salome was pushing Louise on the swing in the front yard. They ran to her as she stopped the pony by the front gate.

"Aenti Joann, did you get a new horse?" Louise asked as she petted the animal's nose.

"Nee, Cricket belongs to Andrew Weaver. He only loaned him to me. Where is your father?"

"He and Mama are weeding the corn patch behind the barn."

"Danki." She watched the two girls return to their play. What if it had been one of them injured by a thrown brick? Who might be next? She made up her mind. She would tell the sheriff what she knew. It was little enough, but someone had to try to put a stop to what was happening.

Joan hurried around the barn and met her brother and sister-in-law as they were heading in with their hoes over their shoulders. She quickly explained what had happened. They were both as shocked as she had been.

Hebron found his voice first. "You must stop working at that place."

She couldn't believe she'd heard him right. "Why?"

"It is too worldly for you. To have dealings with the *Englisch* law twice in one week tells me it is best you stay here and help on the farm."

"I'm sorry, Hebron. I gave my word to Otis Miller that I would do a good job for him. I intend to honor my promise. I will be very late tonight. Don't wait supper on me."

She turned on her heels and left them staring after her, though she knew she hadn't heard the last of Hebron's opinions on the subject.

By the time Joann got back to town, the sheriff had gone and Gerald was nailing a large piece of wood over the broken window. He took a pair of nails from his mouth and said, "Leonard's wife just called and said that Otis is in the emergency room at the hospital in

Millersburg. He's still unconscious, but they say his condition is good."

"Praise God for that news. What did the sheriff have to say?"

"He took the brick, but he has little hope of finding who did this unless someone comes forward to say that they saw the crime committed."

"Did he think this was related to the school fire?"

"If he does, he didn't say so." Gerald put the nails back in his mouth and finished hammering the one he had started into the woodwork.

Joann went inside. No one had started cleaning up, so she got a broom and a dustpan and began sweeping up shards of glass. She had most of it cleaned up, when someone came in the front door. Expecting Roman, she turned around quickly to ask about Otis, but it was a young *Englisch* woman. Joann said, "I'm sorry. We're closed for business today."

The woman shoved her hands in the front pockets of her jeans and hunched her shoulders. Her eyes swept around the room and focused on the blood Joann hadn't had a chance to wash off the floor.

"I heard that the old man who runs this place was hurt. Is that true?" the woman asked.

Joann dumped her dustpan full of glass into the trashcan. "*Ja,* they took him to the hospital in Millersburg."

The woman finally looked at her. "Is he going to be okay?"

"We don't know yet, but he is in God's hands, so we do not fear for him. Do you know Otis Miller? I can give his family a message if you want."

She started backing toward the door. "No, that's okay. I don't know him."

She turned around and ran into Roman who was just coming in. Her face turned ashen white. She bolted past Roman and out the door. Joann stepped to the unbroken window and watched her. She got into a red car parked halfway down the block and took off. Joann grabbed a piece of paper and wrote down the license plate number.

Roman came to stand beside her. "Who was that?"

"I don't know, but does that look like the car that almost ran us off the road on the way to school?"

"I didn't get a good look at the car."

She turned to face him. "She wanted to know if the old man who worked here had been hurt. She seemed upset when I told her what I knew. How is Otis?"

"Awake and worried sick that *Family Hour* and the paper won't go out on time. The doctor said they needed to run more tests. They're going to keep him for a few days."

"We can see that the magazine and paper get out on time. There's nothing wrong with the presses. I'm willing to stay late, and I'm sure everyone else is."

"*Danki,* that will mean a lot to my uncle. What did you write down?" He pointed to the notepad in her hand.

"I wrote down the license plate number of that woman's car."

"What do you intend to do with it?"

She gazed at his face trying to judge what his reaction would be if she admitted what she'd been thinking.

"You plan to give it to the sheriff, don't you?"

"I think the woman knew more about today's event than she let on," Joann said.

"Many in our church will tell you it's none of our business. We must forgive the transgressors. My uncle has said this from his hospital bed."

"I do forgive them. I just don't want anyone else to get hurt."

He held out his hand. "Give it to me."

Joann's shoulders slumped in defeat. She reluctantly handed it over without looking at him.

Roman stifled a twinge of pity and took the note from her. He didn't want her getting in to trouble with her family or with the church.

"What are you going to do with it?" Joann challenged Roman with a hard stare.

"That is my business. Forget the number, forget you ever wrote it down." He waited for the outburst he could see brewing behind her eyes.

Instead, she lowered her gaze. "I need to get the rest of this cleaned up."

"Is the sheriff on our mailing list for the *Family Hour* magazine?"

"*Nee,* but he gets our newspaper."

"Then I want the notice from the farmer whose hay was burned put in the magazine and not in the newspaper."

"I'll have Gerald reset the type."

"*Goot.*"

She started to turn away, but Roman caught her by the arm. "I want to thank you for letting my parents know about Otis. He was grateful to have his sister at his side."

"You don't owe me thanks. I would've done the same for anyone."

Her tone had a sting to it. Clearly, she was implying that he wouldn't. He didn't say anything else. It didn't matter what she thought of him. He would do what was best for all of them.

Once the office was cleaned, they set to work finishing the magazine layout and printing the twenty pages both front and back that would be bound into the final project. Joann was everywhere, running proofs, carrying paper, refilling the ink when Leonard hollered that it was low and pausing to speak to the steady stream of people who stopped in to inquire about Otis and offer help. By late afternoon, the hardware store owner was supervising the installation of a new window.

Roman tried his best to keep up with the flow. Otis normally ran the saddle binder, the machine that stapled the magazine pages together. Roman had already spent some time thinking about how he could operate it with one hand.

Joann had shown him how to use the machine on his first day of work. She laid the open pages across the bar with her right hand and pressed the stapler with her foot. The machine moved the papers into the proper position and inserted a pair of wire staples. She then removed the pages with her left hand and laid the finished product in a container, making the task seem almost effortless. It wasn't for him.

He found a leftover length of plywood to make a slide and positioned it against the end of the machine. He had seen that he didn't have to take the papers off the bar. He simply put the next set on the machine and when it moved the work into the proper position, it kicked the previous magazine off the bar, onto the slide and down into the box. He could bind the pages almost as fast as Otis and Joann had done. He was feeling quite pleased with his ingenuity.

Leonard, his arms loaded with boxes of paper, didn't see Roman's invention until he banged his shin on it.

He muttered under his breath as he hobbled to a nearby chair.

He dropped the boxes and rubbed his leg with both hands. "Who put that dumb board in the way? Are you trying to cripple me?"

"*Nee,* one cripple at this company is enough," Roman said.

He added another set of pages to the binder and stomped on the foot pedal with extra force.

Joann came and picked up the boxes Leonard had dropped. "It's a clever idea, Roman, but you should have warned us you put it here. A few words would have spared our friend this pain," she said.

Leonard stood and took the boxes from Joann. Grudgingly, he said, "I'm sorry about the crippled re-mark."

"Forget it. We've got work to do," Roman said, then continued to bind sets as his embarrassment subsided. Joann's gaze clashed with his briefly before she walked away. She was right. He should have warned them, but he knew she was speaking about more than a bruised shin.

The license number was still in his pant pocket. Would turning it over to the law prevent another at-tack? He struggled with his conscience as he tried to decide the right thing to do.

Chapter 10

Was he ever going to speak to her again?

Joann endured the rest of the day without a word from Roman. Mostly, she kept her head down and stayed out of his way. He knew she'd been talking about the license number when she made that comment about warning folks. She'd seen the look of annoyance that flashed across his face.

It seemed that every time she made a little progress with understanding him, they clashed over something else. She should just give up and accept that they would never get along.

It was almost eight-thirty in the evening before they stopped working, but when they closed the front door, stacks of the *Family Hour* had been printed, stapled and addressed. All that was left was to take them to the post office first thing in the morning.

The sun was setting by the time they gathered in

front of the building. Cricket was still waiting patiently at the hitching rail. However, the two-wheeled cart Andrew had loaned Joann wasn't equipped for nighttime driving.

"Roman, I have an extra set of battery-operated flashing lights you can use to get you home," Gerald said.

"Danki," Roman went with Gerald to get them and the two men made short work of affixing them to the tailgate of the cart.

Leonard and Mabel stood with Joann. Mabel said, "We're going to run over to the hospital and see if Otis needs anything. Can we give you a lift home?"

The couple already had a sixty-mile round trip ahead of them after a long and tiring day. They didn't need to go out of their way to drop her off. "No, you go on. I'll be fine. See you in the morning and please send word if Otis is worse. Tell him we are all praying for him," Joann said.

Mabel kissed Joann's cheek. "We will."

After she and Leonard drove away, Joann stood on the sidewalk and watched Roman climb into the cart. She said, "Good night. I'll see you tomorrow."

"Get in." His first words in four hours.

"Nee, really, the walk will do me good."

He sighed heavily with frustration. "Get in. I'm not letting you walk home in the dark."

It wasn't exactly an invitation, but she really didn't want to walk after such a long day. She climbed up onto the small benchlike seat. The cart was much narrower than the normal buggy. She and Roman were pressed together from hip to knee. The high arms of the seat left no room for her to move away from him. The result was a long, dark and exquisitely uncomfortable ride. He didn't say a word, and she couldn't think of anything to say that wouldn't sound foolish.

When they finally reached her brother's lane, she jumped down. "*Danki,* I appreciate the ride. I'll be driving myself after this, so you won't have to pick me up. Good night."

She raced up the lane like she had a pack of wild dogs coming after her. When she stepped into her brother's kitchen, she realized she'd been right about one thing. Hebron had more to say on the subject of her job. He was waiting for her.

She endured an hour-long lecture about being content with the simple life their ancestors had envisioned. She knew that Hebron believed what he was saying. She also knew he had her best interests at heart. She accepted his admonishment quietly. When he was finished, she explained she would only be working as a cleaning woman at the office starting on Monday, and he was content with that.

The following morning, she arrived at the office just as Leonard and Gerald were carrying boxes of magazines out to Leonard's small pickup. He would take them to the post office as soon as it opened. The usually dour Leonard was smiling. "Otis is being released from the hospital in the afternoon."

"That's wonderful news." She glanced inside the building. "Where is Roman?"

"He's gone to the hospital to help his aunt get Otis home and settled, so he won't be in today. It's just the three of us."

That would make it another busy day if they were to get the paper out on time, but at least she wouldn't have to be on her tippy-toes around Roman all day. What a relief to have a day without him.

She thought that was what she wanted, but she found herself thinking about him constantly and wondering how he and Otis were getting along. As it turned out, he was on her mind as much when he was gone as he was when he was hovering beside her. No matter what, she couldn't escape him. In all the excitement she hadn't mentioned it was their last day together. Would he care?

On the drive home that evening, she passed the turn-off to the sawmill and was tempted to stop. Would he be there yet? What excuse would she give for showing up like this? She realized how foolish she was being and hurried on, determined to forget about Roman Weaver. Come Monday, she would be back at the bookshop in the afternoons, three days a week. She would clean on Saturday when the printing office was closed. Their paths weren't going to cross very often anymore, and that was a good thing.

That night, she dreamed about meeting the Friendly Fisherman, a kindly Amish man who looked like her grandfather with his long gray beard, who laughed with her and not at her, and who admired her keen mind. She awoke early with a bubbling mixture of hope and dread churning her stomach. The sun wasn't yet up when she slipped out of her brother's house and made her way to the lake.

Please, please, please let there be a letter from him.

As dawn broke, Joann entered her favorite spot and saw a raccoon washing his breakfast of clams on the rocky shore. She smiled. "Good morning, sir. Are you the Friendly Fisherman?"

The raccoon paused, his tiny hands grasping a

cracked shell. He bared his teeth at her, then waddled away to eat in peace somewhere else. She called after him. "*Ja,* go away you old grump. I know a fellow just like you."

Annoyed with herself for letting thoughts of Roman spoil the glorious morning, she crossed the clearing to the log and pulled out her jar. There was a new letter inside. She sat down, unfolded the small pages and began to read the strong, bold writing with eager anticipation.

Dear Happy Angler,

Your idea for a mailbox is quite clever. I never would have thought of it. Now I know I can look forward to your notes come fair weather or foul. I'm truly sorry to hear about your troubles. To own a house is a fine dream, and it must be a hard thing to give up. I pray your circumstances will change.

Don't ever think your concerns are small or unworthy. I thank you for sharing them with me. I'll do you the courtesy of returning the favor. I also work with someone who would benefit from a dunking in the lake. Stubborn, willful, hard to please, quick to call attention to my failings. I sometimes wonder if it wouldn't be better to leave my job, but alas, others are depending on me so I must stay.

You're trying to make the best of a bad situation and develop a friendship with your coworker. You put me to shame. I must confess I've done nothing to better our relationship at work. With your wise words in mind, I plan to change that. I will be kinder. I will listen more and judge less.

If I make the effort, perhaps the tension between the two of us will lessen over time. It's worth a try.

You are right about the sunset. Its beautiful colors were reflected perfectly in the water. It was a remarkable sight. Explain to me why a north wind kept you from fishing. It certainly hasn't been cold. I used to fish a lot, but not as much in recent years. I remember now why I liked it so much when I was a boy. It's the peacefulness. Well, landing a big fish is fun, too, although I have trouble holding a rod these days.

I'll be sure to try the orange hopper. Any tips, fishing or otherwise, will always be welcome from you.

As ever,
Your Friendly Fisherman

Joann laid the pages on her lap and stared out at the lake. A strong south wind was starting to blow, and it made the water gray and choppy. She should go over to the north shore and try fishing for bass along the rocky outcropping there. It was spawning season for them, but she didn't unpack her pole. Instead, she spent a long time thinking about the Friendly Fisherman's letter.

He found her advice sound and wise. That made her feel good. It took away some of the uneasiness she felt about continuing the correspondence.

How was it that a stranger understood her feelings and took her words to heart when so few others did?

She read the note again. So he didn't know the rhyme about the wind in the north. He surely had to be an *Englisch* fellow. Her Amish grandfather had taught her the saying years ago. She assumed everyone knew it.

Her conscience pricked her at the thought that he might be a married man. He hadn't said one way or the other. Although she knew her letters were harmless, not everyone would think so. If he were *Englisch,* she should give up writing to him.

She pushed the nagging doubts aside. She didn't know that for sure. He enjoyed her letters. He looked forward to hearing from her and she enjoyed hearing from him. There was nothing wrong with that. She wouldn't give it up. She had already given up so much.

She took out her pencil and notebook and started a new letter.

When she was finished, she tucked the jar back in the knothole and headed for home, where she had a full day of farm work waiting for her.

Later, her family took Otis and his wife a basket of food. They stayed briefly to visit and to do whatever chores the pair needed help with. Hebron might disagree with Joann working at the paper, but he would never neglect a neighbor in need. Joann had half-hoped to see Roman there, but his mother told her he'd already gone home. Try as she might, Joann couldn't stifle her disappointment. It didn't make sense, but she missed seeing him even if they did sometimes clash.

Roman spent the day helping his father and brother stack lumber at the sawmill. His mother had stayed the night with Otis and his wife. She wouldn't be back until late afternoon. Her men were left alone to fend for themselves when it came to cooking, but they managed. His father knew how to make scrambled eggs and cook bacon. They had the same meal for breakfast and lunch.

Roman was pleased to see that Andrew and Faron

were becoming friends. The two joked around and worked well together. He was glad for his brother. He knew Andrew missed his company.

It felt good to get back to physical labor, but he realized by early afternoon that he'd put too much stress on his arm. It began to ache and throb wildly. He was going to be in for a long, uncomfortable night.

When evening came, his mother returned and soon had a hot supper ready for them. After that, the family retired early, leaving Roman alone in his small house. The days were growing longer and it wasn't yet dark.

He was restless. His arm hurt. There was no point in trying to get to sleep early. He wondered if Happy Angler had left him a new letter. He couldn't believe how much he looked forward to hearing from her. Maybe it was because she didn't know about his disability. They were equals, simply two people who enjoyed the same pastime. Roman didn't feel inferior or pitied. He pictured her as an elderly aunt, someone who loved the outdoors and freely gave good advice. What was she like? Should he try to find out? Would her next letter tell him more?

Finally, he gave in to his curiosity and walked to the lake. He didn't bother taking a fishing pole.

When he reached the clearing, he was happy to find he had a new letter. He lowered himself to the grass and used the log as a backrest while he read the latest note from his friend by flashlight.

Dear Friendly Fisherman,
When I arrived at the lake this morning, I saw a raccoon in our spot. I asked him if he knew you, but he grumbled and waddled away without an-

swering me. Make sure you screw the lid of the jar on tightly if you leave me a letter. Raccoons are curious by nature and enjoy the challenge of opening things.

I'm surprised you don't know the rhyme about fishing and the wind. I thought everyone knew it. This is how it goes.

Wind from the West, fish bite the best.

Wind from the East, fish bite the least.

Wind from the North, don't venture forth.

Wind from the South will blow bait in their mouth.

My grandfather taught it to me when I was little. He would only fish when the wind was in the west or in the south, and he always had good luck. I, on the other hand, have not had much success improving my relationship at work. Don't think me wise. I'm not. I have a terrible tendency to say the worst possible thing at the worst possible moment.

Did you ever wish for the ability to call back the words you've said the second they leave your mouth? I wish that every day. Often, I think it would be better if I couldn't talk at all.

Perhaps that's why I enjoy writing these letters. I can always erase the words before you see them if I make a blunder. I hope you are faring better than I am with your troublesome work partner.

I will limit my advice here to fishing in the future. I've had success with spinner baits and rubber worms on this lake. Both are good choices no matter what the weather and temperature. Another

bait you may want to try is a jig-and-pig. The bass
really seem to like them, even in the winter.
As always, your friend,
A Happy Angler

Roman chuckled at the idea of questioning a raccoon about his identity. His unknown friend had a good
imagination and a good sense of humor. As he read the
lines of the fishing rhyme, he vaguely recalled hearing
them in the past. His father didn't enjoy fishing but Roman's grandfather had. Maybe he was the one who had
recited the poem. He died when Roman was only six.
He had very few memories of the man. Roman's grandmother had lived with them until she passed away at
the age of ninety-two.

He pulled his small notebook and pencil from his
pocket and started a new letter. It took him a long time
to get the words just right.

When he finished his note, he tucked the jar securely
in the hollow space. He didn't mind the walk in the dark.
There was a full moon to light his way and he didn't
need to use his flashlight.

To his surprise, he did see a light on the far side of
the lake. Was it his unknown friend? Or was Woolly
Joe looking for a lost lamb? One day, Roman figured he
was bound to meet his friend face-to-face, but he wasn't
sure he wanted to. Discovering her identity would likely
end their unusual friendship. And he didn't want it to
end. He could put his feelings and fears into words on
paper better than he could speak them aloud.

On Sunday morning, Roman joined his family in
the buggy for the eight-mile drive to the preaching service. It was being held for the first time at the home of

Jonathan Dressler, a rare convert to their Amish faith. Jonathan was a horse trainer who took in unwanted and abandoned horses for an equine rescue organization. He had lived among the Amish for several years now and had married Karen Imhoff, the eldest daughter of Eli Imhoff, the previous fall.

The church service lasted the usual three hours. The bishop and two other ministers took turns preaching about forgiveness and about suffering persecution for the sake of their faith. In between, the congregation sang hymns from the *Ausbund,* their sacred songbook.

From his place on the benches near the back of the barn, Roman could see Joann Yoder sitting between her cousin, Sally Yoder, and her friend, Grace Beachy, on the benches to his left. Esta Bowman sat two rows behind them. Several times, he caught Esta smiling at him. Was she tired of Faron already?

Roman was glad he had realized Esta wasn't the woman for him. He was happy he'd discovered that before things had gotten more serious between them. He didn't find her sly smiles, overly sweet voice and flighty ways as attractive as he once did.

He glanced toward Joann. He hated to admit it, but he had her to thank for that. She might not have a sweet and attractive way about her, but she had a knack—a sometimes painful knack—of helping him see the truth. About himself and about others. He had come to respect that about her.

Perhaps it was time he told her that.

At the end of the service, Bishop Zook addressed the crowd once more. "We are taking up two special collections today. One is to help purchase supplies to rebuild and replace what was lost at our school. We will have a workday at the school next Saturday and all are invited to come.

"The second collection is for our annual road use and repair. Our *Englisch* neighbors pay for road maintenance through gasoline taxes, revenue from driver's licenses, and money collected through tolls. However, we use the roads and bridges the same as they do, only we don't have to put gasoline in our horses or pay for a license to drive them. Our horse's shoes damage the roads in ways their car tires don't, so we must pay our fair share to keep them in good order."

Roman flinched at the thought of paying for road repairs. Why should he help the *Englisch* pay for road upkeep? So they could drive even faster and collide with more buggies?

The bishop continued, "Driving on well-maintained roads is a privilege. It is not a right. I urge you to give what you can. Last year our Amish churches in this area raised over a quarter of a million dollars for the fund. That money was divided between the state, the county and the township in which we reside."

Bishop Zook paused and then grinned. "For that amount, you would think I could get the potholes filled on the road that runs past my farm, but I reckon I'll have to give a little more to get that done." A ripple of laughter passed around the room. Roman didn't join in.

When the congregation was dismissed, Roman went out with the intention of speaking to Joann as soon as he had the chance. If he made an effort to mend fences with her, he could tell his pen pal he was making progress in becoming a better man.

In spite of his best intentions, the chance never arrived. Everyone wanted to know about Otis and about what had actually happened. He retold the story many times. By the time he managed to get free, Joann was sitting with her friends and eating, so he went in with his brother and filled his plate. A half hour later, he went in search of her again, but couldn't find her.

He learned later that her sister-in-law had become sick and the family had gone home. He consoled himself with the fact that he would see her at work tomorrow morning.

That evening, he headed to the lake in hopes that there would be another letter for him. He was disappointed to find his own note still in the jar. On the walk home, he pondered why he cared so much about exchanging letters with a stranger. He realized it was because he could say whatever he pleased without the fear of appearing foolish or weak. He had troubles, but so did the Happy Angler. Together they had found a way to share their burdens and make them lighter. Should he suggest meeting in his next letter?

Perhaps not. If his unknown friend wanted to meet, wouldn't she have suggested it by now? Besides, it might be awkward if they found that they knew each other. They would surely stop leaving notes for each other if that were the case.

He found himself wondering why his pen pal hadn't signed her letters in the first place. Roman hadn't signed his first note because he didn't want to take credit for a simple kind deed. So what reason did the Happy Angler have to keep her identity secret? Was it as simple as Roman's reason? Or was there a darker motive behind the omission?

The thought troubled him until late in the night.

The following morning, he drove to work through

the pouring rain and arrived mud-splattered and damp. His uncle was already there ahead of him along with Leonard and Gerald.

Roman said, "*Onkel,* should you be here? Didn't the doctor tell you to rest for a few days?"

"I'm sick of resting. I need to get back to work."

"Velda was driving you nuts, wasn't she?" Leonard said with a knowing wink.

Otis laughed then winced and put a hand to the bandage on his head. "*Ja,* she means well, but it was time to get out of the house. She can fuss over a body more than anyone I've ever met. Are the pillows too high? Would you like some tea? Shall I close the window? Do you need another pillow? Shall I open a window?"

"It's nice to have the love of a good woman," Gerald said.

Otis grinned. "I'm blessed and I know it, but even people who are in love irritate each other once in a while."

Roman glanced at the front door. "Speaking of irritating women, Joann isn't here yet. I wonder if something is wrong."

"She has gone back to her work at the bookshop. I'm not expecting her until noon today," Otis said.

"Are you serious?" Roman stared at Otis in stunned disbelief.

Otis nodded. "Perfectly serious. She has returned to her old position, but she'll do the cleaning here on Saturdays."

Leonard muttered under his breath, "We finally had someone who could do nearly everything in this office, and she goes back to shelving books and mopping floors. I don't think it's right but no one asked my opinion."

Roman wasn't sure what to think. Was this what she meant when she said she wouldn't always be around? Why hadn't she mentioned anything about it?

Otis scowled at Leonard. "Roman will soon master all of the tasks that Joann did."

Maybe he would and maybe he wouldn't. Her feet might be smaller than his, but she had left some mighty big shoes to fill. Was he the reason for her job change? Had she decided she couldn't work with him? It disturbed him to think that might be true. He hadn't been exactly friendly toward her.

"Now, let's get to work," Otis said. "We're going to be reprinting the schoolbooks this week, all of them, grades one through eight. I have the list here. Leonard, the plates are stored in the back of the bookshop."

Roman glanced at the clock. His uncle had said she'd be in after noon. Fine, he could wait a little longer. He had a lot to discuss with her when she came in.

Chapter 11

Would there be a letter waiting for her today? Oh, how she hoped there would be.

Joann left her brother's house an hour before she needed to leave for work. Instead of driving into town, she headed her pony and cart to the lake. It was raining steadily, but she didn't care. She had a sturdy umbrella.

She glanced out from under it at the leaden sky.

"Please, Lord, if I'm driving all this way in the rain, let there be a letter waiting for me today."

She needed something to cheer her, something to get her through the day.

Thoughts of Roman had occupied far too much of her time over the past several days. He needed to let go of the anger he carried, but she didn't know how to help him. She prayed for him and for herself. She wasn't angry about what had happened to the school and to Otis, only saddened by the harmful actions of others.

She offered up her forgiveness for the people who had committed the crimes. That should have been enough, but it wasn't. She wanted to prevent other incidents.

She hadn't forgotten the license plate number she had written down. If she gave it to the *Englisch* sheriff, would it be because she was following God's will or her own? Was she harboring a desire to prevent other such attacks, or was she seeking revenge? She wasn't sure of her own motives.

Vengeance was the Lord's. It had no place in her heart. However, she was human enough to admit she wanted the person who had injured Otis to face worldly justice.

She put her worries aside as she stopped in front of the gate leading to Joseph Shetler's pasture. Before she got down from the cart, a figure loomed out of the rain in front of her.

The shepherd's hired man stood with his shoulders hunched against the weather and water dripping from the brim of his dark hat. "How can I help you?"

Was this the author of her letters? Her heart beat faster. She'd never met him, she'd only heard stories about his reclusive ways. Carl King was much younger than she had expected. "I was on my way to the lake to do a little fishing."

"In this weather?" His voice was deep and gravelly, and held a hint of distrust.

She gave him a nervous smile. "I reckon the fish are already wet, so they shouldn't mind."

"You've been coming here a lot."

"Is that a problem?" What would she do if he turned her away?

"I guess not." He swung open the gate. "Just make

sure that you don't let the sheep out when you leave. Keep an eye out for a ewe and lamb. They're missing from our flock."

Relieved that he wasn't going to stop her, she said, "I'll do that. Please tell Joseph that Joann Yoder says hello."

"I know who you are."

He certainly wasn't a friendly fellow. She would be surprised if it turned out that he was her pen pal. "You're Carl King, aren't you?"

"Yes."

Slapping the reins against her pony, she sent him through the open gate. As Carl swung it closed behind her, she looked over her shoulder. "Have you noticed anyone else coming here a lot?"

"No."

He looked impatient to end their meeting. She was keeping him standing in the rain. "Did you happen to pull a rod and reel out of the lake recently while you were fishing?" If he were the Friendly Fisherman, would he admit it?

"Nope."

"*Danki*. Have a pleasant day." In a way, she was thankful that he wasn't the one, but it was odd that he hadn't seen anyone coming and going frequently. He lived in the shepherd's hut near the pasture gate.

"Is there another way in to the lake?" she asked as she turned around. Carl was already gone. He had vanished into the mist as silently as he had appeared.

Happily, she found a letter waiting for her when she arrived at the log. She sat down and eagerly began to read, taking care to keep it out of the rain.

Dear Happy Angler,
I'm surprised Mr. Raccoon didn't stay and speak to you. I'll tell him that he was rude. I'm sure he will have more to say to you the next time you meet.

Joann grinned. It seemed her pen pal shared her sense of humor.

As for my work-related troubles, they have doubled. It is amazing how cruel and heartless some people can be. It saddens and sickens me. More than ever, I find I need the peace this place brings me. I'm bound up in a struggle between what I know is right and what others think is right.

That was exactly the dilemma she faced. To do what she thought was right, or to do what others told her was right. They were so much alike, this unknown writer and she. It was as if they faced the same challenges. It surely had to be someone she knew. But *Englisch* or Amish?

I never thought I lacked moral courage, but I fear that I do. Forgiveness is an easy word to say, but it's hard to mean it deep in your heart. I say it, but I don't mean it. I don't know if I ever will and that frightens me.

As for our troublesome coworkers, I suggest a trade. You can take my headache for a week and I'll take yours. I hope you don't think I'm making fun of your troubles. I'm not. I'm just grumpy and aching today. I think we're in for a weather change.

Don't be too hard on yourself. We all say things we don't mean. As for your coworker. Look for his strengths instead of his weaknesses. I know you'll find them.

It was good advice. Roman was irritating and reluctant to take her advice, but he had to have his own strengths. She would look for them more diligently.

And when she couldn't find any, she would think more about chucking him headfirst into the lake.

Shame swept over her at her unkind thoughts. Somehow, even when Roman wasn't around, he brought out the worst in her. She continued reading.

I plan to invest in a few jig-and-pigs. Thanks for the tip. Truthfully, I haven't been fishing lately, but I'll let you know what I catch in the future.
A Friendly Fisherman.
P.S. Please don't judge me harshly.

How could she judge him harshly? It was clear he struggled as she did with doing the right thing. She wrote out a heartfelt reply.

She folded the finished letter, tucked it into the jar and placed it inside the fallen log. She wished she could speak to her unknown friend in person. Wouldn't it be wonderful to meet here and enjoy a day of fishing together. She considered adding a request to meet, but shyness stopped her. He might enjoy exchanging letters, but who would enjoy spending time with a plain, lonely old maid? She didn't want his eagerness to read her notes turning to pity for her. It was better this way.

For now. If he would reveal his identity, she might find the courage to reveal hers.

The rain stopped as she climbed back into her cart and headed toward town. Today, she would look for a hidden strength in Roman. If she discovered a positive quality about him, perhaps he would be on her mind less often.

When she arrived in town, she turned down the alley at the side of the building where Otis had a small shed for his employees' horses. She settled her pony on the fresh straw someone had laid down that morning. She made sure he had a pail of water and an armful of hay to munch on.

She entered the back door of the bookstore. Mabel was busy dusting the bookshelves in the small store. She held out a second dust rag for Joann. "I thought I would get started cleaning. I haven't had a customer all morning, and I'm bored to tears."

Joann slipped on a large apron and tied it behind her. She took the rag from Mabel. "I never complain if someone wants to clean."

"There is enough dust for both of us. I started by the front windows. If you want to start with the back shelves, we'll meet in the middle. How does that sound?"

"It sounds like a *goot* plan. Have you heard how Otis is doing?"

"I think he's doing okay. Leonard popped over earlier to tell me Otis had come in to work."

Joann frowned. "I thought he had strict orders from Dr. Zook to rest this week."

"You know men. They ignore their doctor's orders and do what they want to do anyway. Then they complain like small children when they don't get better. I have half a mind to go over there and drag him home by the ear. He scared the life out of me when I saw him lying amid all that broken glass and blood."

Joann began dusting. She pulled out a handful of books, wiped down the shelf and replaced the volumes. "Have they found out who did it?"

Mabel stood on a step stool to wipe off the top of the bookcase. "Not that I've heard. I hope someone wasn't deliberately trying to hurt him. It does make me wonder since Roman is working here, too."

Joann paused in her work. "Why would that make a difference?"

"Because of the trial. Brendan Smith is known to dislike the Amish. He comes from a family that makes no bones about feeling the same way. It's sad, really. If they would just take the time to get to know their neighbors, I think they would feel differently."

"Is there a young woman in his family with white-blond hair, about my height, very pretty?"

"Not that I recall. Why?"

Joann dropped to her knees and began dusting the bottom shelves and books. "A young woman like that stopped in to ask about Otis that afternoon."

"A lot of people stopped in here to ask about Otis. I don't remember seeing anyone like that. The whole community was upset by what had happened. *Englisch* and Amish folks."

"It was probably just a coincidence, but I saw a car like the one she was in the morning of the school fire."

"Did you tell the sheriff?"

Joann shook her head. She had hoped to put her suspicions about the young woman to rest. All she had now was more questions.

"Joann, I don't mean to pry, but I was surprised when Otis told me that you wanted your job here at the bookstore back. I know you loved working in the printing office. Did it have anything to do with Roman Weaver coming to work there?"

It was the question she had been dreading. What should she say? The truth was always the best answer, but she didn't want to make it sound like Roman had forced her out. Otis had the right to hire anyone he wanted.

"It was time for a change." She finished dusting the bottom shelf and moved to the next bookcase.

"After only a few months?"

"I wasn't needed once Roman learned his way around. I'm happy doing this. It gives me more time to go fishing."

Mabel shook her head. "You and your fishing. I don't see how anyone can like touching slimy, smelly fish. Yuck."

Joann was saved from having to explain her fascination with the sport by the bell over the entrance. Mabel went to take care of her customer. Joann finished dusting, ran the vacuum sweeper over the carpet runners between the rows of shelves and mopped the uncarpeted areas of the floor. She was cleaning the two large windows facing the street when she saw Roman walk past. He caught sight of her at the same moment and stopped. To her dismay, he turned around to enter the shop.

Roman stood inside the entrance to the bookstore and watched Joann scrubbing the window so vigorously he was astounded that she hadn't worn a hole through it. She was deliberately ignoring him.

Mabel was helping another customer. "I'll be with you in a minute," she said.

He nodded and stepped over to the nearest bookshelves where he had a clear view of Joann. Was she still upset with him about the license plate number he'd taken from her? He'd been waiting all day to talk to her. Now that she was within sight, he suddenly didn't know why he'd been so keen on it. He rubbed a hand over his jaw and started browsing through the titles in front of him without really seeing them. He glanced her way several times, but she continued to work at cleaning the windows.

Finally, he spoke. "It must be on the outside."

She stopped scrubbing and glanced at him. "Were you talking to me?"

He replaced the book he held and picked up another. "You've been working on the same window pane for five minutes. If the spot hasn't come off by now, it must be on the outside."

She took a step back from the window. "You're right."

"What did you say?"

"I said you're right," she repeated in a louder voice.

He chuckled. "How hard was that to say?"

She rolled her eyes and picked up her supplies. "Laugh if you like, I have work to do."

He put the book away. "Otis told me you decided to come back to your old job. Why?"

"How is he today?"

She avoided his question by asking one of her own, he noticed. "He has a bad headache. I tried to get him to leave, but he insists on staying."

"Stubborn must run in your family," she said.

"Tell me, why does someone who loves research,

reading and writing as much as you do, give it up to scrub floors?"

She glared at him, her green eyes snapping. "There's nothing wrong with cleaning floors. Cleanliness is next to godliness."

He held up his hand. "I didn't say there was anything wrong with it. I only wondered why you chose it over working on the magazine and newspaper."

She looked down at the floor. "It was time for a change."

"Are you sure it's not because I work there now?"

She still didn't look at him. "I accepted this job before you accepted yours."

He wasn't sure he believed her, but he decided to give her the benefit of the doubt. He picked up another book and pretended to read the back cover. "Otis wants me to write an article for next month's magazine."

"On what?"

Mabel came over to him. "Are you interested in child-rearing?"

He looked at the book in his hand and hastily returned it to the shelf. "I'm just browsing."

"That's fine. Let me know if I can be of assistance." Mabel walked back to the counter and sat down. He turned to find Joann smothering a grin.

He liked her smile. He liked the way it made her eyes sparkle. Her grin slowly faded. She looked down. "What are you writing an article about?"

"The law and our responsibilities."

"Because of what's been happening?"

"I assume that's why Otis chose the topic. Perhaps because of my accident, as well."

"It is a relevant topic."

"What is your opinion? Should an Amish person call or notify the police when they are the victim of a crime? Does that go against our teachings of nonresistance and nonviolence? The Bible says in Matthew 5:39, 'But I say unto you, That ye resist not evil: but whosoever shall smite thee on thy right cheek, turn to him the other also.'"

She folded her arms and nibbled at her lower lip. "If you're asking me what I want done about the license plate number I wrote down, I would like to give it to the sheriff."

"There is a larger question besides what you or I would *like* to do. It's about what we *should* do."

"You believe we should do nothing."

"I'm not sure."

"By doing nothing, aren't we leading weaker souls into temptation?"

"How so?"

"Might someone decide it's easier to rob an Amish home because he thinks that crime won't be reported? What is our responsibility to him?"

"You think we should take temptation out of his way."

"Yes, but how? By keeping our money out of sight and in a safe place, or by letting it be known his crime will be reported to the *Englisch* law? Paul urged Christians to give civil authorities their dues with regard to taxes, respect and honor."

The fire was back in her green eyes. Why had he ever thought she was homely? He said, "You've given me a lot to think about."

"I look forward to reading your article. Do you have your answer?"

"I think so. We should feel we can report a crime and

answer police questions if we're asked, but we shouldn't seek revenge. We shouldn't file charges or seek damages from others. I think in this way we will remain true to the teachings of Christ."

"You have forgotten the most important thing."

"What's that?"

"We must forgive those who harm us."

Trust her to point out his failings. Why did he think she might understand his struggle? He took a step back. "I haven't forgotten. Enjoy your new job." He left the bookstore, slamming the door behind him.

He worked the rest of the afternoon on the article his uncle had assigned him. Three times he painstakingly typed out his thoughts and three times he tore the page out of the typewriter, wadded it up and tossed it toward the trash can. He left work that evening hoping something would occur to him out at the lake.

He was happy to discover a new letter waiting for him when he reached his now favorite spot. This time, he had taken his pole and hoped to get in a few hours of fishing before dark. He opened his note.

My Friend,

It seems we share the same sense of the absurd. Mr. Raccoon has not put in another appearance. Clearly, he is ashamed of his earlier behavior and is trying to avoid me.

I'm sorry your troubles at work are getting worse instead of better. I, too, am saddened by the cruel and senseless behavior I've seen lately. Are we perhaps talking about the same events in our community? I'm referring to the Amish schoolhouse fire and the injury of Otis Miller when someone threw a brick through the window of his business. These nameless individuals may think they are hurting the Amish, but they are only hurting themselves. I feel sorry for them.

As for your personal struggle, I urge you to do what you know is right. That is usually the truest course. If you can, seek the wisdom of men you admire and take their words to heart. Very few people have lived a life free of pain. Some may even have faced the same issue that is troubling you. We do not travel though this world alone.

Forgiveness is not easy. Some hurts are so deep that we can see only despair and question why God has chosen this for us. Forgiveness is God's mighty gift to the giver. It heals the one who was harmed. It can also heal those who have caused harm if they acknowledge what they have done and seek redemption.

I hope you continue to draw comfort from this beautiful spot, and I hope you find my letters as comforting as I find yours. I will heed your sage advice and seek the strengths of the man who annoys me. If I don't find any, I'm willing to make the trade. You name the time and place.

The hardware store in Hope Springs carries a good selection of fishing tackle. You can find several kinds of jig-n-pigs there.

May God bless you and keep you.
The Happy Angler

Reading one of the Happy Angler's letters always made him feel better. He didn't have to struggle with his doubts and problems alone. This letter made him almost certain that the Happy Angler was an Amish woman from his community.

She was someone who was familiar with the recent crime spree. She was also someone who advocated forgiveness even as she acknowledged how difficult that could be. Roman's curiosity continued to grow about the identity of his friend. Who could she be? He thought of some of the kindhearted single women in his church district. There was Sally Yoder, Grace Beachy and a whole slew of girls his brother's age. Then there was Lea Belier, the teacher. She would have free time to fish now that school was out for the summer, but who would annoy her at her job? Was she working somewhere else over the summer?

If he started asking his mother questions about the local single maids, she would start harping about grandchildren again. He would simply have to wonder and hope his unknown friend would one day reveal her identity.

Of course, it could be Joann Yoder.

That thought made him flinch. He couldn't see her starting up a correspondence with a stranger. Sure, Leonard was sometimes difficult to work with, but Joann had taken another job. Nothing in this letter indicated the author planned to change where she worked.

He mulled over the advice he'd been given. His friend was a very wise person, indeed. Roman spent the next hour fishing without much success. He caught only three small fish and tossed them all back. As the sun began to set, he wrote:

Dear Happy Angler,
You are so right. We do not travel through this world alone. You are proof of that. Yes, I was

talking about the Amish schoolhouse fire and the brick-throwing incident. What will it take to restore peace in our community?

As for forgiveness, I'm working on that. You write with great conviction about the grace forgiveness brings us. I think you are right.

God bless you and keep writing. I do find comfort in your words.
Your Friendly Fisherman

He tucked the brief letter in their makeshift mailbox. He was starting to care a great deal about the woman who wrote such comforting words. Someday, he would tell her in person about the peace her words brought him.

That evening after supper, he waited for a chance to speak to his father alone. His father was a wise man. If anyone could help him with his dilemma, he could.

He followed his dad into the living room. "*Daed,* can I ask you a question?"

His father settled himself in his favorite chair. "Of course."

"I think I know who is behind the attack on Otis and the fire at the school."

"Who?"

"It's a member of Brendan Smith's family. I don't know what to do with the information."

Menlo stroked his beard. "You are considering giving it to the police?"

"*Ja.* I fear others may be attacked."

"I understand your fears. We must trust that God will keep us from harm."

"I know, but is that enough?"

Menlo was silent for a long time. Roman waited for his answer. Finally, Menlo spoke. "If I see a house on fire, I will pray for everyone's safety, but I will sound the alarm and try to save what I can, be it my neighbor or his goods, and I will work to keep the fire from spreading. *Gott* put me where I could see the flames and help. You must pray for guidance and ask yourself if *Gott* has put you where you can see the flames."

"*Danki,* Papa. I will do that."

The following morning when Roman arrived at the office, he learned Otis wouldn't be in. Leonard was waiting for him with a note from his aunt. As he read it, Gerald came in.

"What's up?" Gerald looked from Leonard to Roman.

"Otis's headache has gotten worse. My aunt is taking him back to the hospital at the urging of Dr. Zook. She says that Otis wants me to take charge of the business until he returns."

Roman rubbed the back of his neck. The job was beyond him. Without Otis here, he really needed someone who knew what they were doing. Leonard and Otis were both waiting for him to say something. "How are we coming on the schoolbooks?"

"I printed twenty copies of all the first-grade books yesterday," Leonard said.

"I will get the covers on and get them bound today," Gerald said, then looked as if he wanted to say something else.

"What?" Roman asked.

Gerald and Leonard shared a speaking glance. "Otis wanted all the books done by this weekend," Gerald said. "I don't think we can do it. Not in addition to getting the paper out and finishing all the other orders we have."

"What do you suggest?" Roman wasn't above asking for help.

"Get Joann in here," Leonard stated. "She knows what needs to get done and how to do it."

Roman nodded. "Okay, I will ask her to help us."

"You will?" Gerald asked in surprise. "I didn't think the two of you got along."

Roman scowled at him. "I won't let my uncle's business suffer because of my personal feelings for the woman. Leonard, get started on the second-grade books today. Are there any that we don't have plates for?"

Leonard shook his head. "We have plates for everything that Leah has been using. It's a good thing too, otherwise it would cost more and take more time to set all that type."

"Guess we should get busy," Gerald said. "I sure hope Joann agrees to help."

As the men went to work, Roman sat down at his desk and noticed a note with his name on it. He unfolded the wrinkled paper and saw it was his first attempt at writing his article on law and order. There was a note in the margin. "This one is the best. Use it."

There was no signature, but he knew the note had come from Joann. She must have come in to straighten up after he left and found his discarded attempts to write his article, then salvaged one.

He read through the rough draft again. She was right. This version said what he wanted to say without sounding judgmental and without preaching. He put a new piece of paper in his typewriter and finished the article.

When he was done, he felt a keen sense of accomplishment that he'd rarely known.

He opened his desk drawer and pulled out the license plate number that Joann had written down. Had God put him and Joann here so that they might see the flames of this evil and sound the alarm?

Roman prayed he was doing the right thing. He stapled the license number inside a copy of the *Family Hour* magazine and addressed it to Sheriff Bradley, then put it in the mailbox.

He drew a deep breath. Now, he needed to convince Joann to come back to work for him. He wasn't at all certain that she would.

Chapter 12

She was late.

Joann stabled her pony without giving him his hay or grain. He whinnied in protest as she closed the stall door. "I'll be back later to feed you. I promise."

It was only the second day of her part-time job and she was thirty minutes late. Otis would not be happy with her.

She should have waited to go to the lake until after work, but she had been eager to check for another letter and to her delight, there had been one waiting for her. She had lost track of time while writing an answer and now she was late. The letter was tucked in her pocket and the words came back to her now.

Dear Happy Angler,
You are so right. We do not travel through this world alone. You are proof of that.

Her words brought him comfort. She smiled at the thought as she rushed in through the back door of the bookstore and jerked open the supply room door. She grabbed her cleaning supplies and a broom from the corner, spun around and ran into Roman. The handle of her broom smacked the side of his head. She stood speechless with surprise and remorse.

He rubbed his temple. "Come into my uncle's office. I need to talk to you."

That didn't sound good. "I really am sorry. It was an accident."

"I'm just glad it wasn't a brick."

"Let me put this stuff back and I'll be right there." At least he hadn't asked why she was late.

She replaced her cleaning supplies and followed him to the office next door. Otis wasn't in. Roman sat behind his uncle's desk. His grave expression set off alarm bells in her head. "Where is your uncle?"

"He is back in the hospital. Apparently, there was some slow bleeding in his brain. My aunt called the bookstore and told Mabel they are taking him into surgery."

"Oh, no!" Joann sank onto a nearby chair. "What can I do to help?"

"I was hoping you would ask that. Can you come back to work in your old position? I don't know what your pay was, but I will match it."

"Of course. Just tell me what you need me to do."

"My uncle has left me in charge, but I am woefully unprepared to run this business."

He wasn't just being modest, he was worried. She could see it in his eyes. "I will do whatever I can to help. What projects are being run this week, and where do they stand?"

"All the schoolbooks are being reprinted," Roman began. "Otis wanted all of them done by Saturday. We have the first-grade books printed. Gerald is running them through the binder now. Leonard has started on the second-grade books. Fortunately, we have plates for all of them through the eighth grade. If worse comes to worst, we can delay delivery for a few weeks since the children aren't in school. Besides the newspaper, we have two hundred and fifty wedding invitations that need to be done by tomorrow, fifty new menus for the Shoofly Pie Café that were promised for Thursday and a half dozen miscellaneous business announcements."

"In other words, a lot."

A smile tugged at the corner of his mouth. "*Ja,* teacher, we have a lot to do."

She didn't mind her nickname this time. He wasn't being sarcastic. This Roman Weaver, a man determined to do the best for someone else, was a man she could like.

She rose to her feet. "I'll start setting the type for the wedding invitations. We can use the proof press to run them since there aren't very many. If you start on the layout for the newspaper, we should be able to get it out on time."

"*Danki,* Joann. For agreeing to help, and for commenting on my magazine article. I couldn't see the forest for the trees when I wrote it."

She felt herself blushing. She wasn't used to him being nice. "That is often the case with writers. That's why it's helpful to have someone read your stuff."

"I'll remember that."

"Once Otis gets back, I'm sure he'll proofread your work."

Roman's eyes darkened with worry. "I wish we could hear how he is doing."

She longed to ease his burdens. "We can manage without you for a few hours if you want go to the hospital."

He gave her a halfhearted smile. "I'm sure you could manage without me for a lot longer than a few hours, but I feel I have to stay here. This business is important to my uncle. Mabel will let us know something as soon as she hears."

Joann studied him in a new light. Her Friendly Fisherman had suggested that she look for Roman's strengths. She had found them in his writing and even more so in his love for his uncle. She looked forward to telling her friend how well his suggestion had worked.

They received good news about Otis an hour later. His surgery had gone well. He was in intensive care, but he was expected to make a full recovery. The tension in the office lightened perceptibly after that.

When they closed up for the evening, they had made significant inroads into their workload. Leonard was ready to start printing the seventh-grade books, and Joann had finished the wedding announcements. They walked together out the back door to where the horses were stabled. Joann had managed to get away long enough to feed her pony. He seemed eager to be on his way home. She was surprised to realize she wasn't eager to leave. She was enjoying Roman's company.

"Since you're working with us again, why don't I pick you up tomorrow?" Roman said as he headed for his horse's stall.

She frowned as she considered how she could make time to get to the lake now. She couldn't. Her letters would have to wait until things settled back to normal.

Roman led his mare out of the stall. "If you don't want to, that's fine."

"No, I want to, I mean, that's fine and it's nice of you to offer."

"But what?"

She smiled to reassure him. "Never mind. It's something I had planned to do in the mornings since I wasn't working, but it can wait. The usual time?"

He nodded. "*Ja,* the usual time."

She looked forward to spending time in his company more than she cared to admit.

The various jobs at the office kept them busy for the rest of the week, but it gave them something to talk about on their way to and from work. Roman remained approachable and interested in what she had to say. At least it seemed that way.

On Friday, Joann found him in Otis's office, seated behind his uncle's desk. He didn't look comfortable there. She couldn't blame him. His uncle's illness had forced him into a position he wasn't ready for.

He looked up. "Did you need something?"

"Do you have a minute to talk about the schoolbooks we're reprinting?"

He frowned at the paper he held. "Do we really need sixteen reams of copy paper this month?"

"That sounds about right."

"Okay." He jotted a note and closed the order book. "What was it you wanted to discuss?"

She took a step inside the office. "There are some

changes that need to be made in the booklet on learning to drive a horse and buggy safely."

"I read through the book. I didn't see anything that needed changing. Besides, we have the plates for that one. It will cost more if we make changes and we've already agreed on a price with Eli Imhoff for the project."

"I wish you would read through it again."

"I don't have time," he said with exasperation.

"You, of all people, know how important it is to share the road properly."

He scowled at her. "I *was* sharing the road properly until Brendan Smith decided to knock the open door off my buggy with his truck. Either he didn't know or he didn't care that I was standing on the other side of that door."

"There's no denying you suffered a bad experience."

"Thank you, but that doesn't help me move my fingers."

"All I'm asking is for you to take a look at the booklet again, with your own experience in mind, and see if you don't think we can make it better."

"You will nag me until you get your way, won't you?"

She pressed her lips into a tight line. "I would hardly call it nagging."

"Is there anything else?"

"That's all I wanted."

"Fine. Now, I've got work to do."

"And I'll be out here taking a nap," she muttered as she turned away. How could he charm her one day and irritate her so much the next?

Roman heard Joann's remark, but he didn't respond to it. He had far too much on his mind. His uncle's health wasn't improving as rapidly as his doctor had hoped. Roman didn't have time to reread each schoolbook and make sure they were accurate. They had been good enough in the past. They would be good enough now.

Only, Joann had planted the seed of doubt in his mind. He couldn't dismiss it. He opened a copy of *Learning to Drive a Horse and Buggy* and started reading. Bishop Zook's words came back to him. Driving on well-maintained roads was a privilege, it wasn't a right. The Amish had to share the responsibility for the roadway upkeep and safety, too. Nothing in the textbook addressed this fundamental piece of information.

He, like many Amish, was guilty of being proud that he shunned cars and drove a buggy. Didn't he expect cars to travel at his pace and pass him safely no matter how long he slowed their progress?

The *Englisch* did not intend to slow down to the Amish pace of life. The Amish had to take as much, or even more, responsibility for safety on the roads. It annoyed him that Joann was the one to point it out.

His conscience pricked him as an overlooked truth wormed its way into his thoughts. It wasn't so much that she was annoying. What he found annoying was that she was so often right.

Later that afternoon, he stopped beside her desk. "Rewrite the section that you think needs to be changed, and I'll look it over."

Her eyes grew round. "Really? We're going to change it?"

"You were right, it needs to be updated."

"Oh, that was hard for you to say, wasn't it?"

He struggled to hide a smile. "You have no idea."

"I'm glad you took this job. It suits you."

"Are you going to the school benefit on Saturday?" he asked.

"*Ja,* I planned on it."

"Do you want to help me take the books out there?"

She hesitated, then nodded. "Sure. Shall I meet you here?"

"I'll pick you up at the usual time."

"Can we make it an hour later?" she asked hopefully. "I have something I'd like to do first."

"I don't see why not."

"Great." She smiled brightly and his mood lightened.

He found he was reluctant to walk away. "My mother wants to come with me. *Daed* and Andrew will be along later with the lumber that's needed."

"That will be fine."

He still didn't move.

She raised one eyebrow. "Is there something else?"

He cleared his throat. "*Nee,* I'll let you get back to your nap."

"*Danki.*" She swooped the paperwork on her desk into one large pile and laid her head on it.

He chuckled as he went back to his uncle's office. He had no idea she had such a cute sense of humor. There was more to her than he once suspected.

In spite of the heavy workload, they were able to get everything finished on time.

Roman's good mood lasted until Saturday morning. His mother was bustling around getting food, plates and glasses ready to help feed the people who would be working at the school that day.

She handed him a picnic basket to put in his buggy

and said, "Esta Barkman asked if she could ride along with us. I told her we'd pick her up. I hope that's okay."

Esta and Joann in the same buggy. That should make for an interesting ride to the school. His mother was humming as she worked. That wasn't like her.

He suddenly had a bad feeling about the day.

Joann hurried toward the lake early on Saturday morning. She hadn't had a chance to check for a new letter since she had resumed her old job. It had only been a few days, but it seemed much too long.

When she reached the log, she was disappointed when she saw her letter was still in the same place. The Friendly Fisherman hadn't returned. She sat down and added a short note to the end of her first letter. Content that her friend would know how she had taken his message to heart, she replaced the jar and hurried home.

An hour later, she waited at the end of the lane as Roman pulled up beside her. His mother sat beside him. "*Guder mariye,* Joann," she called out.

"Good morning, Marie Rose. Have you news of your brother?" Joann climbed into the buggy with them.

"He's doing well and has been moved out of intensive care."

"That is wonderful news."

"Roman tells me you are helping at the printing office again until Otis returns."

She had her old job back, but this wasn't how she wanted it. "Roman has things well in hand. I'm just doing what I can to help."

"We have one more stop to make," Roman said. He seemed out of sorts this morning.

His mother said brightly, "We are picking up Esta

Barkman. She wanted to go with me to the hospital after we finish at the school. She's such a thoughtful young woman, and such a good cook, too." She smiled at her son.

Joann wanted to slink away and hide. She hadn't exchanged a single word with Esta since that day in the barn.

Roman turned into the Barkman lane. Esta was waiting on the porch swing. She looked lovely in a crisp new dress of pale lavender. Joann had chosen one of her work dresses to wear. The plain gray fabric and black apron looked shabby next to Esta's cool color.

Esta came down the walk with a wicker basket over her arm. "Hello, everyone. Joann, I'm surprised to see you."

"Roman and I are taking the new books out to the school."

"How kind of you. Very wise to wear your old dress for such work. Isn't she practical, Roman?" She stood beside the buggy looking up at them.

Joann realized they couldn't all sit up front. She got down and climbed in back expecting Esta to sit in back with her.

"*Danki,* Joann." Esta smiled brightly at her and took her place beside Roman's mother up front.

When Roman set the horse in motion, Esta and his mother were engaged in conversation, Joann folded her arms across her chest and stuck her tongue out at Esta's back.

At the publishing office, Joann and Roman loaded the boxes of books while his mother and Esta continued their chat. They were getting ready to leave when Mabel came out with another box of books. "These are some I wanted to donate to the school. They're mostly storybooks and a few songbooks, things I know the kids will enjoy."

Joann put them beside her on the seat. "*Danki,* Mabel. I know Leah will be most grateful."

When they arrived at the school, the work was well under way. A scaffold had been built across the burned opening at the side of the building. Men in straw hats, white shirts and dark pants with suspenders swarmed around the building like ants. Eli Imhoff and Bishop Zook supervised the work and made sure that everyone knew their job.

The sounds of hammers and saws filled the air along with the chatter and laughter of the children who were playing on the school-ground equipment. Long tables had been set up beneath the shade of a nearby tree and women in dark dresses and white *kapps* laid out the food, and made sure everyone had plenty of lemonade or coffee.

Roman's mother and Esta carried their baskets of food toward the tables. Leah came out of the school with Sarah and Sally at her side. "Oh good, you have the books. Bring them inside."

Joann carried the boxes while Roman went to join the men. She and the other women were soon busy shelving books and sorting through the donations that continued to come in.

Later, when they went out to get refreshments, she saw Roman had been put in charge of painting the building. He had seven young boys of various ages wielding paintbrushes beside him. As Joann watched, Esta approached him with a glass of lemonade and a sly smile.

"I can't believe she has set her sights on him again," Sally said as she folded her arms and shook her head.

Joann tried to pretend she didn't care. "His mother likes her. I think she feels it would be a good match."

Sarah stood beside them nibbling on an oatmeal raisin cookie. "I had hoped that you two might hit it off, Joann."

Joann sighed. Sarah always had matchmaking on her mind. "Roman is not my type. He's not sensitive. He doesn't appreciate my quirky sense of humor." She closed her mouth. She had almost revealed her secret.

Sally turned to stare at Joann. "Is there someone who does appreciate your quirky sense of humor?"

Joann couldn't help the blush that heated her cheeks. Sally and Sarah exchanged excited glances and leaned close to Joann. Sarah said, "Out with it. Who is he? Where did you meet him?"

Now she was in a pickle. They both knew something was up. She was going to have to tell the truth, or some version of the truth.

"I haven't actually met him, but I know a lot about him."

"What does that mean?" Sally asked.

"We've been exchanging letters."

Sarah clapped her hands together. "A pen pal courtship, how wonderful. Who is he? Where does he live?"

Joann shook her head. "I'd rather not say."

Sally's eyes narrowed. "Why not? What is this paragon's name?"

"I'd rather not say," Joann answered in a weak voice.

Sarah nodded. "We won't tease you anymore."

Sally fisted her hands on her hips. "You're making it up."

Joann's chin came up. "I am not."

"Well, there is something fishy about this. How come we haven't heard about him before?"

Joann made sure that no one else was close enough to overhear. "We've been leaving letters for each other in a hollow log at the lake."

Sarah put her arm around Joann's shoulder. "How romantic."

Sally shook her head. "I'm not buying it."

"It's true," Joann insisted. "I lost my new fishing rod in the lake. I was heartbroken. He went fishing and recovered it. Instead of keeping it, he left it with a note beside it. When I went back to the lake, I found my rod and his note. I wrote him a thank-you letter in the same place. It sort of took off from there."

Sarah's gaze grew troubled. "But you know who he is, right?"

"Not exactly." Joann had never considered how lame it would sound when she tried to explain.

Sally scowled at her. "Are you telling us that you're exchanging letters with a complete stranger who happens to fish at the same lake that you do?"

"That about sums it up. I think I'll have another cookie." She started for the table.

Sally grabbed her arm. "Are you crazy? He could be some kind of nut."

Joann didn't want to hear it. "He's not a nut. He's sensitive and troubled and he shares what he's going through with me. What is so wrong with that?"

Sarah clapped a hand over her mouth. "Oh my goodness. He's *Englisch.*"

Joann stared at the ground. "I don't think so. His letters sound… Amish."

"Old Amish? Young Amish? Single Amish? Married Amish? Ex-Amish?" Sally waited for an answer. Joann didn't have one.

"I don't know."

Sarah and Sally each grabbed Joann's arm and pulled

her to a more secluded spot. Sarah said, "You don't know his name, but he knows yours. Right?"

"I sign my letters the Happy Angler. He signed his letters the Friendly Fisherman."

"Are you telling us he doesn't even know he's writing to a woman?" Sarah's mouth dropped open.

Joann closed her eyes. "I told him I was an Amish woman. It's only letters. I was afraid he would stop writing if he knew. It started out innocent enough. Why are you making it sound so sordid?"

Sally shook her head. "You have to stop. He could be anybody."

Joann walked a few steps away from them. "You don't understand. We have a connection. I don't want to stop writing him."

"Then you have find out who he is."

"I'm not doing anything wrong. I'm exchanging letters with someone who likes to fish as much as I do. We share a joke, talk about our problems, offer suggestions and support. There is nothing wrong with what I'm doing."

Sarah and Sally exchanged pitying glances. Before they could say anything else, Leah joined them. "It's almost done. You can't even tell where the fire was. I'm so thankful for all the people who have come out today. Come, Bishop Zook is going to offer a blessing."

Sarah and Sally followed her, but Joann stayed where she was. In her heart, she knew they were right. She had to end the secrecy. If their friendship was a good thing, it would bear up in the light of day.

If it didn't, she didn't know what she would do.

Chapter 13

Roman managed to stay busy and out of Esta's reach for most of the day. He was thankful when she and his mother left to visit Otis in the hospital with some of his English friends. Before she got in the car, his mother gave his arm a squeeze. With a happy smile, she said, "It's wonderful to see you and Esta together again."

"We're not together."

His mother leaned closer. "She told me that things have been rough between the two of you, but she's willing to work it out."

Esta was already in the backseat of the car. She had the grace to blush. She scooted over to make room for his mother when she got in. He closed the car door and watched as they drove away. It didn't matter if she charmed his mother or not. He didn't see a future with her.

On the ride home, he glanced frequently at Joann. She seemed deep in thought. A small frown put a crease between her eyebrows. He wanted to smooth it away. "Is something troubling?" he asked.

She glanced at him and shook her head. "I have a hard decision to make and I'm not sure what to do."

"That sounds serious. Is there anything I can do to help?"

"I appreciate the offer, but this is something I have to work out for myself."

"If this is about your job, you can stay on until Otis comes back."

"I will be happy to help out again if you get in a bind, but there isn't enough work to keep all of us busy now that the schoolbooks have been finished. On Monday I'll be at the bookstore again."

"You don't mind?"

She sighed. "I believe everything happens for a reason."

"If only we could see what that reason was." He pulled Meg to a stop at the end of Hebron's lane.

"Then we wouldn't need faith, would we?" she asked gently.

"I reckon not. You don't need to come in Monday unless you really want to. I gave Leonard and Gerald the day off. They've both put in a lot of long hours, and so have you."

She nodded and got down. She paused and turned to face him. "I'm glad that Esta has come to her senses. You two make a nice couple."

"You and my mother," he said in disgust. "I'd like to choose my own wife, if you don't mind."

"I know it isn't any of my business, but I hope you don't hold the things I said in anger against Esta. I was wrong to repeat gossip. I would hate to think that I ruined something between you."

"You didn't ruin anything. You just have a way of making me look at things differently. Good night."

"Good night."

He turned the horse around and drove toward home. As he drew even with the road that led to the lake, he stopped and turned in. He wanted to see if he had a letter. More than that, he wanted to tell his friend about the decisions he'd made.

It took him a while to find the right place. He was used to coming down from the north end of the lake. Once he spotted the faint path leading around the east shore, he left his buggy and walked through the trees.

Roman hoped he might run into his friend on a Saturday evening, but the small glade was empty. There was a note in the jar.

Dear Friendly Fisherman,
I hope your coworker is becoming less of a headache. I think I may have misjudged mine. We are finding our way with each other. I couldn't have done it without you. My mother always used to say a friend is like a rainbow, always there for you after a storm. Thanks, my friend.
A Happy Angler
P.S. I followed your sound advice and searched for my coworker's strengths. I'm happy to say I have discovered that there is much more to him than I first thought. He is committed to taking care of his family, he has a wonderful sense of humor and he is a fine worker. Thank you. Without your wise words, I might have continued to overlook his good qualities and focused only on his failings. I find that I like him a lot.

Roman sat back with a smile. He took out his notebook and pen and wrote.

My Friend,
We really do have a lot in common. How wise
God was to put us in touch with each other. I don't
see my coworker as a headache anymore. In fact,
I'm finding I like her a lot, too. Much more than
I ever thought I would.

He tapped his lips with the tip of his pen as he decided what else to say.

"I've decided to meet my pen pal."
Joann could barely believe she'd spoken aloud. She
glanced at her cousin Sally to gauge her reaction. Sally
and her family had come for a visit. It was the off Sunday, the one without a church service, and families frequently traveled to visit each other on that day. The
women were gathering morel mushrooms in the woods
beyond the house. Sally's little sister and Joann's nieces
were playing tag up ahead of them.

"Are you sure you want to do that? What if he is
Englisch?" Sally's tone was grave.

Joann walked along with her eyes scanning the
ground. "If he is *Englisch,* well, I can have an *Englisch*
friend."

"Just stop writing him." Sally bent to pick two mo-
rels from the base of a tree.

"You haven't read his letters. We share so many of
the same doubts and hopes. It has nothing to do with
being Amish or being *Englisch.* We're two people trying to find a way to accept God's plan for us."

"I know you feel a connection to this person, but he may not feel the same connection to you."

"I don't believe that." Joann spotted a small cluster of mushrooms and moved toward them.

Sally followed her. "Has your pen pal ever suggested that you meet?"

Joann had trouble meeting Sally's eyes. "No."

Sally stopped and took Joann's hands between her own. "I am the last person who should be giving anyone advice on matters of the heart, but I'm afraid only heartache will come from this meeting."

"I'm not some giddy teenager. This isn't a matter of the heart."

"Isn't it? Aren't you secretly hoping that your pen pal is a handsome, single man?"

Joann pulled away from Sally. "What if I am?"

"Oh, Joann." Sally shook her head sadly. "He's far more likely to be old, fat, bald and married with a half dozen children or just as many grandchildren."

Tears blurred Joann's vision. "Don't you see? I have to find out. I know that I'm not pretty. I know that I'm not likely to marry. This person respects what I think and how I feel. If it's an Amish grandfather who loves fishing as much as I do, that will be wonderful. We'll be friends and go fishing together as often as possible and I won't feel so lonely."

"And if he should be a handsome, unmarried *Englischer?*"

Joann didn't answer. Both she and Sally knew such a relationship would be forbidden. The only way she could sustain such a relationship would be to leave their Amish community.

Joann turned away from Sally. "I have to know."

She had pined for Levi, but Sarah was the wife God chose for him. Now, she was growing fond of Roman and it seemed that Esta was the one for him.

Joann picked another mushroom and dropped it in her basket. Who was the man for her? "Tomorrow, I'll leave him a note asking to meet."

"If he refuses?"

"I'll stop writing him."

If he agreed to meet, what would happen after that?

Roman didn't have to go in to work early on Monday, so he made his way to the lake. The Happy Angler frequented their spot in the mornings. He had hopes of running into her today. He wanted to meet his friend in person.

He reached the grove of trees and followed the path toward their fishing hole. He rounded the last bend in the path and stopped in his tracks. A woman was sitting on the fallen log. She had her back to him, but she was dressed plain in a gray dress with a white kapp covering her hair.

He took a step off the path into the cover of the woods. His unknown friend was here? It didn't seem possible.

He checked the area for signs of other people. He didn't see anyone else.

The woman turned around with a jar in her hand. It wasn't a stranger. It was Joann, and she held his letter.

Joann Yoder was the Happy Angler? He couldn't believe it.

She tucked the jar in the hollow of the log and picked up a fishing pole, the very pole he had pulled from the lake a few weeks ago. He was too stunned to move.

He tried to think of everything he had written. Written about her! Not much of it had been flattering. He couldn't quite wrap his mind around the fact that she was the one reading his musings. She really would dunk him in the lake if she found out.

Did she know he was the one reading her letters?

No, he didn't think so. He hadn't said anything specific about himself. He took a step back. He had to think this over. He'd become increasingly fond of Happy Angler. How could she be Joann? He tried to reconcile the two in his mind. He had learned to respect Joann. She had a sharp mind and a fine measure of humor. He'd even started to care about her as a woman, but he wasn't sure she returned such feelings. She practically had him married to Esta, but something in the way she looked at him the other evening gave him hope. He'd seen longing in her eyes, but was it a longing for him?

What would she think when she discovered she had been writing to him all this time?

Would she be pleased or mortified? The last thing he wanted was to cause a new break between them. This was going to take some careful thinking. He needed to be certain how she felt about him before he let on that he was the Friendly Fisherman.

He needed to be certain she *was* the Happy Angler. Maybe she'd simply stumbled on this location and accidentally found the letter jar.

He dropped to a crouch and waited for her to leave. She fished for a while, but didn't catch anything. Soon, she put her rod and tackle box inside the large end of the log and stuffed some grass into the opening.

She hadn't stumbled on this place by accident. He crouched lower as she walked by. When he was certain

she had gone, he went to the log and pulled out the jar.
His note was gone and there was a brief one in its place.

Dear Friend,
As much as I have enjoyed our correspondences,
I feel it's time we met in person. I have so much
I want to say to you.
Sincerely,
The Happy Angler

The handwriting was the same. Without a doubt,
Joann was the one. Someday, he hoped they would look
back on these days and laugh about their secret correspondence, but he wasn't laughing yet. He was in
trouble.

He pondered how he could make this come out right
as he walked home. The longer he thought about it, the
more panicked he became. His brother was crossing the
yard. He stopped. "I thought you had gone to work?"

Roman pulled off his hat and raked his fingers
through his hair "Not yet. It's her. I couldn't believe
my eyes."

"What are you talking about?" His brother looked at
him as if he'd gone crazy. Maybe he had.

Roman began pacing. "Joann Yoder."

"I still have no idea what you are talking about."

Roman spun to face him. "I went to the lake today,
and she was there. I can't believe this."

"I'm still not following you. Why should you care if
Joann Yoder was fishing at the lake?"

"She wasn't fishing. She was writing a letter."

"I wrote one last month. It's not that amazing that
she knows how to do it."

Roman shook his head. "Remember the letter I left for the person whose rod and reel I pulled out of the lake?"

"Sure. He left you a lure as thanks."

"That wasn't the only letter I wrote. We've been exchanging notes ever since, only I thought I was writing to a woman who liked to fish. I never once thought the letters I received came from Joann Yoder."

"Wait a minute. You've been exchanging love letters with Joann Yoder and you didn't know it? What a hoot!" Andrew started laughing.

"They weren't love letters." He began pacing again.

"It's still funny. You and the old maid leaving notes for each other in a hollow log. That's priceless. Did she know it was you?"

Andrew's question stopped him. Did she? He found it hard to believe. There hadn't been anything in her demeanor or her notes that suggested she was aware of his identity. "I don't think so."

"I reckon you should tell her the truth. I wouldn't want to be in your shoes when she finds out. She's bound to think it was a prank on your part."

That was exactly what he was afraid of. Roman tried to sort out his feelings. The comforting letters that had sustained him through the past few weeks showed him a completely new side of Joann. He thought he knew her. Now he realized he barely knew her at all. That would have to change, and she would have to get to know him, too.

Andrew chuckled. "I've got to get back to work. Tell me how it turns out. The old maid and you, what a hoot."

After his brother left, Roman went in his house and pulled open the drawer of his desk. He took out the letters Joann had written and began to study them. The sound of a car approaching made him look out the window. The sheriff was getting out of his SUV. Roman went to the door and stepped out on the porch to greet him. "Good day, Nick Bradley. What can we do for you?"

"I stopped by the office. Mable from next door said you had given everyone the day off. I hope everything is okay."

"Everything is fine."

"That's good to hear. I got a copy of your uncle's magazine in the mail this week. It had a license plate number stapled inside. Would you know anything about that?"

"*Ja,* I put it there for you."

"I figured it might be from you. Can you tell me if you know a woman named Jenny Morgan?"

"*Nee.* Who is she? Was she involved in that sad business?"

"I mean to find out if she was involved or not. Thanks for your time, Roman." He touched the brim of his hat, got into his vehicle and drove away.

"What are you reading?"

Joann looked up to find Roman watching her intently. How long had he been standing there?

She was getting ready to start her half day at the bookstore, but she had come to town early so she could stop at the library first. It was such a beautiful summer day that she had decided to read for a few minutes on the bench outside.

She marked her place in the book with the ribbon and closed it. "How are you?"

"Fine. Is it a good book?"

She slipped it into her bag. "I like it."

"Would I like it?" There was something different about his voice today. It was softer, gentler and yet teasing.

Or maybe she was just imagining things. "I doubt it."

"It must be one of those romance novels."

She raised her chin. "There is nothing wrong with a story about two people falling in love."

"I didn't say there was. I believe in love. Who wrote it? Maybe I've even read it." He reached for her book bag. She grabbed the strap. After a brief tug-of-war, he wrestled it away from her.

She crossed her arms and glared at him. "Has anyone told you that you are a bully?"

"Nope." He opened the bag and pulled out her book. His eyes widened in surprise. "Successful Freshwater Bass Fishing. That has to be the most romantic title I've ever heard. Don't tell me how it ends. I have to read it now."

"Ha! Ha!" She snatched the book away from him. He let her take it.

She stuffed the book back in her bag. "Very funny."

"I try. Seriously, I didn't know you liked fishing."

"Everyone likes fishing."

He sat down beside her. "A lot of people like to go fishing, but not a lot of people like to read about it."

"Well, I like to do both." She rose and started walking.

He stood and followed her. "Where are you going?"

"To work."

"I'll walk with you."

She scowled at him. What was wrong with him today? He wore a goofy grin, but he looked nervous.

He fell into step beside her. "Tell me more about the fishing you do."

"Why?"

"You may find this hard to believe, but I enjoy fishing, too."

"What an amazing coincidence!"

"I'm serious. My grandfather used to take me when I was little. I loved sitting on the riverbank beside him and listening to his stories. I didn't even mind if we didn't catch anything."

"Really?" She looked at him in surprise.

"Okay, I enjoyed myself a lot more when the fish were biting."

"That wasn't what I meant. I was just surprised because that's how I learned to love fishing. My grandfather took me with him. He was very old then, and he walked with a cane, but he could look at a stretch of water and tell you right where the fish were. He had a gift. I was named after his wife. I think that's why he liked being with me. Those were the very best days." Joann blinked away the tears in her eyes and hoped Roman hadn't noticed.

He said, "I'm sure he liked being with you because you were a charming child."

She cocked her head to the side. "Now I know you're making fun of me."

"How can you say that?"

"I wasn't a charming child. I was plain." And all but invisible to the people she wanted most to be loved by. Her mother had been sick throughout Joann's childhood. Her father spent all his time caring for her and ignoring his lonely daughter.

"If your grandfather inspired your passion for fishing, who inspired your passion for books?"

"I'm not sure. As soon as I learned to read it was like the entire world opened up and invited me in. I could read about places that are far away, have adventures along with the people in the stories. I was hooked."

"I didn't discover books until I started working for Otis. He opened my eyes to what books can do for people."

"That's what I loved about working for him. How is he?"

"Doing well. He should be out of the hospital by the end of the week."

"That's great."

By this time they had reached the printing office. Roman held the door open for her. She said, "I'm working at the bookstore today."

"Oh, right. Say, my brother and I sometimes go fishing. Maybe you can join us one of these days."

"Sure." She smiled and turned away. He was just being polite. She knew the trip would never materialize.

"Great. I'll see you tomorrow." He went into the office and closed the door.

A second later, the door popped open again. He leaned out and said, "I mean it, teacher. We'll go fishing soon."

She giggled and nodded. "Okay, soon."

She spent the rest of the day smiling as she worked. Her heart was warmed by his thoughtfulness.

Chapter 14

On Saturday afternoon, Joann was on her hands and knees sweeping paper shreds from beneath the largest press when she heard her name called in a secretive whisper. She looked behind her to see Sally peeking under the press.

"How did it go? Your meeting with your pen pal. How did it go? Is he fat and bald?"

Joann crawled out and stood up. "I have no idea. He hasn't been back or at least he hasn't left another letter. Why are you whispering?"

Sally looked around then took a step closer. "Believe me, Joann, exchanging secret letters with a total stranger is not the kind of thing you want getting out. Do you think he's avoiding you?"

Joann shrugged. "I have no idea."

"What are you going to do?"

"Finish cleaning this press and then mop the floors."

Sally wrinkled her nose. "Don't be smart. I mean about your mystery guy."

"There isn't much I can do except wait for him to contact me."

"I'm going to go crazy if he doesn't do it soon."

Joann had trekked to the lake and back every morning for the past six days. "How do you think I feel? Maybe he's just busy."

"Maybe his wife found out. Maybe he fell in the lake and drowned. Maybe he read the note and moved to Montana."

Joann rolled her eyes. "Sally, stop it."

Her cousin pointed a finger at her. "This is all your fault."

"Go home. I've got work to do."

"You'll tell me as soon as you hear from him, right?"

"I promise."

Sally tipped her head to one side as she studied Joann. "Is that a new dress? I've never seen you in that color before. It's nice. Mauve suits you."

"Danki." Joann smoothed the front of her matching apron. Sally waved as she headed for the door. Joann waved back. When she was alone, she spun around once to make the skirt flare out. It was a pretty color. She knew it was vain, but she hoped Roman would notice and like it, too.

When Joann finished her work and left the building, she found Roman waiting outside the office in his buggy with Andrew beside him.

Roman jumped down. "Good afternoon. My brother and I are on our way to do some fishing. I thought I'd swing by and see if you wanted to join us."

"Now?"

"*Ja.* We're going to a creek not far from here."

"I know you said you would invite me soon, but I wasn't expecting this soon."

Roman smiled at her. "It was a last-minute decision on my part. I understand if you're busy and don't want to come."

Of course, I want to come. Don't read more into this than it is, Joann. He's asking me to go fishing, like I'm one of the boys. He's not asking me out on a date.

She struggled to hide her excitement. "I'd like to go, but I don't have a pole."

"That's okay. We have an extra rod. Come on, it will be fun."

She looked at his brother. "Andrew, are you sure you don't mind?"

"I'm just along for the ride. This is Roman's idea."

Roman scowled at him. "He doesn't mind a bit."

Andrew shrugged. "Okay, I don't mind."

Roman waited and watched silently as she struggled with her decision. If he pushed any harder, he knew she would refuse. Andrew wasn't helping anything. He'd have a thing or two to say to him when they got home.

Gaining Joann's trust was what Roman was after, but he had to take it one small step at a time.

She nodded and said, "*Ja,* I reckon I could go for a little while."

He could have jumped for joy, but instead he said, "Fine. Hop in."

Andrew drove as they headed east out of town. A half mile later, they pulled off to the side of the road and tethered the horse, then, the three of them left the buggy and walked across the field to a shady spot on the creek.

The bank was grassy, green and inviting beneath a grove of maple trees. Roman saw the way Joann relaxed once she had a pole in her hand. He was happy to sit on the bank and watch her while pretending to keep an eye on his cork. Andrew moved farther downstream to try his luck there and to give them some privacy.

Roman said, "There's nothing better than a day spent fishing, if you ask me."

She was studying the rod holder strapped to his leg. "Do you mind if I ask what that is for?"

"Not at all. This is Andrew's invention. It holds my rod so I can crank with one hand."

"How interesting. I'd like to see it in action."

"You will if the fish cooperate."

Joann's cork went under. He sat up. "You've got one."

She jumped to her feet and set the hook. The tip of her rod bent nearly double. Her reel screeched as the fish took more line and ran with it.

Roman was on his feet beside her. "Andrew, bring the net!"

Joann laughed aloud. She hadn't had so much fun in ages. "He's a big one. I don't think I can hold him."

"Yes, you can. Don't let the line go slack. He'll snap it if you do. Work him toward the bank." Roman coached her along.

She managed to crank in a small amount of line. "I'm trying."

Andrew arrived with a dip net. "Wow, you've hooked a monster."

Roman took the net from him and moved to the edge of the bank. "Bring him a little closer."

Joann pulled with all her might, backing up to bring

the fish within his reach. He leaned out over the water. She said, "Roman, be careful. You'll fall in."

"Don't worry about me. Land your fish."

She fought on with both men shouting encouragement. Each time she got the fish close to the bank, it darted out again into deeper water.

By this time, Andrew was behind Roman holding on to the waistband of his pants to keep his brother from tumbling headlong into the stream. The fish finally surfaced. Andrew shouted, "It's a carp."

"And a mighty big one," Roman added.

Joann's arms were getting tired. "I could've told you that. Get him in the net or he's going to get away."

The fish was running out of steam. She pulled him closer. Roman leaned out as far as he could. Suddenly, the lip of the bank gave way. Roman fell and pulled Andrew in with him.

Joann shrieked. Roman came up with a net in his hand and the fish safely in the net. His straw hat went floating downstream. Joann sat in the grass and laughed until tears ran down her face. Andrew waded after Roman's hat and pulled it out of the water. He was grinning from ear to ear.

As the two men struggled out of the creek, she pressed a hand to her mouth. "All that for a poor old carp that isn't good to eat anyway."

The men didn't seem to care. They were admiring the size of their prize. Andrew said, "I reckon he's twenty-five pounds."

"At least," Roman agreed. He smiled brightly at her.

Joann's heart took a funny leap. No one had ever smiled at her that way. She couldn't help herself. She had to glance behind her to see if he was looking at someone else. No one was there. She turned back to him. He wasn't looking through her. He was looking right at her with those shining blue eyes that put the sky to shame.

In that instant, she realized she was falling hard for Roman and she had no idea what to do about it.

She gloried in the feeling for a heartbeat and then reality reared its ugly head. She was doomed to love in vain. Someone like Roman would never fall for someone like her.

Joann's practical side quickly asserted itself. "We need to get you guys home and out of those wet things."

"Reckon you're right." Roman seemed reluctant to call a halt to the day.

"Put my poor fish back in the creek. He's gasping already."

Roman carried the carp to the water's edge. Andrew said, "I kinda hate to put him back after all the trouble we went to catch him."

She had to agree, but she would be forever grateful to the silver beauty for showing her how wonderful love could feel, if only for a little while.

When they arrived back at Hebron's farm an hour later, Roman got out and walked with her to the door.

She said, "Thanks for taking me fishing. I had a great time."

"So did I. Are you doing anything tomorrow evening?"

She gave him a puzzled look. "Nothing special, why?"

"I thought you might enjoy going on a picnic after church services. The weather is supposed to be nice."

Was he serious? "A picnic? With you?"

"Ja."

"And who else?" She could understand the invitation if it was to a party.

"No one. Just you and I."

She didn't dare hope that he returned her affections. What was he up to? "Why?"

"Joann, I enjoy your company when we aren't trading insults. What do you say?"

Was he making fun of her? He looked perfectly serious, worried even, as if he were afraid she would say no. "Did Sarah put you up to this?"

He shook his head. "No one put me up to it. If you don't want to go, just say so. I will be disappointed, but I'll live."

"You really want to take me on a picnic?" Joy began to spread through her body.

"I do."

A giddy sensation she hadn't felt since she was a teenager made her smile. "I reckon a picnic sounds like fun."

He smiled brightly. "Great. I'll pick you up at noon, if that's okay with you?"

"Noon will be fine. What shall I bring?"

"Just yourself." He stood there smiling at her, looking so handsome it made her heart ache.

She said, "You should get home. Andrew looks miserable."

"You're right. See you tomorrow." He tipped his hat, climbed into his buggy and drove away.

Joann wasn't sure if she actually touched the floor when she went inside her brother's home. Roman Weaver had asked her to go out with him. Just him. No one else. She had a date.

She felt like singing, like spinning in circles until

she fell to the floor, too dizzy to move. She was going on a picnic with Roman.

She ate her supper without tasting a thing. That night, she lay in bed unable to sleep as anticipation chased sleep away. It was a long time before she finally closed her eyes and slept.

She was awake before dawn brightened the sky. Her giddiness had vanished in the night. What was she thinking? Why had she agreed to go? She was barreling toward heartache. He couldn't possibly care for someone like her.

He must have been joking. He wouldn't come at noon. He wouldn't show up at all. She'd made a terrible mistake by agreeing to go. Right now, he and his brother were sitting somewhere laughing at her gullibility.

When twelve o'clock finally arrived, Hebron came in from finishing his chores. Joann helped her sister-in-law prepare lunch. She was setting the table when Salome burst in. "Aunt Joann, there's someone here to see you."

Joann stopped breathing. "Who is it?"

"It's Roman Weaver." Salome's eyes danced with excitement. "He's driving a courting buggy."

Hebron scowled at Joann. "Why has he come to see you?"

She smoothed the front of her apron to hide her trembling hands. "He's taking me on a picnic."

"Is he really?" Salome demanded.

"*Ja,* he really is." She looked at her sister-in-law. "I don't expect to be back until late, so don't wait supper on me."

Everyone was staring at her with their mouths open. Joann pulled her book bag off the hook by the door and rushed outside before her courage failed.

* * *

Roman slipped a finger under the collar of his shirt to loosen it. He hadn't been this nervous since...ever. It occurred to him that he was rushing things, but he didn't want to keep the truth from Joann a moment longer. He had come to care deeply for her. He wanted their relationship to be based on trust and understanding. He wanted to be more than her friend. Much more.

As she came out the door, she gave him a beautiful smile. His heart flipped over in his chest and started beating like mad. She took his breath away.

She slid in beside him in the buggy. "What a glorious day."

"It sure is." It wasn't the weather that filled him with happiness. It was having her beside him.

"Any ill effects?" Her voice sounded breathy and nervous. Her cheeks were pink and her eyes sparkled. He sure hoped he was the reason.

"From what?"

She giggled. "Your swim with the fishes."

"*Nee,* I'm fine and so is Andrew. We'll have to do that again."

She looked down at her hands. "I'd like that. Where are we going?"

"I thought we might go out to the lake."

Her head snapped up. She stared at him with wide eyes. "The lake?"

Suddenly, it didn't seem like such a great plan. "If that's okay with you?"

"It's okay. *Ja,* it's fine. I like going to the lake."

"So do I. It's peaceful there."

She fell silent, and he drove the rest of the way with growing misgivings.

When they reached the south shore, he parked in the shade of an oak tree. She said, "This is a good spot. Shall I put the blanket out here?"

"No, it's prettier on the east side of the lake. Let's take our stuff over there."

Some of the joy left her eyes. "Okay."

He hated that he was tricking her, but he had arranged for the Friendly Fisherman to introduce himself. It had seemed so clever when he thought of it. He prayed he was doing the right thing. He took the picnic basket from the back of the buggy and started following the path around the lake. When they reached the clearing with the fallen tree, he looked down at her. "I like this spot, don't you?"

She relaxed a little. "It's fine."

He said, "You put out our things. I left the lemonade in the buggy. I'll be right back."

Joann couldn't believe Roman had brought her to the same spot where she exchanged letters with her secret friend. Once he was out of sight, she laid open the blanket and went to the log. Reaching into the knothole, she brought out her mail jar. There was a new note inside. She opened the lid and took it out.

My dear friend,
I would be delighted to meet you face to face. We do have a lot to talk about. So turn around.
F.F.

Turn around. Her heart skipped a beat and stumbled onward. Slowly, she looked up. Roman was standing at the edge of the trees. He lifted his hand in a brief wave. "Hi."

A terrible buzzing filled her ears. This couldn't be happening. He hadn't brought her here for a picnic. He'd brought her here to humiliate her. She should have known better. What a fool she was.

She pressed a hand to her forehead. "It was you! All this time I thought I was reading heartfelt letters from some stranger. Only I wasn't. I was the victim of your sick joke."

He took a step toward her. "No, Joann, it wasn't like that."

She was so embarrassed she thought she might die from shame. When she thought of the things she had confided to him it made her ill. "Did you know it was me all along?"

"Of course not."

"You knew before today, didn't you?"

"I couldn't tell you. I wasn't sure you even liked me."

He knew and he'd said nothing. How humiliating. "I have a newsflash for you, Roman Weaver. I still don't like you. You are mean and underhanded and dishonest. I can't believe I ever thought I did like you. Never speak to me again."

Joann dashed past him and began running through the trees. She heard him calling, but she didn't slow down. She ran past his buggy and across the pasture until she was so out of breath that she had to stop and lean against the gate.

What an idiot she was. He must be laughing his head off. Tears blinded her. She wiped them away. "I don't cry. I never cry."

Only today, she did.

* * *

Roman couldn't believe how things had gone from so good to so bad in a heartbeat. He gathered up the remains of their picnic and followed Joann. She had to listen to him. He had to make her understand that he had been afraid of losing her friendship. Only now, it seemed that he'd lost so much more.

She wasn't waiting at the buggy. He repeatedly called her name, but she didn't answer.

So much for his bright idea. He left the lake and drove to her brother's house. She wasn't there. She hadn't come back and they didn't know where she might be.

Defeated, Roman went home. Perhaps if he gave her enough time, she would cool off and be able to see that he did care for her.

The next day, he waited impatiently for her to come to work. She didn't show up. He started to worry. He left work early and went back to her brother's house only to be told she still hadn't come home. No one in the family had seen her.

Where could she be? Who would she seek out? Sally perhaps?

He set his tired horse in motion once more and drove out to Sally's home.

Sally was hanging clothes on the line when he drove in the yard. He left the buggy and crossed the lawn with long strides. "Is she here?"

Sally looked at him as if he were crazy. "Is who here?"

"I don't want to play games. Is Joann here?"

"She is not. What's going on?"

"I need to speak to her. I need to make her understand that I care about her. I hurt her without meaning to."

"How?"

Roman hesitated but finally explained what had been going on. Sally was every bit as upset as Joann had been. "You weasel. First, you take her job, she loses the home she's always wanted and then you toy with her affections. I wouldn't want to see you again either."

"Wait a minute. What do you mean I took her job?"

"Her job at the newspaper. She was fired so you could have it. Did you really think she only wanted to clean up after you?"

"I thought it was odd, but she said it was what she wanted."

"No, the job you could care less about is the job she wanted. The job she needed."

"So she could buy a house of her own," he said softly, remembering her letter.

Sally's attitude softened. "You really didn't know?"

"That my uncle put her on the cleaning staff so that I could have her job? No. It never crossed my mind."

"Not only did you get her job, she had to teach you how do it. It wasn't fair of Otis Miller to do that."

"No wonder she seemed to resent me. How can I make this right? I do care about her. You must believe me."

"To start with, you're gonna have to eat a lot of crow."

"I can't tell her how sorry I am if I can't find her. Do you know where she is?"

"Maybe I do, and maybe I don't. If you are sincere about patching things up with her, I'll see what I can do to help."

The truth dawned on him in a blinding flash. "Sally,

not only am I sincere about patching things up with her, I want her to be my wife. And I don't care who knows it."

"Well, that puts a slightly different slant on things. Okay, I'll help, but you have to go home now."

"Go home? I can't. Not until I've talked to her."

"Men are so clueless sometimes. You have to give her a little cooling-off time. Joann is a smart woman, but she doesn't have a lot of confidence. She's felt unwanted most of her life. Thinking that someone loves her for herself is not something that she's used to doing. Give her some time to let the idea sink in. If she still isn't willing to talk to you in a few days' time, then drastic measures will be needed."

He didn't like the sound of that. "What kind of drastic measures?"

"Nothing for you to worry about. Go home and wait until I contact you. Trust me."

He didn't want to go home. He wanted to find Joann and make her understand how much he loved her, but it didn't look like that would happen tonight. It was with a heavy heart that he left and drove away.

When he arrived at the sawmill, he saw the sheriff talking to his father. Andrew came and took the horse from Roman. "The sheriff wants to talk to you."

"All right."

Roman walked toward the sheriff and his father. "How can I help you, Nick Bradley?"

"I came to let you know we arrested someone for the arson at the school and for the vandalism at your uncle's business."

"Who?"

"Robert Smith, Brendan's younger brother. The

woman who came by the printing office after the attack is his girlfriend. The farmer out on Bent Tree Road was able to give me a description of the car they saw speeding away. When I ran the license plate number I received in the mail, her name came up. Her car matched the description of the one at the haystack fire. When I confronted her, she told me everything."

Roman shoved his hands in his pockets. "Did she say why?"

"She thought they were having some harmless fun. They were getting their kicks out of torching a few haystacks. It wasn't until Robert wanted to burn down the school that she started getting worried. She was the one who called in the tip to us that day. After Otis was hurt, she got scared and broke it off with Robert."

"Why does he hate us so?" Menlo asked.

"She said he hates the Amish because they won't fight for their country. He tried to join the Army, but he was rejected. He thinks the Amish are a bunch of hypocrites."

Shame filled Roman. "If I had asked for leniency for his brother, maybe none of this would've happened."

"In my book, Brendan got what he deserved. He didn't know and he didn't care that you were standing at the side of the road when he sideswiped you. He thought it would be funny to knock the door off your buggy because the Amish don't report crimes to the law. Usually. This time you stopped a crime, Roman. According to Jenny, Robert was planning to torch this place next."

Menlo laid a hand on Roman's shoulder. "God was merciful to us."

The sheriff nodded. "I just wanted you to know that the people around here are safer thanks to you."

As Sheriff Bradley walked away, Roman called after him, "Sheriff, will you do me a favor?"

"If I can. What is it?"

"Will you tell the attorney for Brendan and his brother that I will be pleased to come speak on their behalves? Forgiveness is about more than words. It has taken me a while to understand that."

The sheriff nodded and smiled. "I'll be happy to pass on the message."

Chapter 15

Joann sat on the window seat of Sarah's old house and watched the activity on the street below. She was grateful that Sarah and Levi had allowed her to stay in the empty house. Levi had brought over a cot for her to sleep on. It was all she needed at the moment. A place to hide until her heartache healed.

A buggy pulled up in front of Levi's shop and her cousin Sally stepped out. Tears pricked Joann's eyes. She didn't want to see anybody. She hoped that Sarah wouldn't reveal where she was.

Her hope was in vain. Only a few minutes after entering Levi's shop, Sally emerged with Sarah and they both crossed the street toward her.

She heard the front door open downstairs. Sally's voice called out, "Joann, are you here?"

Maybe if she stayed silent, they would go away. She

should've known better. Sally came tromping up the stairs. "I know you're up here, Joann. Answer me."

"Joann doesn't live here anymore. She ran away and joined the circus."

The bedroom door flew open and Sally breezed in. "I've often thought that being an Amish circus performer would be a truly difficult way to live. But if that's what you want, I'll support you."

Joann sighed. "Go away, Sally. I don't want to talk to anyone."

Sally sat beside her on the window bench. "So don't talk, just listen."

Sarah came into the bedroom and stood with her arms folded. "Don't bully her, Sally."

Sally sat back. "You're right. I am trying to bully her into believing that she is a terrific person and that any man would be blessed to have her be part of his life. Even Roman Weaver."

Joann said, "I appreciate the sentiment, but that is hardly the case. I'm a sad, pathetic excuse of a woman who fell in love with an idea, not with a real man."

Sally said, "I have to admit that he's not much of a catch. Who would want a man who can't hold you in his arms?"

Joann glared at Sally. "He only needs one good arm to put around me. If he lost both arms he would still be smarter and more determined than any man I know."

Sally smiled. "That's a pretty strong defense of someone you don't see as a real man."

"You know what I mean."

Sarah came and sat down on the other side of Joann. "I only have one question for you. Do you love him?"

"How can I love someone who lies to me, who tricks me into thinking that he is something he's not?"

Sarah took Joann's hands in her own. "That wasn't exactly a no."

"Okay, I love him, but that doesn't change anything."

"She's right," Sally said. "We just have to figure out what to do now."

Joann stood and crossed the room before turning to face them. "I've come to a decision."

"Not the circus," Sally said dryly.

"No, not the circus. I have an aunt who lives near Bird-in-Hand, Pennsylvania. She left the Amish years ago. My brothers have forbidden anyone to speak about her, but I believe she'll take me in. I'm family, after all."

Sally slapped her hands on her knees. "Wonderful. Now that that's taken care of, all you have to do is write her and wait for an answer."

Joann frowned at her. "Are you that eager to be rid of me?"

"Of course not," Sarah said. "We just want what is best for you."

Sally stood. "In the meantime, we need to get you a pair of new dresses. You can't go to her looking like a pauper. I'll bring some material over tomorrow and we can get you ready to start a new and different life. Wow, I envy you that."

Sally's eyes grew sad. Before Joann could ask her what was wrong, she perked up and said, "I'll be back first thing tomorrow morning."

She charged out of the room, but Sarah remained. "Joann, you are welcome to stay with Levi and me for as long as you like. I hope you know that."

"I appreciate that, Sarah, but I need to move on with my life. There isn't anything for me here."

"I think you're wrong about that, but I'll accept whatever decision you make."

Sarah left and Joann was alone again.

Roman was almost out of patience.

Sally had told him to have faith and wait until she contacted him, but it had been a week and there was still no sign of Joann. Each day he grew more afraid that he had lost her forever. He was proofreading an article for the magazine when the front door of the shop opened. He looked up hoping it was Joann, but it was finally Sally.

"It's about time. Where is she?" he demanded.

Sally gave him a look of disgust. "I have no idea what she sees in you."

"I'm sorry. Hello, Sally, how may I help you?" He forced a smile to his stiff lips.

"You need to go fishing right now."

"Is this some kind of joke, because if it is…" His voice trailed off. He was in no position to issue an ultimatum and she knew it.

"Joann is packed and ready to go to her aunt's home in Pennsylvania. Her aunt's letter arrived today. She wants to leave on this evening's bus. All that she's lacking is her fishing pole. She went to collect."

"To her brother, Hebron's place?"

Sally shook her head. "He's the one who threw it in the lake. Long story. She said she kept it in a hollow log at the lake. Since that was where you exchanged letters, I assume you know where she is going."

He got up from his desk and grabbed his hat. "I could kiss you, Sally."

"Yuck. Not interested. You should hurry. She left Sarah's home thirty minutes ago."

When Roman reached the lake he prayed he wasn't too late. He rounded the last bend in the path and held his breath.

She was sitting on the fallen log by the edge of the water. For a moment, he was too scared to speak. What if he couldn't make her understand? What if he had to spend the rest of his life without her?

Unless he could convince her of his love, that was exactly what would happen.

He prayed for the strength and wisdom to say what she needed to hear. Suddenly, a deep calm came over him. He knew in his heart that she was the woman God had chosen for him. He took a deep breath and walked into the clearing. "Are they biting today?"

She tensed but didn't look at him. "I don't know."

At least she wasn't running away. He took a seat a few feet away from her on a log.

"What do you want, Roman?" There was so much pain in her voice that he wanted to wrap his arm around her and hold her close, but he knew that would be a mistake.

"I want you to be happy, Joann. I know you don't believe that, but it's the truth."

"You hurt me." Her voice quivered.

"I know, and I am so sorry."

She crossed her arms and raised her chin. "If you have come seeking my forgiveness, I give it freely."

He chose his words carefully. "I didn't come seeking forgiveness."

For the first time she looked at him. "Then why are you here?"

"Because you are here. No matter where I go, I'm lonely if I'm not with you."

She bowed her head. Her voice was barely more than a whisper. "Stop pretending. I'm not the kind of woman a man like you falls for."

How could he make her understand? He moved to stand in front of her and then dropped to his knees. "Oh, sweet Joann, you are exactly the kind of woman I have fallen for. I need you."

"Don't," she whispered, turning her face away.

"I have to say this and you have to hear it. I need someone smart and steadfast who will overlook my mistakes. I need someone kind and patient, someone who can teach me to be a better man. I need you, my darling teacher."

She looked down at her clenched hands. "You could have your pick of the pretty girls for miles around. You don't have to settle for someone like me."

"Why would I want a pretty girl when I have a beautiful woman right in front of me?"

"I may be a lot of things, but I'm not beautiful."

"I know you don't think you are, but my eyes see the face of an angel when I look at you. If you would but smile at me, my heart would be made whole again."

"I don't believe you." She started to rise, but he grabbed her hand.

"What can I say that will make you believe me?"

"Nothing."

He let go and sank back on his heels. "Is it because I'm crippled?"

"Don't be ridiculous, Roman."

"How is it ridiculous to lay open my heart and then have you trod on it?"

He rose to his feet and walked to the edge of the water. With his head bowed, he said, "If my disability repels you, I can accept that."

He felt the touch of her hand on his back. He turned to face her.

Joann had never been more confused and more frightened in her life. Here was everything she wanted and everything she knew she could never have. "I don't find you repulsive. No woman could."

"Then why won't you marry me?"

She bit her lip and looked down. "I'm not the marrying kind. I was born to be an old maid."

He put his finger under her chin and forced her to look at him. "For such an intelligent woman, that is the stupidest thing I've ever heard you say."

There were tears in his eyes. It broke her heart to see him in pain. "It's true."

"No, the truth is that I love you and you love me. You're just afraid to say it."

He was right. She was terrified. What if he changed his mind? What if he realized what a poor bargain she really was? How could she face loving him and losing him?

He kissed her cheek. "Be brave, my darling, Joann. You were chosen by God to be my mate. Have faith in God's mercy. Believe that I love you, that I vow before God to love, honor, and cherish you my entire life. Please, I beg you, say that you love me, too."

How could she refuse him anything? She searched her soul and found the faith and courage she needed.

She closed her eyes and took a plunge into the unknown. "All right. I love you, Roman Weaver."

He cupped her cheek with his hand and kissed her gently. He drew back and gazed into her eyes. "You have made me the happiest man in the world."

She smiled as he pulled her close and wrapped his arm around her. Her arms moved up to circle his neck. It felt so right and so wonderful to hold him. It was like a marvelous dream and she was very much afraid she would wake up to find it wasn't true.

"Tell me the truth, Joann. Does it bother you that I only have one arm to hold you with?"

She pulled back a little so that she could see his face. "*Nee,* it does not bother me. What bothers me is that someday you may not wish to hold me."

"That day will never come."

"How can you be so sure?"

"How can you be sure the sun will rise tomorrow?"

"I guess I can't be. I just have faith that it will."

"Then I ask that you have faith in me, too, for I will love you until the day I die."

"Oh, Roman, what have I done to deserve such joy?"

"I don't know, but I am ever thankful that God has smiled upon us."

She looked out over the waters of the lake. "I'm going to miss coming here to read your letters."

"I don't see why we have to stop writing each other. Our wedding won't be until late November."

"Our wedding. That has a wonderful sound to it."

"It does, doesn't it? Mrs. Roman Weaver. I like the sound of that, too."

She laid her head against his chest. "Mrs. Roman Weaver. I *love* the sound that. You know what's funny?"

"What?"

"Sarah told me that we would be a good match." She looked up at him and smiled.

He kissed the tip of her nose. "Remind me to thank her."

"What is your favorite kind of pie?"

"I like them all, but I guess I would have to say my favorite is pumpkin."

"Pumpkin. I like pumpkin pie. That will be easy enough."

"Do I want to know why you're asking that question?"

"Levi said the way to a man's heart is through his stomach. That looks fade but good cooking never does."

"Obviously, he doesn't know what he's talking about. I've never tasted your cooking. You found the way to my heart with pen and ink and a fishing rod."

She chuckled. "I thought the Friendly Fisherman was an ancient Amish grandfather who shared his wisdom with me. What did you think the Happy Angler was like?"

Suddenly she stepped away from him and fisted her hand on her hips. "You said I was someone who would benefit from a dunking in the lake. That I was stubborn, willful, hard to please, and quick to call attention to your failings."

He reached out and pulled her back against him. "And what part of that isn't true? Be honest, soon-to-be Mrs. Roman Weaver."

"I'm not stubborn."

"Yes, you are, and I love that about you."

"I'm not hard to please."

"Have you ever considered marrying anyone else in Hope Springs?"

"No."

"There are a lot of nice fellows hereabouts. Do you agree?"

She nodded. "There are some nice boys around here."

"And yet you have only agreed to marry me. Therefore, you are hard to please, but you knew that and waiting for the right man to come along was worth the wait."

"You have yet to prove that you are worth the wait."

He cupped the back of her head and leaned down until his forehead rested against hers. "Then I had best get started, hadn't I?"

"*Ja,* you should," she answered and gladly raised her face for his kiss.

A long time later, Roman pulled his horse to a stop in front of Sarah and Levi's home. Joanne hated to see the day end, but she knew it had to.

"I'm glad I had the chance to live in Sarah's house before it was sold."

Roman studied her for a moment. "Is this the house you wanted to buy?"

"This is the one." She smiled at him. "But I will enjoy living anywhere you are."

"I've been thinking about that. My arm may not ever be better than it is now. My younger brother can handle the sawmill with my dad. Otis would like me to take over his business when the time comes."

"You do a wonderful job there."

He leaned close and kissed her nose. "I had a good teacher."

She blushed and laid her head on his shoulder. "There

are many things that we will learn together. How to raise children, how to bring them up to value our way of life, how to grow old together."

"As long as I learn those lessons with you by my side, I will be a content man. Will you work with me at the printing office until our children arrive?"

"Gladly." Her heart turned over with happiness at his request. What could be better than working at his side?

"*Goot,* for I need my teacher and my friend beside me."

"I will always be there for you, my love."

"If I'm going to be working in town for the rest of my life, I'm thinking I may need to buy a house that's closer to where I work. Any suggestions?"

Joann wrapped her arms around his and squeezed. "I know the perfect house, and it's for sale."

"Only God is perfect, my love."

She looked up into the eyes of the most wonderful man she would ever meet. The man God had chosen for her. "It may not be perfect, but with you there, the fence painted white, pansies along the walk, our children playing there and a birdhouse in the corner of the yard, it will be very, very close."

* * * * *

We hope you enjoyed reading

Love

by *New York Times* bestselling author
SHERRYL WOODS

and

Plain Admirer

by *USA TODAY* bestselling author
PATRICIA DAVIDS.

Both were originally Harlequin® series stories!

From passionate, suspenseful and dramatic
love stories to inspirational or historical,
Harlequin offers different lines to
satisfy every romance reader.

New books in each line are available every month.

LOVE INSPIRED
INSPIRATIONAL ROMANCE

Uplifting stories of faith, forgiveness and hope.

SPECIAL EXCERPT FROM

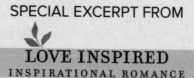

LOVE INSPIRED
INSPIRATIONAL ROMANCE

*With her emotional support dog at her side,
Jalissa Tucker will do whatever it takes to ensure the
survival of the local animal rescue—even ally herself
with her nemesis, firefighter Jeremy Rider. As working
together dredges up old hurts, putting the past aside
could be the key to their future joy…*

*Read on for a sneak preview of
An Unlikely Alliance by Toni Shiloh,
available July 2022 from Love Inspired!*

What are you thinking?

Apparently, she wasn't. Jalissa straightened her shoulders and slipped her mental armor on. Just because Rider had been perfectly charming with her family didn't mean she'd let that soften her toward him. He was still arrogant, immature and a touch reckless.

"Morning, Tucker," Rider said when he opened her door. "Captain Simms's wife is already here and has set up the perfect spot for the shoot." Rider pointed toward the rear of the van. "Animals in the back?"

"Yes. They're all in crates."

He opened the back doors then shook his head. "How did you survive the ride with all that noise?"

"Found my happy place." And one day she'd see Hawaii in person. She loosened Flo and moved back so the dog could exit the van through the driver's side.

"You know what happiness is?" Rider smirked.

"Hardy har-har." Jalissa rounded the back to start unloading the animals. "Where am I putting them?"

"Oh, don't worry about it." Rider cupped his mouth. "Young, Trent, Barns, come help!"

She wiggled a finger in her eardrum. "I think your voice carries well enough without you shouting."

"Maybe, but I have no idea where they are in the firehouse. Now you don't have to carry the animals. Plus, the guys already know where everything is set up."

"Then I can leave?" She had a load of laundry she could do.

"Oh, no." He tsked at her. "We need your assistance with the animals."

Jalissa slowly inched backward but stopped when Flo nudged her. *One…two…* She could do this. Be near the firehouse for help. She didn't actually have to go *inside*, did she? Flo licked her fingertips.

"All right," Jalissa said slowly. "I'll just stay out of everyone's way unless I'm needed."

"You'll be needed." He stared into her eyes.

She blinked slowly. What was going on with her? First thinking Rider was good-looking, and now they were having some kind of moment. She needed to fix this real quick. "I'm sure. It's not like I can trust you to be competent."

The firemen rounded the back of the van, ignoring her conversation with Rider. They quietly began unloading the crates.

Rider rocked back on his heels, sliding his hands into his pockets. "Shots fired in, what?" He pulled an arm up to glance at his watch. "Five minutes. Must be some kind of record for you."

"Whatever." She gave him a wide berth and followed the last fireman from the side parking lot to the front of the firehouse.

She inhaled. *One…two…three…four…* Exhale. *Five…six… seven…eight…* Flo bumped into her hand as if to let Jalissa know she wasn't alone. She buried her fingers in the soft fur as they strolled up the walkway.

Don't miss
An Unlikely Alliance *by Toni Shiloh,*
available July 2022
wherever Love Inspired books and ebooks are sold.

LoveInspired.com

Love Harlequin romance?

DISCOVER.

Be the first to find out about promotions, news and exclusive content!

Facebook.com/HarlequinBooks

Twitter.com/HarlequinBooks

Instagram.com/HarlequinBooks

Pinterest.com/HarlequinBooks

YouTube.com/HarlequinBooks

ReaderService.com

EXPLORE.

Sign up for the Harlequin e-newsletter and download a free book from any series at **TryHarlequin.com**

CONNECT.

Join our Harlequin community to share your thoughts and connect with other romance readers!
Facebook.com/groups/HarlequinConnection

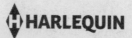